EYELESS IN GAZA

Born in 1894, Aldous Huxley belonged to a
family of great talent: he was the grandson of
the famous Thomas Henry Huxley; the son of
Leonard Huxley, the editor of *Cornhill Maga-
zine*; and the brother of Sir Julian Huxley. He
was educated at Eton and Balliol, and before
devoting himself entirely to his own writing
worked as a journalist and dramatic critic.

Aldous Huxley first attracted attention with a
volume of stories called *Limbo* (1920) and followed this up with his novel *Crome Yellow*
(1921). *Antic Hay* and *Those Barren Leaves*
followed in 1923 and 1925 respectively. His three
most outstanding novels are *Point Counter Point*
(1928), *Brave New World* (1932), and *Eyeless in
Gaza* (1936). His travel books include *Jesting
Pilate* (1926), and *Beyond the Mexique Bay*
(1934). *Grey Eminence* and *The Devils of Loudun* are historical studies, and in *The Doors of
Perception* and *Heaven and Hell* he discussed the
nature and significance of visionary experience.
He died in 1963.

His last books were *Brave New World Revisited* (1959), *Collected Essays* (1960), *On Art
and Artists* (1961), *Island* (1962), and *Literature
and Science* (1963).

BY ALDOUS HUXLEY

Limbo, 1920
Leda, 1920
*Crome Yellow, 1921
Mortal Coils, 1922
*Antic Hay, 1923
On the Margin, 1923
Little Mexican, 1924
*Those Barren Leaves, 1925
Along the Road, 1925
Two or Three Graces, 1926
Jesting Pilate, 1926
Proper Studies, 1927
*Point Counter Point, 1928
Do What You Will, 1929
*Brief Candles, 1930
Music at Night, 1931
The Cicadas, 1931
The World of Light, 1931
*Brave New World, 1932
Texts and Pretexts, 1932
Beyond the Mexique Bay, 1934
The Olive Tree, 1936
*Eyeless in Gaza, 1936
Ends and Means, 1937
*After Many a Summer, 1939
Grey Eminence, 1941
The Art of Seeing, 1943
Time Must Have a Stop, 1945
The Perennial Philosophy, 1946
Science, Liberty and Peace, 1947
The Gioconda Smile, 1948
Ape and Essence, 1948
Themes and Variations, 1950
*The Devils of Loudun, 1952
*The Doors of Perception, 1954
The Genius and the Goddess, 1955
*Heaven and Hell, 1956
Collected Short Stories, 1957
Brave New World Revisited, 1959
Collected Essays, 1960
On Art and Artists, 1961
*Island, 1962
Literature and Science, 1963

*Published in Penguin Books

ALDOUS HUXLEY

EYELESS IN GAZA
A NOVEL

PENGUIN BOOKS

IN ASSOCIATION WITH CHATTO & WINDUS

Penguin Books Ltd, Harmondsworth, Middlesex, England
Penguin Books Australia Ltd, Ringwood, Victoria, Australia
Penguin Books Canada Ltd, 41 Steelcase Road West, Markham, Ontario, Canada
Penguin Books (N.Z.) Ltd, 182–190 Wairau Road, Auckland 10, New Zealand

—

First published by Chatto & Windus 1936
Published in Penguin Books 1955
Reprinted 1959, 1962, 1965, 1968, 1971, 1972, 1974, 1975

—

Copyright © Mrs Laura Huxley, 1936

—

Made and printed in Great Britain
by C. Nicholls & Company Ltd
Set in Linotype Granjon

'Eyeless in Gaza at the Mill with slaves'
MILTON

EYELESS IN GAZA

*

CHAPTER ONE
August 30th 1933

THE snapshots had become almost as dim as memories. This young woman who had stood in a garden at the turn of the century was like a ghost at cockcrow. His mother, Anthony Beavis recognized. A year or two, perhaps only a month or two, before she died. But fashion, as he peered at the brown phantom, fashion is a topiary art. Those swan-like loins! That long slanting cascade of bosom – without any apparent relation to the naked body beneath! And all that hair, like an ornamental deformity on the skull! Oddly hideous and repellent it seemed in 1933. And yet, if he shut his eyes (as he could not resist doing), he could see his mother languidly beautiful on her *chaise-longue*; or, agile, playing tennis; or swooping like a bird across the ice of a far-off winter.

It was the same with these snapshots of Mary Amberley, taken ten years later. The skirt was as long as ever, and within her narrower bell of drapery woman still glided footless, as though on castors. The breasts, it was true, had been pushed up a bit, the redundant posterior pulled in. But the general shape of the clothed body was still strangely improbable. A crab shelled in whalebone. And this huge plumed hat of 1911 was simply a French funeral of the first class. How could any man in his senses have been attracted by so profoundly anti-aphrodisiac an appearance? And yet, in spite of the snapshots, he could remember her as the very embodiment of desirability. At the sight of that feathered crab on wheels his heart had beaten faster, his breathing had become oppressed.

Twenty years, thirty years after the event, the snapshots revealed only things remote and unfamiliar. But the unfamiliar (dismal automatism!) is always the absurd. What he remembered, on the contrary, was the emotion felt when the unfamiliar was still the familiar, when the absurd, being taken for granted, had nothing absurd about it. The dramas of memory are always Hamlet in modern dress.

How beautiful his mother had been – beautiful under the convoluted wens of hair and in spite of the jutting posterior, the long slant of bosom. And Mary, how maddeningly desirable even in a carapace, even beneath funereal plumes! And in his little fawn-coloured covert coat and scarlet tam-o'-shanter; as Bubbles, in grass-green velveteen and ruffles; at school in his Norfolk suit with the knickerbockers that ended below the knees in two tight tubes of box-cloth; in his starched collar and his bowler, if it were Sunday, his red-and-black school-cap on other days – he too, in his own memory, was always in modern dress, never the absurd little figure of fun these snapshots revealed. No worse off, so far as inner feeling was concerned, than the little boys of thirty years later in their jerseys and shorts. A proof, Anthony found himself reflecting impersonally, as he examined the top-hatted and tail-coated image of himself at Eton, a proof that progress can only be recorded, never experienced. He reached out for his note-book, opened it and wrote: 'Progress may, perhaps, be perceived by historians; it can never be felt by those actually involved in the supposed advance. The young are born into the advancing circumstances, the old take them for granted within a few months or years. Advances aren't *felt* as advances. There is no gratitude – only irritation if, for any reason, the newly invented conveniences break down. Men don't spend their time thanking God for cars; they only curse when the carburettor is choked.'

He closed the book and returned to the top-hat of 1907.

*

There was a sound of footsteps and, looking up, he saw Helen Ledwidge approaching with those long springing strides of hers across the terrace. Under the wide hat her face was bright with the reflection from her flame-coloured beach pyjamas. As though she were in hell. And in fact, he went on to think, she *was* there. The mind is its own place; she carried her hell about with her. The hell of her grotesque marriage; other hells too, perhaps. But he had always refrained from inquiring too closely into their

6

nature, had always pretended not to notice when she herself offered to be his guide through their intricacies. Inquiry and exploration would land him in heaven knew what quagmire of emotion, what sense of responsibility. And he had no time, no energy for emotions and responsibilities. His work came first. Suppressing his curiosity, he went on stubbornly playing the part he had long since assigned himself – the part of the detached philosopher, of the preoccupied man of science who doesn't see the things that to everyone else are obvious. He acted as if he could detect in her face nothing but its external beauties of form and texture. Whereas, of course, flesh is never wholly opaque; the soul shows through the walls of its receptacle. Those clear grey eyes of hers, that mouth with its delicately lifted upper lip, were hard and almost ugly with a resentful sadness.

The hell-flush was quenched as she stepped out of the sunlight into the shadow of the house; but the sudden pallor of her face served only to intensify the embittered melancholy of its expression. Anthony looked at her, but did not rise, did not call a greeting. There was a convention between them that there should never be any fuss; not even the fuss of saying good morning. No fuss at all. As Helen stepped through the open glass doors into the room, he turned back to the study of his photographs.

'Well, here I am,' she said without smiling. She pulled off her hat and with a beautiful impatient movement of her head shook back the ruddy-brown curls of her hair. 'Hideously hot!' She threw the hat on to the sofa and crossed the room to where Anthony was sitting at his writing-table. 'Not working?' she asked in surprise. It was so rare to find him otherwise than immersed in books and papers.

He shook his head. 'No sociology today.'

'What are you looking at?' Standing by his chair, she bent over the scattered snapshots.

'At my old corpses.' He handed her the ghost of the dead Etonian.

After studying it for a moment in silence, 'You looked nice then,' she commented.

'*Merci, mon vieux!*' He gave her an ironically affectionate pat on the back of the thigh. 'At my private school they used to call me Benger.' Between his finger-tips and the rounded resilience of her flesh the silk interposed a dry sliding smoothness, strangely disagreeable to the touch. 'Short for Benger's Food. Because I looked so babyish.'

'Sweet,' she went on, ignoring his interruption, 'you looked really sweet then. Touching.'

'But I still am,' Anthony protested, smiling up at her.

She looked at him for a moment in silence. Under the thick dark hair the forehead was beautifully smooth and serene, like the forehead of a meditative child. Childish too, in a more comical way, was the short, slightly tilted nose. Between their narrowed lids the eyes were alive with inner laughter, and there was a smile also about the corners of the lips – a faint ironic smile that in some sort contradicted what the lips seemed in their form to express. They were full lips, finely cut; voluptuous and at the same time grave, sad, almost tremulously sensitive. Lips as though naked in their brooding sensuality; without defence of their own and abandoned to their helplessness by the small, unaggressive chin beneath.

'The worst of it is,' Helen said at last, 'that you're right. You *are* sweet, you *are* touching. God knows why. Because you oughtn't to be. It's all a swindle really, a trick for getting people to like you on false pretences.'

'Come !' he protested.

'You make them give you something for nothing.'

'But at least I'm always perfectly frank about its being nothing. I never pretend it's a Grand Passion.' He rolled the *r* and opened the *a*'s grotesquely. 'Not even a *Wahlverwandschaft,*' he added, dropping into German, so as to make all this romantic business of affinities and violent emotions sound particularly ridiculous. 'Just a bit of fun.'

'Just a bit of fun,' Helen echoed ironically, thinking, as she spoke, of that period at the beginning of the affair, when she had stood, so to speak, on the threshold of being in love with him – on the threshold, waiting to be called in. But how firmly (for all his silence and studied gentleness), how definitely and decidedly he had shut the door against her ! He didn't want to be loved. For a moment she had been on the verge of rebellion ; then, in that spirit of embittered and sarcastic resignation with which she had learned to face the world, she accepted his conditions. They were the more acceptable since there was no better alternative in sight; since, after all, he was a remarkable man and, after all, she was very fond of him; since, also, he knew how to give her at least a physical satisfaction. 'Just a bit of fun,' she repeated, and gave a little snort of laughter.

Anthony shot a glance at her, wondering uncomfortably whether she meant to break the tacitly accepted agreement between them and refer to some forbidden topic. But his fears were unjustified.

'Yes, I admit it,' she went on after a little silence. 'You're honest all right. But that doesn't alter the fact that you're always getting something for nothing. Call it an unintentional swindle. Your face is your fortune, I suppose. Handsome is as handsome doesn't in your case.' She bent down once more over the photographs. 'Who's that?'

He hesitated a moment before replying; then, with a smile, but feeling at the same time rather uncomfortable, 'One of the not-grand passions,' he answered. 'Her name was Gladys.'

'It would have been!' Helen wrinkled up her nose contemptuously. 'Why did you throw her over?'

'I didn't. She preferred someone else. Not that I very much minded,' he was adding, when she interrupted him.

'Perhaps the other man sometimes talked to her when they were in bed.'

Anthony flushed. 'What do you mean?'

'Some women, oddly enough, like being talked to in bed. And seeing that you didn't ... You never do, after all.' She threw Gladys aside and picked up the woman in the clothes of 1900. 'Is that your mother?'

Anthony nodded. 'And that's yours,' he said, pushing across the picture of Mary Amberley in her funereal plumes. Then, in a tone of disgust, 'All this burden of past experience one trails about with one!' he added. 'There ought to be some way of getting rid of one's superfluous memories. How I hate old Proust! Really detest him.' And with a richly comic eloquence he proceeded to evoke the vision of that asthmatic seeker of lost time squatting, horribly white and flabby, with breasts almost female but fledged with long black hairs, for ever squatting in the tepid bath of his remembered past. And all the stale soapsuds of countless previous washings floated around him, all the accumulated dirt of years lay crusty on the sides of the tub or hung in dark suspension in the water. And there he sat, a pale repellent invalid, taking up spongefuls of his own thick soup and squeezing it over his face, scooping up cupfuls of it and appreciatively rolling the grey and gritty liquor round his mouth, gargling, rinsing his nostrils with it, like a pious Hindu in the Ganges. . . .

'You talk about him,' said Helen, 'as if he were a personal enemy.'

Anthony only laughed.

In the silence that followed, Helen picked up the faded snapshot of her mother and began to pore over it intently, as though it were some mysterious hieroglyph which, if interpreted, might provide a clue, unriddle an enigma.

Anthony watched her for a little; then, rousing himself to activity, dipped into the heap of photographs and brought out his Uncle James in the tennis clothes of 1906. Dead now – of cancer, poor old wretch, and with all the consolations of the Catholic religion. He dropped that snapshot and picked up another. It showed a group in front of dim Swiss mountains – his father, his stepmother, his two half-sisters. 'Grindelwald, 1912' was written on the back in Mr Beavis's neat hand. All four of them, he noticed, were carrying alpenstocks.

'And I would wish,' he said aloud, as he put the picture down, 'I would wish my days to be separated each from each by unnatural impiety.'

Helen looked up from her undecipherable hieroglyph. 'Then why do you spend your time looking at old photographs?'

'I was tidying my cupboard,' he exclaimed. 'They came to light. Like Tutankhamen. I couldn't resist the temptation to look at them. Besides, it's my birthday,' he added.

'Your birthday?'

'Forty-two today.' Anthony shook his head. 'Too depressing! And since one always likes to deepen the gloom. . . .' He picked up a handful of the snapshots and let them fall again. 'The corpses turned up very opportunely. One detects the finger of Providence. The hoof of chance, if you prefer it.'

'You liked her a lot, didn't you?' Helen asked after another silence, holding out the ghostly image of her mother for him to see.

He nodded and, to divert the conversation, 'She civilized me,' he explained. 'I was half a savage when she took me in hand.' He didn't want to discuss his feelings for Mary Amberley – particularly (though this, no doubt, was a stupid relic of barbarism) with Helen. 'The white woman's burden,' he added with a laugh. Then, picking up the alpenstock group once again, 'And this is one of the things she delivered me from,' he said. 'Darkest Switzerland. I can never be sufficiently grateful.'

'It's a pity she couldn't deliver herself,' said Helen, when she had looked at the alpenstocks.

'How is she, by the way?'

Helen shrugged her shoulders. 'She was better when she came out of the nursing home this spring. But she's begun again, of course. The same old business. Morphia; and drink in the intervals. I saw her in Paris on the way here. It was awful!' She shuddered.

Ironically affectionate, the hand that still pressed her thigh seemed all of a sudden extremely out of place. He let it fall.

'I don't know which is worse,' Helen went on after a pause. 'The dirt – you've no idea of the state she lives in! – or that malice, that awful lying.' She sighed profoundly.

With a gesture that had nothing ironical about it, Anthony took her hand and pressed it. 'Poor Helen!'

She stood for a few seconds, motionless and without speech, averted; then suddenly shook herself as though out of sleep. He felt her limp hand tighten on his; and when she turned round on him, her face was alive with a reckless and deliberate gaiety. 'Poor Anthony, on the contrary!' she said, and from deep in her throat produced a queer unexpected little sound of swallowed laughter. 'Talk of false pretences!'

He was protesting that, in her case, they were true, when she bent down and, with a kind of angry violence, set her mouth against his.

CHAPTER TWO

April 4th 1934

Fɪᴠᴇ words sum up every biography. *Video meliora proboque;
deteriora sequor.* Like all other human beings, I know what I
ought to do, but continue to do what I know I oughtn't to do.
This afternoon, for example, I went to see poor Beppo, miserably convalescent from 'flu. I knew I ought to have sat with him
and let him pour out his complaints about youth's ingratitude
and cruelty, his terror of advancing old age and loneliness, his
awful suspicions that people are beginning to find him a bore,
no longer *à la page.* The Bolinskys had given a party without
inviting him, Hagworm hadn't asked him to a week-end since
November. . . . I knew I ought to have listened sympathetically,
and proffered good advice, implored him not to make himself
miserable over inevitabilities and trifles. The advice, no doubt,
wouldn't have been accepted – as usual; but still, one never
knows, therefore ought never to fail to give it. Instead of which
I squared conscience in advance by buying him a pound of
expensive grapes and told a lie about some committee I had to
run off to, almost immediately. The truth being that I simply
couldn't face a repetition of poor B's self-commiserations. I
justified my behaviour, as well as by five bob's worth of fruit, by
righteous thoughts : at fifty, the man ought to know better than
continue to attach importance to love affairs and invitations to
dinner and meeting the right people. He oughtn't to be such an
ass; therefore (impeccable logic) it wasn't incumbent upon me
to do what I knew I should do. And so I hurried off after only a
quarter of an hour with him – leaving the poor wretch to
solitude and his festering self-pity. Shall go to him tomorrow for
at least two hours.

'Besetting sin' – can one still use the term? No. It has too
many unsatisfactory overtones and implications – blood of lamb,
terrible thing to fall into hands of living God, hell fire, obsession
with sex, offences, chastity instead of charity. (Note that poor
old Beppo, turned inside out = Comstock or St Paul.) Also
'besetting sin' has generally implied that incessant, egotistic

brooding on self which mars so much piety. See in this context the diary of Prince, that zealous evangelical who subsequently founded the Abode of Love – under Guidance, as the Buchmanites would say; for his long-repressed wish for promiscuous copulation at last emerged into consciousness as a command from the Holy Ghost (with whom in the end he came to identify himself) to 'reconcile flesh with God'. And he proceeded to reconcile it – in public, apparently, and on the drawing-room sofa.

No, one can't use the phrase, nor think in the terms it implies. But that doesn't mean, of course, that persistent tendencies to behave badly don't exist, or that it isn't one's business to examine them, objectively, and try to do something about them. That remark of old Miller's, as we were riding to see one of his Indian patients in the mountains : 'Really and by nature every man's a unity; but you've artificially transformed the unity into a trinity. One clever man and two idiots – that's what you've made yourself. An admirable manipulator of ideas, linked with a person who, so far as self-knowledge and feeling are concerned, is just a moron; and the pair of you associated with a half-witted body. A body that's hopelessly unaware of all it does and feels, that has no accomplishments, that doesn't know how to use itself or anything else.' Two imbeciles and one intellectual. But man is a democracy, where the majority rules. You've got to do something about that majority. This journal is a first step. Self-knowledge an essential preliminary to self-change. (Pure science and then applied.) That which besets me is indifference. I can't be bothered about people. Or rather, won't. For I avoid, carefully, all occasions for being bothered. A necessary part of the treatment is to embrace all the bothersome occasions one can, to go out of one's way to create them. Indifference is a form of sloth. For one can work hard, as I've always done, and yet wallow in sloth; be industrious about one's job, but scandalously lazy about all that isn't the job. Because, of course, the job is fun. Whereas the non-job – personal relations, in my case – is disagreeable and laborious. More and more disagreeable as the habit of avoiding personal relations ingrains itself with the passage of time. Indifference is a form of sloth, and sloth in its turn is one of the symptoms of lovelessness. One isn't lazy about what one loves. The problem is : how to love? (Once more the word is suspect – greasy from being fingered by generations of Stigginses.) There ought to be some way of dry-cleaning and disinfecting words. Love, purity, goodness, spirit – a pile of dirty linen waiting for the laundress. How, then, to – not 'love', since it's an unwashed handkerchief – feel, say, persistent affectionate interest in people? How make the anthropological approach to them, as old Miller would say? Not easy to answer.

April 5th

Worked all morning. For it would be silly not to put my materials into shape. Into a new shape, of course. My original conception was of a vast *Bouvard et Pécuchet*, constructed of historical facts. A picture of futility, apparently objective, scientific, but composed, I realize, in order to justify my own way of life. If men had always behaved either like half-wits or baboons, if they couldn't behave otherwise, then I was justified in sitting comfortably in the stalls with my opera-glasses. Whereas if there were something to be done, if the behaviour could be modified ... Meanwhile a description of the behaviour and an account of the ways of modifying it will be valuable. Though not so valuable as to justify complete abstention from all other forms of activity.

In the afternoon to Miller's, where I found a parson, who takes Christianity seriously and has started an organization of pacifists. Purchas by name. Middle-aged. Slightly the muscular-jocular Christian manner. (How hard to admit that a man can use clichés and yet be intelligent!) But a very decent sort of man. More than decent, indeed. Rather impressive.

The aim is to use and extend Purchas's organization. The unit a small group, like the Early Christian *agape*, or the communist cell. (Note that all successful movements have been built up in rowing eights or football elevens.) Purchas's groups preface meetings with Christian devotions. Empirically, it is found that a devotional atmosphere increases efficiency, intensifies spirit of cooperation and self-sacrifice. But devotion in Christian terms will be largely unacceptable. Miller believes possible a non-theological praxis of meditation. Which he would like, of course, to couple with training, along F. M. Alexander's lines, in use of the self, beginning with physical control and achieving through it (since mind and body are one) control of impulses and feelings. But this is impracticable. The necessary teachers don't exist. 'We must be content to do what we can from the mental side. The physical will let us down, of course. The flesh is weak in so many more ways than we suppose.'

I agreed to contribute the money, prepare some literature and go round speaking to groups. The last is most difficult, as I have always refused to utter in public. When Purchas has gone, asked Miller if I should take lessons in speaking.

Answer. 'If you take lessons before you're well and physically coordinated, you'll merely be learning yet another way of using yourself badly. Get well, achieve coordination, use yourself properly; you'll be able to speak in any way you please. The difficulties, from stage fright to voice production, will no longer exist.'

Miller then gave me a lesson in use of the self. Learning to sit in a chair, to get out of it, to lean back and forward. He warned me it might seem a bit pointless at first. But that interest and understanding would grow with achievement. And that I should find it the solution of the *video meliora proboque; deteriora sequor* problem : a technique for translating good intentions into acts, for being sure of doing what one knows one ought to do.

Spent the evening with Beppo. After listening to catalogues of miseries, suggested that there was no cure, only prevention. Avoid the cause. His reaction was passionate anger : I was robbing life of its point, condemning him to suicide. In answer I hinted that there was more than one point. He said he would rather die than give up his point; then changed his mood and wished to God he could give it up. But for what? I suggested pacifism. But he was a pacifist already, always had been. Yes, I knew that; but a passive pacifist, a negative one. There was such a thing as active and positive pacifism. He listened, said he'd think about it, thought perhaps it might be a way out.

CHAPTER THREE

August 30th 1933

From the flat roof of the house the eye was drawn first towards the west, where the pines slanted down to the sea – a blue Mediterranean bay fringed with pale bone-like rocks and cupped between high hills, green on their lower slopes with vines, grey with olive trees, then pine-dark, earth-red, rock-white or rosy-brown with parched heath. Through a gap between the nearer hills, the long straight ridge of the Sainte-Baume stood out metallically clear, but blue with distance. To north and south, the garden was hemmed in by pines; but eastwards, the vine-yards and the olive orchards mounted in terraces of red earth to a crest; and the last trees stood, sometimes dark and brooding, sometimes alive with tremulous silver, against the sky.

There were mattresses on the roof for sun-bathing; and on one of these they were lying, their heads in the narrow shade of the southern parapet. It was almost noon; the sunlight fell steep out of the flawless sky; but a faint breeze stirred and died and swelled again into motion. Lapped in that fitfully tempered heat, skin seemed to acquire a livelier sensibility, almost an independent consciousness. As though it were drinking a new life from the sun. And that strange, violent, flamy life from outer space seemed to strike through the skin, to permeate and transmute the flesh beneath, till the whole body was a thing of alien sun-stuff and the very soul felt itself melting out of its proper identity and becoming something else, something of a different, an other-than-human kind.

There are so few possible grimaces, such a paucity, in com-parison with all the thoughts and feelings and sensations, such a humiliating poverty of reflexes, even of consciously expressive gestures! Still lucid in his self-estrangement, Anthony observed the symptoms of that death-bed in which he also had his part as assassin and fellow-victim. Restlessly she turned her head on the cushions, this way, that way, as though seeking, but always vainly, some relief, however slight, some respite, if only for a moment, from her intolerable suffering. Sometimes, with the

16

gesture of one who prays despairingly that a cup may be removed, she clasped her hands, and raising them to her mouth gnawed at the clenched knuckles or pressed a wrist between her parted teeth as if to stifle her own crying. Distorted, the face was a mask of extremest grief. It was the face, he suddenly perceived, as he bent down towards those tormented lips, of one of Van der Weyden's holy women at the foot of the Cross.

And then, from one moment to the next, there was a stillness. The victim no longer rolled her tortured head on the pillow. The imploring hands fell limp. The agonized expression of pain gave place to a superhuman and rapturous serenity. The mouth became grave like that of a saint. Behind the closed eyelids what beatific vision had presented itself?

They lay for a long time in a golden stupor of sunlight and fulfilled desire. It was Anthony who first stirred. Moved by the dumb unthinking gratitude and tenderness of his satisfied body he reached out a caressing hand. Her skin was hot to the touch like fruit in the sun. He propped himself up on his elbow and opened his eyes.

'You look like a Gauguin,' he said after a moment. Brown like a Gauguin and, curiously, it struck him, flat like a Gauguin too; for the sunburn suppressed those nacreous gleams of carmine and blue and green that give the untanned white body its peculiar sumptuousness of relief.

The sound of his voice broke startlingly into Helen's warm delicious trance of unconsciousness. She winced almost with pain. Why couldn't he leave her in peace? She had been so happy in that other world of her transfigured body; and now he was calling her back – back to this world, back to her ordinary hell of emptiness and drought and discontent. She left his words unanswered and, shutting her eyes yet tighter against the menace of reality, tried to force her way back to the paradise from which she had been dragged.

Brown like a Gauguin, and flat. . . . But the first Gauguin he ever saw (and had pretended, he remembered, to like a great deal more than he actually did) had been with Mary Amberley that time in Paris – that exciting and, for the boy of twenty that he then was, extraordinary and apocalyptic time.

He frowned to himself; this past of his was becoming importunate! But when, in order to escape from it, he bent down to kiss Helen's shoulder, he found the sun-warmed skin impregnated with a faint yet penetrating smell, at once salty and smoky, a smell that transported him instantaneously to a great chalk pit in the flank of the Chilterns, where, in Brian Foxe's company, he had spent an inexplicably pleasurable hour striking two flints together and sniffing, voluptuously, at the place where the spark had left its characteristic tang of marine combustion.

'L-like sm-moke under the s-sea,' had been Brian's stammered comment when he was given the flints to smell.

Even the seemingly most solid fragments of present reality are riddled with pitfalls. What could be more uncompromisingly *there*, in the present, than a woman's body in the sunshine? And yet it had betrayed him. The firm ground of its sensual immediacy and of his own physical tenderness had opened beneath his feet and precipitated him into another time and place. Nohing was safe. Even this skin had the scent of smoke under the sea. This living skin, this present skin; but it was nearly twenty years since Brian's death.

A chalk pit, a picture gallery, a brown figure in the sun, a skin, here, redolent of salt and smoke, and here (like Mary's, he remembered) savagely musky. Somewhere in the mind a lunatic shuffled a pack of snapshots and dealt them out at random, shuffled once more and dealt them out in a different order, again and again, indefinitely. There was no chronology. The idiot remembered no distinction between before and after. The pit was as real and vivid as the gallery. That ten years separated flints from Gauguins was a fact, not given, but discoverable only on second thoughts by the calculating intellect. The thirty-five years of his conscious life made themselves immediately known to him as a chaos – a pack of snapshots in the hands of a lunatic. And who decided which snapshots were to be kept, which thrown away? A frightened or libidinous animal, according to the Freudians. But the Freudians were victims of the pathetic fallacy, incorrigible rationalizers always in search of sufficient reasons, of comprehensible motives. Fear and lust are the most easily comprehensible motives of all. Therefore . . . But psychology had no more right to be anthropomorphic, or even exclusively zoomorphic, than any other science. Besides a reason and an animal, man was also a collection of particles subject to the laws of chance. Some things were remembered for their utility or their appeal to the higher faculties of the mind; some, by the presiding animal, remembered (or else deliberately forgotten) for their emotional content. But what of the innumerable remembered things without any particular emotional content, without utility, or beauty, or rational significance? Memory in these cases seemed to be merely a matter of luck. At the time of the event certain particles happened to be in a favourable position. Click! the event found itself caught, indelibly recorded. For no *reason* whatever. Unless, it now rather disquietingly occurred to him, unless of course the reason were not before the event, but after it, in what had been the future. What if that picture gallery had been recorded and stored away in the cellars of his mind for the sole and express purpose of being brought up into consciousness at this present moment? Brought up, today, when he was forty-two and secure, forty-two and fixed, unchangeably himself, brought up along with those critical years of his adolescence, along with the woman who had been his teacher, his first mistress, and was now a hardly human creature festering to death, alone, in a dirty burrow? And what if that absurd childish game with the flints had had a point, a profound purpose, which was simply to be recollected here on this blazing roof, now as his lips made contact with Helen's sun-warmed flesh? In order that he might be forced, in the midst of this act of detached and irresponsible sensuality, to think of Brian and of the things that Brian had lived for; yes, and had died for – died for, another image suddenly reminded him, at the foot of just such a cliff as that beneath which they had played as children in the chalk pit. Yes, even Brian's suicide, he now realized with horror, even the poor huddled body on the rocks, was mysteriously implicit in this hot skin.

One, two, three, four – counting each movement of his hand, he began to caress her. The gesture was magical, would transport him, if repeated sufficiently often, beyond the past and the future, beyond right and wrong, into the discrete, the self-

19

sufficient, the atomic present. Particles of thought, desire, and feeling moving at random among particles of time, coming into casual contact and as casually parting. A casino, an asylum, a zoo; but also, in a corner, a library and someone thinking. Some-one largely at the mercy of the croupiers, at the mercy of the idiots and the animals; but still irrepressible and indefatigable. Another two or three years and the Elements of Sociology would be finished. In spite of everything; yes, in spite of everything, he thought with a kind of defiant elation, and counted thirty-two, thirty-three, thirty-four, thirty-five ...

CHAPTER FOUR

November 6th 1902

Horns with a frizzle of orange hair between; the pink muzzle lowered inquiringly towards a tiny cup and saucer; eyes expres-sive of a more than human astonishment. 'THE OX', it was pro-claimed in six-inch lettering, 'THE OX IN THE TEA-CUP'. The thing was supposed to be a reason for buying beef extract – *was* a reason.

Ox in Cup. The words, the basely comic image, spotted the Home Counties that summer and autumn like a skin disease. One of a score of nasty and discreditable infections. The train which carried Anthony Beavis into Surrey rolled through mile-long eczemas of vulgarity. Pills, soaps, cough drops and – more glaringly inflamed and scabby than all the rest – beef essence, the cupped ox.

'Thirty-one ... thirty-two,' the boy said to himself, and wished he had begun his counting when the train started. Between Waterloo and Clapham Junction there must have been hundreds of oxen. Millions.

Opposite, leaning back in his corner, sat Anthony's father. With his left hand he shaded his eyes. Under the drooping brown moustache his lips moved.

'Stay for me there,' John Beavis was saying to the person who, behind his closed lids, was sometimes still alive, sometimes the cold, immobile thing of his most recent memories:

20

Stay for me there; I shall not fail
To meet thee in that hollow vale.

There was no immortality, of course. After Darwin, after the Fox Sisters, after John Beavis's own father, the surgeon, how could there be? Beyond that hollow vale there was nothing. But all the same, oh, all the same, stay for me, stay for me, stay, stay!

'Thirty-three.'

Anthony turned away from the hurrying landscape and was confronted by the spectacle of that hand across the eyes, those moving lips. That he had ever thought of counting the oxen seemed all at once shameful, a betrayal. And Uncle James, at the other end of the seat, with his *Times* – and his face, as he read, twitching every few seconds in sudden spasms of nervousness. He might at least have had the decency not to read it *now* – now, while they were on their way to ... Anthony refused to say the words; words would make it all so clear, and he didn't want to know too clearly. Reading *The Times* might be shameful; but the other thing was terrible, too terrible to bear thinking about, and yet so terrible that you couldn't help thinking about it.

Anthony looked out of the window again, through tears. The green and golden brightness of St Martin's summer swam in an obscuring iridescence. And suddenly the wheels of the train began to chant articulately. 'Dead-a-dead-a-dead,' they shouted, 'dead-a-dead-a-dead ...' For ever. The tears overflowed, were warm for an instant on his cheeks, then icy cold. He pulled out his handkerchief and wiped them away, wiped the fog out of his eyes. Luminous under the sun, the world before him was like one vast and intricate jewel. The elms had withered to a pale gold. Huge above the fields, and motionless, they seemed to be meditating in the crystal light of the morning, seemed to be remembering, seemed, from the very brink of dissolution, to be looking back and in a last ecstasy of recollection living over again, concentrated in this shining moment of autumnal time, all the long-drawn triumph of spring and summer.

'DEAD-A-DEAD', in a sudden frenzy yelled the wheels, as the train crossed a bridge, 'A-DEAD-A-DEAD!'

Anthony tried not to listen – vainly; then tried to make the wheels say something else. Why shouldn't they say, *To stop the train pull down the chain*? That was what they usually said. With a great effort of concentration he forced them to change their refrain.

'To stop the train pull down the chain, to stop the train pull down a-dead-a-dead-a-dead . . .' It was no good.

Mr Beavis uncovered his eyes for a moment and looked out of the window. How bright the autumnal trees! Cruelly bright they would have seemed, insultingly, except for something desperate in their stillness, a certain glassy fragility that, oh! invited disaster, that prophetically announced the coming darkness and the black branches moving in torture among stars, the sleet like arrows along the screaming wind.

Uncle James turned the page of his *Times*. The Ritualists and the Kensitites were at it again, he saw; and was delighted. Let dog eat dog. 'MR CHAMBERLAIN AT UNIVERSITY COLLEGE SCHOOL.' What was the old devil up to now? Unveiling a tablet to the Old Boys who had been killed in the war. 'Over one hundred young men went to the front, and twelve of them laid down their lives for the country in South Africa (cheers).' Deluded idiots, thought Uncle James, who had always been passionately a pro-Boer.

Painted, among the real cows in their pasture, the enormous horns, the triangular auburn frizz, the inquiring nostrils, the tea-cup. Anthony shut his eyes against the vision.

'No, I won't,' he said with all the determination he had previously used against the wheels. He refused to know the horror; he refused to know the ox. But what was the good of refusing? The wheels were still shouting away. And how could he suppress the fact that this ox was the thirty-fourth, on the right, from Clapham Junction? A number is always a number, even on the way to . . . But counting was shameful, counting was like Uncle James's *Times*. Counting was shirking, was betraying. And yet the other thing, the thing they ought to be thinking about, was really too terrible. Too *unnatural*, somehow.

'Whatever we may have thought, or still think, as to the causes, the necessity, the justice of the war which is now happily at an end, I think that we must all have a feeling of profound satisfaction that when the country called its children to arms, the manhood of the nation leaped to it in response. . . .' His face twitching with exasperation, Uncle James put down *The Times* and looked at his watch.

'Two and a half minutes late,' he said angrily.

'If only it were a hundred years late,' thought his brother. 'Or ten years early – no, twelve, thirteen. The first year of our marriage.'

James Beavis looked out of the window. 'And we're still at least a mile from Lollingdon,' he went on.

As though to a sore, to an aching tooth, his fingers travelled again to the chronometer in his waistcoat pocket. Time for its own sake. Always imperiously time, categorically time – time to look at one's watch and see the time. . . .

The wheels spoke more and more slowly, became at last inarticulate. The brakes screamed.

'Lollingdon, Lollingdon,' the porter called.

But Uncle James was already on the platform. 'Quick!' he shouted, striding, long-legged, beside the still moving train. His hand went once more to that mystical ulcer for ever gnawing at his consciousness. 'Quick!'

A sudden resentment stirred in his brother's mind. 'What does he want me to be quick for?' As if they were in danger of missing something – some pleasure, some precariously brief entertainment.

Anthony climbed down after his father. They walked towards the gate, along a wall of words and pictures. A GUINEA A BOX AND A BLESSING TO MEN THE PICKWICK THE OWL AND KILLS MOTHS BUGS BEETLES A SPADE A SPADE AND BRANSON'S CAMP COFFEE THE OX IN . . . And suddenly here were the horns, the expressive eyes, the cup – the thirty-fifth cup – 'No, I won't, I won't' – but all the same, the thirty-fifth, the thirty-fifth from Clapham Junction on the right-hand side.

The cab smelt of straw and leather. Of straw and leather and of the year eighty-eight, was it? yes, eighty-eight; that Christmas when they had driven to the Champernownes' dance – he and she and her mother – in that cold, with the sheepskin rug across their knees. And as though by accident (for he had not yet dared to make the gesture deliberately) the back of his hand had brushed against hers; had brushed, as though by accident, had casually rested. Her mother was talking about the difficulty of

23

getting servants – and when you did get them, they didn't know anything, they were lazy. She hadn't moved her hand! Did that mean she didn't mind? He took the risk; his fingers closed over hers. They were disrespectful, her mother went on, they were ... He felt an answering pressure and, looking up, divined in the darkness that she was smiling at him.

'Really,' her mother was saying,' I don't know what things are coming to nowadays.' And he had seen, by way of silent comment, the mischievous flash of Maisie's teeth; and that little squeeze of the hand had been deliciously conspiratorial, secret, and illicit.

Slowly, hoof after hoof, the old horse drew them; slowly along lanes, into the heart of the great autumnal jewel of gold and crystal; and stopped at last at the very core of it. In the sunshine, the church tower was like grey amber. The clock, James Beavis noticed with annoyance, was slow. They passed under the lych-gate. Startlingly and hideously black, four people were walking up the path in front of them. Two huge women (to Anthony they all seemed giantesses) rose in great inky cones of drapery from the flagstones. With them, still further magnified by their top-hats, went a pair of enormous men.

'The Champernownes,' said James Beavis; and the syllables of the familiar name were like a sword, yet another sword, in the very quick of his brother's being. 'The Champernownes and – let's see – what's the name of that young fellow their daughter married? Anstey? Annerley?' He glanced inquiringly at John; but John was staring fixedly in front of him and did not answer.

'Amersham? Atherton?' James Beavis frowned with irritation. Meticulous, he attached an enormous importance to names and dates and figures; he prided himself on his power to reproduce them correctly. A lapse of memory drove him to fury. 'Atherton? Anderson?' And what made it more maddening was the fact that the young man was so good-looking, carried himself so well – not in that stupid, stiff, military way, like his father-in-law, the General, but gracefully, easily ... 'I shan't know what to call him,' he said to himself; and his right cheek began to twitch, as though some living creature had been confined beneath the skin and were violently struggling to escape.

24

They walked on. It seemed to Anthony that he had swallowed his heart – swallowed it whole, without chewing. He felt rather sick, as though he were expecting to be caned.

The black giants halted, turned, and came back to meet them. Hats were raised, hands shaken.

'And dear little Anthony!' said Lady Champernowne, when at last it was his turn. Impulsively, she bent down and kissed him.

She was fat. Her lips left a disgusting wet place on his cheek. Anthony hated her.

'Perhaps I ought to kiss him too,' thought Mary Amberley, as she watched her mother. One was expected to do such odd things when one was married. Six months ago, when she was still Mary Champernowne and fresh from school, it would have been unthinkable. But now . . . one never knew. In the end, however, she decided that she wouldn't kiss the boy, it would really be too ridiculous. She pressed his hand without speaking, smiling only from the remote security of her secret happiness. She was nearly five months gone with child, and had lived for these last two or three weeks in a kind of trance of drowsy bliss, inexpressibly delicious. Bliss in a world that had become beautiful and rich and benevolent out of all recognition. The country, as they drove that morning in the gently swaying landau, had been like paradise; and this little plot of green between the golden trees and the tower was Eden itself. Poor Mrs Beavis had died, it was true; so pretty still, so young. How sad that was! But sadness, somehow, did not touch this secret bliss of hers, remained profoundly irrelevant to it, as though it were the sadness of somebody in another planet.

Anthony looked up for a moment into the smiling face, so bright in its black setting, so luminous with inner peace and happiness, then was overcome with shyness and dropped his eyes.

Fascinated, meanwhile, Roger Amberley observed his father-in-law and wondered how it was possible for anyone to live so unfailingly in character; how one could contrive to be a real general and at the same time to look and sound so exactly like a general on the musical comedy stage. Even at a funeral, even while he was saying a few well-chosen words to the bereaved husband – pure Grossmith! Under his fine brown moustache his lips twitched irrepressibly.

'Looks badly cut up,' the General was thinking, as he talked to John Beavis; and felt sorry for the poor fellow, even while he still disliked him. For of course the man was an affected bore and a prig, too clever, but at the same time a fool. Worst of all, not a man's man. Always surrounded by petticoats. Mother's petticoats, aunts' petticoats, wives' petticoats. A few years in the army would have done him all the good in the world. Still, he did look most horribly cut up. And Maisie had been a sweet little thing. Too good for him, of course. . . .

They stood for a moment, then all together slowly moved towards the church. Anthony was in the midst of them, a dwarf among the giants. Their blackness hemmed him in, obscured the sky, eclipsed the amber tower and the trees. He walked as though at the bottom of a moving well. Its black walls rustled all around him. He began to cry.

He had not wanted to know – had done his best not to know, except superficially, as one knows, for example, that thirty-five comes after thirty-four. But this black well was dark with the concentrated horror of death. There was no escape. His sobs broke out uncontrollably.

Mary Amberley, who had been lost in the rapturous contemplation of golden leaves patterned against the pale sky, looked down for a moment at this small creature weeping on another planet, then turned away again.

'Poor child!' his father said to himself; and then, overbidding as it were, 'Poor motherless child!' he added deliberately, and was glad (for he wanted to suffer) that the words should cost him so much pain to pronounce. He looked down at his son, saw the grief-twisted face, the full and sensitive lips so agonizingly hurt, and above this tear-stained distortion the broad high forehead, seemingly unmoved in its smooth purity; saw, and felt his heart wrung with an additional pain.

'Dear boy!' he said aloud, thinking, as he spoke, how this grief would surely bring them nearer together. It was so difficult somehow with a child – so hard to be natural, to establish a contact. But surely, surely this sadness, and their common memories . . . He squeezed the small hand within his own.

They were at the church door. The well disintegrated.

'One might be in Tibet,' thought Uncle James as he took off his hat. 'Why not one's boots as well?'

Inside the church was an ancient darkness, smelly with centuries of rustic piety. Anthony took two breaths of that sweet-stale air, and felt his midriff heave with a qualm of disgust. Fear and misery had already made him swallow his heart; and now this smell, this beastly smell that meant that the place was full of germs. ... 'Reeking with germs!' He heard her voice – her voice that always changed when she talked about germs, became different, as though somebody else was speaking. At ordinary times, when she wasn't angry, it sounded so soft and somehow lazy – laughingly lazy, or tiredly lazy. Germs made it suddenly almost fierce, and at the same time frightened. 'Always spit when there's a bad smell about,' she had told him. 'There might be typhoid germs in the air.' His mouth, as he recalled her words, began to water. But how could he spit here, in church? There was nothing to do but swallow his spittle. He shuddered as he did so, with fear and a sickening disgust. And suppose he really should be sick in this stinking place? The apprehension made him feel still sicker. And what did one have to do during the service? He had never been to a funeral before.

James Beavis looked at his watch. In three minutes the hocus-pocus was timed to begin. Why hadn't John insisted on a plain-clothes funeral? It wasn't as if poor Maisie had ever set much store by this kind of thing. A silly little woman; but never religiously silly. Hers had been the plain secular silliness of mere female frivolity. The silliness of reading novels on sofas, alternating with the silliness of tea-parties and picnics and dances. Incredible that John had managed to put up with that kind of foolery – had even seemed to like it! Women cackling like hens round the tea-table. James Beavis frowned with angry contempt. He hated women – was disgusted by them. All those soft bulges of their bodies. Horrible. And the stupidity, the brainlessness. But anyhow, poor Maisie had never been one of the curate-fanciers. It was those awful relations of hers. There were deans in the family – deans and deanesses. John hadn't wanted to offend them. Weak-minded of him. One ought to be offensive on a matter of principle.

The organ played. A little procession of surplices entered through the open door. Some men carried in what seemed a great pile of flowers. There was singing. Then silence. And then, in an extraordinary voice, 'Now is Christ risen from the dead,' began the clergyman; and went on and on, all about God, and death, and beasts at Ephesus, and the natural body. But Anthony hardly heard, because he could think of nothing except those germs that were still there in spite of the smell of the flowers, and of the spittle that kept flowing into his mouth and that he had to swallow in spite of the typhoid and influenza, and of that horrible sick feeling in his stomach. How long would it last?

'Like a goat,' James Beavis said to himself as he listened to the intoning from the lectern. He looked again at that son-in-law of the Champernownes. Anderton, Abdy . . . ? What a fine, classical profile!

His brother sat with bent head and a hand across his eyes, thinking of the ashes in the casket there beneath the flowers – the ashes that had been her body.

The service was over at last. 'Thank goodness!' thought Anthony, as he spat surreptitiously into his handkerchief and folded away the germs into his pocket, 'Thank goodness!' He hadn't been sick. He followed his father to the door and, rapturously, as he stepped out of the twilight, breathed the pure air. The sun was still shining. He looked around and up into the pale sky. Overhead, in the church tower, a sudden outcry of jackdaws was like the noise of a stone flung glancingly on to a frozen pond and skidding away with a reiteration of glassy chinking across the ice.

'But, Anthony, you mustn't throw stones on the ice,' his mother had called to him. 'They get frozen in, and then the skaters . . .'

He remembered how she had come swerving round towards him, on one foot – swooping, he had thought, like a sea-gull; all in white: beautiful. And now . . . The tears came into his eyes again. But, oh, why had she insisted on his trying to skate?

'I don't want to,' he had said; and when she asked why, it had been impossible to explain. He was afraid of being laughed at, of course. People made such fools of themselves. But how could he have told her that? In the end he had cried – in front of everyone. It couldn't have been worse. He had almost hated her that morning. And now she was dead, and up there in the tower the jackdaws were throwing stones on last winter's ice.

They were at the grave-side now. Once more Mr Beavis pressed his son's hand. He was trying to forestall the effect upon the child's mind of these last, most painful moments.

'Be brave,' he whispered. The advice was tendered as much to himself as to the boy.

Leaning forward, Anthony looked into the hole. It seemed extraordinarily deep. He shuddered, closed his eyes; and immediately there she was, swooping towards him, white, like a sea-gull, and white again in the satin evening-dress when she came to say good night before she went out to dinner, with that scent on her as she bent over him in bed, and the coolness of her bare arms. 'You're like a cat,' she used to say when he rubbed his cheek against her arms. 'Why don't you purr while you're about it?'

'Anyhow,' thought Uncle James with satisfaction, 'he was firm about the cremation.' The Christians had been scored off there. Resurrection of the body, indeed! In A.D. 1902!

When his time came, John Beavis was thinking, this was where he would be buried. In this very grave. His ashes next to hers.

The clergyman was talking again in that extraordinary voice. 'Thou knowest, Lord, the secrets of our hearts ...' Anthony opened his eyes. Two men were lowering into the hole a small terra-cotta box, hardly larger than a biscuit tin. The box touched the bottom; the ropes were hauled up.

'Earth to earth,' bleated the goat-like voice, 'ashes to ashes.'

'My ashes to her ashes,' thought John Beavis. 'Mingled.'

And suddenly he remembered that time in Rome, a year after they were married; those June nights and the fire-flies, under the trees, in the Doria Gardens, like stars gone crazy.

'Who shall change our vile body that it may be like unto his glorious body ...'

'Vile, *vile*?' His very soul protested.

Earth fell, one spadeful, then another. The box was almost covered. It was so small, so dreadfully and unexpectedly tiny ...

the image of that enormous ox, that minute tea-cup, rose to Anthony's imagination. Rose up obscenely and would not be exorcized. The jackdaws cried again in the tower. Like a sea-gull she had swooped towards him, beautiful. But the ox was still there, still in its tea-cup, still base and detestable; and he himself yet baser, yet more hateful.

John Beavis released the hand he had been holding and, laying his arm round the boy's shoulders, pressed the thin little body against his own – close, close, till he felt in his own flesh the sobs by which it was shaken.

'Poor child! Poor motherless child!'

CHAPTER FIVE

December 8th 1926

'You wouldn't dare,' Joyce said.

'I would.'

'No, you wouldn't.'

'I tell you I would,' Helen Amberley insisted more emphatically.

Maddeningly sensible, 'You'd be sent to prison if you were caught,' the elder sister went on. 'No, not to prison,' she corrected herself. 'You're too young. You'd be sent to a reformatory.'

The blood rushed up to Helen's face. 'You and your reformatories!' she said in a tone that was meant to be contemptuous, but that trembled with irrepressible anger. That reformatory was a personal affront. Prison was terrible; so terrible that there was something fine about it. (She had visited Chillon, had crossed the Bridge of Sighs.) But a reformatory – no! that was utterly ignoble. A reformatory was on the same level as a public lavatory or a station on the District Railway. 'Reformatories!' she repeated. It was typical of Joyce to think of reformatories. She always dragged anything amusing and adventurous down into the mud. And, what made it so much worse, she was generally quite right in doing so: the mud was facts, the mud was common sense. 'You think I wouldn't dare to do it, because *you* wouldn't dare,' Helen went on. 'Well, I *shall* do it. Just to show you. I shall steal something from every shop we go to. Every one. So there.'

Joyce began to feel seriously alarmed. She glanced questioningly at her sister. A profile, pale now and rigid, the chin defiantly lifted, was all that Helen would let her see. 'Now, look here,' she began severely.

'I'm not listening,' said Helen, speaking straight ahead into impersonal space.

'Don't be a little fool!'

There was no answer. The profile might have been that of a young queen on a coin. They turned into the Gloucester Road and walked towards the shops.

But suppose the wretched girl really meant what she said? Joyce changed her strategy. 'Of course I know you dare,' she said conciliatorily. There was no answer. 'I'm not doubting it for a moment.' She turned again towards Helen; but the profile continued to stare ahead with eyes unwaveringly averted. The grocer's was at the next corner, not twenty yards away. There was no time to lose. Joyce swallowed what remained of her pride. 'Now, look here, Helen,' she said, and her tone was appealing, she was throwing herself on her sister's generosity. 'I do wish you wouldn't.' In her fancy she saw the whole deplorable scene. Helen caught red-handed; the indignant shopkeeper, talking louder and louder; her own attempts at explanation and excuse made unavailing by the other's intolerable behaviour. For, of course, Helen would just stand there, in silence, not uttering a word of self-justification or regret, calm and contemptuously smiling, as though she were a superior being and everybody else just dirt. Which would enrage the shopkeeper still more. Until at last he'd send for a policeman. And then ... But what would Colin think when he heard of it? His future sister-in-law arrested for stealing! He might break off the engagement. 'Oh, please, don't do it,' she begged; 'please!' But she might as well have begged the image of King George on a half-crown to turn round, and wink at her. Pale, determined, a young queen minted in silver, Helen kept on. 'Please!' Joyce repeated, almost tearfully. The thought that she might lose Colin was a torture. 'Please!' But the smell of groceries was already in her nostrils;

they were on the very threshold. She caught her sister by the sleeve; but Helen shook her off and marched straight in. With a sinking of the heart, Joyce followed as though to her execution. The young man at the cheese and bacon counter smiled welcomingly as they came in. In her effort to avert suspicion, to propitiate in advance his inevitable indignation, Joyce smiled back with an effusive friendliness. No, that was overdoing it. She readjusted her face. Calm; easy; perfectly the lady, but at the same time affable; affable and (what was that word?), oh! yes, *gracious* – like Queen Alexandra. Graciously she followed Helen across the shop. But why, she was thinking, why had she ever broached the subject of crime? Why, knowing Helen, had she been mad enough to argue that, if one were properly brought up, one simply couldn't be a criminal? It was obvious what Helen's response would be to *that*. She had simply asked for it.

It was to the younger sister that their mother had given the shopping list. 'Because she's almost as much of a scatter-brain as I am,' Mrs Amberley had explained, with that touch of complacency that always annoyed Joyce so much. People had no right to boast about their faults. 'It'll teach her to be a good housekeeper – God help her!' she added with a little snort of laughter.

Standing at the counter, Helen unfolded the paper, read, and then, very haughtily and without a smile, as though she were giving orders to a slave, 'Coffee first of all,' she said to the assistant. 'Two pounds – the two-and-fourpenny mixture.'

The girl, it was evident, was offended by Helen's tone and feudal manner. Joyce felt it her duty to beam at her with a double, compensatory graciousness.

'Do try to behave a little more civilly,' she whispered when the girl had gone for the coffee.

Helen preserved her silence, but with an effort. Civil, indeed! To this horrible little creature who squinted and didn't wash enough under the arms? Oh, how she loathed all ugliness and deformity and uncleanliness! Loathed and detested . . .

'And for heaven's sake,' Joyce went on, 'don't do anything idiotic. I absolutely forbid . . .'

But even as she spoke the words, Helen stretched out a hand and without any attempt at concealment took the topmost of an elaborate structure of chocolate tablets that stood, like the section of a spiral pillar, on the counter – took it and then, with the same slow deliberation of movement, put it carefully away in her basket.

But before the crime was fully accomplished Joyce had turned and walked away.

'I might say I'd never seen her before,' she was thinking. But of course that wouldn't do. Everybody knew they were sisters. 'Oh, Colin,' she cried inwardly, 'Colin!'

A pyramid of tinned lobster loomed up before her. She halted. 'Calm,' she said to herself. 'I must be calm.' Her heart was thumping with terror, and the dark magenta lobsters on the labels of the tins wavered dizzily before her eyes. She was afraid to look round; but through the noise of her heart-beats she listened anxiously for the inevitable outcry.

'I don't know if you're interested in lobster, Miss,' a confidential voice almost whispered into her left ear.

Joyce started violently; then managed, with an effort, to smile and shake her head.

'This is a line we can heartily recommend, Miss. I'm sure if you were to try a tin ...'

'And now,' Helen was saying, very calmly and in the same maddeningly feudal tone, 'I need ten pounds of sugar. But that you must send.'

They walked out of the shop. The young man at the cheese and bacon counter smiled his farewell; they were nice-looking girls and regular customers. With a great effort, Joyce contrived to be gracious yet once more. But they were hardly through the door when her face disintegrated, as it were, into a chaos of violent emotion.

'Helen!' she said furiously. 'Helen!'

But Helen was still the young queen on her silver florin, a speechless profile.

'Helen!' Between the glove and the sleeve, Joyce found an inch of her sister's bare skin and pinched, hard.

Helen jerked her arm away, and without looking round, a profile still, 'If you bother me any more,' she said in a low voice, 'I shall push you into the gutter.'

Joyce opened her mouth to speak, then changed her mind

and, absurdly, shut it again. She knew that if she did say anything more, Helen unquestionably would push her into the gutter. She had to be content with shrugging her shoulders and looking dignified.

The greengrocer's was crowded. Waiting for her turn to be served, Helen had no difficulty in bagging a couple of oranges.

'Have one?' she proposed insultingly to Joyce as they walked out of the shop.

It was Joyce's turn to be a profile on a coin.

At the stationer's there were, unfortunately, no other clients to distract the attention of the people behind the counter. But Helen was equal to the situation. A handful of small change suddenly went rolling across the floor; and while the assistants were hunting for the scattered pennies, she helped herself to a rubber and three very good pencils.

It was at the butcher's that the trouble began. Ordinarily Helen refused to go into the shop at all; the sight, the sickening smell of those pale corpses disgusted her. But this morning she walked straight in. In spite of the disgust. It was a point of honour. She had said *every* shop, and she wasn't going to give Joyce an excuse for saying she had cheated. For the first half-minute, while her lungs were still full of the untainted air she had inhaled outside in the street it was all right. But, oh God, when at last she had to breathe ... God! She put her handkerchief to her nose. But the sharp rasping smell of the carcasses leaked through the barrier of perfume, superimposing itself upon the sweetness, so that a respiration that began with *Quelques Fleurs* would hideously end with dead sheep or, opening in stale blood, modulated insensibly into the key of jasmine and ambergris.

A customer went out; the butcher turned to her. He was an oldish man, very large, with a square massive face that beamed down at her with a paternal benevolence.

'Like Mr Baldwin,' she said to herself, and then, aloud but indistinctly through her handkerchief, 'A pound and a half of rumpsteak, please.'

The butcher returned in a moment with a mass of gory flesh. 'There's a beautiful piece of meat, Miss!' He fingered the dank, red lump with an artist's loving enthusiasm. 'A really *beautiful* piece.' It was Mr Baldwin fingering his Virgil, thumbing his dog's-eared Webb.

'I shall never eat meat again,' she said to herself, as Mr Baldwin turned away and began to cut up the meat. 'But what shall I take?' She looked round. 'What on earth . . .? Ah!' A marble shelf ran, table-high, along one of the walls of the shop. On it, in trays, pink or purply brown, lay a selection of revolting viscera. And among the viscera a hook – a big steel S, still stained, at one of its curving tips, with the blood of whatever drawn and decapitated corpse had hung from it. She glanced round. It seemed a good moment – the butcher was weighing her steak, his assistant was talking to that disgusting old woman like a bull-dog, the girl at the cash desk was deep in her accounts. Aloof and dissociated in the doorway, Joyce was elaborately overacting the part of one who interrogates the sky and wonders if this drizzle is going to turn into something serious. Helen took three quick steps, picked up the hook, and was just lowering it into her basket when, full of solicitude, 'Look out, Miss,' came the butcher's voice, 'you'll get yourself dirty if you touch those hooks.'

That start of surprise was like the steepest descent of the Scenic Railway – sickening! Hot in her cheeks, her eyes, her forehead, came a rush of guilty blood! She tried to laugh.

'I was just looking.' The hook clanked back on to the marble.

'I wouldn't like you to spoil your clothes, Miss.' His smile was fatherly. More than ever like Mr Baldwin.

Nervously, for lack of anything better to do or say, Helen laughed again, and, in the process, drew another deep breath of corpse. Ugh! She fortified her nose once more with *Quelques Fleurs*.

'One pound and eleven ounces, Miss.'

She nodded her assent. But what could she take? And how was she to find the opportunity?

'Anything more this morning?'

Yes, that was the only thing to do – to order something more. That would give her time to think, a chance to act. 'Have you any . . .' she hesitated '. . . any sweetbreads?'

Yes, Mr Baldwin did have some sweetbreads, and they were

on the shelf with the other viscera. Near the hook. 'Oh, I don't know,' she said, when he asked her how much she needed. 'Just the ordinary amount, you know.'

She looked about her while he was busy with the sweetbreads, despairingly. There was nothing in this beastly shop, nothing except the hook, that she *could* take. And now that he had seen her with it in her hands, the hook was out of the question. Nothing whatever. Unless ... That was it! A shudder ran through her. But she frowned, she set her teeth. She was determined to go through with it.

'And now,' when he had packed up the sweetbreads, 'now,' she said, 'I must have some of those!' She indicated the packets of pale sausages piled on a shelf at the other end of the shop.

'I'll do it while his back is turned,' she thought. But the girl at the cash desk had emerged from her accounts and was looking round the shop. 'Oh, damn her, damn her!' Helen fairly screamed in her imagination, and then, 'Thank goodness!' the girl had turned away. A hand shot out; but the averted glance returned, '*Damn* her!' The hand dropped back. And now it was too late. Mr Baldwin had got the sausages, had turned, was coming back towards her.

'Will that be all, Miss?'

'Well, I wonder?' Helen frowned uncertainly, playing for time. 'I can't help thinking there was something else ... something else ...' The seconds passed; it was terrible; she was making a fool of herself, an absolute idiot. But she refused to give up. She refused to acknowledge defeat.

'We've some beautiful Welsh mutton in this morning,' said the butcher in that artist's voice of his, as though he were talking of the Georgics.

Helen shook her head: she really couldn't start buying mutton now.

Suddenly the girl at the cash desk began to write again. The moment had come. 'No,' she said with decision, 'I'll take another pound of sausages.'

'Another?' Mr Baldwin looked surprised.

No wonder! she thought. They'd be surprised at home too.

'Yes, just one more,' she said, and smiled ingratiatingly, as though she were asking a favour. He walked back towards the shelf. The girl at the cash desk was still writing, the old woman who looked like a bull-dog had never stopped talking to the assistant. Quickly – there was not a second to lose – Helen turned towards the marble shelf beside her. It was for one of those kidneys that she had decided. The thing slithered obscenely between her gloved fingers – a slug, a squid. In the end she had to grab it with her whole hand. Thank heaven, she thought, for gloves! As she dropped it into the basket, the idea came to her that for some reason she might have to take the horrible thing in her mouth, raw as it was and oozy with some unspeakable slime, take it in her mouth, bite, taste, swallow. Another shudder of disgust ran through her, so violent this time that it seemed to tear something at the centre of her body.

Tired of acting the meteorologist, Joyce was standing under her umbrella looking at the chrysanthemums in the florist's window next door. She had prepared something particularly offensive to say to Helen when she came out. But at the sight of her sister's white unhappy face she forgot even her legitimate grievances.

'Why, Helen, what *is* the matter?'

For all answer Helen suddenly began to cry.

'What is it?'

She shook her head and, turning away, raised her hand to her face to brush away the tears.

'Tell me . . .'

'Oh!' Helen started and cried out as though she had been stung by a wasp. An expression of agonized repugnance wrinkled up her face. 'Oh, too filthy, *too* filthy,' she repeated, looking at her fingers. And setting her basket down on the pavement, she unbuttoned the glove, stripped it off her hand, and, with a violent gesture, flung it away from her into the gutter.

CHAPTER SIX

November 6th 1902

THE guard whistled, and obediently the train began to move – past Keating, at a crawl; past Branson; past Pickwick, Owl and

Waverley; past Beecham, Owbridge, Carter, Pears, in accelerated succession; past Humphrey's Iron Buildings, past Lollingdon for Choate; past Eno's almost at twenty miles an hour; past Pears, Pears, Pears, Pears, Pears – and suddenly the platform and its palings dipped and were lost, swallowed in the green country. Anthony leaned back in his corner and sighed thankfully. It was escape at last; he had climbed out of that black well into which they had pushed him, and he was free again. The wheels sang cheerfully in his ears. 'To stop the train pull down the chain penálty for impróper use five póunds five pounds FIVE POUNDS FIVE POUNDS ...' But how perfectly awful luncheon at Granny's had been!

'Work,' James Beavis was saying. 'It's the only thing at a time like this.'

His brother nodded. 'The only thing,' he agreed. Then, after a moment's hesitation, 'One's had a pretty bad knock,' he added self-consciously, in that queer jargon which he imagined to be colloquial English. John Beavis's colloquialisms mostly came out of books. That 'bad knock' was a metaphor drawn from the boxing contests he had never witnessed. 'Luckily,' he went on, 'one's got a great deal of work on hand at the moment.' He thought of his lectures. He thought of his contributions to the Oxford Dictionary. The mountains of books, the slips, his huge card index, the letters from fellow philologists. And the exhaustive essay on Jacobean slang. 'Not that one wants to "shirk" anything,' he added, putting the colloquial word between the audible equivalents of inverted commas. James mustn't think that he was going to drown his grief in work. He groped for a phrase. 'It's ... it's a sacred music that one's facing!' he brought out at last.

James kept nodding with quick jerks of the head, as though he knew in advance everything his brother would or possibly could say. His face twitched with sudden involuntary tics. He was wasted by nervous impatience as though by a consumption, eaten away by it to the very bone. 'Quite,' he said, 'quite.' And gave one last nod. There was a long silence.

'Tomorrow,' Anthony was thinking, 'there'll be algebra with old Jimbug.' The prospect was disagreeable; he wasn't good at maths, and, even at the best of times, even when he was only joking, Mr Jameson was a formidable teacher. 'If Jimbug gets baity with me, like that time last week ...' Remembering the scene, Anthony frowned; the blood came up into his cheeks. Jimbug made sarcastic remarks at him and pulled his hair. He had begun to blub. (Who wouldn't have blubbed?) A tear had fallen on to the equation he was trying to work out and made a huge round blot. That beast Staithes had ragged him about it afterwards. Luckily Foxe had come to his rescue. One laughed at Foxe because he stammered; but he was really extraordinarily decent.

At Waterloo, Anthony and his father took a hansom. Uncle James preferred to walk. 'I can get to the Club in eleven minutes,' he told them. His hand went to his waistcoat pocket. He looked at his watch; then turned and without saying another word went striding away down the hill.

'Euston!' John Beavis called up to the cabman.

Stepping cautiously on the smooth slope, the horse moved forward; the cab heaved like a ship. Inaudibly, Anthony hummed the 'Washington Post'. Riding in a hansom always made him feel extraordinarily happy. At the bottom of the hill, the cabby whipped his horse into a trot. They passed a smell of beer, a smell of fried fish; drove through 'Goodbye, Dolly Gray' on a cornet and swung into the Waterloo Road. The traffic roared and rattled all about them. If his father had not been there, Anthony would have sung out aloud.

The end of the afternoon was still smokily bright above the house-tops. And, all at once, here was the river, shining, with the black barges, and a tug, and St Paul's like a balloon in the sky, and the mysterious Shot Tower.

On the bridge, a man was throwing bread to the sea-gulls. Dim, almost invisible, they came sliding through the air; turned, with a tilt of grey wings, leaning against their speed, and suddenly flashed into brilliance, like snow against the dark fringes of the sky; then wheeled away again out of the light, towards invisibility. Anthony looked and stopped humming. Swerving towards you on the ice a skater will lean like that.

And suddenly, as though, disquietingly, he too had understood the inner significance of those swooping birds, 'Dear boy,'

Mr Beavis began, breaking a long silence. He pressed Anthony's arm. 'Dear boy!'

With a sinking of the heart Anthony waited for what he would say next.

'We must stand together now,' said Mr Beavis.

The boy made a vague noise of acquiescence.

'Close together. Because we both ...' he hesitated, 'we both loved her.'

There was another silence. 'Oh, if only he'd stop!' Anthony prayed. Vainly. His father went on.

'We'll always be true to her,' he said. 'Never ... never let her down? – will we?'

Anthony nodded.

'Never!' John Beavis repeated emphatically. 'Never!' And to himself he recited yet once more those lines that had haunted him all these days:

> Till age, or grief, or sickness must
> Marry my body to that dust
> It so much loves; and fill the room
> My heart keeps empty in thy tomb.
> Stay for me there!

Then aloud and in a tone almost of defiance, 'She'll never be dead for us,' he said. 'We'll keep her living in our hearts – won't we?'

'Living for us,' his father continued, 'so that we can live for her – live finely, nobly, as she would want us to live.' He paused on the brink of a colloquialism – the sort of colloquialism, he intended it to be, that a schoolboy would understand and appreciate. 'Live .. well, like a pair of regular "bricks",' he brought out unnaturally. 'And bricks,' he continued, extemporizing an improvement on the locution, 'bricks that are also "pals". Real "chums". We're going to be "chums" now, Anthony, aren't we?'

Anthony nodded again. He was in an agony of shame and embarrassment. 'Chums.' It was a school-story word. *The Fifth Form at St Dominic's.* You laughed when you read it, you howled derisively. *Chums!* And with his father! He felt himself blushing. Looking out of the side window, to hide his discomfort, he saw one of the grey birds come swooping down, out of the sky, towards the bridge; nearer, nearer; then it leaned, it swerved away to the left, gleamed for a moment, transfigured, and was gone.

*

At school everyone was frightfully decent. Too decent, indeed. The boys were so tactfully anxious not to intrude on his emotional privacy, not to insult him with the display of their own high spirits, that, after having made a few constrained and unnatural demonstrations of friendliness, they left him alone. It was almost, Anthony found, like being sent to Coventry. They could hardly have made it worse for him if he had been caught stealing or sneaking. Never, since the first days of his first term, had he felt so hopelessly out of it all as he felt that evening.

'Pity you missed the match this afternoon,' said Thompson as they sat down to supper; he spoke in the tone he would have used to a visiting uncle.

'Was it a good game?' Anthony asked with the same unnatural politeness.

'Oh, jolly good. They won, though. Three-two.' The conversation languished. Uncomfortably, Thompson wondered what he should say next. That limerick of Butterworth's, about the young lady of Ealing? No, he couldn't possibly repeat that; not today, when Beavis's mother ... Then what? A loud diversion at the other end of the table providentially solved his problem. He had an excuse to turn away. 'What's that?' he shouted with unnecessary eagerness. 'What's that?' Soon they were all talking and laughing together. From beyond an invisible gulf Anthony listened and looked on.

'Agnes!' someone called to the maid. 'Agnes!'

'Aganeezer Lemon-squeezer,' said Mark Staithes – but in a low voice, so that she shouldn't hear; rudeness to the servants was a criminal offence at Bulstrode, and for that reason all the more appreciated, even *sotto voce*. That lemon-squeezer produced an explosion of laughter. Staithes himself, however, preserved his gravity. To sit unsmiling in the midst of the laughter he himself had provoked gave him an extraordinary sense of power and superiority. Besides, it was in the family tradition. No Staithes ever smiled at his own joke or epigram or repartee.

Looking round the table, Mark Staithes saw that that wretched,

41

baby-faced Benger Beavis wasn't laughing with the rest, and for a second was filled with a passionate resentment against this person who had dared not to be amused by his joke. What made the insult more intolerable was the fact that Benger was so utterly insignificant. Bad at football, not much use at cricket. The only thing he was good at was work. Work! And did such a creature dare to sit unsmiling when he ... Then, all of a sudden, he remembered that the poor chap had lost his mother, and, relaxing the hardness of his face, he gave him, across the intervening space, a little smile of recognition and sympathy. Anthony smiled back, then looked away, blushing with an obscure discomfort as though he had been caught doing something wrong. The consciousness of his own magnanimity and the spectacle of Benger's embarrassment restored Staithes to his good humour.

'Agnes!' he shouted. 'Agnes!'

Large, chronically angry, Agnes came at last.

'More jam, please, Agnes.'

'Jore mam,' cried Thompson. Everybody laughed again, not because the joke was anything but putrid, but simply because everybody wanted to laugh.

'And breadney.'

'Yes, more breaf.'

'More breaf, please, Agnes.'

'Breaf, indeed!' said Agnes indignantly, as she picked up the empty bread-and-butter plate. 'Why can't you say what you mean?'

There was a redoubling of the laughter. They couldn't say what they meant – absolutely couldn't, because to say 'breaf' or 'breadney' instead of bread was a Bulstrodian tradition and the symbol of their togetherness, the seal of their superiority to all the rest of the uninitiated world.

'More Pepin le Bref!' shouted Staithes.

'Pepin le Breadney, le Breadney!'

The laughter became almost hysterical. They all remembered that occasion last term, when they had come to Pepin le Bref in their European History. Pepin le Bref – le *Bref!* First Butterworth had broken down, then Pembroke-Jones, then Thompson – and finally the whole of Division II, Staithes with the rest of them, uncontrollably. Old Jimbug had got into the most appalling bait. Which made it, now, even funnier.

'Just a lot of silly babies!' said Agnes; and, finding them still laughing when, a moment later, she came back with more bread, 'Just babies!' she repeated in a determined effort to be insulting. But her stroke did not touch them. They were beyond her, rapt away in the ecstasy of causeless laughter.

Anthony would have liked to have laughed with them, but somehow did not dare to do more than smile, distantly and politely, like someone in a foreign country, who does not understand the joke, but wants to show that he has no objection to other people having a bit of fun. And a moment later, feeling hungry, he found himself unexpectedly struck dumb above his empty plate. For to have asked for more breaf, or another chunk of breadney, would have been, for the sacred pariah he had now become, at once an indecency and an intrusion – an indecency, because a person who has been sanctified by his mother's death should obviously not talk slang, and an intrusion, because an outsider has no right to use the special language reserved to the elect. Uncertainly, he hesitated. Then at last, 'Pass me the bread, please,' he murmured; and blushed (the words sounded so horribly stupid and unnatural) to the roots of his hair.

Leaning towards his neighbour on the other side, Thompson went on with his whispered recitation of the limerick. '. . . all over the ceiling,' he concluded; and they shrieked with laughter.

Thank goodness, Thompson hadn't heard. Anthony felt profoundly relieved. In spite of his hunger, he did not ask again.

There was a stir at the high table; old Jimbug rose to feet. A hideous noise of chair-legs scraping across boards filled the hall, solidly, it seemed; then evaporated into the emptiness of complete silence. 'For all that we have received . . .' The talk broke out again, the boys stampeded towards the door.

In the corridor, Anthony felt a hand on his arm. 'Hullo, B-benger.'

'Hullo, Foxe.' He did not say, 'Hullo, Horse-Face,' because of what happened this morning. Horse-Face woud be as inappropriate to the present circumstances as Breaf.

'I've got s-something to sh-show you,' said Brian Foxe, and

his melancholy, rather ugly face seemed suddenly to shine, as he smiled at Anthony. People laughed at Foxe because he stammered and looked like a horse. But almost everybody liked him. Even though he was a bit of a swot and not much good at games. He was rather pi, too, about smut; and he never seemed to get into trouble with the masters. But in spite of it all, you had to like him, because he was so awfully decent. Too decent, even; for it really wasn't right to treat New Bugs the way he did – as though they were equals. Beastly little ticks of nine the equals of boys of eleven and twelve; imagine! No, Foxe was wrong about the New Bugs; of that there could be no doubt. All the same, people liked old Horse-Face.

'What have you got?' asked Anthony; and he felt so grateful to Horse-Face for behaving towards him in a normal, natural way, that he spoke quite gruffly, for fear the other might notice what he was feeling.

'Come and see,' Brian meant to say; but he got no further than 'C-c-c-c . . .' The long agony of clicks prolonged itself. At another time, Anthony might have laughed, might have shouted, 'Listen to old Horse-Face trying to be sea-sick!' But today he said nothing; only thought what awful bad luck it was on the poor chap. In the end, Brian Foxe gave up the attempt to say, 'Come and see,' and, instead, brought out. 'It's in my p-play-box.'

They ran down the stairs to the dark lobby where the play-boxes were kept.

'Th-there!' said Brian, lifting the lid of his box.

Anthony looked, and at the sight of that elegant little ship, three-masted, square-rigged with paper sails, 'I say,' he exclaimed, 'that's a beauty! Did you make her yourself?'

Brian nodded. He had had the carpenter's shop to himself that afternoon – all the tools he needed. That was why she was so professional-looking. He would have liked to explain it all, to share his pleasure in the achievement with Anthony; but he knew his stammer too well. The pleasure would evaporate while he was laboriously trying to express it. Besides, 'carpenter' was a terrible word. 'We'll t-try her to-n-night,' he had to be content with saying. But the smile which accompanied the words seemed at once to apologize for their inadequacy and to make

44

up for it. Anthony smiled back. They understood one another.

Carefully, tenderly, Brian unstepped the three matchstick masts and slipped them, sails and all, into the inner pocket of his jacket; the hull went into his breeches. A bell rang. It was bed-time. Obediently, Brian shut his play-box. They started to climb the stairs once more.

'I w-won f-five more g-games today with my old c-c-c ... my ch-cheeser,' he emended, finding 'conker' too difficult.

'Five !' cried Anthony. 'Good for the old Horse-Face !'

Forgetting that he was an outcast, a sacred pariah, he laughed aloud. He felt warm and at home. It was only when he was undressing in his cubicle that he remembered – because of the tooth powder.

'Twice a day,' he heard her saying, as he dipped his wet brush into the pink carbolic-smelling dust. 'And if you possibly can, after lunch as well. Because of the germs.'

'But, Mother, you can't expect me to go up and clean them after *lunch* !'

The wound to his vanity (did she think his teeth were so dirty?) had made him rude. He found a retrospective excuse in the reflection that it was against the school rules to go up to the dorms during the day.

On the other side of the wooden partition that separated his cubicle from Anthony's, Brian Foxe was stepping into his pyjamas. First the left leg, then the right. But just as he was starting to pull them up, there came to him, suddenly, a thought so terrible that he almost cried aloud. 'Suppose *my* mother were to die !' And she *might* die. If Beavis's mother had died, of course she might. And at once he saw her, lying in her bed at home. Terribly pale. And the death-rattle, that death-rattle one always read about in books – he heard it plainly; and it was like the noise of one of those big wooden rattles that you scare birds with. Loud and incessant, as though it were made by a machine. A human being couldn't possibly make such a noise. But all the same, it came out of her mouth. It was the death-rattle. She was dying.

His trousers still only half-way up his thighs, Brian stood there, quite still, staring at the brown varnished partition in front of him with eyes that filled with tears. It was too terrible.

The coffin; and then the empty house; and, when he went to bed, nobody to come and say good night.

Suddenly shaking himself out of immobility, he pulled up his trousers and tied the string with a kind of violence.

'But she *isn't* dead!' he said to himself. 'She *isn't*!'

Two cubicles away, Thompson gave vent to one of those loud and extraordinarily long-drawn farts for which, at Bulstrode, he had such a reputation. There were shouts, a chorus of laughter. Even Brian laughed – Brian who generally refused to see that there was anything funny about that sort of noise. But he was filled at this moment with such a sense of glad relief, that any excuse for laughter was good enough. She was still alive! And though she wouldn't have liked him to laugh at anything so vulgar, he simply had to allow his thankfulness to explode. Uproariously he guffawed; then, all at once, broke off. He had thought of Beavis. *His* mother was really dead. What must *he* be thinking? Brian felt ashamed of having laughed, and for such a reason.

Later, when the lights had been put out, he climbed on to the rail at the head of his bed, and, looking over the partition into Anthony's cubicle, 'I s-say,' he whispered, 'sh-shall we see how the new b-b-b ... the new sh-ship goes?'

Anthony jumped out of bed and, the night being cold, put on his dressing-gown and slippers; then, noiselessly, stepped on to his chair and from the chair (pushing aside the long baize curtain) to the window-ledge. The curtain swung back behind him, shutting him into the embrasure.

It was a high narrow window, divided by a wooden transom into two parts. The lower and larger part consisted of a pair of sashes; the small upper pane was hinged at the top and opened outwards. When the sashes were closed, the lower of them formed a narrow ledge, half-way up the window. Standing on this ledge, a boy could conveniently get his head and shoulders through the small square opening above. Each window – each pair of windows, rather – was set in a gable, so that when you leaned out, you found the slope of the tiles coming steeply down on either side, and immediately in front of you, on a level with the transom, the long gutter which carried away the water from the roof.

The gutter! It was Brian who had recognized its potentialities. A sod of turf carried surreptitiously up to bed in a bulging pocket, a few stones – and there was your dam. When it was built, you collected all the water-jugs in the dormitory, hoisted them one by one and poured their contents into the gutter. There would be no washing the next morning; but what of that? A long narrow sea stretched away into the night. A whittled ship would float, and those fifty feet of watery boundlessness invited the imagination. The danger was always rain. If it rained hard, somebody had somehow to sneak up, at whatever risk, and break the dam. Otherwise the gutter would overflow, and an overflow meant awkward investigations and unpleasant punishments.

Perched high between the cold glass and the rough hairy baize of the curtains, Brian and Anthony leaned out of their twin windows into the darkness. A brick mullion was all that separated them, they could speak in whispers.

'Now then, Horse-Face,' commanded Anthony. 'Blow!'

And like the allegorical Zephyr in a picture, Horse-Face blew. Under its press of paper sail, the boat went gliding along the narrow water-way.

'Lovely!' said Anthony ecstatically; and bending down till his cheek was almost touching the water, he looked with one half-shut and deliberately unfocused eye until, miraculously, the approaching toy was transformed into a huge three-master, seen phantom-like in the distance and bearing down on him, silently, through the darkness. A great ship – a ship of the line – one hundred and ten guns – under a cloud of canvas – the North-East Trades blowing steadily – bowling along at ten knots – eight bells just sounding from ... He started violently as the foremast came into contact with his nose. Reality flicked back into place again.

'It looks just like a real ship,' he said to Brian as he turned the little boat round in the gutter. 'Put your head down and have a squint. I'll blow.'

Slowly the majestic three-master travelled back again.

'It's like the Fighting T-t-t ... You know that p-picture.'

Anthony nodded; he never liked to admit ignorance.

'T-temeraire,' the other brought out at last.

'Yes, yes,' said Anthony, rather impatiently, as though he had known it all the time. Bending down again, he tried to recapture that vision of the huge hundred-and-ten-gunner bowling before the North-East Trades; but without success; the little boat refused to be transfigured. Still, she was a lovely ship. 'A beauty,' he said out loud.

'Only she's a b-bit l-lopsided,' said Brian, in modest depreciation of his handiwork.

'But I rather like that,' Anthony assured him. 'It makes her look as though she were heeling over with the wind.' Heeling over : – it gave him a peculiar pleasure to pronounce the phrase. He had never uttered it before – only read it in books. Lovely words! And making an excuse to repeat them, 'Just look!' he said, 'how she heels over when it blows really hard.'

He blew, and the little ship almost capsized. The hurricane, he said to himself … struck her full on the starboard beam … carried away the fore top-gallant sails and the spinnakers … stove in our only boat … heeled till the gunwale touched the water. … But it was tiring to go on blowing as hard as that. He looked up from the gutter; his eyes travelled over the sky; he listened intently to the silence. The air was extraordinarily still; the night, almost cloudless. And what stars! There was Orion, with his feet tangled in the branches of the oak tree. And Sirius. And all the others whose names he didn't know. Thousands and millions of them.

'Gosh!' he whispered at last.

'W-what on earth do you s-suppose they're f-for?' said Brian, after a long silence.

'What – the stars?'

Brian nodded.

Remembering things his Uncle James had said, 'They're not *for* anything,' Anthony answered.

'But they m-must be,' Brian objected.

'Why?'

'Because e-everything is for s-something.'

'I don't believe that.'

'W-well, th-think of b-b-bees,' said Brian with some difficulty.

Anthony was shaken; they had been having some lessons in botany from old Bumface – making drawings of pistils and

48

things. Bees – yes; they were obviously for something. He wished he could remember exactly what Uncle James had said. The iron somethings of nature. But iron whats?

'And m-mountains,' Brian was laboriously continuing. 'It w-wouldn't r-rain properly if there w-weren't any m-mountains.'

'Well, what do *you* think they're for?' Anthony asked, indicating the stars with an upward movement of the chin.

'P-perhaps there are p-people.'

'Only on Mars.' Anthony's certainty was dogmatic.

There was a silence. Then, with decision, as though he had at last made up his mind to have it out, at any cost, 'S-sometimes,' said Brian, 'I w-wonder wh-whether they aren't really al-live.' He looked anxiously at his companion : was Benger going to laugh? But Anthony, who was looking up at the stars, made no sound or movement of derision; only nodded gravely. Brian's shy defenceless little secret was safe, had received no wound. He felt profoundly grateful; and suddenly it was as though a great wave were mounting, mounting through his body. He was almost suffocated by that violent uprush of love and ('Oh, suppose it had been *my* mother!') of excruciating sympathy for poor Benger. His throat contracted; the tears came into his eyes. He would have liked to reach out and touch Benger's hand; only, óf course, that sort of thing wasn't done.

Anthony meanwhile was still looking at Sirius. 'Alive,' he repeated to himself. 'Alive.' It was like a heart in the sky, pulsing with light. All at once he remembered that young bird he had found last Easter holidays. It was on the ground and couldn't fly. His mother had made fun of him because he didn't want to pick it up. Big animals he liked, but for some reason it gave him the horrors to touch anything small and alive. In the end, making an effort with himself, he had caught the bird. And in his hand the little creature had seemed just a feathered heart, pulsing against his palm and fingers, a fistful of hot and palpitating blood. Up there, above the fringes of the trees, Sirius was just such another heart. Alive. But of course Uncle James would just laugh.

Stung by this imaginary mockery and ashamed of having been betrayed into such childishness, 'But how can they be alive?' he asked resentfully, turning away from the stars.

Brian winced. 'Why is he angry?' he wondered. Then aloud, 'Well,' he started, 'if G-god's alive . . .'

'But my pater doesn't go to church,' Anthony objected.

'N-no, b-b-but . . .' How little he wanted to argue, now!

Anthony couldn't wait. 'He doesn't believe in that sort of thing.'

'But it's G-god that c-counts; n-not ch-church.' Oh, if only he hadn't got this horrible stammer! He could explain it all so well; he could say all those things his mother had said. But somehow, at the moment, even the things that she had said were beside the point. The point wasn't saying; the point was caring for people, caring until it hurt.

'My uncle,' said Anthony, 'he doesn't even believe in God. I don't either,' he added provocatively.

But Brian did not take up the challenge. 'I s-say,' he broke out impulsively, 'I s-say, B-b-b- . . .' The very intensity of his eagerness made him stammer all the worse. 'B-benger,' he brought out at last. It was an agony to feel the current of his love thus checked and diverted. Held up behind the grotesquely irrelevant impediment to its progress, the stream mounted, seemed to gather force and was at last so strong within him that, forgetting althogether that it wasn't done, Brian suddenly laid his hand on Anthony's arm. The fingers travelled down the sleeve, then closed round the bare wrist; and thereafter, every time his stammer interposed itself between his feeling and its object, his grasp tightened in a spasm almost of desperation.

'I'm so t-terribly s-sorry about your m-mother,' he went on. 'I d-didn't w-want to s-say it be-before. N-not in f-front of the o-others. You know, I was th-th-th . . .' He gripped on Anthony's wrist more tightly; it was as though he were trying to supplement his strangled words by the direct eloquence of touch, were trying to persuade the other of the continued existence of the stream within him, of its force, unabated in spite of the temporary checking of the current. He began the sentence again and acquired sufficient momentum to take him past the barrier. 'I was th-thinking just n-now,' he said, 'it m-might have been *my* mother. Oh, B-b-beavis, it m-must be too awful!'

Anthony looked at him, in the first moment of surprise, with an expression of suspicion, almost of fear on his face. But as the other stammered on, this first hardening of resistance melted away, and now, without feeling ashamed of what he was doing, he began to cry.

Balanced precariously in the tall embrasure of the windows, the two children stood there for a long time in silence. The cheeks of both of them were cold with tears; but on Anthony's wrist the grip of that consoling hand was obstinately violent, like a drowning man's.

Suddenly, with a thin rattling of withered leaves, a gust of wind came swelling up out of the darkness. The little three-master started, as though it had been woken out of sleep, and noiselessly, with an air of purposeful haste, began to glide, stern-foremost, along the gutter.

*

The servants had gone to bed; all the house was still. Slowly, in the dark, John Beavis left his study and climbed past the mezzanine landing, past the drawing-room, stair after stair, towards the second floor. Outside, in the empty street, the sound of hoofs approached and again receded. The silence closed in once more – the silence of his solitude, the silence (he shuddered) of her grave.

He stood still, listening for long seconds to the beating of his heart; then, with decision, mounted the last two stairs, crossed the dark landing and, opening the door, turned on the light. His image confronted him, staring palely from the dressing-table mirror. The silver brushes were in their usual place, the little trays and pin-cushions, the row of cut-glass bottles. He looked away. One corner of the broad pink quilt was turned back; he saw the two pillows lying cheek by cheek, and above them, on the wall, that photogravure of the Sistine Madonna they had bought together, in the shop near the British Museum. Turning, he saw himself again, at full length, funereally black, in the glass of the wardrobe. The wardrobe ... He stepped across the room and turned the key in the lock. The heavy glass door swung open of its own accord, and suddenly he was breathing the very air of her presence, that faint scent of orris-root, quickened secretly, as it were, by some sharper, warmer perfume. Grey, white, green, shell-pink, black – dress after dress. It was as though she had died ten times and ten times been hung there, limp, gruesomely headless, but haloed still, ironically, with the sweet, breathing symbol of her life. He stretched out his hand and touched the smooth silk, the cloth, the muslin, the velvet; all those various textures. Stirred, the hanging folds gave out their perfume more strongly; he shut his eyes and inhaled her real presence. But what was left of her had been burnt, and the ashes were at the bottom of that pit in Lollingdon churchyard.

'Stay for me there,' John Beavis whispered articulately in the silence.

His throat contracted painfully; the tears welled out between his closed eyelids. Shutting the wardrobe door, he turned away and began to undress.

He was conscious, suddenly, of an overwhelming fatigue. It cost him an immense effort to wash. When he got into bed, he fell asleep almost at once.

Towards the morning, when the light of the new day and the noises from the street had begun to break through the enveloping layers of his inner darkness, John Beavis dreamed that he was walking along the corridor that led to his lecture-room at King's College. No, not walking: running. For the corridor had become immensely long and there was some terrible urgent reason for getting to the end of it quickly, for being there in time. In time for what? He did not know; but as he ran, he felt a sickening apprehension mounting, as it were, and expanding and growing every moment more intense within him. And when at last he opened the door of the lecture-room, it wasn't the lecture-room at all, but their bedroom at home, with Maisie lying there, panting for breath, her face flushed with the fever, dark with the horrible approach of asphyxiation, and across it, like two weals, bluish and livid, the parted lips. The sight was so dreadful that he started broad awake. Daylight shone pale between the curtains; the quilt showed pink; there was a gleam in the wardrobe mirror; outside, the milkman was calling, 'Mu-ilk, Mui-uilk!' as he went his rounds. Everything was reassuringly familiar, in its right place. It had been no more than a bad dream. Then, turning his head, John Beavis saw that the other half of the broad bed was empty.

*

The bell came nearer and nearer, ploughing through the deep warm drifts of sleep, until at last it hammered remorselessly on his naked and quivering consciousness. Anthony opened his eyes. What a filthy row it made! But he needn't think of getting up for at least another five minutes. The warmth under the sheets was heavenly. Then – and it spoilt everything – he remembered that early school was algebra with Jimbug. His heart came into his throat. Those awful quadratics! Jimbug would start yelling at him again. It wasn't fair. And he'd blub. But then it occurred to him that Jimbug probably wouldn't yell at him today – because of what, he suddenly remembered, had happened yesterday. Horse-Face had been most awfully decent last night, he went on to think.

But it was time to get up. One, two, three and, ugh, how filthily cold it was! He was just diving upwards into his shirt when somebody tapped very softly at the door of his cubicle. One last wriggle brought his head through into daylight. He went and opened. Staithes was standing in the passage. Staithes – grinning, it was true, in apparent friendliness; but still ... Anthony was disturbed. Mistrustfully, but with a hypocritical smile of welcome, 'What's up?' he began; but the other put a finger to his lips.

'Come and look,' he whispered. 'It's marvellous!'

Anthony was flattered by this invitation from one who, as captain of the football eleven, had a right to be, and generally was, thoroughly offensive to him. He was afraid of Staithes and disliked him – and for that very reason felt particularly pleased that Staithes should have taken the trouble to come to him like this, of his own accord. ...

Staithes's cubicle was already crowded. The conspiratorial silence seethed and bubbled with a suppressed excitement. Thompson had had to stuff his handkerchief into his mouth to keep himself from laughing, and Pembroke-Jones was doubling up in paroxysms of noiseless mirth. Wedged in the narrow space between the foot of the bed and the washstand, Partridge was standing with one cheek pressed against the partition. Staithes touched him on the shoulder. Partridge turned round and came out into the centre of the cubicle; his freckled face was distorted with glee and he twitched and fidgeted as though his bladder were bursting. Staithes pointed to the place he had vacated and Anthony squeezed in. A knot in the wood of the partition had been prized out, and, through the hole you could see all that was going on in the next cubicle. On the bed, wearing only a woollen undervest and his rupture appliance, lay Goggler Ledwidge. His eyes behind the thick glass of his spectacles were shut; his lips were parted. He looked tranquilly happy and serene, as though he were in church.

'Is he still there?' whispered Staithes.

Anthony turned a grinning face and nodded; then pressed his eyes more closely to the spy-hole. What made it so specially funny was the fact that it should be Goggler – Goggler, the school buffoon, the general victim, predestined by weakness and timidity to inevitable persecution. This would be something new to bait him with.

'Let's give him a fright,' suggested Staithes, and climbed up on to the rail at the head of the bed.

Partridge, who played centre forward for the first eleven, made a movement to follow him. But it was to Anthony that Staithes unexpectedly turned. 'Come on, Beavis,' he whispered. 'Come up here with me.' He wanted to be specially decent to the poor chap – because of his mater. Besides, it pleased him to be able to snub that lout, Partridge.

Anthony accepted the flattering invitation with an almost abject alacrity and got up beside him. The others perched unsteadily at the foot of the bed. At a signal from Staithes all straightened themselves up and, showing their heads above the partition, hooted their derision.

Recalled thus brutally from his squalidly tender little Eden of enemas and spankings (it had, as yet, no female inhabitants), Goggler gave vent to a startled cry; his eyes opened, frantic with terror; he went very white for a moment, then blushed. With his two hands he pulled down his vest; but it was too short to cover his nakedness or even his truss. Absurdly short, like a baby's vest. ('We'll try to make them last this one more term,' his mother had said. 'These woollen things are so frightfully expensive.' She had made great sacrifices to send him to Bulstrode.)

'Pull, pull!' Staithes shouted in sarcastic encouragement of his efforts.

'Why wouldn't Henry VIII allow Anne Boleyn to go into his henhouse?' said Thompson. Everyone knew the answer, of course. There was a burst of laughter.

Staithes lifted one foot from its perch, pulled off the leather-soled slipper, took aim and threw. It hit Goggler on the side of the face. He gave a cry of pain, jumped out of bed and stood with hunched shoulders and one skinny little arm raised to cover his head, looking up at the jeering faces through eyes that had begun to overflow with tears.

'Buzz yours too!' shouted Staithes to the others. Then, seeing the new arrival standing in the open doorway of his cubicle, 'Hullo, Horse-Face,' he said, as he took off the other slipper; 'come and have a shot.' He raised his arm; but before he could throw, Horse-Face had jumped on to the bed and caught him by the wrist.

'No, s-stop!' he said. 'Stop.' And he caught also at Thompson's arm. Leaning over Staithes's shoulder, Anthony threw – as hard as he could. Goggler ducked. The slipper thumped against the wooden partition behind him.

'B-beavis!' cried Horse-Face – so reproachfully, that Anthony felt a sudden twinge of shame.

'It didn't hit him,' he said by way of excuse; and for some queer reason found himself thinking of that horrible deep hole in Lollingdon churchyard.

Staithes had found his tongue again. 'I don't know what you think you're doing, Horse-Face,' he said angrily, and jerked the slipper out of Brian's hand. 'Why can't you mind your own business?'

'It isn't f-fair,' Brian answered.

'Yes, it is.'

'F-five against one.'

'But you don't know what he was doing.'

'I d-don't c-c-c . . . don't mind.'

'You would care, if you knew,' said Staithes; and proceeded

to tell him what Goggler had been doing – as dirtily as he knew how.

Brian dropped his eyes and his cheeks went suddenly very red. To have to listen to smut always made him feel miserable – miserable and at the same time ashamed of himself.

'Look at old Horse-Face blushing!' called Partridge; and they all laughed – none more derisively than Anthony. For Anthony had had time to feel ashamed of his shame; time to refuse to think about that hole in Lollingdon churchyard; time, too, to find himself all of a sudden almost hating old Horse-Face. 'For being so disgustingly pi,' he would have said, if somebody had asked him to explain his hatred. But the real reason was deeper, obscurer. If he hated Horse-Face, it was because Horse-Face was so extraordinarily decent; because Horse-Face had the courage of convictions which Anthony felt should also be *his* convictions – which, indeed, would be his convictions if only he could bring himself to have the courage of them. It was just because he liked Horse-Face so much that he now hated him. Or, rather, because there were so many reasons why he should like him – so few reasons, on the contrary, why Horse-Face should return the liking. Horse-Face was rich with all sorts of fine qualities that he himself either lacked completely or else, which was worse, possessed, but somehow was incapable of manifesting. That sudden derisive burst of laughter was the expression of a kind of envious resentment against a superiority which he loved and admired. Indeed, the love and the admiration in some sort produced the resentment and the envy – produced, but ordinarily kept them below the surface in an unconscious abeyance, from which, however, some crisis like the present would suddenly call them.

'You should have seen him,' concluded Staithes. Now that he felt in a better humour he laughed – he could afford to laugh.

'In his truss,' Anthony added, in a tone of sickened contempt. Goggler's rupture was an aggravation of the offence.

'Yes, in his beastly old truss!' Staithes confirmed approvingly. There was no doubt about it; combined as it was with the spectacles and the timidity, that truss made the throwing of slippers not only inevitable, but right, a moral duty.

'He's disgusting,' Anthony went on, warming pleasantly to his righteous indignation.

For the first time since Staithes had started on his description of Goggler's activities Brian looked up. 'B-but w-why is he more disgusting than anyone else?' he asked in a low voice. 'A-after all,' he went on, and the blood came rushing back into his cheeks as he spoke, 'he i-isn't the . . . the o-only one.'

There was a moment's uncomfortable silence. Of course he wasn't the only one. But he was the only one, they were all thinking, who had a truss, and goggles, and a vest that was too short for him; the only one who did it in broad daylight and let himself be caught at it. There *was* a difference.

Staithes counter-attacked on another front. 'Sermon by the Reverend Horse-Face!' he said jeeringly, and at once recovered the initiative, the position of superiority. 'Gosh!' he added in another tone, 'it's late. We must buck up.'

CHAPTER SEVEN

April 8th 1934

FROM A.B.'S DIARY

CONDITIONED reflex. What a lot of satisfaction I got out of old Pavlov when first I read him. The ultimate debunking of all human pretensions. We were all dogs and bitches together. Bow-wow, sniff the lamp-post, lift the leg, bury the bone. No nonsense about free will, goodness, truth, and all the rest. Each age has its psychological revolutionaries. La Mettrie, Hume, Condillac, and finally the Marquis de Sade, latest and most sweeping of the eighteenth-century debunkers. Perhaps, indeed, the ultimate and absolute revolutionary. But few have the courage to follow the revolutionary argument to Sade's conclusions. Meanwhile, science did not stand still. *Dix-huitième* debunking, apart from Sade, proved inadequate. The nineteenth century had to begin again. Marx and the Darwinians. Who are still with us – Marx obsessively so. Meanwhile the twentieth century has produced yet another lot of debunkers – Freud and, when he began to flag, Pavlov and the Behaviourists. Conditioned reflex: – it seemed, I remember, to put the lid on everything. Whereas actually, of course, it merely restated the doctrine of free will. For if reflexes can be conditioned, then, obviously, they can be re-conditioned. Learning to use the self properly, when one has been using it badly – what is it but reconditioning one's reflexes?

Lunched with my father. More cheerful than I've seen him recently, but old and, oddly, rather enjoying it. Making much of getting out of his chair with difficulty, of climbing very slowly up the stairs. A way, I suppose, of increasing his sense of importance. Perhaps also a way of commanding sympathy whenever he happens to want it. Baby cries so that mother shall come and make a fuss of him. It goes on from the cradle to the grave. Miller says of old age that it's largely a bad habit. Use conditions function. Walk about as if you were a martyr to rheumatism and you'll impose such violent muscular strains upon yourself that a martyr to rheumatism you'll really be. Behave like an old man and your body will function like an old man's, you'll think and feel as an old man. The lean and slippered pantaloon – literally a part that one plays. If you refuse to play it and learn how to act on your refusal, you won't become a pantaloon. I suspect this is largely true. Anyhow, my father is playing his present part with gusto. One of the great advantages of being old, provided that one's economic position is reasonably secure and one's health not too bad, is that one can afford to be serene. The grave is near, one has made a habit of not feeling anything very strongly; it's easy, therefore, to take the God's-eye view of things. My father took it about peace, for example. Yes, men were mad, he agreed; there would be another war quite soon – about 1940, he thought. (A date, significantly, when he was practically certain to be dead!) Much worse than the last war, yes; and would probably destroy the civilization of Western Europe. But did it really matter so much? Civilization would go on in other continents, would build itself up anew in the devastated areas. Our time scale was all wrong. We should think of ourselves, not as living in the thirties of the twentieth century, but as at a point between two ice ages. And he ended up by quoting Goethe – *alles Vergängliche ist nur ein Gleichnis*. All which is doubtless quite true, but not the whole truth. Query: how to combine belief that the world is to a great extent illusory with belief that it is none the less essential to improve the illusion? How to be simultaneously dispassionate and not indifferent, serene like an old man and active like a young one?

CHAPTER EIGHT

August 30th 1933

'These vile horse-flies!' Helen rubbed the reddening spot on her arm. Anthony made no comment. She looked at him for a little in silence. 'What a lot of ribs you've got!' she said at last.

'Schizothyme physique,' he answered from behind the arm with which he was shielding his face from the light. 'That's why I'm here. Predestined by the angle of my ribs.'

'Predestined to what?'

'To sociology; and in the intervals to this.' He raised his hand, made a little circular gesture and let it fall again on the mattress.

'But what's "this"?' she insisted.

'This?' Anthony repeated. 'Well ...' He hesitated. But it would take too long to talk about that temperamental divorce between the passions and the intellect, those detached sensualities, those sterilized ideas. 'Well, *you*,' he brought out at last.

'Me?'

'Oh, I admit it might have been someone else,' he said, and laughed, genuinely amused by his own cynicism.

Helen also laughed, but with a surprising bitterness. 'I *am* somebody else.'

'Meaning what?' he asked, uncovering his face to look at her.

'Meaning what I say. Do you think *I* should be here – the real I?'

'Real I!' he mocked. 'You're talking like a theosophist.'

'And you're talking like a fool,' she said. 'On purpose. Because, of course, you aren't one.' There was a long silence. I, real I? But where, but how, but at what price? Yes, above all, at what price? Those Cavells and Florence Nightingales. But it was impossible, that sort of thing; it was, above all, ridiculous.

59

She frowned to herself, she shook her head; then, opening her eyes, which had been shut, looked for something in the external world to distract her from these useless and importunate thoughts within. The foreground was all Anthony. She looked at him for a moment; then, reaching out with a kind of fascinated reluctance, as though towards some irresistibly strange but distasteful animal, she touched the pink crumpled skin of the great scar that ran diagonally across his thigh, an inch or two above the knee. 'Does it still hurt?' she asked.

'When I'm run down. And sometimes in wet weather.' He raised his head a little from the mattress and, at the same time bending his right knee, examined the scar. 'A touch of the Renaissance,' he said reflectively. 'Slashed trunks.'

Helen shuddered. 'It must have been awful!' Then, with a sudden vehemence, 'How I hate pain!' she cried, and her tone was one of passionate, deeply personal resentment. 'Hate it,' she repeated for all the Cavells and Nightingales to hear.

She had pushed him back into the past again. That autumn day at Tidworth eighteen years before. Bombing instruction. An imbecile recruit had thrown short. The shouts, his panic start, the blow. Oddly remote it all seemed now, and irrelevant, like something seen through the wrong end of a telescope. And even the pain, all the months of pain, had shrunk almost to non-existence. Physically, it was the worst thing that had ever happened to him – and the lunatic in charge of his memory had practically forgotten it.

'One can't remember pain,' he said aloud.

'*I* can.'

'No, you can't. You can only remember its occasion, its accompaniments.'

Its occasion at the midwife's in the rue de la Tombe-Issoire, its accompaniments of squalor and humiliation. Her face hardened as she listened to his words.

'You can never remember its actual quality,' he went on. 'No more than you can remember the quality of a physical pleasure. Today, for example, half an hour ago – you can't *remember*. There's nothing like a re-creation of the event. Which is lucky.' He was smiling now. 'Think, if one could fully remember perfumes or kisses. How wearisome the reality of them would be! And what woman with a memory would ever have more than one baby?'

Helen stirred uneasily. 'I can't imagine how any woman ever does,' she said in a low voice.

'As it is,' he went on, 'the pains and pleasures are new each time they're experienced. Brand new. Every gardenia is the first gardenia you ever smelt. And every confinement . . .'

'You're talking like a fool again,' she interrupted angrily. 'Confusing the issue.'

'I thought I was clarifying it,' he protested. 'And anyhow, what *is* the issue?'

'The issue's me, you, real life, happiness. And you go chattering away about things in the air. Like a fool!'

'And what about you?' he asked. 'Are you such a clever one at real life? Such an expert in happiness?'

In the mind of each of them his words evoked the image of a timorous figure, ambushed behind spectacles.

That marriage! What on earth could have induced her? Old Hugh, of course, had been sentimentally in love. But was that a sufficient reason? And, afterwards, what sort of disillusions? Physiological, he supposed, for the most part. Comic, when you thought of them in relation to old Hugh. The corners of Anthony's mouth faintly twitched. But for Helen, of course, the joke could only have been disastrous. He would have liked to know the details – but at second hand, on condition of not having to ask for or be offered her confidences. Confidences were dangerous, confidences were entangling – like fly-paper; yes, like fly-paper. . . .

Helen sighed; then, squaring her shoulders and in a tone of resolution, 'Two blacks don't make a white,' she said. 'Besides, I'm my own affair.'

Which was all for the best, he thought. There was a silence.

'How long were you in hospital with that wound?' she asked in another tone.

'Nearly ten months. It was disgustingly infected. They had to operate six times altogether.'

'How horrible!'

Anthony shrugged his shoulders. At least it had preserved him from those trenches. But for the grace of God . . . 'Queer,' he added, 'what unlikely forms the grace of God assumes sometimes! A half-witted bumpkin with a hand-grenade. But for him I should have been shipped out to France and slaughtered – almost to a certainty. He saved my life.' Then, after a pause, 'My freedom too,' he added. 'I'd let myself be fuddled by those beginning-of-war intoxications. "Honour has come back, as a king, to earth." But I suppose you're too young ever to have heard of poor Rupert. It seemed to make sense then, in 1914. "Honour has come back ..." But he failed to mention that stupidity had come back too. In hospital, I had all the leisure to think of that other royal progress through the earth. Stupidity has come back, as a king – no; as an emperor, as a divine Führer of all the Aryans. It was a sobering reflection. Sobering and profoundly liberating. And I owed it to the bumpkin. He was one of the great Führer's most faithful subjects.' There was a silence. 'Sometimes I feel a bit nervous – like Polycrates – because I've had so much luck in my life. All occasions always seem to have conspired *for* me. Even *this* occasion.' He touched the scar. 'Perhaps I ought to do something to allay the envy of the Gods – throw a ring into the sea next time I go bathing.' He uttered a little laugh. 'The trouble is, I don't possess a ring.'

CHAPTER NINE

April 2nd 1903

At Paddington, Mr Beavis and Anthony got into an empty third-class compartment and waited for the train to start. For Anthony a railway journey was still profoundly important, still a kind of sacrament. The male soul, in immaturity, is *naturaliter ferrovialis*. This huge and god-like green monster, for example, that now came snorting into the station and drew up at Platform 1 – but for Watt and Stephenson it would never have rolled thus majestically into its metropolitan cathedral of sooty glass. But the intensity of delight which Anthony felt as he watched the divine creature approach, as he breathed its stink of coal smoke and hot oil, as he heard and almost unconsciously imitated the ch-ff, ch-ff, ch-ff of its steamy panting, was a sufficient proof that the boyish heart must have been, in some mysterious way, prepared for the advent of Puffing Billy and the Rocket, that the actual locomotive, when it appeared, must have corresponded (how satisfyingly!) with some dim prophetic image of a locomotive, pre-existing in the mind of children from the beginning of palaeolithic time. Ch-ff, ch-ff; then silence; then the terrible, the soul-annihilating roar of escaping steam. Wonderful! Lovely!

Bonneted, in black, like a pair of Queen Victorias, two fat and tiny old ladies passed slowly, looking for a compartment where they would not have their throats cut or be compelled to listen to bad language. Mr Beavis looked very respectable indeed. They paused, held a consultation; but, leaning out of the window, Anthony made such a face at them that they moved away again. He smiled triumphantly. Keeping the compartment to oneself was one of the objects of the sacred game of travelling – was the equivalent, more or less, of a Royal Marriage at bezique; you scored forty, so to speak, each time you left a station without a stranger in your carriage. Having lunch in the dining-car counted as much as a Sequence – two hundred and fifty. And Double Bezique – but this, as yet, Anthony had never scored – was being in a slip carriage.

The guard whistled, the train began to move.

'Hurrah!' Anthony shouted.

The game had begun well: a Royal Marriage in the very first round. But a few minutes later he was regretting those two old ladies. For, rousing himself suddenly from his abstracted silence, John Beavis leaned forward and, touching his son's knee, 'Do you remember what day of the month it is?' he asked in a low and, to Anthony, inexplicably significant tone.

Anthony looked at him doubtfully; then started to overact the part of the Calculator, frowning over a difficult problem. There was something about his father that seemed to make such over-acting inevitable.

'Let me see,' he said unnaturally, 'we broke up on the thirty-first – or was it the thirtieth? That was Saturday, and today's Monday ...'

'Today's the second,' said his father in the same slow voice.

Anthony felt apprehensive. If his father knew the date, why had he asked?

'It's exactly five months today,' Mr Beavis went on.

Five months? And then, with a sudden sickening drop of the heart, Anthony realized what his father was talking about. The Second of November, the Second of April. It was five months since she had died.

'Each second of the month – one tried to keep the day sacred.'

Anthony nodded and turned his eyes away with a sense of guilty discomfort.

'Bound each to each by natural piety,' said Mr Beavis.

What on earth was he talking about now? And, oh, why, why did he have to say these things? So awful; so indecent – yes, indecent; one didn't know where to look. Like the times when Granny's stomach made those awful bubbling noises after meals . . .

Looking into his son's averted face, Mr Beavis perceived signs of resistance and was hurt, was saddened, and felt the sadness turn into an obscure resentment that Anthony should not suffer as acutely as he did. Of course the child was still very young, not yet able to realize the full extent of his loss; but all the same, all the same . . .

To Anthony's unspeakable relief the train slowed down for its first stop. The suburbs of Slough passed slowly and ever slowlier before his eyes. Against all the rules of the sacred game, he prayed that somebody might get into their compartment. And, thank heaven, somebody did get in – a gross, purple-faced man whom on any other occasion Anthony would have hated. Today he loved him.

Shielding his eyes with his hand, Mr Beavis retired again into a private world of silence.

In the carriage, on the way from Twyford station, his father added insult to injury.

'You must always be on your very best behaviour,' he recommended.

'Of course,' said Anthony curtly.

'And always be punctual,' Mr Beavis continued. 'And don't be greedy at meal-times.' He hesitated, smiled in anticipation of what he was about to say, then launched his colloquialism: 'however excellent the "grub" may be.' There was a little silence. 'And be polite to the Abigails,' he added.

They turned off the road into a drive that wound between tall shrubberies of rhododendrons. Then, across an expanse of tree-islanded grass, appeared a façade of Georgian stucco. The house was not large, but solid, comfortable and at the same time elegant. Built, you divined, by someone who could quote Horace, aptly, on every occasion. Rachel Foxe's father, Mr Beavis reflected, as he looked at it, must have left quite a lot of money. Naval architecture – and didn't the old boy invent something that the Admiralty took up? Foxe, too, had been well off: something to do with coal. (How charming those daffodils looked in the grass there, under the tree!) But a dour, silent, humourless man who had not, Mr Beavis remembered, understood his little philological joke about the word 'pencil'. Though if he'd known at the time that the poor fellow had a duodenal ulcer, he certainly wouldn't have risked it.

Mrs Foxe and Brian came to meet them as the carriage drew up. The boys went off together. Mr Beavis followed his hostess into the drawing-room. She was a tall woman, slender and very upright, with something so majestic in her carriage, so nobly austere in the lines and expression of her face, that Mr Beavis always felt himself slightly intimidated and ill at ease in her presence.

'It was so very good of you to ask us,' he said. 'And I can't tell you how much it will mean for ...' he hesitated for an instant; then (since it was the second of the month), with a little shake of the head and in a lower tone, 'for this poor motherless little fellow of mine,' he went on, 'to spend his holidays here with you.'

Her clear brown eyes had darkened, as he spoke, with a sympathetic distress. Always firm, always serious, the coming together of her full, almost floridly sculptured lips expressed more than ordinary gravity. 'But I'm so delighted to have him,' she said in a voice that was warm and musically vibrant with feeling. 'Selfishly glad – for Brian's sake.' She smiled, and he noticed that even when she smiled her mouth seemed some-how to preserve, through all its sensibility, its profound capacity for suffering and enjoyment, that seriousness, that determined purity which characterized it in repose. 'Yes, selfishly,' she repeated. 'Because, when he's happy, I am.'

Mr Beavis nodded; then, sighing, 'One's thankful,' he said, 'to have as much left to one as that – the reflection of someone else's happiness.' Magnanimously, he was giving Anthony the right not to suffer – though of course when the boy was a little older, when he could realize more fully . . .

Mrs Foxe did not continue the conversation. There was something rather distasteful to her in his words and manner, something that jarred upon her sensibilities. But she hastened to banish the disagreeable impression from her mind. After all, the important, the essential fact was that the poor man had suffered, was still suffering. The false note, if falsity there were, was after the fact – in the mere expression of the suffering.

She proposed a stroll before tea, and they walked through the garden and out into the domesticated wilderness of grass and trees beyond. In a glade of the little copse that bounded the property to the north, three crippled children were picking primroses. With a gruesome agility they swung themselves on their crutches from clump to clump of the pale golden flowers, yelling as they went in shrill discordant rapture.

They were staying, Mrs Foxe explained, in one of her cottages. 'Three of my cripples,' she called them.

At the sound of her voice the children looked up, and at once came hopping across the open space towards her.

'Look, Miss, look what I found!'

'Look here, Miss!'

'What's this called, Miss?'

She answered their questions, asked others in return, promised to come that evening to see them.

Feeling that he too ought to do something for the cripples, Mr Beavis began to tell them about the etymology of the word 'primrose'. '*Primerole* in Middle English,' he explained. 'The "rose" crept in by mistake.' They stared at him uncomprehendingly. 'A mere popular blunder,' he went on; then, twinkling, 'a "howler,"' he added. 'Like our old friend,' he smiled at them knowingly, 'our old friend "causeway".'

There was a silence. Mrs Foxe changed the subject.

'Poor little mites!' she said, when at last they let her go. 'They're so happy, they make one want to cry. And then, after a week, one has to pack them off again. Back to their slum. It seems too cruel. But what can one do? There are so many of them. One can't keep one lot at the expense of the others.'

They walked on for a time in silence, and Mrs Foxe found herself suddenly thinking that there were also cripples of the spirit. People with emotions so lame and rickety that they didn't know how to feel properly; people with some kind of hunch or deformity in their power of expression. John Beavis perhaps was one of them. But how unfair she was being! How presumptuous too! Judge not that ye be not judged. And anyhow, if it were true, that would only be another reason for feeling sorry for him.

'I think it must be tea-time,' she said aloud; and, to prevent herself from passing any more judgements, she started to talk to him about those Cripple Schools she had been helping to organize in Notting Dale and St Pancras. She described the cripple's life at home – the parents out at work; not a glimpse of a human face from morning till night; no proper food; no toys, no books, nothing to do but to lie still and wait – for what? Then she told him about the ambulance that now went round to fetch the children to school, about the special desks, the lessons, the arrangements for supplying a decent dinner.

'And our reward,' she said, as she opened the door into the house, 'is that same heart-breaking happiness I was speaking of just now. I can't help feeling it as a kind of reproach, an accusation. Each time I see that happiness, I ask myself what right I have to be in a position to give it so easily, just by spending a little money and taking a tiny bit of pleasant trouble. Yes, what right?' Her warm clear voice trembled a little as she uttered the question. She raised her hands in an interrogative gesture, then let them fall again and walked quickly into the drawing-room.

Mr Beavis followed her in silence. A kind of tingling warmth had expanded within him as he listened to her last words. It was like the sensation he had when he read the last scene of *Measure for Measure*, or listened to Joachim in the Beethoven Concerto.

67

Mr Beavis could only stay two nights. There was an important meeting of the Philological Society. And then, of course, his work on the Dictionary. 'The old familiar grind,' he explained to Mrs Foxe in a tone of affected self-pity and with a sigh that was hardly even meant to carry conviction. The truth was that he enjoyed his work, would have felt lost without it. 'And you're really sure,' he added, 'that Anthony won't be too much of a burden to you?'

'Burden? But look!' And she pointed through the window to where the two boys were playing bicycle polo on the lawn. 'And it's not only that,' she went on. 'I've really come to be very much attached to Anthony in these two days. There's something so deeply touching about him. He seems so vulnerable somehow. In spite of all that cleverness and good sense and determination of his. There's part of him that seems terribly at the mercy of the world.' Yes, at its mercy, she repeated to herself, thinking, as she did so, of that broad and candid forehead, of those almost tremulously sensitive lips, of that slight, unforceful chin. He could be easily hurt, easily led astray. Each time he looked at her, he made her feel almost guiltily responsible for him.

'And yet,' said Mr Beavis, 'there are times when he seems strangely indifferent.' The memory of that episode in the train had not ceased to rankle. For though, of course, he wanted the child to be happy, though he had decided that the only happiness he himself could know henceforward would come from the contemplation of the child's happiness, the old resentment still obscurely persisted : he felt aggrieved because Anthony had not suffered more, because he seemed to resist and reject suffering when it was brought to him. 'Strangely indifferent,' he repeated.

Mrs Foxe nodded. 'Yes,' she said, 'he wears a kind of armour. Covers up his vulnerability in the most exposed place and at the same time uncovers it elsewhere, so that the slighter wounds shall act as a kind of distraction, a kind of counter-irritant. It's self-protection. And yet' (her voice deepened, thrillingly), 'and yet I believe that in the long run he'd be better and spiritually healthier, yes, and happier too, if he could bring himself to do just the opposite – if he'd armour himself against the little distracting wounds, the little wounds of pleasure as well as the little wounds of pain, and expose his vulnerableness only to the great and piercing blows.'

'How true that is!' said Mr Beavis, who found that her words applied exactly to himself.

There was a silence. Then, harking back to his original question, 'No, no,' said Mrs Foxe with decision, 'so far from feeling him as a burden, I'm really enchanted to have him here. Not only for what he is in himself, but also for what he is to Brian – and incidentally for what Brian is to him. It's delightful to see them. I should like them to be together every holidays.' Mrs Foxe paused for a moment; then, 'Seriously,' she went on, 'if you've made no plans for the summer, why don't you think of this? We've taken a little house at Tenby for August. Why shouldn't you and Anthony find a place there too?'

Mr Beavis thought the idea an excellent one; and the boys, when it was broached to them, were delighted.

'So it's only good-bye till August,' said Mrs Foxe as she saw him off. 'Though of course,' she added, with a warmth that was all the greater for being the result of a deliberate effort of cordiality, 'of course we shall meet before then.'

The carriage rattled away down the drive; and for a hundred yards or more Anthony ran beside it, shouting 'Good-bye' and waving his handkerchief with a vehemence that Mr Beavis took as the sign of a correspondingly intense regret to see him go. In fact, however, it was just a manifestation of overflowing energy and high spirits. Circumstances had filled him, body and mind, with the deep joy of being happily alive. This joy required physical expression, and his father's departure gave him an excuse for running and waving his arms. Mr Beavis was extremely touched. But if only, he went on sadly to think, if only there were some way of canalizing this love, and his own for the boy, so that it might irrigate the aridities of their daily intercourse! Women understood these things so much better. It had been touching to see how the poor child had responded to Mrs Foxe's affection. And perhaps, he went on to speculate, perhaps it was just because there had been no woman to direct his feelings that Anthony had seemed to be so uncaring. Perhaps a child could never adequately mourn his mother for the very reason that he was motherless. It was a vicious circle. Mrs Foxe's influence would be good, not only in this matter, but in a thousand other ways as well. Mr Beavis sighed. If only it were possible for a man and a woman to associate; not in marriage, but for a common purpose, for the sake of motherless, of fatherless children! A good woman – admirable, extraordinary even. But in spite of that (almost because of that), it could only be an association for a common purpose. Never a marriage. And anyhow there was Maisie – waiting for him there; he would not fail ... But an association for the sake of the children – that would be no betrayal.

Anthony walked back to the house whistling 'The Honeysuckle and the Bee'. He was fond of his father – fond, it is true, by force of habit, as one is fond of one's native place, or its traditional cooking – but still, genuinely fond of him. Which did nothing however, to diminish the discomfort he always felt in Mr Beavis's presence.

'Brian!' he shouted, as he approached the house – shouted a bit self-consciously; for it seemed queer to be calling him Brian instead of Foxe or Horse-Face. Rather unmanly, even a shade discreditable.

Brian's answering whistle came from the school-room.

'I vote we take the bikes,' Anthony called.

At school, people used to mock at old Horse-Face for his bird mania. 'I say, you fellows,' Staithes would say, taking Horse-Face by the arm, 'guess what I saw today! Two spew-tits and a piddle-warbler.' And a great howl of laughter would go up – a howl in which Anthony always joined. But here, where there was nobody to shame him out of being interested in spring migrants and nest-boxes and heronries, he took to bird-watching with enthusiasm. Coming in, wet and muddy from the afternoon's walk, 'Do you know what we heard, Mrs Foxe?' he would ask triumphantly, before poor Brian had had time to get out a stammered word. 'The first whitethroat!' or 'The first willow wren!' and Rachel Foxe would say, 'How splendid!' in such a way that he was filled with pride and happiness. It was as though those piddle-warblers had never existed.

After tea, when the curtains had been drawn and the lamps brought in, Mrs Foxe would read to them. Anthony, who had always been bored to death by Scott, found himself following the 'Fortunes of Nigel' with the most passionate attention.

Easter approached, and, for the time being, 'Nigel' was put away. Mrs Foxe gave them readings, instead, from the New Testament. 'And he saith unto them, My soul is exceeding sorrowful unto death : tarry ye here, and watch. And he went forward a little and fell on the ground, and prayed that, if it were possible, the hour might pass from him. And he said, Abba, Father, all things are possible unto thee; take away this cup from me : nevertheless not what I will, but what thou wilt.' The lamplight was a round island in the darkness of the room, and towards it, from the fire, projected a vague promontory of luminous redness. Anthony was lying on the floor, and from the high Italian chair beside the lamp the words came down to him, transfigured, as it were, by that warm, musical voice, charged with significances he had never heard or seen in them before. 'And it was the third hour, and they crucified him.' In the ten heart-beats of silence that followed he seemed to hear the blows of the hammer on the nails. Thud, thud, thud ... He passed the fingers of one hand across the smooth palm of the other; his body went rigid with horror, and through the stiffened muscles passed a violent spasm of shuddering.

'And when the sixth hour was come, there was darkness over the whole land until the ninth hour.' Mrs Foxe lowered her book. 'That's one of those additions I was telling you about,' she said, 'one of those embroideries on the story. One must think of the age in which the writers of the gospels lived. They believed these things could happen; and, what's more, they thought they ought to happen on important occasions. They wanted to do honour to Jesus; they wanted to make his story seem more wonderful. But to us nowadays, these things make it seem less wonderful; and we don't feel that they do him honour. The wonderful thing for us,' she went on, and her voice thrilled with a deep note of fervour, 'is that Jesus was a man, no more able to do miracles and no more likely to have them done for him than the rest of us. Just a man – and yet he could do what he did, he could be what he was. That's the wonder.'

There was a long silence; only the clock ticked and the flame rustled silkily in the grate. Anthony lay on his back and stared at the ceiling. Everything was suddenly clear. Uncle James was right; but the other people were right too. She had shown how it was possible for both of them to be right. Just a man – and yet . . . Oh, he too, he too would do and be!

Mrs Foxe picked up the book once more. The thin pages crackled as she turned them.

'Now upon the first day of the week, very early in the morning, they came upon the sepulchre, bringing the spices which they had prepared, and certain others with them. And they found the stone rolled away from the sepulchre.'

The stone . . . But at Lollingdon there was earth; and only ashes in that little box – that little box no bigger than a biscuit tin. Anthony shut his eyes in the hope of excluding the odious vision; but against the crimson darkness the horns, the triangular frizz of auburn curls stood out with an intenser vividness. He lifted his hand to his mouth, and, to punish himself, began to bite the forefinger, harder, harder, until the pain was almost intolerable.

That evening, when she came to say good night to him, Mrs Foxe sat down on the edge of Anthony's bed and took his hand. 'You know, Anthony,' she said after a moment of silence, 'you mustn't be afraid of thinking about her.'

'Afraid?' he mumbled, as though he hadn't understood. But he *had* understood – understood, perhaps, more than she had meant. The blood rushed guiltily into his cheeks. He felt frightened, as though somehow she had trapped him, found him out – frightened and therefore resentful.

'You mustn't be afraid of suffering,' she went on. 'Thinking about her will make you sad: that's inevitable. And it's right. Sadness is necessary sometimes – like an operation; you can't be well without it. If you think about her, Anthony, it'll hurt you. But if you don't think about her, you condemn her to a second death. The spirit of the dead lives on in God. But it also lives on in the minds of the living – helping them, making them better and stronger. The dead can only have this kind of immortality if the living are prepared to give it them. Will you give it her, Anthony?'

Mutely, and in tears, he nodded his answer. It was not so much the words that had reassured him as the fact that the words were hers and had been uttered in that compelling voice. His fears were allayed, his suspicious resentment died down. He felt safe with her. Safe to abandon himself to the sobs that now mounted irresistibly in his throat.

'Poor little Anthony!' She stroked his hair. 'Poor little Anthony! There's no help for it; it'll always hurt – always. You'll never be able to think of her without some pain. Even time can't take away all the suffering, Anthony.'

She paused, and for a long minute sat there in silence, thinking of her father, thinking of her husband. The old man, so massive, so majestic, like a prophet – then in his wheeled chair, paralysed and strangely shrunken, his head on one side, dribbling over his white beard, hardly able to speak ... And the man she had married, out of admiration for his strength, out of respect for his uprightness; had married, and then discovered that she did not, could not love. For the strength, she had found, was cold and without magnanimity; the uprightness, harsh and cruel uprightness. And the pain of the long last illness had hardened and embittered him. He had died implacable, resisting her tenderness to the last.

'Yes, there'll always be pain and sadness,' she went on at last. 'And after all,' a warm note of pride, almost of defiance, came into her voice, 'can one wish that it should be otherwise? You wouldn't want to forget your mother, would you, Anthony? Or not to care any more? Just in order to escape a little suffering. You wouldn't want that?'

Sobbing, he shook his head. And it was quite true. At this moment he didn't want to escape. It was in some obscure way a relief to be suffering this extremity of sorrow. And he loved her because she had known how to make him suffer.

Mrs Foxe bent down and kissed him. 'Poor little Anthony!' she kept repeating. 'Poor little Anthony!'

It rained on Good Friday; but on Saturday the weather changed, and Easter Day was symbolically golden, as though on purpose, as though in a parable. Christ's resurrection and the re-birth of Nature – two aspects of an identical mystery. The sunshine, the clouds, like fragments of marbly sculpture in the pale blue sky, seemed, in some profound and inexpressible way, to corroborate all that Mrs Foxe had said.

They did not go to church; but, sitting on the lawn, she read aloud, first a bit of the service for Easter Day, then some extracts from Renan's *Life of Jesus*. The tears came into Anthony's eyes as he listened, and he felt an unspeakable longing to be good, to do something fine and noble.

On the Monday, a party of slum children were brought down to spend the day in the garden and the copse. At Bulstrode one would have called them scadgers and offensively ignored their existence. Beastly little scadgers; and when they were older, they would grow into louts and cads. Here, however, it was different. Mrs Foxe transformed the scadgers into unfortunate children who would probably never get a second glimpse of the country in all the year.

'Poor kids!' Anthony said to her when they arrived. But in spite of the compassion he was doing his level best to feel, in spite of his determined goodwill, he was secretly afraid of these stunted yet horribly mature little boys with whom he had offered to play, he feared and therefore disliked them. They seemed immeasurably foreign. Their patched, stained clothes, their shapeless boots, were like a differently coloured skin; their cockney might have been Chinese. The mere appearance of them made him feel guiltily self-conscious. And then there was the way they looked at him, with a derisive hatred of his new suit and his alien manners; there was the way the bolder of them whispered together and laughed. When they laughed at Brian for his stammer, he laughed with them; and in a little while they laughed no more, or laughed only in a friendly and almost sympathetic way. Anthony, on the contrary, pretended not to notice their mockery. A gentleman, he had always been taught explicitly as well as by constant implication and the example of his elders, a gentleman doesn't pay any attention to that kind of thing. It is beneath his dignity. He behaved as though their laughter were non-existent. They went on laughing.

He hated that morning of rounders and hide-and-seek. But worse was to follow at lunch-time. He had offered to help in the serving of the table. The work in itself was unobjectionable enough. But the smell of poverty when the twenty children were assembled in the dining-room was so insidiously disgusting

74

– like Lollingdon church, only much worse – that he had to slip out two or three times in the course of the meal to spit in the lavatory basin. 'Reeking with germs!' he heard his mother's angrily frightened voice repeating. 'Reeking with germs!' And when Mrs Foxe asked him a question, he could only nod and make an inarticulate noise with his mouth shut; if he spoke, he would have to swallow. Swallow what? It was revolting only to think of it.

'Poor kids!' he said once more, as he stood with Mrs Foxe and Brian watching their departure. 'Poor kids!' and felt all the more ashamed of his hypocrisy when Mrs Foxe thanked him for having worked so hard to entertain them.

And when Anthony had gone up to the school-room, 'Thank *you* too, my darling,' she said, turning to Brian. 'You were really splendid.'

Flushing with pleasure, Brian shook his head. 'It was all y-you,' he said; and suddenly, because he loved her so much because she was so good, so wonderful, he found his eyes full of tears.

Together they walked out into the garden. Her hand was on his shoulder. She smelt faintly of eau-de-Cologne, and all at once (and this also, it seemed, was part of her wonderfulness) the sun came out from behind a cloud.

'Look at those heavenly daffodils!' she cried, in that voice that made everything she said seem, to Brian, truer, in some strange way, than the truth itself. ' "And now my heart with pleasure fills . . ." Do you remember, Brian?'

Flushed and with bright eyes, he nodded. ' "And d-dances . . ." '

' "Dances with the daffodils." ' She pressed him closer to her. He was filled with an unspeakable happiness. They walked on in silence. Her skirts rustled at every step – like the sea, Brian thought; the sea at Ventnor, that time last year, when he couldn't sleep at night because of the waves on the beach. Lying there in the darkness, listening to the distant breathing of the sea, he had felt afraid, and above all sad, terribly sad. But, associated with his mother, the memories of that fear, that profound and causeless sadness, became beautiful; and at the same time, in some obscure way, they seemed to reflect their new beauty back on to her, making her seem yet more

75

wonderful in his eyes. Rustling back and forth across the sunny lawn, she took on some of the mysterious significance of the windy darkness, the tirelessly returning waves.

'Poor little Anthony!' said Mrs Foxe, breaking the long silence. 'It's hard, it's terribly hard.' Hard also for poor Maisie, she was thinking. That graceful creature, with her languors, her silences, her dreamy abstractions, and then her sudden bursts of laughing activity – what had such a one to do with death? Or with birth, for that matter? Maisie with a child to bring up – it hardly made more sense than Maisie dead.

'It must be t-t-t . . .' but 'terrible' wouldn't come, 'it must be d-dreadful,' said Brian, laboriously circumventing the obstacle, while his emotion ran on ahead in an imaginary outburst of un-uttered and unutterable words, 'n-not to have a m-mother.'

Mrs Foxe smiled tenderly, and, bending down, laid her cheek for a moment against his hair. 'Dreadful also not to have a son,' she said, and realized, as she did so, that the words were even truer than she had intended them to be – that they were true on a plane of deeper, more essential existence than that on which she was now moving. She had spoken for the present; but if it would be terrible not to have him now, how incomparably more terrible it would have been *then*, after her father had had his stroke and during the years of her husband's illness! In that time of pain and utter spiritual deprivation her love for Brian had been her only remaining possession. Ah, terrible, terrible indeed, then, to have no son !

CHAPTER TEN

June 16th 1912

Books. The table in Anthony's room was covered with them. The five folio volumes of Bayle, in the English edition of 1738. Rickaby's translation of the *Summa contra Gentiles*. De Gourmont's *Problème du Style. The Way of Perfection.* Dostoevsky's *Notes from Underground.* Three volumes of Byron's *Letters.* The works of St John of the Cross in Spanish. The plays of Wycherley. Lee's *History of Sacerdotal Celibacy.*

If only, Anthony thought as he came in from his walk, if only one had two sets of eyes! Janus would be able to read *Candide* and the *Imitation* simultaneously. Life was so short, and books so countlessly many. He pored voluptuously over the table, opening at random now one volume, now another. 'He would not lie down,' he read; 'then his neck was too large for the aperture, and the priest was obliged to drown his exclamations by still louder exhortations. The head was off before the eye could trace the blow; but from an attempt to draw back the head, notwithstanding it was held forward by the hair, the first head was cut off close to the ears; the other two were taken off more cleanly. The first turned me quite hot and thirsty and made me shake so that I could hardly hold the opera glass. . . .' 'Happiness being the peculiar good of an intelligent nature, must attach to the intelligent nature on the side of something that is peculiar to it. But appetite is not peculiar to intelligent nature, but is found in all things, though diversely in diverse beings. The will, as being an appetite, is not a peculiar appurtenance of an intelligent nature, except so far as it is dependent on the intelligence; but intelligence in itself is peculiar to an intelligent nature. Happiness therefore consists in an act of the intellect substantially and principally rather than in an act of the will. . . .' 'Even in my most secret soul I have never been able to think of love as anything but a struggle, which begins with hatred and ends with moral subjection. . . .' ' "I will not be a cuckold, I say; there will be danger in making me a cuckold." "Why, wert thou well cured of thy last clap?" . . .' '*La primera noche o purgación es amarga y terrible para el sentido, como ahora diremos. La segunda no tiene comparación, porque es horrenda y espantable para el espíritu.* . . .' 'I think I have read somewhere that preciseness has been carried so far that ladies would not say, *J'ai mangé des confitures*, but *des fitures*. At this rate, above one-half of the words of the Dictionary of the French Academy should be struck out. . . .'

In the end, Anthony settled down to *The Way of Perfection of St Teresa*. When Brian came in, an hour later, he had got as far as the Prayer of Quiet.

'B-busy?' Brian asked.

Anthony shook his head.

77

The other sat down. 'I c-came to s-see if there was anything more to s-settle about to-m-morrow.' Mrs Foxe and Joan Thursley, Mr and Mrs Beavis were coming down to Oxford for the day. Brian and Anthony had agreed to entertain them together.

Hock or Sauterne cup? Lobster mayonnaise or cold salmon? And if it rained, what would be the best thing to do in the afternoon?

'Are you c-coming to the F-fabians this evening?' Brian asked, when the discussion of the next day's plans was at an end.

'Of course,' said Anthony. There was to be voting, that evening, for next term's president. 'It'll be a close fight between you and Mark Staithes. You'll need all the votes you can . . .'

Interrupting him, 'I've st-stood down,' said Brian.

'Stood down? But why?'

'V-various reasons.'

Anthony looked at him and shook his head. 'Not that I'd have ever dreamt of putting up,' he said. 'Can't imagine anything more boring than to preside over any kind of organization.' Even belonging to an organization was bad enough. Why should one be bullied into making choices when one didn't want to choose; into binding oneself to a set of principles when it was so essential to be free; into committing oneself to associate with other people when as likely as not one would want to be alone; into promising in advance to be at given places at given times? It was with the greatest difficulty that Brian had persuaded him to join the Fabians; for the rest he was unattached. 'Inconceivably boring,' he insisted. 'But still, once in the running, why stand down?'

'Mark'll be a b-better president than I.'

'He'll be ruder, if that's what you mean.'

'B-besides, he was so a-awfully k-keen on g-getting elected,' Brian began; then broke off, suddenly conscience-stricken. Anthony might think he was implying a criticism of Mark Staithes, was assuming the right to patronize him. 'I mean, he kn-knows he'll do the j-job so well,' he went on quickly. 'W-whereas I . . . So I r-really didn't see why . . .'

'In fact you thought you might as well humour him.'

78

'No, n-no!' cried Brian in a tone of distress. 'Not th-that.'

'Cock of the dunghill,' Anthony continued, ignoring the other's protest. 'He's got to be cock – even if it's only of the tiniest little Fabian dunghill.' He laughed. 'Poor old Mark! What an agony when he can't get to the top of his dunghill! One's lucky to prefer books.' He patted St Teresa affectionately. 'Still, I wish you hadn't stood down. It would have made me laugh to see Mark trying to pretend he didn't mind when you'd beaten him. You're reading a paper, aren't you,' he went on, 'after the voting?'

Relieved by the change of subject, Brian nodded. 'On Syn . . .' he began.

'On sin?'

'Synd-dicalism.'

They both laughed.

'Odd, when you come to think of it,' said Anthony when their laughter subsided, 'that the mere notion of talking to socialists about sin should seem so . . . well, so outrageous, really. Sin . . . socialism.' He shook his head. 'It's like mating a duck with a zebra.'

'You could t-talk about sin if you st-started from the other end.'

'Which end?'

'The s-social end. O-organizing a s-society so well that the i-individual simply c-couldn't commit any sins.'

'But do you honestly think such a society could exist?'

'P-perhaps,' said Brian doubtfully, but reflected that social change could hardly abolish those ignoble desires of his, couldn't even legitimate those desires, except within certain conventional limits. He shook his head. 'N-no, I don't kn-know,' he concluded.

'I can't see that you could do more than just transfer people's sins from one plane to another. But we've done that already. Take envy and ambition, for example. They used to express themselves on the plane of physical violence. Now, we've reorganized society in such a way that they have to express themselves for the most part in terms of economic competition.'

'Which we're g-going to ab-abolish.'

'And so bring physical violence back into fashion, eh?'

'Th-that's what you *h-hope*, d-don't you?' said Brian; and laughing, 'You're awful!' he added.

There was a silence. Absently, Brian picked up *The Way of Perfection*, and, turning over the pages, read a line here, a paragraph there. Then with a sigh he shut the book, put it back in its place and, shaking his head, 'I c-can't underst-stand,' he said, 'why you read this sort of st-stuff. S-seeing that you d-don't b-believe in it.'

'But I do believe,' Anthony insisted. 'Not in the orthodox explanations, of course. Those are obviously idiotic. But in the facts. And in the fundamental metaphysical theory of mysticism.'

'You m-mean that you can g-get at t-truth by some s-sort of d-direct union with it?'

Anthony nodded. 'And the most valuable and important sort of truth only in that way.'

Brian sat for a time in silence, his elbows on his knees, his long face between his hands, staring at the floor. Then, without looking up, 'It s-seems to me,' he said at last, 'that you're r-running with the h-hare and h-h-h . . . and h-h . . .'

'Hunting with the hounds,' Anthony supplied.

The other nodded. 'Using sc-cepticism against r-religion – ag-gainst any s-sort of i-idealism, really,' he added, thinking of the barbed mockery with which Anthony loved to puncture any enthusiasm that seemed to him excessive. 'And using th-this st-stuff' – he pointed to *The Way of Perfection* – 'a-against s-scientific argument, when it s-suits your b-b-b . . .' 'book' refused to come: 'when it s-suits your bee-double-o-kay.'

Anthony relit his pipe before answering. 'Well, why shouldn't one make the best of both worlds?' he asked, as he threw the spent match into the grate. 'Of *all* the worlds. Why not?'

'W-well, c-consistency, s-single-mindedness . . .'

'But I don't value single-mindedness. I value completeness. I think it's one's duty to develop all one's potentialities – *all* of them. Not stupidly stick to only one. Single-mindedness!' he repeated. 'But oysters are single-minded. Ants are single-minded.'

'S-so are s-saints.'

'Well, that only confirms my determination not to be a saint.'

'B-but h-how can you d-do anything if you're not s-single-minded? It's the f-first cond-dition of any ach-achievement.'

'Who tells you I want to achieve anything?' asked Anthony. 'I don't. I want to *be*, completely. And I want to *know*. And so far as getting to know is doing, I accept the conditions of it, single-mindedly.' With the stem of his pipe he indicated the books on the table.

'You d-don't accept the c-conditions of *th-that* kind of kn-knowing,' Brian retorted, pointing once more at *The Way of Perfection*. 'P-praying and f-fasting and all th-that.'

'Because it isn't knowing; it's a special kind of experience. There's all the difference in the world between knowing and experiencing. Between learning algebra, for example, and going to bed with a woman.'

Brian did not smile. Still staring at the floor, 'B-but you th-think,' he said, 'that m-mystical experiences b-brings one into c-contact with the t-truth?'

'And so does going to bed.'

'D-does it?' Brian forced himself to ask. He disliked this sort of conversation, disliked it more than ever now that he was in love with Joan – in love, and yet (he hated himself for it) desiring her basely, wrongly. . . .

'If it's the right woman,' the other answered with an airy knowingness, as though he had experimented with every kind of female. In fact, though he would have been ashamed to admit it, he was a virgin.

'S-so you needn't b-bother about the f-fasting,' said Brian, suddenly ironical.

Anthony grinned. 'I'm quite content with only *knowing* about the way of perfection,' he said.

'I think I should w-want to exp-experience it too,' said Brian, after a pause.

Anthony shook his head. 'Not worth the price,' he said. 'That's the trouble of all single-minded activity; it costs you your liberty. You find yourself driven into a corner. You're a prisoner.'

'But if you w-want to be f-free, you've g-got to be a p-prisoner. It's the c-condition of freedom – t-true freedom.'

'True freedom!' Anthony repeated in the parody of a clerical voice. 'I always love that kind of argument. The contrary of a thing isn't the contrary; oh, dear me, no! It's the thing itself, but as it *truly* is. Ask a diehard what conservatism is; he'll tell you it's *true* socialism. And the brewers' trade papers; they're full of articles about the beauty of True Temperance. Ordinary temperance is just a gross refusal to drink; but *true* temperance, *true* temperance is something much more refined. True temperance is a bottle of claret with each meal and three double whiskies after dinner. Personally, I'm all for true temperance, because I hate temperance. But I like being free. So I won't have anything to do with true freedom.'

'Which doesn't p-prevent it from being t-true freedom,' the other obstinately insisted.

'What's in a name?' Anthony went on. 'The answer is, Practically everything, if the name's a good one. Freedom's a marvellous name. That's why you're so anxious to make use of it. You think that, if you call imprisonment true freedom, people will be attracted to the prison. And the worst of it is you're quite right. The name counts more with most people than the thing. They'll follow the man who repeats it most often and in the loudest voice. And of course "True Freedom" is actually a better name than freedom *tout court*. Truth – it's one of the magical words. Combine it with the magic of "freedom" and the effect's terrific.' After a moment's silence, 'Curious,' he went on, digressively and in another tone, 'that people don't talk about true truth. I suppose it sounds too queer. True truth; true truth,' he repeated experimentally. 'No, it obviously won't do. It's like beri-beri, or Wagga-Wagga. Nigger talk. You couldn't take it seriously. If you want to make the contrary of truth acceptable, you've got to call it spiritual truth, or inner truth, or higher truth, or even . . .'

'But a m-moment ago you were s-saying that there *w-was* a k-kind of higher truth. S-something you could only g-get at m-mystically. You're c-contradicting yourself.'

Anthony laughed. 'That's one of the privileges of freedom. Besides,' he added, more seriously, 'there's that distinction between knowing and experiencing. Known truth isn't the same as experienced truth. There ought to be two distinct words.'

'You m-manage to wr-wriggle out of e-everything.'

'Not out of *everything*,' Anthony insisted. 'There'll always be those.' He pointed again to the books. 'Always knowledge. The prison of knowledge – because of course knowledge is also a prison. But I shall always be ready to stay in that prison.'

'A-always?' Brian questioned.

'Why not?'

'Too m-much of a l-luxury.'

'On the contrary. It's a case of scorning delights and living laborious days.'

'Which are thems-selves del-lightful.'

'Of course. But mayn't one take pleasure in one's work?'

Brian nodded. 'It's not exactly th-that,' he said. 'One doesn't w-want to exp-ploit one's privileges.'

'Mine's only a little one,' said Anthony. 'About six pounds a week,' he added, specifying the income that had come to him from his mother.

'P-plus all the r-rest.'

'Which rest?'

'The l-luck that you happen to l-like this sort of thing.' He reached out and touched the folio Bayle. 'And all your g-gifts.'

'But I can't artificially make myself stupid,' Anthony objected. 'Nor can you.'

'N-no, but we can use what we've g-got for s-something else.'

'Something we're not suited for,' the other suggested sarcastically.

Ignoring the mockery, 'As a k-kind of th-thank-offering,' Brian went on with a still intenser passion of earnestness.

'For what?'

'For all that we've been g-given. M-money, to start with. And then kn-knowledge, t-taste, the power to c-c . . .' He wanted to say 'create', but had to be content with 'to do things'. 'B-being a scholar or an artist – it's l-like purs-suing your p-personal salvation. But there's also the k-kingdom of G-god. W-waiting to be realized.'

'By the Fabians?' asked Anthony in a tone of pretended ingenuousness.

'Am-mong others.' There was a long half-minute of silence. 'Shall I say it?' Brian was wondering. 'Shall I tell him?' And suddenly, as though a dam had burst, his irresolution was swept away. 'I've decided,' he said aloud, and the feeling with which he spoke the words was so strong that it lifted him, almost without his knowledge, to his feet and sent him striding rest-lessly about the room, 'I've decided that I shall g-go on with ph-philosophy and l-literature and h-history till I'm thirty. Then it'll be t-time to do something else. S-something more dir-rect.'

'Direct?' Anthony repeated. 'In what way?'

'In getting at p-people. In r-realizing the k-kingdom of G-god . . .' The very intensity of his desire to communicate what he was feeling reduced him to dumbness.

Listening to Brian's words, looking up into the serious and ardent face, Anthony felt himself touched, profoundly, to the quick of his being . . . felt himself touched, and, for that very reason, came at once under a kind of compulsion, as though in self-defence, to react to his own emotion, and his friend's, with a piece of derision. 'Washing the feet of the poor, for example,' he suggested. 'And drying them on your hair. It'll be awkward if you go prematurely bald.'

Afterwards, when Brian had gone, he felt ashamed of his ignoble ribaldry – humiliated, at the same time, by the un-reflecting automatism with which he had brought it out. Like those pithed frogs that twitch when you apply a drop of acid to their skin. A brainless response.

'Damn!' he said aloud, then picked up his book.

He was deep once more in *The Way of Perfection* when there was a thump at the door and a voice, deliberately harshened so as to be like the voice of a drill-sergeant on parade, shouted his name.

'These bloody stairs of yours!' said Gerry Watchett as he came in. 'Why the devil do you live in such a filthy hole?'

Gerry Watchett was fair-skinned, with small, unemphatic features and wavy golden-brown hair. A good-looking young man, but good-looking, in spite of his height and powerful build, almost to girlish prettiness. For the casual observer, there was an air about him of Arcadian freshness and innocence, strangely belied, however, upon a closer examination, by the hard insolence in his blue eyes, by the faint smile of derision and contempt that kept returning to his face, by the startling coarseness of those thick-fingered, short-nailed hands.

Anthony pointed to a chair. But the other shook his head. 'No, I'm in a hurry. Just rushed in to say you've got to come to dinner tonight.'

'But I can't.'

Gerry frowned. 'Why not?'

'I've got a meeting of the Fabians.'

'And you call that a reason for not coming to dine with me?'

'Seeing I've promised to . . .'

'Then I can expect you at eight?'

'But really . . .'

'Don't be a fool! What does it matter? A mothers' meeting?'

'But what excuse shall I give?'

'Any bloody thing you like. Tell them you've just had twins.'

'All right, then,' Anthony agreed at last. 'I'll come.'

'Thank you very kindly,' said Gerry, with mock politeness. 'I'd have broken your neck if you hadn't. Well, so long.' At the door he halted. 'I'm having Bimbo Abinger, and Ted, and Willie Monmouth, and Scroope. I wanted to get old Gorchakov too; but the fool's gone and got ill at the last moment. That's why I had to ask you,' he added with a quiet matter-of-factness that was far more offensive than any emphasis could have been; then turned, and was gone.

'Do you l-like him?' Brian had asked one day when Gerry's name came up between them. And because the question evoked an uneasy echo in his own consciousness, Anthony had answered, with a quite unnecessary sharpness, that of course he liked Gerry. 'Why else do you suppose I go about with him?' he had concluded, looking at Brian with irritable suspicion. Brian made no reply; and the question had returned like a boomerang upon the asker. Yes why *did* he go about with Gerry? For of course he didn't like the man; Gerry had hurt and humiliated him, was ready, he knew, to hurt and humiliate him again on the slightest provocation. Or rather without any provocation at all – just for fun, because it amused him to humiliate people, because he had a natural talent for inflicting pain. So why, why?

Mere snobbery, as Anthony was forced to admit to himself, was part of the discreditable secret. It was absurd and ridiculous; but the fact remained, nevertheless, that it pleased him to associate with Gerry and his friends. To be the intimate of these young aristocrats and plutocrats, and at the same time to know himself their superior in intelligence, taste, judgement, in all the things that *really* mattered, was satisfying to his vanity.

Admitting his intellectual superiority, the young barbarians expected him to pay for their admiration by amusing them. He was their intimate, yes; but as Voltaire was the intimate of Frederick the Great, as Diderot of the Empress Catherine. The resident philosopher is not easily distinguishable from the court fool.

With genuine appreciation, but at the same time patronizingly, offensively, 'Good for the Professor!' Gerry would say after one of his sallies. Or, 'Another drink for the old Professor' – as though he were an Italian organ-grinder, playing for pennies.

The prick of remembered humiliation was sharp like an insect's sting. With sudden violence Anthony heaved himself out of his chair and began to walk, frowning, up and down the room.

A middle-class snob tolerated because of his capacities as an entertainer. The thought was hateful, wounding. 'Why do I stand it?' he wondered. 'Why am I such a damned fool? I shall write Gerry a note to say I can't come.' But time passed; the note remained unwritten. For, after all, he was thinking, there were also advantages, there were also satisfactions. An evening spent with Gerry and his friends was exhilarating, was educative. Exhilarating and educative, not because of anything they said or thought – for they were all stupid, all bottomlessly ignorant; but because of what they were, of what their circumstances had made them. For, thanks to their money and their position, they were able actually to live in such freedom as Anthony had only imagined or read about. For them, the greater number of the restrictions which had always hedged him in did not even exist. They permitted themselves as a matter of course licences which he took only in theory, and which he felt constrained even then to justify with all the resources of a carefully perverted metaphysic, an ingeniously adulterated mystical theology. By the mere force of social and economic circumstances, these ignorant barbarians found themselves quite naturally behaving as he did not dare to behave even after reading all Nietzsche had said about the Superman, or Casanova about women. Nor did they have to study Patanjali or Jacob Boehme in order to find excuses for the intoxications of wine and sensuality : they just got drunk and had their girls, like that, as though they were in the Garden of Eden. They faced life, not diffidently and apologetically, as Anthony faced it, not wistfully, from behind invisible bars, but with the serenely insolent assurance of those who know that God intended them to enjoy themselves and had decreed the unfailing acquiescence of their fellows in all their desires.

True, they also had their confining prejudices; they too on occasion were as ready as poor old Brian to lock themselves up in the prison of a code. But code and prejudices were of their own particular caste; therefore, so far as Anthony was concerned, without binding force. Their example delivered him from the chains that his upbringing had fastened upon him, but was powerless to bind him with those other chains in which they themselves walked through life. In their company the compulsions of respectability, the paralysing fear of public opinion, the inhibitory maxims of middle-class prudence fell away from him; but when Bimbo Abinger indignantly refused even to listen to the suggestion that he should sell the monstrous old house that was eating up three-quarters of his income, when Scroope complained that he would have to go into Parliament, because in his family the eldest sons had always sat in the House of Commons before coming into the title, Anthony could only feel the amused astonishment of an explorer watching the religious antics of a tribe of blackamoors. A rational being does not allow himself to be converted to the cult of Mumbo Jumbo; but he will have no objection to occasionally going a bit native. The worship of Mumbo Jumbo means the acceptance of taboos; going native means freedom. 'True freedom !' Anthony grinned to himself; his good humour and equanimity had returned. A snob, a middle-class snob. No doubt. But there was a reason for his snobbery, a justification. And if the lordly young barbarians tended to regard him as a sort of high-class buffoon – well, that was the price he had to pay for their gift of freedom. There was no price to be paid for associating with the Fabians; but then, how little they had to give to him! Socialist doctrines might to some extent theoretically liberate the intellect; but the example of the young barbarians was a liberation in the sphere of practice.

'So frightfully sorry,' he scribbled in his note to Brian. 'Suddenly remembered I'd booked myself for dinner tonight.' ('Booked' was one of his father's words – a word he ordinarily detested for its affectation. Writing a lie, he had found it coming spontaneously to his pen.) 'Alas' (that was also a favourite locution of his father's), 'shan't be able to listen to you on *sin*! Wish I could get out of this, but don't see how. Yours, A.'

*

By the time the fruit was on the table they were all pretty drunk. Gerry Watchett was telling Scroope about that German baroness he had had on the boat, on the way to Egypt. Abinger had no audience, but was reciting limericks: the Young Lady of Wick, the Old Man of Devizes, the Young Man called Maclean – a whole dictionary of national biography. Ted and Willie were having a violent quarrel about the best way of shooting grouse. Alone of the party, Anthony was silent. Speech would have compromised the delicate happiness he was then enjoying. That last glass of champagne had made him the inhabitant of a new world, extraordinarily beautiful and precious and significant. The apples and oranges in the silver bowl were like enormous gems. Each glass, under the candles, contained, not wine, but a great yellow beryl, solid and translucent. The roses had the glossy texture of satin and the shining hardness and distinctness of form belonging to metal or glass. Even sound was frozen and crystalline. The Young Lady of Kew was the equivalent, in his ears, of a piece of sculptured jade, and that violently futile discussion about grouse seemed like a waterfall in winter. *Le transparent glacier des vols qui n'ont pas fui*, he thought with heightened pleasure. Everything was supernaturally brilliant and distinct, but at the same time how remote, how strangely irrelevant! Bright against the outer twilight of the room, the faces grouped about the table might have been things seen on the other side of a sheet of plate-glass, in an illuminated aquarium. And the aquarium was not only without, it was also, mysteriously, within him. Looking through the glass at those sea flowers and submarine gems, he was himself a fish – but a fish of genius, a fish that was also a god. ICHTHUS – *Iesous Christos theou huios soter*. His divine fish-soul hung there, poised in its alien element, gazing, gazing through huge eyes that perceived everything, understood everything, but having no part in what it saw. Even his own hands lying there on the table in front of him had ceased, in any real sense, to be *his*. From his aquarium fastness he viewed them with the same detached and happy admiration as he felt for the fruits and flowers, or those other transfigured bits of still life, the faces of his friends. Beautiful hands! contrived – how marvellously! – to perform their innumerable functions – the pointing of double-barrelled guns at flying birds, the caressing of the thighs of German baronesses in liners, the playing of imaginary scales upon the tablecloth, so. Enchanted, he watched the movements of his fingers, the smooth sliding of the tendons under the skin. Exquisite hands! But no more truly a part of himself, of the essential fish-soul in its timeless aquarium, than the hands of Abinger peeling that banana, the hands of Scroope carrying a match to his cigar. I am not my body, I am not my sensations, I am not even my mind; I am that I am. I *om* that I *om*. The sacred word OM represents Him. God is not limited by time. For the One is not absent from anything, and yet is separated from all things. ...

'Hi, Professor!' A piece of orange-peel struck him on the cheek. He started and turned round. 'What the hell are you thinking about?' Gerry Watchett was asking in that purposely harsh voice which it amused him to put on like a hideous mask.

The momentarily troubled waters of the aquarium had already returned to rest. A fish once more, a divine and remotely happy Fish, Anthony smiled at him with serene indulgence.

'I was thinking about Plotinus,' he said.

'Why Plotinus?'

'Why Plotinus? But, my dear sir, isn't it obvious? Science is reason, and reason is multitudinous.' The fish had found a tongue; eloquence flowed from the aquarium in an effortless stream. 'But if one happens to be feeling particularly *un*multitudinous – well, what else is there to think about except Plotinus? Unless, of course, you prefer the pseudo-Dionysius, or Eckhart, or St Teresa. The flight of the alone to the Alone. Even St Thomas is forced to admit that no mind can see the divine substance unless it is divorced from bodily senses, either by death or by some rapture. Some rapture, mark you! But a rapture is always a rapture, whatever it's due to. Whether it's champagne, or saying OM, or squinting at your nose, or looking at a crucifix, or making love – preferably in a boat, Gerry; I'm the first to admit it; preferably in a boat. What are the wild waves saying? Rapture! Ecstasy! Fairly yelling it. Until, mark you, until, the breath of this corporeal frame and even the motion of our human blood almost suspended, we are laid asleep in body, and become a living soul, while with an eye made quiet ...'

'There was a Young Fellow of Burma,' Abinger suddenly declaimed.

'Made quiet,' Anthony repeated more loudly, 'by the power of harmony ...'

'Whose betrothed had good reasons to murmur.'

'And the deep power of joy,' shouted Anthony, 'we see ...'

'But now that they're married he's

'Been taking cantharides ...'

'We see into the life of things. The life of things, I tell you. The life of things. And damn all Fabians!' he added.

*

Anthony got back to his lodgings at about a quarter to midnight, and was unpleasantly startled, as he entered the sitting-room, to see someone rising with the violent impatience of a Jack-in-the-box from an armchair.

'God, what a fright ...!'

'At last!' said Mark Staithes. His emphatically featured face wore an expression of angry impatience. 'I've been waiting nearly an hour.' Then, with contempt, 'You're drunk,' he added.

'As though *you'd* never been drunk!' Anthony retorted. 'I remember ...'

'So do I,' said Mark Staithes, interrupting him. 'But that was in my first year.' In his first year, when he had felt it necessary to prove that he was manly – manlier than the toughest of them, noisier, harder drinking. 'I've got something better to do now.'

'So *you* imagine,' said Anthony.

The other looked at his watch. 'I've got about seven minutes,' he said. 'Are you sober enough to listen?'

Anthony sat down with dignity and in silence.

Short, but square-shouldered and powerful, Mark stood over him, almost menacingly. 'It's about Brian,' he said.

'About Brian?' Then with a knowing smile, 'That reminds me,' Anthony added, 'I ought to have congratulated you on being our future president.'

'Fool!' said Mark angrily. 'Do you think I go about accepting charity? When he withdrew, I withdrew too.'

'And let that dreary little Mumby walk into the job?'

'What the devil do I care about Mumby?'

'What do any of us care about anybody?' said Anthony sententiously. 'Nothing, thank God. Absolutely noth ...'

'What does he mean by insulting me like that?'

'Who? Little Mumby?'

'No; Brian, of course.'

'He thinks he's being nice to you.'

'I don't want his damned niceness,' said Mark. 'Why can't he behave properly?'

'Because it amuses him to behave like a Christian.'

'Well, then, tell him for God's sake to try it on someone else in future. I don't like having Christian tricks played on me.'

'You want a cock to fight, in fact.'

'What do you mean?'

'Otherwise it's no fun being on top of the dunghill. Whereas Brian would like us all to be jolly little capons together. Well, so far as dunghills are concerned, I'm all for Brian. It's when we come to the question of the hens that I begin to hesitate.'

Mark looked at his watch again. 'I must go.' At the door he turned back. 'Don't forget to tell him what I've told you. I like Brian, and I don't want to quarrel with him. But if he tries being charitable and Christian again . . . '

'The poor boy will forfeit your esteem for ever,' concluded Anthony.

'Buffoon!' said Staithes, and slamming the door behind him, hurried downstairs.

Left alone, Anthony took the fifth volume of the *Historical Dictionary* and began to read what Bayle had to say about Spinoza.

CHAPTER ELEVEN

December 8th 1926

'*Condar intra* meum *latus!* It is the only place of refuge left to us.' Anthony rolled the sheet off his typewriter, added it to the other sheets lying before him on the table, clipped them together and started to read through what he had written. Chapter XI of his Elements of Sociology was to deal with the Individual and his conceptions of Personality. He had spent the day jotting down unmethodically a few preliminary reflections.

'*Cogito ergo sum*,' he read. 'But why not *caco ergo sum*? *Eructo ergo sum*? Or, escaping solipsism, why not *futuo ergo sumus*? Ribald questions. But what *is* "personality"?

'MacTaggart knows his personality by direct acquaintance; others by description. Hume and Bradley don't know theirs at all, and don't believe it really exists. Mere splitting, all this, of a bald man's imaginary hairs. What matters is that "Personality" happens to be a common word with a generally accepted meaning.

'People discuss my "personality". What are they talking about? Not *homo cacans*, nor *homo eructans*, not even, except very superficially, *homo futuens*. No, they are talking about *homo sentiens* (impossible Latin) and *homo cogitans*. And when, in public, I talk about "myself", I talk about the same two *homines*. My "personality", in the present conventional sense of the word, is what I think and feel – or, rather, what I confess to thinking and feeling. *Caco, eructo, futuo* – I never admit that the first person singular of such verbs is really *me*. Only when, for any reason, they palpably affect my feelings and thinking do the processes they stand for come within the bounds of my "personality". (This censorship makes ultimate nonsense of all literature. Plays and novels just aren't true.)

'Thus, the "personal" is the creditable, or rather the potentially creditable. Not the morally undifferentiated.

'It is also the enduring. Very short experiences are even less personal than discreditable or merely vegetative experiences. They become personal only when accompanied by feeling and thought, or when reverberated by memory.

'Matter, analysed, consists of empty space and electric charges. Take a woman and a washstand. Different in kind. But their component electric charges are similar in kind. Odder still, each of these component electric charges is different in kind from the whole woman or washstand. Changes in quantity, when sufficiently great, produces changes in quality. Now, human experience is analogous to matter. Analyse it – and you find yourself in the presence of psychological atoms. A lot of these atoms constitute normal experience, and a selection from normal experience constitutes "personality". Each individual atom is unlike normal experience and still more unlike personality. Conversely, each atom in one experience resembles the corresponding atom in another. Viewed microscopically, a woman's body is just like a washstand, and Napoleon's experience is just like Wellington's. Why do we imagine that solid matter exists? Because of the grossness of our sense organs. And why do we imagine that we have coherent experiences and personality? Because our minds work slowly and have very feeble powers of analysis. Our world and we who live in it are the creations of stupidity and bad sight.

'Recently, however, thinking and seeing have been improved. We have instruments that will resolve matter into very small parts and a mathematical technique that allows us to think about still smaller parts.

'Psychologists have no new instruments, only new techniques of thought. All their inventions are purely mental – techniques of analysis and observation, working hypotheses. Thanks to the novelists and professional psychologists, we can think of our experience in terms of atoms and instants as well as in terms of lumps and hours. To be a tolerably good psychologist was possible, in the past, only for men of genius. Compare Chaucer's psychology with Gower's, even Boccaccio's. Compare Shakespeare's with Ben Jonson's. The difference is one not only of quality, but also of quantity. The men of genius knew *more* than their merely intelligent contemporaries.

'Today, there is a corpus of knowledge, a technique, a working hypothesis. The amount a merely intelligent man can know is enormous – more than an unlearned man of genius relying solely on intuition.

'Were the Gowers and Jonsons hampered by their ignorance? Not at all. Their ignorance was the standard knowledge of their times. A few monsters of intuition might know more than they; but the majority knew even less.

'And here a digression – sociologically speaking, more important than the theme digressed from. There are fashions in personality. Fashions that vary in time – like crinolines and hobble skirts – and fashions that vary in space – like Gold Coast loincloths and Lombard Street tail-coats. In primitive societies everyone wears, and longs to wear, the same personality. But each society has a different psychological costume. Among the Red Indians of the North-West Pacific Coast the ideal personality was that of a mildly crazy egotist competing with his rivals on the plane of wealth and conspicuous consumption. Among the Plains Indians, it was that of an egotist competing with others in the sphere of warlike exploits. Among the Pueblo Indians, the ideal personality was neither that of an egotist, nor of a conspicuous consumer, nor of a fighter, but of the perfectly gregarious man who makes great efforts never to distinguish himself, who knows the traditional rites and gestures and tries to be exactly like everyone else.

'European societies are large and racially, economically, professionally heterogeneous; therefore orthodoxy is hard to impose, and there are several contemporaneous ideals of personality. (Note that Fascists and Communists are trying to create one single "right" ideal – in other words, are trying to make industrialized Europeans behave as though they were Dyaks or Eskimos. The attempt, in the long run, is doomed to failure; but in the meantime, what fun they will get from bullying the heretics!)

'In our world, what are the ruling fashions? There are, of course, the ordinary clerical and commercial modes – turned out by the little dressmakers round the corner. And then *la haute couture. Ravissante personnalité d'intérieur de chez Proust, Maison Nietzsche et Kipling: personnalité de sport. Personnalité de nuit, création de Lawrence. Personnalité de bain, par Joyce.* Note the interesting fact that, of these, the *personnalité de sport* is the only one that can really count as a personality in the accepted sense of the word. The others are to a greater or less extent impersonal, because to a greater or less extent atomic. And this brings us back to Shakespeare and Ben Jonson. A pragmatist would have us say that Jonson's psychology was "truer" than Shakespeare's. Most of his contemporaries did in fact perceive themselves and were perceived as Humours. It took Shakespeare to see what a lot there was outside the boundaries of the Humour, behind the conventional mask. But Shakespeare was in a minority of one – or, if you set Montaigne beside him, of two. Humours "worked"; the complex, partially atomized personalities of Shakespeare didn't.

'In the story of the emperor's new clothes the child perceives that the man is naked. Shakespeare reversed the process. His contemporaries thought they were just naked Humours; he saw that they were covered with a whole wardrobe of psychological fancy dress.

'Take Hamlet. Hamlet inhabited a world whose best psychologist was Polonius. If he had known as little as Polonius, he would have been happy. But he knew too much; and in this consists his tragedy. Read his parable of the musical instruments. Polonius and the others assumed as axiomatic that man was a penny whistle with only half a dozen stops. Hamlet knew that, potentially as least, he was a whole symphony orchestra.

'Mad, Ophelia lets the cat out of the bag. "We know what we are, but know not what we may be." Polonius knows very clearly what he and other people *are*, within the ruling conventions. Hamlet knows this, but also what they may be – outside the local system of masks and humours.

'To be the only man of one's age to know what people may be as well as what they conventionally are! Shakespeare must have gone through some disquieting quarters of an hour.

'It was left to Blake to rationalize psychological atomism into a philosophical system. Man, according to Blake (and, after him, according to Proust, according to Lawrence), is simply a succession of states. Good and evil can be predicated only of states, not of individuals, who in fact don't exist, except as the places where the states occur. It is the end of personality in the old sense of the word. (Parenthetically – for this is quite outside the domain of sociology – is it the beginning of a new kind of personality? That of the total man, unbowdlerized, unselected, uncanalized, to change the metaphor, down any one particular drainpipe of *Weltanschauung* – of the man, in a word, who actually is what he may be. Such a man is the antithesis of any of the variants on the fundamental Christian man of our history. And yet in a certain sense he is also the realization of the ideal personality conceived by the Jesus of the Gospel. Like Jesus's ideal personality, the total, unexpurgated, non-canalized man is (1) not pharisaic, that is to say, not interested in convention and social position, not puffed up with the pride of being better than other men; (2) humble, in his acceptance of himself, in his refusal to exalt himself above his human station; (3) poor in spirit, inasmuch as "he" – his ego – lays no lasting claims on anything, is content with what, for a personality of the old type, would seem psychological and philosophical destitution; (4) like a little child, in his acceptance of the immediate datum of experience for its own sake, in his refusal to take thought for the morrow, in his readiness to let the dead bury their dead; (5) not a hypocrite or a liar, since there is no fixed model which individuals must pretend to be like.)

'A question : did the old personality ever really exist? In the year *m* men feel *x* in context *z*. In the year *n* they feel the same *x* in quite a different context *p*. But *x* is a major emotion – vitally significant for personality. And yet *x* is felt in contexts that change with the changing conventions of fashion. "Rather death than dishonour." But honour is like women's skirts. Worn short, worn long, worn full, worn narrow, worn with petticoats, worn minus drawers. Up to 1750 you were expected to feel, you did feel, mortally dishonoured if you saw a man pinching your sister's bottom. So intense was your indignation, that you had to try to kill him. Today, our honours have migrated from the fleshy parts of our female relations' anatomy, and have their seats elsewhere. And so on, indefinitely.

'So what *is* personality? And what is it *not*?

'It is *not* our total experience. It is *not* the psychological atom or instant. It is *not* sense impressions as such, nor vegetative life as such.

'It *is* experience in the lump and by the hour. It *is* feeling and thought.

'And who makes this selection from total experience, and on what principle? Sometimes *we* make it – whoever *we* are. But as often it is made for us – by the collective unwisdom of a class, a whole society. To a great extent, "personality" is not even our personal property.

'Vaguely, but ever more widely, this fact is now coming to be realized. At the same time, ever-increasing numbers of people are making use of the modern techniques to see themselves and others microscopically and instantaneously, as well as in the lump and by the hour. Moreover, having a working hypothesis of the unconscious, increasing numbers are becoming aware of their secret motives, and so are perceiving the large part played in their lives by the discreditable and vegetative elements of experience. With what results? That the old conception of personality has begun to break down. And not only the conception, also the fact. "Strong personalities", even "definite personalities", are becoming less common. Fascists have to go out of their way to manufacture them, deliberately, by a suitable process of education. An education that is simplification, Eskimization; that entails the suppression of pyschological knowledge and the inculcation of respect for psychological ignorance. Odious policy – but, I suspect, inevitable and, sociologically speaking, *right*. For our psychological acumen is probably harmful to society. Society has need of simple Jonsonian Humours, not of formless collections of self-conscious states. Yet another example of the banefulness of too much knowledge and too much scientific technique.

'Once more, Hamlet casts a light. Polonius is much more obviously and definitely a person than the prince. Indeed, Hamlet's personality is so indefinite that critics have devoted thousands of pages to the discussion of what it really was. In fact, of course, Hamlet didn't have a personality – knew altogether too much to have one. He was conscious of his total experience, atom by atom and instant by instant, and accepted no guiding principle which would make him choose one set of patterned atoms to represent his personality rather than another. To himself and to others he was just a succession of more or less incongruous states. Hence that perplexity at Elsinore and among the Shakespearian critics ever since. Honour, Religion, Prejudice, Love – all the conventional props that shore up the ordinary personality have been, in this case, gnawed through. Hamlet is his own termite, and from a tower has eaten himself down to a heap of sawdust. Only one thing prevents Polonius and the rest from immediately perceiving the fact : whatever the state of his mind, Hamlet's body is still intact, unatomized, macroscopically present to the senses. And perhaps, after all, this is the real reason for our belief in personality : – the existence and persistence of bodies. And perhaps whatever reality there is in the notion of coherent individual continuity is just a function of this physical persistence. "Such hair, such a wonderful figure ! I think Mrs Jones has a *lovely* poyssonality." When I heard that, in the bus going up Fifth Avenue, it made me laugh. Whereas I probably ought to have listened as though to Spinoza. For what *is* the most personal thing about a human being? Not his mind – his body. A Hearst, a Rothermere, can mould my feelings, coerce my thinking. But no amount of propaganda can make my digestion or metabolism become identical to theirs. *Cogito, ergo Rothermere est*. But *caco, ergo sum*.

'And here, I suspect, lies the reason for that insistence, during recent years, on the rights of the body. From the Boy Scouts to the fashionable sodomites, and from Elizabeth Arden to D. H. Lawrence (one of the most powerful personality-smashers, incidentally : there are no "characters" in his books). Always and everywhere the body. Now the body possesses one enormous merit; it is indubitably *there*. Whereas the personality, as a mental structure, may be all in bits – gnawed down to Hamlet's heap of sawdust. Only the rather stupid and insentient, nowadays, have strong and sharply defined personalities. Only the barbarians among us "know what they are". The civilized are conscious of "what they may be", and so are incapable of knowing what, for practical, social purposes, they actually are – have forgotten how to select a personality out of their total atomic experience. In the swamp and welter of this uncertainty the body stands firm like the Rock of Ages.

> *Jesu, pro me perforatus,*
> *Condar intra tuum latus.*

Even faith hankers for warm caverns of perforated flesh. How much more wildly urgent must be the demands of a scepticism that has ceased to believe even in its own personality! *Condar intra* MEUM *latus!* It is the only place of refuge left to us.'

Anthony laid the typescript down, and, tilting backwards, rocked himself precariously on the hind legs of his chair. Not so bad, he was thinking. But there were obviously omissions, there were obviously unjustifiable generalizations. He had written of the world in general as though the world in general were like himself – from the desire, of course, that it should be. For how simple it would be if it were! How agreeable! Each man a succession of states enclosed in the flesh of his own side. And if any other principle of coherence were needed, there was always some absorbing and delightful intellectual interest, like sociology, for example, to supplement the persisting body. *Condar intra meum laborem.* Instead of which ... He sighed. In spite of *Hamlet*, in spite of *The Prophetic Books*, in spite of *Du côté de chez Swann* and *Women in Love*, the world was still full of Jonsonian Humours. Full of the villains of melodrama, the equally deplorable heroes of films, full of Poincarés, of Mussolinis, of Northcliffes, full of ambitious and avaricious michief-makers of every size and shape.

An idea occurred to him. He let his tilted chair fall forward and picked up his fountain-pen.

'Last infirmity of noble mind, the primary, perhaps only, source of sin,' he scribbled. 'Noble mind = *evil* mind. Tree known by fruits. What are fruits of fame-seeking, ambition, desire to excel? Among others, war, nationalism, economic competition, snobbery, class hatred, colour prejudice. Comus quite right to preach sensuality; and how foolish of Satan to tempt a, by definition, *ahimsa*-practising Messiah with fame, dominion, ambition – things whose inevitable fruits are violence and coercion! Compared with fame-seeking, pure sensuality all but harmlesss. Were Freud right and sex supreme, we should live almost in Eden. Alas, only half-right. Adler also half-right. *Hinc illae lac.*'

He looked at his watch. Twenty past seven – and he had to be in Kensington by eight! In his bath, he wondered what the evening would be like. It was twelve years now since he had quarrelled with Mary Amberley. Twelve years, during which he had seen her only at a distance – in picture galleries, once or twice; and across the drawing-room of a common friend. 'I don't ever want to speak to you again,' he had written in that last letter to her. And yet, a few days since, when her reconciliatory invitation had unexpectedly appeared with the other letters on his breakfast table, he had accepted immediately; accepted in the same tone as that in which the invitation itself was couched – casually, matter-of-factly, with no more explicit reference to the past than a 'Yes, it's a long time since I last dined at Number 17.' And after all, why not? What was the point of doing things finally and irrevocably? What right had the man of 1914 to commit the man of 1926? The 1914 man had been an embodied state of anger, shame, distress, perplexity. His state today was one of cheerful serenity, mingled, so far as Mary Amberley was concerned, with considerable curiosity. What would she be like now – at forty-three, was it? And was she really as amusing as he remembered her? Or had his admiration been only one of the fruits – the absurd, delicious fruits – of youthful inexperience? Would his swan turn out a goose? Or still a swan – but moulted, but (poor Mary!) middle-aged? Still wondering, he hurried downstairs and into the street.

CHAPTER TWELVE

August 30th 1933

A FAINT rustling caressed the half-conscious fringes of their torpor, swelled gradually, as though a shell were being brought closer and closer to the ear, and became at last a clattering roar that brutally insisted on attention. Anthony opened his eyes for just long enough to see that the aeroplane was almost immediately above them, then shut them again, dazzled by the intense blue of the sky.

'These damned machines !' he said. Then, with a little laugh, 'They'll have a nice God's-eye view of us here,' he added.

Helen did not answer; but behind her closed eyelids she smiled. Pop-eyed and with an obscene and gloating disapproval ! The vision of that heavenly visitant was irresistibly comic.

'David and Bathsheba,' he went on. 'Unfortunately at a hundred miles an hour ... '

A strange yelping sound punctuated the din of the machine. Anthony opened his eyes again, and was in time to see a dark shape rushing down towards him. He uttered a cry, made a quick and automatic movement to shield his face. With a violent but dull and muddy impact the thing struck the flat roof a yard or two from where they were lying. The drops of a sharply spurted liquid were warm for an instant on their skin, and then, as the breeze swelled up out of the west, startlingly cold. There was a long second of silence. 'Christ!' Anthony whispered at last. From head to foot both of them were splashed with blood. In a red pool at their feet lay the almost shapeless carcass of a fox-terrier. The roar of the receding aeroplane had diminished to a raucous hum, and suddenly the ear found itself conscious once again of the shrill rasping of the cicadas.

Anthony drew a deep breath; then, with an effort and still rather unsteadily, contrived to laugh. 'Yet another reason for disliking dogs,' he said, and, scrambling to his feet, looked down, his face puckered with disgust, at his blood-bedabbled body. 'What about a bath?' he asked, turning to Helen.

She was sitting quite still, staring with wide-open eyes at the horribly shattered carcass. Her face was very pale, and a glancing spurt of blood had left a long red streak that ran diagonally from the right side of the chin, across the mouth, to the corner of the left eye.

'You look like Lady Macbeth,' he said, with another effort at jocularity. '*Allons*.' He touched her shoulder. 'Out, vile spot. This beastly stuff's drying on me. Like seccotine.'

For all answer, Helen covered her face with her hands and began to sob.

For a moment Anthony stood quite still, looking at her crouched there, in the hopeless abjection of her blood-stained nakedness, listening to the painful sound of her weeping. 'Like seccotine': his own words re-echoed disgracefully in his ears. Pity stirred within him, and then an almost violent movement of love for this hurt and suffering woman, this *person*, yes, this person whom he had ignored, deliberately, as though she had no existence except in the context of pleasure. Now, as she knelt there sobbing, all the tenderness he had ever felt for her body, all the affection implicit in their sensualities and never expressed, seemed suddenly to discharge themselves, in a kind of lightning flash of accumulated feeling, upon this person, this embodied spirit, weeping in solitude behind concealing hands.

He knelt down beside her on the mattress, and, with a gesture that was meant to express all that he now felt, put an arm round her shoulder.

But at his touch she winced away as if from a defilement. With a violent, shuddering movement she shook her head.

'But, Helen ... ' he protested, in the stupid conviction that there must be some mistake, that it was impossible that she shouldn't be feeling what he was feeling. It was only a question of making her understand what had happened to him. He laid his hand once more on her shoulder. 'But I care, I'm so fond ... ' Even now he refused to commit himself to the word 'love'.

'Don't touch me,' she cried almost inarticulately, leaning away from him.

He withdrew his hand, but remained there, kneeling beside her, in perplexed and miserable silence. He remembered the time when she had wanted to be allowed to love, and how he had evaded her, had refused to take more of the person that she was, or to give more of himself, than the occasional and discontinuous amorousness of their bodies. She had ended by accepting his terms – accepting them so completely that now ...

'Helen,' he ventured once more. She *must* be made to understand.

Helen shook her head again. 'Leave me alone,' she said; then, as he did not move, she uncovered a face now grotesquely smudged with blood and looked at him. 'Why can't you go away?' she asked, making an effort to express a cold dispassionate resentment of his intrusion upon her. Then, suddenly, her tears began to flow again. 'Oh, please go away!' she implored. Her voice broke, and turning aside, she once more buried her face in her hands.

Anthony hesitated for a moment; then, realizing that he would only make things worse if he stayed on, rose to his feet and left her. 'Give her time,' he said to himself, 'give her time.'

He took a bath, dressed and went down to the sitting-room. The snapshots were lying as they had left them, scattered over the table. He sat down and methodically began to sort them out, subject by subject, into little heaps. Mary in plumes; Mary veiled, clambering into a pre-war Renault; Mary bathing at Dieppe in a half-sleeved bodice and bloomers that were covered to the knee by a little skirt. His mother in a garden; feeding the pigeons in the Piazza San Marco; and then her grave at Lollingdon churchyard. His father with an alpenstock; roped to a guide on a snow slope; with Pauline and the two children. Uncle James on his bicycle; Uncle James wearing a speckled straw hat; rowing on the Serpentine; talking, ten years later, with convalescent soldiers in a hospital garden. Then Brian; Brian with Anthony's own former self at Bulstrode; Brian in a punt with Joan and Mrs Foxe; Brian climbing in the Lakes. That girl he had had an affair with in New York, in 1927, was it? His grandmother. His aunts. Half a dozen snaps of Gladys ...

Half an hour later he heard Helen's steps, cautious at first and slow on the precipitous stairs leading down from the roof, then swift along the passage. Water splashed in the bath.

Time, she must have time. He decided to behave towards her as though nothing had happened. It was almost cheerfully, therefore, that he greeted her as she entered the room.

'Well?' he questioned brightly, looking up from his photographs. But the sight of that pale and stonily collected face filled him with misgiving.

'I'm going,' she said.

'Now? Before lunch?'

She nodded.

'But why?'

'I prefer it,' was all she answered.

Anthony was silent for a moment, wondering whether he ought to protest, to insist, to tell her the things he had tried to tell her on the roof. But the stoniness of her composure proclaimed in advance that the attempt would be useless. Later, when she had got over the first shock, when she had been given time ... 'All right, then,' he said aloud. 'I'll drive you back to the hotel.'

Helen shook her head. 'No, I shall walk.'

'Not in this heat!'

'I shall walk,' she repeated in a tone of finality.

'Well, if you also prefer to swelter ... ' He tried to smile, without much success.

She passed through the glass doors on to the terrace, and suddenly that pale stony face was as though fire-flushed by the reflection from her pyjamas. In hell again, he said to himself, as he followed her.

'Why do you come out?' she asked.

'I'll take you as far as the gate.'

'There's no need.'

'I prefer it.'

She did not return his smile, but walked on without speaking. Two small bushy plants of buddleia grew on either side of the steps that led down from the terrace. On the hot air the scent of the flowers (itself, so it seemed, intrinsically hot) was of an intense and violent sweetness.

'Delicious,' Anthony said aloud as they stepped into the perfumed aura of the blossoms. 'Almost too delicious. But look!' he called in another voice, and caught her sleeve. 'Do look!'

New from the chrysalis, bright and still untattered, a swallow-tail had settled on one of the clusters of mauve flowers. The pale yellow wings, with their black markings, their eyes of blue and crimson, were fully outstretched in the sunlight. Their forward edges had the curve of a sabre, and from the tips the line slanted elegantly backwards towards the two projecting tails of the lower wings. The whole butterfly seemed the symbol, the hiero-glyph of gay and airy speed. The spread wings were tremulous as though from an uncontrollable excess of life, of passionate energy. Rapidly, ravenously, but with an extraordinary precision of purposeful movement, the creature plunged its uncoiled proboscis into the tiny trumpet-shaped flowers that composed the cluster. A quick motion of the head and thorax, and the probe had been thrust home, to be withdrawn a moment later and plunged as swiftly and unerringly between the lips of an-other and yet another flower, until all the blooms within striking distance had been explored and it was necessary to hasten on towards a yet unrifled part of the cluster. Again, again, to the very quick of the expectant flowers, deep to the sheathed and hidden sources of that hot intoxicating sweetness! Again, again, with what a tireless concupiscence, what an intense passion of aimed and accurate greed!

For a long minute they watched in silence. Then, suddenly, Helen stretched out her hand and flicked the cluster on which the butterfly was settled. But before her finger had even touched the flowers, the light, bright creature was gone. A quick flap of the wings, then a long soaring swoop; another spurt of flutter-ing movement, another long catenary of downward and upward slanting flight, and it was out of sight behind the house.

'Why did you do that?' he asked.

Pretending not to have heard his question, Helen ran down the steps and along the gravelled path. At the gate of the garden she halted and turned back.

'Good-bye, Anthony.'

'When are you coming again?' he asked.

Helen looked at him for a few seconds without speaking, then shook her head. 'I'm not coming,' she said at last.

'Not coming again?' he repeated. 'What do you mean?'

But she had already slammed the gate behind her and with

long springing strides was hurrying along the dusty road under the pine trees.

Anthony watched her go, and knew that, for the moment at least, it was no good even trying to do anything. It would only make things worse if he followed her. Later on, perhaps; this evening, when she had had time . . . But walking back along the garden path, through the now unheeded perfume of the buddleias, he wondered uneasily whether it would be much good, even later on. He knew Helen's obstinacy. And then what right had he now, after all these months of disclaiming, of actively refusing any rights whatever?

'But I'm a fool,' he said aloud as he opened the kitchen door, 'I'm mad.' And he made an effort to recover his sanity by disparaging and belittling the whole incident. Unpleasant, admittedly. But not unpleasant enough to justify Helen in behaving as though she were acting Ibsen. Doing a slight Doll's House, he said to himself – trying to reduce it all to a conveniently ridiculous phrase – when there was no doll and no house; for she really couldn't complain that old Hugh had ever shut her up, or that he himself had cherished any designs on her liberty. On the contrary, he had insisted on her being free. Her liberty was also his; if she had become his slave, he would necessarily have become hers.

As for his own emotions, up there on the roof – that uprush of tenderness, that longing to know and love the suffering person within that all at once irrelevantly desirable body – these had been genuine, of course; were facts of direct experience. But after all, they could be explained, explained away, as the mere exaggerations, in a disturbing moment, of his very natural sympathy with her distress. The essential thing was time. Given a little time, she would listen once more to what he wanted to say, and he would no longer want to say any of the things she had just now refused to listen to.

He opened the refrigerator and found that Mme Cayol had prepared some cold veal and a cucumber and tomato salad. Mme Cayol had a vicarious passion for cold veal, was constantly giving it him. Anthony, as it happened, didn't much like it, but he preferred eating it to discussing the bill of fare with Mme Cayol. Whole weeks would sometimes pass without the necessity arising for him to say more than *Bon jour* and *À demain, Mme Cayol*, and *Il fait beau aujourd' hui*, or *Quel vent!*, whichever the case might be. She came for two hours each morning, tidied up, prepared some food, laid the table and went away again. He was served, but almost without being aware of the servant. The arrangement, he considered, was as nearly perfect as any earthly arrangement could be. Cold veal was a small price to pay for such service.

At the table in the shade of the great fig tree on the terrace, Anthony settled down with determination to his food, and as he ate, turned over the pages of his latest note-book. There was nothing, he assured himself, like work – nothing, to make oneself forget a particular and personal feeling, so effective as a good generalization. The word 'freedom' caught his eye, and remembering the satisfaction he had felt, a couple of months before, when he had got those ideas safely on to paper, he began to read.

'Acton wanted to write the History of Man in terms of a History of the Idea of Freedom. But you cannot write a History of the Idea of Freedom without at the same time writing a History of the Fact of Slavery.

'The Fact of Slavery. Or rather of Slaveries. For, in his successive attempts to realize the Idea of Freedom, man is constantly changing one form of slavery for another.

'The primal slavery is the slavery to the empty belly and the unpropitious season. Slavery to nature, in a word. The escape from nature is through social organization and technical invention. In a modern city it is possible to forget that such a thing as nature exists – particularly nature in its more inhuman and hostile aspects. Half the population of Europe lives in a universe that's entirely home-made.

'Abolish slavery to nature. Another form of slavery instantly arises. Slavery to institutions: religious institutions, legal institutions, military institutions, economic institutions, educational, artistic, and scientific institutions.

'All modern history is a History of the Idea of Freedom from Institutions. It is also the History of the Fact of Slavery to Institutions.

'Nature is senseless. Institutions, being the work of men, have meaning and purpose. Circumstances change quicker than institutions. What once was sense is sense no longer. An outworn institution is like a person who applies logical reasoning to the non-existent situation created by an *idée fixe* or hallucination. A similar state of things comes about when institutions apply the letter of the law to individual cases. The institution would be acting rationally if the circumstances envisaged by it really existed. But in fact they don't exist. Slavery to an institution is like slavery to a paranoiac, who suffers from delusions but is still in possession of all his intellectual faculties. Slavery to nature is like slavery to an idiot who hasn't even enough mind to be able to suffer from delusions.

'Revolt against institutions leads temporarily to anarchy. But anarchy is slavery to nature, and to a civilized man slavery to nature is even less tolerable than slavery to institutions. The escape from anarchy is through the creation of new institutions. Sometimes there is no period of anarchy – no temporary enslavement to nature; men pass directly from one set of institutions to another.

'Institutions are changed in an attempt to realize the Idea of Freedom. To appreciate the fact of the new slavery takes a certain time. So it comes about that in all revolts against institutions there is a kind of joyful honeymoon, when people believe that freedom has at last been attained. "Bliss was it in that dawn to be alive." And not only in the dawn of the French Revolution. What undiluted happiness, for example, in the dawn of the Franciscan movement, in the dawn of the Reformation, in the dawn of Christianity and Islam ! Even in the dawn of the Great War. The honeymoon may last for as much as twenty or thirty years. Then the fact of the new slavery imposes itself on men's consciousness. It is perceived that the idea of freedom was not realized by the last change, that the new institutions are just as enslaving as the old. What is to be done ? Change the new institutions for yet newer ones. And when *that* honeymoon is over ? Change the yet newer for newer still. And so on – indefinitely, no doubt.

'In any given society the fact of freedom exists only for a very small number of individuals. Propitious economic circumstances are the condition of at least a partial freedom. But if the freedom is to be more nearly complete, there must also be propitious intellectual, psychological, biographical circumstances. Individuals for whom all these circumstances are favourable are not the slaves of institutions. For them, institutions exist as a kind of solid framework on which they can perform whatever gymnastics they please. The rigidity of society as a whole makes it possible for these privileged few to wander out of intellectual and customary moral bounds without risk either for themselves or for the community at large. All particular freedoms – and there is no freedom that is not particular – is enjoyed on the condition of some form of general slavery.'

Anthony shut his book, feeling that he couldn't read even one line more. Not that his words seemed any less true now than they had done when he wrote them. In their own way and on their particular level they were true. Why then did it all seem utterly false and wrong? Not wishing to discuss this question with himself, he went into the house and sat down to Usher's *History of Mechanical Inventions*.

At half past four he suddenly remembered that dead dog. A few hours more, and in this heat ... He hurried out to the toolhouse. The ground in the untended garden was sun-baked almost to the consistency of brick; by the time he had dug the hole he was dripping with sweat. Then, spade in hand, he went up to the roof. There lay the dog. The blood-stains on its fur, on the parapet, on the mattresses had turned the colour of rust. After several ineffectual attempts, he succeeded in scooping up the carcass with his spade and throwing it, flies and all – for the flies refused to be disturbed – over the parapet. He went downstairs and out into the garden; there, as though he were obstinately competing in some hideous egg-and-spoon race, he scooped the thing up once more and carried it, horribly dangling across the iron of his spade, to the grave. When he came back to the house he felt so sick that he had to drink some brandy. After that he went down to the sea and took a long swim.

At six, when he was dressed again, he took his car and drove down to the hotel to have a talk with Helen. By this time, he calculated, she would have got over her first shock, she would be ready to listen to him. Forgetting all about the Doll's House and the sanity it had been intended to preserve, he was filled, as he drove, with an extraordinary elation. In a few minutes he would be seeing her again. Would be telling her of the discoveries he had suddenly made that morning: the discovery that he cared for her, the discovery that he had been a fool and worse, unspeakably worse than a fool. ... It would be difficult, it would be all but impossible to say these things about himself; but for that very reason the thought that he was going to say them filled him with profound happiness.

He drew up at the door of the hotel and hurried into the hall.

'*Madame Ledwidge est-elle dans sa chambre, mademoiselle?*'

'*Mais non, monsieur, Madame vient de partir.*'

'*Elle vient de partir?*'

'*Madame est allée prendre le rapide à Toulon.*'

Anthony looked at his watch. The train had already started. In a wretched little car like his there was no hope of getting to Marseille before it left again for Paris.

'*Merci, mademoiselle, merci,*' he said, lapsing by force of habit into that excessive politeness by means of which he protected himself from the disquieting world of the lower classes.

'*Mais de rien, monsieur.*'

He drove home again, wondering miserably whether he oughtn't to be thankful for the deliverance. The postman had called in his absence. There was a letter from his broker, advising him to sell at least a part of that block of gold-mining shares he had inherited from Uncle James. There seemed to be no likelihood of their appreciating any further; in view of which, the wisest course would be to take advantage of the present prices and re-invest in sound English industrials such as ... He threw the letter aside. Occasions, as usual, had been conspiring for him – thrusting good fortune upon him, malignantly. Now, in the depression, he was better off than ever before. Better off when other people were worse off. Freer while they were hopelessly enslaved. The ring of Polycrates ... It looked as though the gods had already begun their vengeance.

He went to bed early, and at two was woken by that horribly familiar dream that had haunted his boyhood and plagued him from time to time even as a grown man. In substance it was always the same. Nothing much was ever visible; but there was generally a knowledge that he was in company, surrounded by dim presences. He took a mouthful of some indeterminate food, and instantly it expanded between his teeth, became progressively more rubbery and at the same time stickier, till it was like a gag smeared with a kind of gum that dried in a thick film on the teeth, tongue, palate. Unspeakably disgusting, this process of asphyxiating expansion, of gluey thickening and clogging, went on and on. He tried to swallow, tried, in spite of the obscure but embarrassing presence of strangers, to disgorge. Without effect. In the end, he was reduced to hooking the stuff out with his finger – lump after ropy lump of it. But always in vain. For the gag continued to expand, the film to thicken and harden. Until at last he was delivered by starting out of sleep. This night, the expanding mouthful had some kind of vague but horrible connexion with the dog. He woke up shuddering. Once awake, he was unable to go to sleep again. A huge accumulation of neglected memories broke through, as it were, into his awareness. Those snapshots. His mother and Mary Amberley. Brian in the chalk pit, evoked by that salty smell of sun-warmed flesh, and again dead at the cliff's foot, among the flies – like that dog . . .

CHAPTER THIRTEEN

May 20th 1934

Made my second yesterday night. Without serious nervousness. It's easy enough, once you've made up your mind that it doesn't matter if you make a fool of yourself. But it's depressing. There's a sense in which five hundred people in a hall aren't concrete. One's talking to a collective noun, an abstraction, not to a set of individuals. Only those already partially or completely convinced of what you're saying even want to understand you. The rest are invincibly ignorant. In private conversation, you could be certain of getting your man to make at least a grudging effort to understand you. The fact that there's an audience confirms the not-understander in his incomprehension. Particularly if he can ask questions after the address. Some of the reasons for this are obvious. Just getting up and being looked at is a pleasure – in many cases, piercing to the point of pain. Excruciating orgasms of self-assertion. Pleasure is heightened if the question is hostile. Hostility is a declaration of personal independence. Makes it clear at the same time that it's only an accident that the questioner isn't on the platform himself – accident or else, of course, deliberate plot on the part of ruffians who want to keep him down. Interruptions and questions are generally of course quite irrelevant. Hecklers (like the rest of us) live in their own private world, make no effort to enter other people's worlds. Most arguments in public are at cross-purposes and in different languages – without interpreters.

Mark was at the meeting, and afterwards, in my rooms, took pleasure in intensifying my depression.

'Might as well go and talk to cows in a field.' The temptation to agree with him was strong. All my old habits of thinking, living, feeling impel me towards agreement. A senseless world, where nothing whatever can be done – how satisfactory ! One can go off and (seeing that there's nothing else to do) compile one's treatise on sociology – the science of human senselessness. With Mark last night I caught myself taking intense pleasure in commenting on the imbecility of my audience and human beings at large. Caught and checked myself. Reflecting that seeds had been sown, that if only one were to germinate, it would have been worth while to hold the meeting. Worth while even if none were to germinate – for my own sake, as an exercise, a training for doing better next time.

I didn't say all this. Merely stopped talking and, I suppose, changed my expression. Mark, who notices everything, began to laugh. Foresaw the time when I'd preface every mention of a person or group with the adjective 'dear'. The dear Communists', 'the dear armament makers', 'dear General Goering'.

I laughed – for he was comic in his best savage manner. But, after all, if you had enough love and goodness, you could be sure of evoking some measure of answering love and goodness from almost everyone you came in contact with – whoever he or she might be. And in that case almost everyone would really be 'dear'. At present, most people seem more or less imbecile or odious; the fault is at least as much in oneself as in them.

May 24th 1934

Put in four hours this morning at working up my notes.

Extraordinary pleasure ! How easily one could slip back into un-interrupted scholarship and idea-mongering ! Into that 'Higher Life' which is simply death without tears. Peace, irresponsibility – all the delights of death here and now. In the past, you had to go into a monastery to find them. You paid for the pleasure of death with obedience, poverty, chastity. Now you can have them gratis and in the ordinary world. Death completely without tears. Death with smiles, death with the pleasures of bed and bottle, death in private with nobody to bully you. Scholars, philosophers, men of science – conventionally supposed to be unpractical. But what other class of men has succeeded in getting the world to accept it and (more astonishing) go on accepting it at its own valuation? Kings have lost their divine right, plutocrats look as though they were going to lose theirs. But Higher Lifers continue to be labelled as superior. It's the fruit of persistence. Persistently paying compliments to themselves, persistently disparaging other people. Year in, year out, for the last sixty centuries. We're High, you're Low; we're of the Spirit, you're of the World. Again and again, like Pears Soap. It's been accepted, now, as an axiom. But, in fact, the Higher Life is merely the better death-substitute. A more complete escape from the responsibilities of living than alcohol or morphia or addiction to sex or property. Booze and dope destroy health. Sooner or later sex addicts get involved in responsibilities. Property addicts can never get all the stamps, Chinese vases, houses, varieties of lilies or whatever it may be, that they want. Their escape is a torment of Tantalus. Whereas the Higher Life escapes into a world where there's no risk to health and the minimum of responsibilities and tortures. A world, what's more, that tradition regards as actually superior to the world of responsible living – higher. The Higher Shirker can fairly wallow in his good conscience. For how easy to find in the life of scholarship and research equivalents for all the moral virtues ! Some, of course, are not equivalent, but identical : perserverance, patience, self-forgetfulness and the like. Good means to ends that may be bad. You can work hard and whole-heartedly at anything – from atomic physics to forgery and white-slaving. The rest are ethical virtues transposed into the mental key. *Chastity* of artistic and mathematical form. *Purity* of scientific research. *Courageousness* of thought. *Bold* hypotheses. Logical *integrity*. *Temperance* of views. Intellectual *humility* before the facts. All the cardinal virtues in fancy dress. The Higher Lifers come to think of themselves as saints – saints of art and science and scholarship. A purely figurative and metaphorical sanctity taken *au pied de la lettre*.

'Blessed are the poor in spirit.' The Higher Lifer even has equivalents for spiritual poverty. As a man of science, he tries to keep himself unbiased by his interests and prejudices. But that's not all. Ethical poverty of spirit entails taking no thought for the morrow, letting the dead bury their dead, losing one's life to gain it. The Higher Lifer can make parodies of these renunciations. I know; for I made them and actually took credit to myself for having made them. You live continuously and responsibly only in the other, Higher world. In this, you detach yourself from your past; you refuse to commit yourself in the future; you have no convictions, but live moment by moment; you renounce your own identity, except as a Higher Lifer, and become just the succession of your states. A more than Franciscan destitution. Which can be combined, however, with more than Napoleonic exultations in imperialism. I used to think I had no will to power. Now I perceive that I vented it on thoughts, rather than people. Conquering an unknown province of knowledge. Getting the better of a problem. Forcing ideas to associate or come apart. Bullying recalcitrant words to assume a certain pattern. All the fun of being a dictator without any risks and responsibilities.

CHAPTER FOURTEEN
December 8th 1926

By dinner-time it was already a Story – the latest addition to Mary Amberley's repertory. The latest, and as good, it seemed to Anthony's critically attentive ear, as the finest classics of the collection. Ever since he received her invitation, he now realized, his curiosity had been tinged with a certain vindictive hope that she would have altered for the worse, either relatively in his own knowledgeable eyes, or else absolutely by reason of the passage of these twelve long years; would have degenerated from what she was, or what he had imagined her to be, at the time when he had loved her. Discreditably enough, as he now admitted to himself, it was with a touch of disappointment that he had found her hardly changed from the Mary Amberley of his memories. She was forty-three. But her body was almost as slim as ever, and she moved with all the old swift agility. With something more than the old agility, indeed; for he had noticed that she was now agile on purpose, that she acted the part of one who is carried away by a youthful impulse to break into quick and violent motion – acted it, moreover, in circumstances where the impulse could not, if natural, possibly have been felt. Before dinner, she took him upstairs to her bedroom to see those nudes by Pascin that she had just bought. The first half of the flight she negotiated at a normal pace, talking as she went; then, as though she had suddenly remembered that slowness on stairs is a sign of middle age, she suddenly started running – no, *scampering*, Anthony corrected himself as he remembered the incident; *scampering* was the word. And when they returned to the drawing-room, no tomboy of sixteen could have thrown herself more recklessly into the sofa or tucked up her legs with a more kittenish movement. The Mary of 1914 had never behaved so youthfully as that. Couldn't have even if she had wanted to, he reflected, in all those skirts and petticoats. Whereas now, in kilts ... It was absurd, of course; but not yet, he judicially decided, painfully absurd. For Mary could still claim to look the youthful part. Only a little worn, her face still seemed to sparkle, through the faint stigmata of fatigue, with the old laughing vitality. And as for her accomplishments – why, this improvisation (and an improvisation it must be, seeing that the event had occurred only that morning), this improvisation on the theme of Helen's stolen kidney was a little masterpiece.

'I shall have the object embalmed,' she was concluding in a mock-serious tone, pregnant with subdued laughter. 'Embalmed and ...'

But like a suddenly opened ginger-beer bottle, bubbling, 'I'll give you an address for the embalming,' put in Beppo Bowles. He smiled, he blinked his eyes, he wriggled. His whole plump and florid person seemed to participate in what he said; he talked with every organ of his body. 'From the *Mortician's Journal*.' He waved a hand and declaimed, 'Embalmers! do your results have that unpleasant putty look? If so . . .'

Mrs Amberley had laughed – a little perfunctorily, perhaps; for she did not like to be interrupted in the middle of a story. Beppo was a darling, of course. So boyish, in spite of his tummy and the bald patch on the top of his head. (So girlish, even, on occasion.) But still . . . She cut him short with a 'Too perfect.' Then, turning back to the rest of the table, 'Well, as I was saying,' she continued, 'I shall have it embalmed and put under one of those glass domes . . .'

'Like life,' Beppo could not refrain from ginger-beerily interjecting. But nobody caught the reference to *Adonais*, and he giggled alone.

'Those domes,' repeated Mrs Amberley without looking at the interrupter, 'one finds in lodging-houses. With birds under them. Stuffed *birds*.' She lingered over the monosyllable, as though she were a German prolonging a modified o; and the birds, the Teutonic bö-öds, became, for some obscure reason, extraordinarily funny.

The voice, Anthony decided, was better than ever. There was a faint hoarseness now, like the bloom on a fruit, like the haze through which, on a summer's day, one sees St Paul's from Waterloo Bridge. The interposition of that curtain of husky gauze seemed to deepen, as it were, and enrich the beauties of the vocal landscape lying behind it. Listening more attentively than ever, he tried to fix the cadences of her speech upon his memory, to analyse them into their component sounds. In his projected Elements of Sociology there was to be a chapter on Mass Suggestion and Propaganda. One of the sections would be devoted to the subject of Fascinating Noises. The fascinatingly excitingly exciting noise, for example, of Savonarola, or Lloyd George. The fascinatingly sedative noise of intoning priests; the fascinatingly hilarious noise of Robey and Little Tich; the fascinatingly aphrodisiac noise of certain actors and actresses, certain singers, certain sirens and Don Juans of private life.

Mary's gift, he decided, was for making a noise that was simultaneously aphrodisiac and comic. She could emit sounds that touched the springs of laughter and desire, but never those of sorrow, of pity, of indignation. In moments of emotional stress (and he recalled those horrible scenes she used to make) her voice passed out of control into a chaos of raucous shrillness. The sound of her words of complaint, reproach, or grief evoked in the hearer only a certain physical discomfort. Whereas with Mrs Foxe, he now went on to think, the noise alone of what she said had been enough to compel your acquiescence and sympathy. Hers was the mysterious gift that hoisted Robespierre into power, that enabled Whitefield, by the mere repetition, two or three times, of some pious exclamation, to reduce the most hardened sceptic to tears. There are fascinating noises capable of convincing a listener of the existence of God.

Those bö-öds! They all laughed, all simply had to laugh, at them. Even Colin Egerton, even Hugh Ledwidge. And yet ever since that man Beavis had come into the drawing-room, Hugh had been in a prickle of uneasiness. Beavis whom he always did his best to avoid ... Why hadn't Mary told him? For a moment he imagined it was a plot. Mary had invited Beavis on purpose to put him to shame – because she knew that the man had been a witness of his humiliations at Bulstrode. There were to be two of them : Staithes (for Staithes, he knew, was expected after dinner) and Beavis. Hugh had grown accustomed to meeting Staithes in his house, didn't mind meeting him. Staithes, there could be no doubt, had forgotten. But Beavis – whenever he met Beavis, it always seemed to Hugh that the man looked at him in a queer way. And now Mary had invited him, on purpose, so that he could remind Staithes; and then the two of them would bait him with their reminiscences – their reminiscences of how he had funked at football; of how he had cried when it was his turn at fire-drill to slide down the rope; of how he had sneaked to Jimbug and had then been made to run the gauntlet between two lines of them, armed with wet towels rolled up into truncheons; of how they had looked over the partition ... He shuddered. But of course, on second, saner thoughts, it couldn't possibly be a plot. Not conceivably. All the same, he was glad when they went down to dinner and he found himself separated from Beavis. Across Helen, conversation would be difficult. And after dinner he would do his best to keep at a distance . . .

As for Colin, he had sat all through the meal in a bewilderment that, as it grew, as he felt himself more and more hopelessly out of it all, was mingled to an ever-increasing extent with exasperation and disapproval, until at last he was saying to himself (what he intended to say aloud to Joyce at the first opportunity), was saying: 'I may be stupid and all that' – and this confession was uttered by his inward voice in a tone of firm contempt, as though it were a confession of strength, not weakness – 'I may be stupid and all that, but at least – well, at least I do know what's within the pale and what's without.' He would say all that to Joyce, and much more; and Joyce (he had glanced at her in the middle of one of Beppo's outrageous stories and caught an eye that was humble, anxious, pleadingly apologetic), Joyce would agree with every word he said. For the poor child was like a kind of changeling – a County changeling left by some inexplicable mistake in the arms of a mad, impossible mother who forced her, against her real nature, to associate with these . . . these . . . (He couldn't find the mentionable word for Beppo.) And he, Colin Egerton, he was the St George who would rescue her. The fact that – like some pure young girl fallen among white slavers – she needed rescuing was one of the reasons why he felt so strongly attracted to her. He loved her, among other reasons, because he so violently loathed that ghastly degenerate (*that* was the word), Beppo Bowles; and his approval of all that Joyce was and did was proportionate to his disapproval (a disapproval strengthened by a certain terror) of Joyce's mother. And yet, now, in spite of the disapproval, in spite of his fear of that sharp tongue of hers, those piercingly ironic glances, he could not help laughing with the rest. Those long-drawn *bö-öds* under their glass domes were irresistible.

For Mrs Amberley the laughter was like champagne – warming, stimulating. 'And I shall have an inscription carved on the base,' she went on, raising her voice against the din: ' "This kidney was stolen by Helen Amberley, at the risk of life and . . ." '

'Oh, do shut up, Mummy!' Helen was blushing with a mixture of pleasure and annoyance. 'Please!' It was certainly nice to be the heroine of a story that everybody was listening to – but then the heroine was also a bit of an ass. She felt angry with her mother for exploiting the assishness.

'. . . and in spite of a lifelong and conscientious objection to butchery,' Mrs Amberley went on. Then, 'Poor darling,' she added in another tone. 'Smells always were her weak point. Butchers, fishmongers, – and shall I ever forget the one and only time I took her to church!'

('One and only time,' thought Colin. 'No wonder she goes and does things like this!')

'Oh, I do admit,' cried Mrs Amberley, 'that a village congregation on a wet Sunday morning – well, frankly, it stinks. Deafeningly! But still . . .'

'It's the odour of sanctity,' put in Anthony Beavis: and turning to Helen, 'I've suffered from it myself. And did your mother make you spit when there were bad smells about? Mine did. It made things very difficult in church.'

'She didn't spit,' Mrs Amberley answered for her daughter. 'She was sick. All over old Lady Worplesdon's astrakhan coat. I was never able to show my face in respectable society again. Thank God!' she added.

Beppo sizzled a protest against her implied imputations. Switched off kidneys, the conversation rolled away along another line.

Helen sat unnoticed, in silence. Her face had suddenly lost all its light; 'I'll never touch meat again,' she had said. And here she was, with a morsel of that gruesome red lump of cow impaled on her fork. 'I'm awful,' she thought. *Pas sérieuse*, old Mme Delécluze had pronounced. And though as a professional girl-finisher the old beast could hardly be expected to say anything else, yet it was true; at bottom it was quite true. 'I'm not serious. I'm not . . .' But suddenly she was aware that the voice which had been sounding, inarticulately and as though from an immense distance, in her right ear was addressing itself to her.

'. . . Proust,' she heard it saying, and realized that it had pronounced the same syllable at least twice before. She looked round, guiltily, and saw, red with embarrassment, the face of

Hugh Ledwidge turned, waveringly and uncertainly, towards her. He smiled foolishly; his spectacles flashed; he turned away. She felt doubly confused and ashamed.

'I'm afraid I didn't quite catch . . .' she contrived to mumble.

'Oh, it doesn't matter,' he mumbled back. 'It's really of no importance.' Of no importance; but it had taken him the best part of five minutes to think of that gambit about Proust. I must say something to her, he had decided, when he saw Beavis safely involved in intimate talk with Mary Amberley and Beppo. 'Must say something.' But what? What did one say to young girls of eighteen? He would have liked to say something personal, something even a bit gallant. About her frock, for example. 'How nice!' No, that was a bit vague and unspecific. 'How it suits your complexion, your eyes!' (What colour were they, by the way?) Or he might ask her about parties. Did she go to many? With (very archly) boy friends? But that, he knew, was too difficult for him. Besides, he didn't much like to think of her with boy friends – preferred her virginal : *du bist wie eine Blume* . . . Or else, seriously but with a smile, 'Tell me,' he might say, 'tell me, Helen, what are young people *really* like nowadays? What *do* they think and feel about things?' And Helen would plant her elbows on the table and turn sideways and tell him exactly all he wanted to know about that mysterious world, the world where people danced and went to parties and were always having personal relations with one another; would tell him everything, everything – or else, more likely, nothing, and he would just be made to feel an impertinent fool. No, no; this wouldn't do, wouldn't do at all. This was just fancy, this was just wish-fulfilment. It was then that the question about Proust had occurred to him. What did she think of Proust? It was a comfortingly impersonal question – one that he could ask without feeling awkward and unnatural. But its impersonality could easily be made to lead to a long discussion – always in the abstract, always, so to speak, in a test-tube – of the most intimately emotional, even (no, no; but still, one never knew; it was revolting; and yet . . .) even physiological matters. Talking of Proust, it would be possible to say everything – everything, but always in terms of a strictly literary criticism. Perfect! He had turned towards Helen.

'I suppose you're as keen on Proust as everybody else.' No answer. From the end of the table came wafts of Mrs Amberley's conversation with Anthony and Beppo: they were discussing the habits of their friends. Colin Egerton was in the middle of a tiger hunt in the Central Provinces. He coughed, then, 'You're a Proustian, I take it? Like the rest of us,' he repeated. But the lowered and melancholy profile gave no sign of life. Feeling most uncomfortably a fool, Hugh Ledwidge tried once more.

'I wish you'd tell me,' he said in a louder voice, that sounded, he thought, peculiarly unnatural, 'what *you* think about Proust.'

Helen continued to stare at some invisible object on the table, just in front of her plate. *Pas sérieuse.* She was thinking of all the unserious things she had ever done in her life, all the silly, the mean, the awful things. A kind of panic embarrassment overwhelmed Hugh Ledwidge. He felt as he might feel if his trousers were to start coming down in Piccadilly – lost. Anybody else, of course, would just touch her arm and say, 'A penny for your thoughts, Helen!' How simple this would be, how sensible! The whole incident would at once be turned into a joke – a joke, moreover, at *her* expense. He would establish once and for all a position of teasing superiority. 'Day-dreaming in the middle of a dinner! About what? About whom?' Very knowing and arch. And she would blush, would giggle – at *his* behest, in response to *his* command. Like a skilled matador, he would wave his little red flag, and she would go plunging here, go charging there, making an absurd and ravishing exhibition of herself, until at last raising his sword ... But simple and sensible and strategically advantageous as all this would be, Hugh Ledwidge found it quite impossible to make the first move. There was her bare arm, thin like a little girl's; but somehow he could not bring himself to put out his hand and touch it. And the jocular offer of that penny – it couldn't be made; his vocal cords would not do it. Thirty seconds passed – seconds of increasing embarrassment and uncertainty. Then suddenly, as though waking from sleep, she had looked round at him. What had he said? But it was impossible to repeat that question again.

'It's of no importance. No importance.' he turned away. But

why, oh why was he such a fool, so ridiculously incompetent? At thirty-five. *Nel mezzo del cammin.* Imagine Dante in the circumstances! Dante, with his steel profile, ploughing forward, like a spiritual battleship. And meanwhile, what on earth should he say to her in place of that now impossible remark about Proust? What in the name of heaven . . . ?

It was she finally who touched *his* arm. 'I'm sorry,' she said with a real contrition. She was trying to make up for her awfulness, for having so frivolously eaten Mr Baldwin's well-thumbed cow. Besides, she liked old Hugh. He was nice. He had taken the trouble to show her the Mexican things at the Museum. 'I have an appointment with Mr Ledwidge,' she had said. And the attendants had all been delightfully deferential. She had been led to his private room – the private room of the Assistant Director of the Department – as though she were some distinguished personage. One eminent archaeologist visiting another. It had really been extraordinarily interesting. Only, of course – and this was another symptom of her awful unseriousness – she had forgotten most of the things he had told her. 'So awfully sorry,' she repeated; and it was genuinely true. She knew what he must be feeling. 'You see,' she explained, 'Granny's deaf. I know how awful it is when I have to repeat something. It sounds so idiotic. Like Mr Shandy and the clock, somehow, if you see what I mean. Do forgive me.' She pressed his arm appealingly, then planting her elbows on the table and turning sideways towards him in just the confidential attitude he had visualized, 'Listen, Hugh,' she said, 'you're serious, aren't you? You know, *sérieux.*'

'Well, I suppose so,' he stammered. He had just seen, rather belatedly, what she meant by that reference to Mr Shandy, and the realization had come as something of a shock.

'I mean,' she went on, 'you could hardly be at the Museum if you weren't serious.'

'No,' he admitted, 'I probably couldn't.' But after all, he was thinking, still preoccupied by Mr Shandy, there's such a thing as theoretical knowledge. (And didn't he know it? Only too well.) Theoretical knowledge corresponding to no genuine experience, unrealized, not lived through. 'Oh God!' he inwardly groaned.

'Well, I'm *not* serious,' Helen was saying. She felt a great need to unburden herself, to ask for help. There were moments – and they recurred whenever, for one reason or another, she felt doubtful of herself – moments when everything round her seemed terribly vague and unreliable. Everything – but in practice, of course, it all boiled down to the unreliability of her mother. Helen was very fond of her mother, but at the same time she had to admit to herself that she was no use. 'Mummy's like a very bad practical joke,' she had once said to Joyce. 'You think you're going to sit on it; but the chair's whisked away and you come down with a horrible bump on your bottom.' But all that Joyce had said was : 'Helen, you simply mustn't use those words.' Ass of a girl ! Though, of course, it had to be admitted, Joyce was a chair that *could* be sat on. But an inadequate chair, a chair only for unimportant occasions – and what was the good of that? Joyce was too young; and even if she'd been much older, she wouldn't really have understood anything properly. And now that she was engaged to Colin, she seemed to understand things less and less. God, what a fool that man was ! But all the same, there, if you liked, *was* a chair. A chair like the rock of ages. But so shaped, unfortunately, that it forced you to sit in the most grotesquely uncomfortable position. However, as Joyce didn't seem to mind the discomfort, that was all right. Chairless in an exhausting world, Helen almost envied her. Meanwhile there was old Hugh. She sat down, heavily.

'What's wrong with me,' she went on, 'is that I'm so hopelessly frivolous.'

'I can't really believe that,' he said; though why he said it he couldn't imagine. For, obviously, he ought to be encouraging her to make confession, not assuring her that she had no sins to confess. It was as though he were secretly afraid of the very thing he had wished for.

'I don't think you're ... '

But unfortunately nothing he said could put her off. She insisted on using him as a chair.

'No, no, it's quite true,' she said. 'You can't imagine how frivolous I am. I'll tell you ... '

Half an hour later, in the back drawing-room, he was writing out for her a list of the books she ought to read. Burnet's *Early*

Greek Philosophers; *Phaedrus, Timaeus, The Apology*, and *The Symposium* in Jowett's translation; the *Nicomachean Ethios*; Cornford's little anthology of the Greek moralists; Marcus Aurelius; Lucretius in any good translation; Inge's *Plotinus*. His manner, as he spoke, was easy, confident, positively masterful. He was like a creature suddenly restored to its proper element.

'Those will give you some idea of the way the ancients thought about things.'

She nodded. Her face as she looked at the pencilled list was grave and determined. She had decided that she would wear spectacles, and have a table brought up to her bedroom, so that she could sit undisturbed, with her books piled up and her writing materials in front of her. Note-books – or, better, a card index. It would be a new life – a life with some meaning in it, some purpose. In the drawing-room somebody started up the gramophone. As though on its own initiative, her foot began to beat out the rhythm. One two three, one two three – it was a waltz. But what was she thinking of? She frowned and held her foot still.

'As for modern thought,' Hugh was saying, 'well, the two indispensable books, from which every modern culture must start, are' – his pencil hurried across the paper – 'Montaigne's *Essays* and the *Pensées* of Pascal. Indispensable, these.' He underlined the names. 'Then you'd better glance at the *Discourse on Method*.'

'Which method?' asked Helen.

But Hugh did not hear her question. 'And take a look at Hobbes, if you have the time,' he went on with ever-increasing power and confidence. 'And then Newton. That's absolutely essential. Because if you don't know the philosophy of Newton, you don't know why science has developed as it has done. You'll find all you need in Burtt's *Metaphysical Foundations of Modern Science*.' There was a little silence while he wrote. Tom had arrived, and Eileen and Sybil. Helen could hear them talking in the other room. But she kept her eyes determinedly fixed on the paper. 'Then there's Hume,' he continued. 'You'd better begin with the *Essays*. They're superb. Such sense, such an immense sagacity!'

'Sagacity,' Helen repeated, and smiled to herself with pleasure. Yes, that was exactly the word she'd been looking for – exactly what she herself would like to be : sagacious, like an elephant, like an old sheepdog, like Hume, if you preferred it. But at the same time, of course, herself. Sagacious, but young; sagacious, but lively and attractive; sagacious, but impetuous and . . .

'I won't inflict Kant on you,' said Hugh indulgently. 'But I think' (he brought the pencil into play again), 'I think you'll have to read one or two of the modern Kantians. Vaihinger's *Philosophy of As If*, for example, and von Uexküll's *Theoretical Biology*. You see, Kant's behind all our twentieth-century science. Just as Newton was behind all the science of the eighteenth and nineteenth . . . '

'Why, Helen !'

They started and looked up – looked up into the smiling, insolently handsome face of Gerry Watchett. Brilliantly blue against the sunburnt skin, the eyes glanced from one to the other with a kind of mockery. Coming a step nearer, he laid his hand familiarly on Helen's shoulder. 'What's the fun? Cross-word puzzles?' He gave the shoulder two or three little pats.

'As though she were his horse,' Hugh said to himself indignantly. And, in effect, that was what the man looked like – a groom. That crisply waving, golden-brownish hair, that blunt-featured face, at once boyish and tough – they were straight from the stable, straight from Epsom Downs.

Helen smiled a smile that was intended to be contemptuously superior – an intellectual's smile. 'You *would* think it was cross-words!' she said. Then, 'By the way,' she added in another tone, 'you know each other, don't you?' she looked inquiringly from Gerry to Hugh.

'We do,' Gerry answered : still keeping his right hand on Helen's shoulder, he raised his left in the derisive caricature of military salute. 'Good evening, Colonel.'

Sheepishly, Hugh returned the salute. All his power and confidence had vanished with his forced return from the world of books to that of personal life; he felt like an albatross on dry land – helplessly awkward, futile, ugly. And yet how easy it should have been to put on a knowing smile, and say signifi-

cantly, 'Yes, I know Mr Watchett very well' – know him, the
tone would imply, for what he is : the gentleman sharepusher,
the professional gambler, and the professional lover. Mary
Amberley's lover at the moment, so it was supposed. 'Know
him very well *indeed*!' That was what it would have been so
easy to say. But he didn't say it : he only smiled and rather
foolishly raised his hand to his forehead.

Gerry, meanwhile, had sat down on the arm of the sofa, and
through the smoke of his cigarette was staring at Helen with a
calm and easy insolence, appraising her, so it seemed, point by
point – hocks, withers, quarters, barrel. 'Do you know, Helen,'
he said at last, 'you're getting prettier and prettier every day.'

Blushing, Helen threw back her head and laughed; then
suddenly stiffened her face into an unnatural rigidity. She was
angry – angry with Gerry for his damned impertinence, angry
above all with herself for having been pleased by the damned
impertinence, for having reacted with such a humiliating automatic punctuality to that offensive flattery. Going red in the
face and giggling like a schoolgirl! And that Philosophy of As
If, those horn-rimmed spectacles, and the new life, and the card
index ...? A man said, 'You're pretty,' and it was as though
they had never been so much as thought of. She turned towards
Hugh; turned for protection, for support. But her eyes no
sooner met his than he looked away. His face took on an expression of meditative absence; he seemed to be thinking of something else. Was he angry with her, she wondered? Had he been
offended because she had been pleased by Gerry's compliment?
But it had been like blinking at the noise of a gun – something
you couldn't help doing. He ought to understand, ought to
realize that she wanted to lead that new life, was simply longing
to be sagacious. Instead of which, he just faded out and refused
to have anything to do with her. Oh, it wasn't fair !

Behind that cold detached mask of his, Hugh was feeling
more than ever like Baudelaire's albatross.

> *Ce voyageur ailé, comme il est gauche et veule!*
> *Lui, naguère si beau, qu'il est comique et laid!*

Ah, those strong and majestic swoopings in the neo-Kantian
azure!

From the next room the gramophone was trumpeting, 'Yes, sir, she's my Baby.' Gerry whistled a couple of bars; then 'What about a spot of fox-trotting, Helen?' he suggested. 'Unless, of course, you haven't finished with the Colonel.' He glanced mockingly at Hugh's averted face. 'I don't want to interrupt ...'

It was Helen's turn to look at Hugh. 'Well ...' she began doubtfully.

But without looking up, 'Oh, not at all, not at all,' Hugh made haste to say; and wondered, even as he did so, what on earth had induced him to proclaim his own defeat before there had been a battle. Leaving her to that groom! Fool, coward! Still, he told himself cynically, she probably preferred the groom. He got up, mumbled something about having to talk to someone about some point that had turned up, and moved away towards the door that gave on to the landing and the stairs.

'Well, if he doesn't want me to stay,' Helen thought resentfully, 'if he doesn't think it's worth his while to keep me.' She was hurt.

'Exit the Colonel,' said Gerry. Then, 'What about that spot of dancing?' He rose, came towards her and held out his hand. Helen took it and pulled herself up from the low chair. 'No, sir, don't say maybe,' he sang as he put his arm about her. They stepped out into the undulating stream of the music. Zig-zagging between chairs and tables, he steered towards the door that led into the other room.

CHAPTER FIFTEEN

June 1903 – January 1904

It had become a rite, a sacrament (that was how John Beavis described it to himself): a sacrament of communion. First, the opening of the wardrobe door, the handling of her dresses. Closing his eyes, he breathed the perfume they exhaled, the faint sweet essence of her body from across the widening abyss of time. Then there were the drawers. These three, on the left, contained her linen. The lavender bags were tied with pale blue ribbon. This lace on the night-gown he now unfolded had touched ... Even in thought, John Beavis avoided the pronunciation of the words 'her breasts', but only imagined the rounded flesh softly swelling and sinking under the intricacies of the patterned thread; then recalled those Roman nights; and finally thought of Lollingdon and the hollow vale, the earth, the terrible dark silence. The night-gown refolded and once more shut away, it was the turn of the two small drawers on the right – of the gloves that had encased her hands, the belts that had girdled her body and that now he wound round his wrist or tightened like a phylactery about his temples. And the rite concluded with the reading of her letters – those touchingly childish letters she had written during their engagement. That consummated the agony for him; the rite was over and he could go to bed with yet another sword in his heart.

But recently, it seemed, the sword had grown blunter. It was as though her death, till now so poignantly alive, had itself begun to die. The rite seemed to be losing its magic : consummation became increasingly difficult of achievement, and, when achieved, was less painful and, for that reason, less satisfying. For the thing which had made life worth living all these months was precisely the pain of his bereavement. Desire and tenderness had suddenly been deprived of their object. It was an amputation – agonizing. And now this pain – and it was all of her that was left him – this precious anguish was slipping away from him, was dying, even as Maisie herself had died.

Tonight it seemed to have vanished altogether. He buried his face in the scented folds of her dresses, he spread out the lace and lawn she had worn next to her skin, he blew into one of her gloves and watched the gradual deflation of this image of her hand – dying, dying, till the skin hung limp again and empty of even the pretence of life. But the rites were without effect; John Beavis remained unmoved. He knew that she was dead and that his bereavement was terrible. But felt nothing of this bereavement – nothing except a kind of dusty emptiness of spirit.

He went to bed unfulfilled, somehow humiliated. Magic rites justify themselves by success; when they fail to produce their proper emotional results, the performer feels that he has been betrayed into making a fool of himself.

Dry, like a mummy, in the dusty emptiness of his own sepulchre, John Beavis lay for a long time, unable to sleep. Twelve; one; two; and then, when he had utterly despaired of it, sleep came, and he was dreaming that she was there beside him; and it was Maisie as she had been the first year of their marriage, the round flesh swelling and subsiding beneath the lace, the lips parted and, oh, innocently consenting. He took her in his arms.

It was the first time since her death that he had dreamed of her except as dying.

John Beavis woke to a sense of shame; and when, later in the day, he saw Miss Gannett evidently waiting for him as usual, in the corridor outside his lecture-room, he pretended not to have noticed her, but hurried past with downcast eyes, frowning, as though preoccupied by some abstruse, insoluble problem in higher philology.

But the next afternoon found him at his Aunt Edith's weekly At Home. And of course – though he expressed a perhaps excessive surprise at seeing her – of course Miss Gannett was there, as he knew she would be; for she never missed one of Aunt Edith's Thursdays.

'You were in a terrible hurry yesterday,' she said, when his surprise had had time to die down.

'Me? When?' He pretended not to know what she meant.

'At the college, after your lecture.'

'But were you there? I didn't see you.'

'Now he thinks I shirked his lecture,' she wailed to some nonexistent third party. Ever since, two months before, she had first met him in Aunt Edith's drawing-room, Miss Gannett had faithfully attended every one of his public lectures. 'To improve my mind,' she used to explain. 'Because,' with a jocularity that was at the same time rather wistful, 'it does so need improving!'

Mr Beavis protested. 'But I didn't say anything of the kind.'

'I'll show you the notes I took.'

'No, please don't do that!' It was his turn to be playful. 'If you knew how my own lectures bored me!'

'Well, you nearly ran over me in the corridor, after the lecture.'

'Oh, *then*!'

'I never saw anyone walk so fast.'

He nodded. 'Yes, I *was* in a hurry; it's quite true. I had a Committee. Rather a special one,' he added impressively.

She opened her eyes at him very wide, and, from playful, her tone and expression became very serious. 'It must be rather a bore sometimes,' she said, 'to be such a very important person – isn't it?'

Mr Beavis smiled down at the grave and awestruck child before him – at the innocent child who was also a rather plump and snubbily pretty young woman of seven and twenty – smiled with pleasure and stroked his moustache. 'Oh, not quite so important as all that,' he protested. 'Not quite such ... ' he hesitated for a moment; his mouth twitched, his eyes twinkled; then the colloquialism came out: 'not quite such a "howling toff" as you seem to imagine.'

There was only one letter that morning. From Anthony, Mr Beavis saw as he tore open the envelope.

BULSTRODE, *June 26th*

DEAREST FATHER, – Thank you for your letter. I thought we were going to Tenby for the holidays. Did you not arrange it with Mrs Foxe? Foxe says she expects us, so perhaps we ought not to go to Switzerland instead as you say we are doing. We had two matches yesterday, first eleven *v.* Sunny Bank, second *v.* Mumbridge, we won both which was rather ripping. I was playing in the second eleven and made six not out. We have begun a book called Lettres de mon Moulin in French, I think it is rotten. There is no more news, so with much love. – Your loving son, ANTHONY.

P.S. – Don't forget to write to Mrs Foxe, because Foxe says he knows she thinks we are going to Tenby.

Mr Beavis frowned as he read the letter, and when breakfast was over, sat down at once to write an answer.

EARL'S COURT SQUARE
27.vi.03.

DEAREST ANTHONY, – I am disappointed that you should have received what I had hoped was a piece of very exciting news with so little enthusiasm. At your age I should certainly have welcomed the prospect of 'going abroad', especially to Switzerland, with unbounded delight. The arrangements with Mrs Foxe were always of the most indeterminate nature. Needless to say, however, I wrote to her as soon as the golden opportunity for exploring the Bernese Oberland in congenial company turned up, as it did only a few days since, and made me decide to postpone the realization of our vague Tenby plans. If you want to see exactly where we are going, take your map of Switzerland, find Interlaken and the Lake of Brienz, move eastward from the end of the lake to Meiringen and thence in a southerly direction towards Grindelwald. We shall be staying at the foot of the Scheideck Pass, at Rosenlaui, almost in the shadow of such giants as the Jungfrau, Weisshorn and Co. I do not know the spot, but gather from all accounts that it is entirely 'spiffing' and paradisal.

I am delighted to hear you did so creditably in your match. You must go on, dear boy, from strength to strength. Next year I shall hope to see you sporting the glories of the First Eleven Colours.

I cannot agree with you in finding Daudet 'rotten'. I suspect that his rottenness mainly consists in the difficulties he presents to a tyro. When you have acquired a complete mastery of the language, you will come to appreciate the tender charm of his style and the sharpness of his wit.

I hope you are working your hardest to make good your sad weakness in 'maths'. I confess that I never shone in the mathematical line myself, so I am able to sympathize with your difficulties. But hard work will do wonders, and I am sure that if you really 'put your back into' algebra and geometry, you can easily get up to scholarship standards by this time next year. – Ever your most affectionate father,   J.B.

'It's too sickening!' said Anthony, when he had finished reading his father's letter. The tears came into his eyes; he was filled with a sense of intolerable grievance.

'W-what does he s-say?' Brian asked.

'It's all settled. He's written to your mater that we're going to some stinking hole in Switzerland instead of Tenby. Oh, I really am too sick about it!' He crumpled up the letter and threw it angrily on the ground, then turned away and tried to relieve his feeling by kicking his play-box. 'Too sick, too sick!' he kept repeating.

Brian was sick too. They were going to have had such a splendid time at Tenby; it had been imaginatively foreseen, preconstructed in the most luxuriant detail; and now, crash! the future good time was in bits.

'S-still,' he said at last, after a long silence, 'I exp-pect you'll enj-joy yourself in S-switzerland.' And, moved by a sudden impulse, for which he would have found it difficult to offer an explanation, he picked up Mr Beavis's letter, smoothed out the crumpled pages and handed it back to Anthony. 'Here's your l-letter,' he said.

Anthony looked at it for a moment, opened his mouth as though to speak, then shut it again, and taking the letter, put it away in his pocket.

The congenial company in which they were to explore the Bernese Oberland turned out, when they reached Rosenlaui, to consist of Miss Gannett and her old school-friend Miss Louie Piper. Mr Beavis always spoke of them as 'the girls', or else, with a touch of that mock-heroic philological jocularity to which he was so partial, 'the damsels' – *dominicellae*, double diminutive of *domina*. The teeny-weeny ladies! He smiled to himself each time he pronounced the word. To Anthony the damsels seemed a pair of tiresome and already elderly females. Piper, the thin one, was like a governess. He preferred fat old Gannett, in spite of that awful mooey, squealing laugh of hers, in spite of the way she puffed and sweated up the hills. Gannett at least was well-meaning. Luckily, there were two other English boys in the hotel. True, they came from Manchester and spoke rather funnily, but they were decent chaps, and they knew an extraordinary number of dirty stories. Moreover, in the woods behind the hotel they had discovered a cave, where they kept cigarettes. Proudly, when he got back to Bulstrode, Anthony announced that he had smoked almost every day of the hols.

One Saturday in November Mr Beavis came down to Bulstrode for the afternoon. They watched the football for a bit, then went for a depressing walk that ended, however, at the King's Arms. Mr Beavis ordered crumpets 'and buttered eggs for this young stalwart' (with a conspiratorial twinkle at the waitress, as though she knew that the word meant 'foundation-worthy'), 'and cherry jam to follow – isn't cherry the favourite?'

Anthony nodded. Cherry *was* the favourite. But so much solicitude made him feel rather suspicious. What could it all be for?

Was he going to say something about his work? About going in for the scholarship next summer? About...? He blushed. But after all, his father couldn't possibly know anything about *that*. Not possibly. In the end he gave it up; he couldn't imagine what it was.

But when, after an unusually long silence, his father leaned forward and said, 'I've got an interesting piece of news for you, dear boy,' Anthony knew, in a sudden flash of illumination, exactly what was coming.

'He's going to marry the Gannett female,' he said to himself.

And so he was. In the middle of December.

'A companion for you,' Mr Beavis was saying. That youthfulness, those fresh and girlish high spirits! 'A companion as well as a second mother.'

Anthony nodded. But 'companion' – what did he mean? He thought of the fat old Gannett, toiling up the slopes behind Rosenlaui, red-faced, smelling of sweat, reeking ... And suddenly his mother's voice was sounding in his ears.

'Pauline wants you to call her by her Christian name,' Mr Beavis went on. 'It'll be ... well, jollier, don't you think?'

Anthony said 'Yes,' because there was obviously nothing else for him to say, and helped himself to more cherry jam.

*

'Third person singular aorist of τίθημι?' questioned Anthony.

Horse-Face got it wrong. It was Staithes who answered correctly.

'Second plural pluperfect of ἔρχομαι?'

Brian's hesitation was due to something graver than his stammer.

'You're putrid tonight, Horse-Face,' said Anthony, and pointed his finger at Staithes, who gave the right answer again. 'Good for you, Staithes.' And repeating Jimbug's stalest joke, 'The sediment sinks to the bottom, Horse-Face,' he rumbled in a parody of Jimbug's deep voice.

'Poor old Horse-Face!' said Staithes, slapping the other on the back. Now that Horse-Face had given him the pleasure of knowing less Greek grammar than he did, Staithes almost loved him.

It was nearly eleven, long after lights out, and the three of them were crowded into the w.c., Anthony in his capacity of examiner sitting majestically on the seat, and the other two squatting on their heels below him, on the floor. The May night was still and warm; in less than six weeks they would be sitting for their scholarship examinations, Brian and Anthony at Eton, Mark Staithes at Rugby. It was after the previous Christmas holidays that Staithes had come back to Bulstrode with the announcement that he was going in for a scholarship. Astonishing news and, for his courtiers and followers, appalling! That work was idiotic, and that those who worked were contemptible, had been axiomatic among them. And now here was Staithes going in for a schol with the other swots – with Benger Beavis, with old Horse-Face, with that horrible little tick, Goggler Ledwidge. It had seemed a betrayal of all that was most sacred.

By his words first of all, and afterwards, more effectively, by his actions, Staithes had reassured them. The scholarship idea was his Pater's. Not because of the money, he had hastened to add. His Pater didn't care a damn about money. But for the honour and glory, because it was a tradition in the Family. His Pater himself and his uncles, his Fraters – they had all got schols. It wouldn't do to let the Family down. Which didn't change the fact that swotting was a stinking bore and that all swotters who swotted because they liked it, as Horse-Face and Beavis seemed to do, or for the sake of the money, like that miserable Goggler, were absolutely worms. And to prove it he had ragged old Horse-Face about his stammer and his piddle-warblers, he had organized a campaign against Goggler for funking at football, he had struck nibs into Beavis's bottom during prep; and though working very hard himself, he had made up for it by playing harder than ever and by missing no opportunity of telling everyone how beastly swotting was, how he had absolutely no chance whatever of getting a schol.

When face had been sufficiently saved, he had changed his tactics towards Beavis and Horse-Face, and after showing himself for some time progressively more friendly towards them, had ended by proposing the creation of a society of mutual assistance in schol swotting. It was he who, at the beginning of the summer term, had suggested the nightly sessions in the w.c. Brian had wanted to include Goggler in these reading-parties; but the other two had protested; and anyhow, the w.c. was demonstrably too small to contain a fourth. He had to be content with helping Goggler in occasional half-hours during the day. Night and the lavatory were reserved for the triumvirate.

To explain this evening's failure with Greek verbs, 'I'm rather t-t-t ...' Brian began; then, forced into apparent affectation, 'rather weary to-n-night,' he concluded.

His pallor and the blue transparency under his eyes testified to the truth of his words; but for Mark Staithes they were obviously an excuse by means of which Horse-Face hoped to diminsh a little the sting of his defeat at the hands of one who had been swotting, not for years, as his rivals had, but only a few months. It was an implied confession of inferiority. Triumphing, Staithes felt that he could be magnanimous. 'Hard luck!' he said solicitously. 'Let's have a bit of a rest.'

From the pocket of his dressing-gown Anthony produced three ginger-nuts, rather soft, it was true, with age, but none the less welcome.

For the thousandth time since it had been decided that he should go in for a scholarship, 'I wish I had a ghost of a chance,' said Staithes.

'You've g-got a very g-good one.'

'No, I haven't. It's just a crazy idea of my Pater's. Crazy!' he repeated, shaking his head. But in fact it was with a tingling, warm sensation of pride, of exultation, that he remembered his father's words. 'We Staitheses ... When one's a Staithes ... You've got as good brains as the rest of us, and as much determination ...' He forced a sigh, and, aloud, 'Not a ghost of a chance,' he insisted.

'Yes, you h-have, honestly.'

'Rot!' he refused to admit even the possibility of the thing. Then, if he failed, he could laughingly say, 'I told you so'; and if he succeeded, as he privately believed he would, the glory would be all the greater. Besides, the more persistently he denied his chances, the oftener they would repeat their delicious assurances of his possible, his probable, success. Success, what was more, in their own line; success, in spite of his consistent refusal, till the beginning of last term, ever to take this ridiculous swotting seriously.

It was Benger who brought the next tribute. 'Jimbug thinks you've got a chance,' he said. 'I heard him talking to old Jacko about it yesterday.'

'What does that old fool Jimbug know about it?' Staithes made a disparaging grimace; but through the mask of contempt his brown eyes shone with pleasure. 'And as for Jacko . . .'

A sudden rattling of the door-handle made them all start. 'I say, you chaps,' came an imploring whisper through the keyhole, 'do buck up! I've got the most frightful belly-ache.'

Brian rose hastily from the floor. 'We must l-let him in,' he began.

But Staithes pulled him down again. 'Don't be a fool!' he said; then, turning towards the door, 'Go to one of the rears downstairs,' he said, 'we're busy.'

'But I'm in a most frightful hurry.'

'Then the quicker you go, the better.'

'You are a swine!' protested the whisper. Then 'Christ!' it added, and they heard the sound of slippered feet receding in a panic rush down the stairs.

Staithes grinned. 'That'll teach him,' he said. 'What about another go at the Greek grammar?'

*

Outraged in advance, James Beavis had felt his indignation growing with every minute he spent under his brother's roof. The house positively reeked of matrimony. It was asphyxiating! And there sat John, fairly basking in those invisible radiations of dark female warmth, inhaling the stuffiness with a quivering nostril, deeply contented, revoltingly happy! Like a marmot, it suddenly occurred to James Beavis, a marmot with its female, crowded fur to fur in their subterranean burrow. Yes, the house was just a burrow – a burrow, with John like a thin marmot at one end of the table and that soft, bulging marmot-woman at the other, and between them, one on either side, himself, outraged and nauseated, and that unhappy little Anthony, like a changeling from the world of fresh air, caught and dragged down and imprisoned in the marmot-warren. Indignation begot equally violent pity and affection for this unhappy child, begot at the same time a retrospective feeling of sympathy for poor Maisie. In her lifetime he had always regarded Maisie as just a fool – hopelessly silly and frivolous. Now, John's marriage and the oppressive connubiality which enveloped the all too happy couple made him forget his judgements on the living Maisie and think of her as a most superior woman (at least, she had had the grace to be slim), posthumously martyred by her husband for the sake of this repulsively fleshy female marmot. Horrible. He did well to be angry.

Pauline meanwhile had refused a second helping of the chocolate soufflé.

'But, my dear, you *must*,' John Beavis insisted.

Pauline heaved the conscious imitation of a sigh of repletion. 'I couldn't.'

'Not even the favourite *chocolatl*?' Mr Beavis always spoke of chocolate in the original Aztec.

Playfully, Pauline eyed the dish askance. 'I *shouldn't*,' she said, implicity admitting that the repletion was not complete.

'Yes, you should,' he wheedled.

'Now he's trying to make me fat!' she wailed with mock reproach. 'He's leading me into temptation!'

'Well, be led.'

This time, Pauline's sigh was a martyr's. 'All right, then,' she said submissively. The maid, who had been waiting impassively for the outcome of the controversy, presented the dish once again. Pauline helped herself.

'There's a good child,' said Mr Beavis, in a tone and with a twinkle that expressed a sportive mock-fatherliness. 'And now, James, I hope you'll follow the good example.'

James's disgust and anger were so intense that he could not trust himself to speak, for fear of saying something outrageous. He contented himself with curtly shaking his head.

'No *chocolatl* for you?' Mr Beavis turned to Anthony. 'But I'm sure *you'll* take pity on the pudding!' And when Anthony did. 'Ah that's good!' he said. 'That's the way ...' – he hesitated for a fraction of second – '... the way to tuck in!'

CHAPTER SIXTEEN

June 17th 1912

Anthony's fluency, as they walked to the station, was a symptom of his inward sense of guilt. By the profusion of his talk, by the brightness of his attention, he was making up to Brian for what he had done the previous evening. It was not as though Brian had uttered any reproaches; he seemed, on the contrary, to be taking special pains not to hint at yesterday's offence. His silence served Anthony as an excuse for postponing all mention of the disagreeable subject of Mark Staithes. Some time, of course, he would have to talk about the whole wretched affair (what a bore people were, with their complicated squabbles!); but, for the moment, he assured himself, it would be best to wait ... to wait until Brian himself referred to it. Meanwhile, his uneasy conscience constrained him to display towards Brian a more than ordinary friendliness, to make a special effort to be interesting and to show himself interested. Interested in the poetry of Edward Thomas as they walked down Beaumont Street; in Bergson opposite Worcester; crossing Hythe Bridge, in the nationalization of coal mines; and finally, under the viaduct and up the long approach to the station, in Joan Thursley.

'It's ext-traordinary,' said Brian, breaking, with what was manifestly an effort, a rather long preparatory silence, 'that you sh-shouldn't ever have met her.'

'*Dis aliter visum*', Anthony answered in his father's best classical style. Though, of course, if he had accepted Mrs Foxe's invitations to stay at Twyford, the gods, he reflected, would have changed their minds.

'I w-want you to l-like one another,' Brian was saying.

'I'm sure we shall.'

'She's not frightfully c-c-c ...' Patiently he began again: 'frightfully c-clever. N-not on the s-surface. You'd th-think she was o-only interested in c-c-c ...' But 'country life' wouldn't allow itself to be uttered; Brian was forced into a seemingly affected circumlocution: 'in rural m-matters,' he brought out at last. 'D-dogs and b-birds and all that.'

Anthony nodded and, suddenly remembering those spew-tits and piddle-warblers of the Bulstrode days, imperceptibly smiled.

'But w-when you g-get to kn-know her better,' Brian went on laboriously, 'you f-find there's a lot m-more in her than you th-thought. She's g-got ext-traordinary feeling for p-p-p ··· for v-verse. W-wordsworth and M-meredith, for example. I'm always ast-tonished how g-good her j-judgements are.'

Anthony smiled to himself sarcastically. Yes, it *would* be Meredith!

The other was silent, wondering how he should explain, whether he should even try to explain. Everything was against him – his own physical disability, the difficulty of putting what he had to say into words, the possibility that Anthony wouldn't even want to understand what he said, that he would produce his alibi of cynicism and just pretended not to be there at all.

Brian thought of their first meeting. The embarrassing discovery of two strangers in the drawing-room when he came in, flushed and his hair still wet with the rain, to tea. His mother pronounced a name: 'Mrs Thursley', The new vicar's wife, he realized, as he shook hands with the thin dowdy woman. Her manners were so ingratiating that she lisped as she spoke; her smile was deliberately bright.

'And this is Joan.'

The girl held out her hand, and as he took it, her slender body swayed away from his alien presence in a movement of shyness that was yet adorably graceful, like the yielding of a young tree before the wind. That movement was the most beautiful and at the same time the most touching thing he had ever seen.

'We've been hearing you're keen on birds,' said Mrs Thursley, with an oppressive politeness and intensifying that all too bright, professionally Christian smile of hers. 'So's Joan. A regular ornithologist.'

Blushing, the girl muttered a protest.

'She *will* be pleased to have someone to talk to about her precious birds. Won't you, Joanie?'

Joan's embarrassment was so great that she simply couldn't speak.

Looking at her flushed, averted face, Brian was filled with compassionate tenderness. His heart began to beat very hard. With a mixture of fear and exultation he realized that something extraordinary, something irrevocable had happened.

And then, he went on to think, there was that time, some four or five months later, when they were staying together at her uncle's house in East Sussex. Away from her parents, she was as though transformed – not into another person; into her own fundamental self, into the happy, expansive girl that it was impossible for her to be at home. For at home she lived under constraint. Her father's chronic grumblings and occasional outbursts of bad temper oppressed her with fear. And though she loved her, she felt herself the prisoner of her mother's affection, was dimly conscious of being somehow exploited by means of it. And finally there was the cold numbing atmosphere of the genteel poverty in which they lived, the unremitting tension of the struggle to keep up appearances, to preserve social superiority. At home, it was impossible for Joan to be fully herself; but there, in that spacious house at Iden, among its quiet, easy-going inhabitants, she was liberated into a transfiguring happiness. Dazzled, Brian fell in love with her all over again.

He thought of the day when they had gone walking in Winchelsea marshes. The hawthorn was in bloom; dotted here and there on the wide, flat expanse of grass, the sheep and their lambs were like white constellations; overhead, the sky was alive with white clouds gliding in the wind. Unspeakably beautiful! And suddenly it seemed to him that they were walking through the image of their love. The world was their love, and their love the world; and the world was significant, charged with depth beyond depth of mysterious meaning. The proof of God's goodness floated in those clouds, crept in those grazing sheep, shone from every burning bush of incandescent blossom – and, in himself and Joan, walked hand in hand across the grass and was manifest in their happiness. His love, it seemed to him, in that apocalyptic moment, was more than merely *his*; it was in some mysterious way the equivalent of this wind and sunshine, these white gleams against the green and blue of spring.

His feeling for Joan was somehow implicit in the world, had a divine and universal significance. He loved her infinitely, and for that reason was able to love everything in the world as much as he loved her.

The memory of that experience was precious to him, all the more so now, since the quality of his feelings had undergone a change. Transparent and seemingly pure as spring water, that infinite love of his had crystallized out, with the passage of time, into specific desires.

> Et son bras et sa jambe, et sa cuisse et ses reins,
> Polis comme de l'huile, onduleux comme un cygne,
> Passaient devant mes yeux clairvoyants et sereins,
> Et son ventre et ses seins, ces grappes de ma vigne.

Ever since Anthony had first made him read the poem, those lines had haunted his imagination; impersonally, at first; but later, they had come to associate themselves, definitely, with the image of Joan. *Polis comme de l'huile, onduleux comme un cygne.* There was no forgetting. The words had remained with him, indelibly, like a remorse, like the memory of a crime.

They entered the station and found that there were nearly five minutes to wait. The two young men walked slowly up and down the platform.

In an effort to lay the shameful phantom of those breasts, that oil-smooth belly, 'My m-mother likes her a l-lot,' Brian went on at last.

'That's *very* satisfactory,' said Anthony; but felt, even as he uttered the words, that he was rather overdoing the approval. If *he* fell in love, he most certainly wouldn't take the girl to be inspected by his father and Pauline. On approval! But it wasn't their business to approve – or disapprove, for that matter. Mrs Foxe was different, of course; one could take her more seriously than Pauline or his father. But, all the same, one wouldn't want even Mrs Foxe to interfere – indeed, he went on to reflect, would probably dislike the interference even more intensely than other people's, just because of that superiority. For the superiority constituted a kind of claim on one, gave her certain rights. One wouldn't be able so easily to ignore her opinion as one could ignore Pauline's, for example. He was very fond of Mrs Foxe, he respected and admired her; but for that very reason he felt her as potentially a menace to his freedom. For she might – indeed, if she knew it, she certainly would – object to his way of looking at things. And though her criticisms would be based on the principles of that liberal Christianity of hers, and though, of course, such modernism was just as preposterous and, in spite of its pretensions to being 'scientific', just as hopelessly beyond the pale of rationality as the most extravagant fetishism – nevertheless, her words, being *hers*, would carry weight, would have to be considered. Which was why he did his best not to place himself in the position of having to listen to them. It was more than a year now since he had accepted one of her invitations to come and stay with them in the country. *Dis aliter visum*. But he looked forward rather nervously to his impending encounter with her.

The train came roaring in; and there, a minute later, they all were, at the other end of the platform – Mr Beavis in a grey suit, and Pauline beside him, very large in mauve, her face apoplectically flushed by the shadow of her mauve parasol, and behind them Mrs Foxe, straight and queenly, and a tall girl in a big flopping hat and a flowered dress.

Mr Beavis adopted for his greetings a humorously mock-heroic manner that Anthony found particularly irritating. 'Six precious souls,' he quoted, as he patted his son's shoulder, 'or rather only four precious souls, but all agog to dash through thick and thin. And what a hot dash – what a dashed hot dash!' he emended, twinklingly.

'Well, Anthony.' Mrs Foxe's voice was musically rich with affection. 'It's an age since I saw you.'

'Yes, an age.' He laughed rather uncomfortably, trying, as he did so, to remember those elaborate reasons he had given for not accepting her invitations. At all costs he mustn't contradict himself. Was it at Easter or at Christmas that the necessity of working at the British Museum had kept him in London? He felt a touch on his arm, and thankful for any excuse to break off the embarrassing conversation, turned quickly away.

'J-joan,' Brian was saying to the girl in the flowered dress, 'h-here's A-anthony.'

'Awfully glad,' he mumbled. 'Heard such a lot about you from ...' Nice hair, he thought; and the hazel eyes were beautifully bright and eager. But the profile was too emphatic; and though the lips were well cut, the mouth was too wide. A bit dairymaidish, was his conclusion; and her clothes were really too home-made. He himself preferred something rather more urban.

'Well, lead on, Macduff,' said Mr Beavis.

They left the station, and slowly, on the shady side of the street, walked towards the centre of the town. Still merrily Gilpinesque, as though (and this particularly irritated Anthony) today's expedition were his first holiday jaunt for twenty years, Mr Beavis expatiated in waggish colloquialisms on the Oxford of his own undergraduate days. Mrs Foxe listened, smiled at the appropriate moments, asked pertinent questions. Pauline complained from time to time of the heat. Her face shone; and, walking in gloomy silence beside her, Anthony remarked with distaste the rather rank intensification of her natural odour. From behind him, he could hear snatches of the conversation between Brian and Joan. '... a great big hawk,' she was saying. Her speech was eager and rapid. 'It must have been a harrier.' 'D-did it have b-bars on its t-t-t ... on its tail?' 'That's it. Dark bars on a light grey ground.' 'Th-then it was a f-female,' said Brian. 'Fe-females have b-bars on their tails.' Anthony smiled to himself sarcastically.

They were passing the Ashmolean, when a woman who was coming very slowly and as though disconsolately out of the museum suddenly waved her hand at them and, calling out first Mr Beavis's name and then, as they all turned round to look at her, Mrs Foxe's, came running down the steps towards them.

'Why, it's Mary Champernowne,' said Mrs Foxe. 'Mary Amberley, I should say.' Or perhaps, she reflected, should *not* say, now that the Amberleys were divorced.

The name, the familiar face, evoked in Mr Beavis's mind only a pleasant sensation of surprised recognition. Raising his hat with a self-consciously comic parody of an old-world flourish, 'Welcome,' he said to the new arrival. 'Welcome, dear lady.'

Mary Amberley took Mrs Foxe's hand. 'Such luck,' she exclaimed breathlessly. Mrs Foxe was surprised by so much cordiality. Mary's mother was her friend; but Mary had always held aloof. And anyhow, since her marriage she had moved in a world that Mrs Foxe did not know, and of which, on principle, she disapproved. 'Such marvellous luck!' the other repeated as she turned to Mr Beavis.

'The luck is ours,' he said gallantly. 'You know my wife, don't you? And the young stalwart?' His eyes twinkled; the corners of his mouth, under the moustache, humorously twitched. He laid a hand on Anthony's arm. 'The young foundation-worthy?'

She smiled at Anthony. A strange smile, he noticed; a crooked smile of unparted lips that seemed as though secretly significant. 'I haven't seen you for years,' she said. 'Not since . . .' Not since the first Mrs Beavis's funeral, as a matter of fact. But one could hardly say so. 'Not since you were *so* high!' And lifting a gloved hand to the level of her eye, she measured, between the thumb and forefinger, a space of about an inch.

Anthony laughed nervously, intimidated, even while he admired, by so much prettiness and ease and smartness.

Mrs Amberley shook hands with Joan and Brian; then turning back to Mrs Foxe, 'I was feeling like Robinson Crusoe,' she said, explaining that abnormal cordiality. 'Marooned.' She lingered with a comical insistence over the long syllable. 'Absolutely marooned. Monarch of all I surveyed.' And while they slowly walked on across St Giles's, she launched out into a complicated story about a stay in the Cotswolds; about an appointment to meet some friends on the way home, at Oxford, on the eighteenth; about her journey from Chipping Campden; about her punctual arrival at the meeting-place, her waiting, her growing impatience, her rage, and finally her discovery that she had come a day too early: it was the seventeenth. 'Too typical of me.'

Everybody laughed a great deal. For the story was full of unexpected fantasies and extravagances; and it was told in a voice that modulated itself with an extraordinary subtlety to fit the words – a voice that knew when to hurry breathlessly and when to drawl, when to fade out into an inaudibility rich with unspoken implications.

Even Mrs Foxe, who didn't particularly want to be amused –

because of that divorce – found herself unable to resist the story.

For Mary Amberley, their laughter was like champagne; it warmed her, it sent a tingling exhilaration through her body. They were bores, of course; they were philistines. But the applause even of bores and philistines is still applause and intoxicating. Her eyes shone, her cheeks flushed. 'Too hopelessly typical of me!' she wailed, when their laughter had subsided; but the gesture of despairing self-disparagement was a caricature; she was really proud of her incompetence, regarded it as part of her feminine charm. 'Well, anyhow,' she concluded, 'there I was – shipwrecked. All alone on a desert island.'

They walked for a moment in silence. The thought that she would have to be asked to lunch was in all their minds – a thought tinged in Mrs Foxe's case with vexation, in Anthony's with embarrassed desire. The lunch was being given in his rooms; as the host, he ought to ask her. And he wanted to ask her – violently wanted it. But what would the others say? Oughtn't he somehow to consult them first? Mr Beavis solved the problem for him by making the suggestion on his own account.

'I think' – he hesitated; then, twinkling, 'I think our festal "spread",' he went on, 'will run to another guest, won't it, Anthony?'

'But I can't impose myself,' she protested, turning from the father to the son. He seemed a nice boy, she thought, sensitive and intelligent. Pleasant-looking too.

'But I assure you . . .' Anthony was earnestly and incoherently repeating, 'I assure you . . .'

'Well, if it's really all right . . .' She thanked him with a smile of sudden intimacy, almost of complicity – as though there were some bond between them, as though, of all the party, they two were the only ones who understood what was what.

After lunch, Joan had to be shown the sights of Oxford; and Mr Beavis had an appointment with a philological colleague in the Woodstock Road; and Pauline thought she would like to take things quietly till tea-time. Anthony was left to entertain Mary Amberley. The responsibility was deliciously alarming.

In the hansom that was taking them to Magdalen Bridge Mrs

145

Amberley turned to him a face that was bright with sudden mischief.

'Free at last,' she said.

Anthony nodded at her and smiled back, understandingly, conspiratorially. 'They *were* rather heavy,' he said. 'Perhaps I ought to apologize.'

'I've often thought of founding a league for the abolition of families,' she went on. 'Parents ought never to be allowed to come near their children.'

'Plato thought so too,' he said, rather pedantically.

'Yes, but he wanted children to be bullied by the state instead of by their fathers and mothers. I don't want them to be bullied by anyone.'

He ventured a personal question. 'Were *you* bullied?' he asked.

Mary Amberley nodded. 'Horribly. Few children have been more loved than I was. They fairly bludgeoned me with affection. Made me a mental cripple. It took me years to get over the deformity.' There was a silence. Then, looking at him with an embarrassingly appraising glance, as though he were for sale, 'Do you know,' she said, 'the last time I saw you was at your mother's funeral.'

The subterranean association between this remark and what had gone before made him blush guiltily, as though at an impropriety in mixed company. 'Yes, I remember,' he mumbled, and was annoyed with himself for feeling so embarrassed, was at the same time rather ashamed that he had allowed even this remotely implied comment upon his mother to pass without some kind of protest, that he had felt so little desire to make a protest.

'You were a horrible, squalid little boy then,' she went on, still looking at him judicially. 'How awful little boys always are! It seems incredible that they should ever turn into presentable human beings. And of course,' she added, 'a great many of them don't. Dismal, don't you find? – the way most people are so hideous and stupid, so utterly and abysmally boring!'

Making a violent effort of will, Anthony emerged from his embarrassment with a creditable dash. 'I hope I'm not one of the majority?' he said, lifting his eyes to hers.

Mrs Amberley shook her head, and with a serious matter-of-factness. 'No,' she answered. 'I was thinking how successfully you'd escaped from the horrors of boyhood.'

He blushed again, this time with pleasure.

'Let's see, how old are you now?' she asked.

'Twenty – nearly twenty-one.'

'And I shall be thirty this winter. Queer,' she added, 'how these things change their significance. When I saw you last, those nine years were a great gulf between us. Uncrossable, it seemed then. We belonged to different species. And yet here we are, sitting on the same side of the gulf as though it were the most natural thing in the world. Which indeed it is, now.' She turned and smiled at him that secret and significant smile of unparted lips. Her dark eyes were full of dancing brightness. 'Ah, there's Magdalen,' she went on, leaving him (to his great relief; for in his excited embarrassment he would not have known what to say) no time to comment on her words. 'How dreary that late Gothic can be! So mean! No wonder Gibbon didn't think much of the Middle Ages!' She was suddenly silent, remembering the occasion when her husband had made that remark about Gibbon. Only a month or two after their marriage. She had been shocked and astonished by his airy criticisms of things she had been brought up to regard as sacredly beyond judgement – shocked, but also thrilled, also delighted. For what fun to see the sacred things knocked about! And in those days Roger was still adorable. She sighed; then, with a touch of irritation, shook off the sentimental mood and went on talking about that odious architecture.

The cab drew up at the bridge; they dismounted and walked down to the boat-house. Lying back on the cushions of the punt, Mary Amberley was silent. Very slowly, Anthony poled his way upstream. The green world slid past her half-shut eyes. Green darkness of trees overarching the olive shadows and tawny-glaucous lights of water; and between the twilight stretches of green vaulting, the wide gold-green meadows, islanded with elms. And always the faint weedy smell of the river; and the air so soft and warm against the face that one was hardly aware any longer of the frontiers between self and not-self, but lay there, separated by no dividing surfaces, melting, drowsily melting into the circumambient summer.

Standing at the stern, Anthony could look down on her, as from a post of vantage. She lay there at his feet, limp and abandoned. Handling his long pole with an easy mastery of which he was proud, he felt, as he watched her, exultantly strong and superior. There was no gulf between them now. She was a woman, he a man. He lifted his trailing punt pole and swung it forward with a movement of easy grace, of unhurried and accomplished power. Thrust it down into the mud, tightened his muscles against its resistance; the punt shot forward, the end of the pole lifted from the river-bed, trailed for a moment, then gracefully, once more, easily, masterfully was swung forward. Suddenly she lifted her eyelids and looked at him, with that detached appraising look that had embarrassed him so much in the cab. His manly confidence evaporated at once.

'My poor Anthony,' she said at last, and her face came closer, as it were, in a sudden smile. 'It makes me hot even to look at you.'

When the punt had been secured, he came forward and sat down in the place she made, drawing her skirts away, on the cushion beside her.

'I don't suppose your father bullies you much,' she said, returning to the theme of their conversation in the cab.

He shook his head.

'Nor blackmails you with too much affection, I imagine.'

Anthony found himself feeling unexpectedly loyal to his father. 'I think he was always very fond of me.'

'Oh, of course,' said Mrs Amberley, impatiently. 'I didn't imagine he knocked you about.'

Anthony could not help laughing. The vision of his father running after him with a club was irresistibly comic. Then, more seriously, 'He never got near enough to knock me about,' he said. 'There was always a great gulf fixed.'

'Yes, one feels he has a talent for fixing gulfs. And yet your step-mother seems to get on with him all right. So did your mother, I believe.' She shook her head. 'But, then, marriage is so odd and unaccountable. The most obviously incompatible couples stick together, and the most obviously compatible fly apart. Boring, tiresome people are adored, and charming ones are hated. Why? God knows. But I suppose it's generally a matter of what Milton calls the Genial Bed.' She lingered, ludicrously, over the first syllable of 'genial'; but Anthony was so anxious not to seem startled by the casual mention of what he had always regarded as, in a lady's presence, the unmentionable, that he did not laugh – for a laugh might have been interpreted as a schoolboy's automatic reaction to smut – did not even smile; but gravely, as though he were admitting the truth of a proposition in geometry, nodded his head and in a very serious and judicial tone said, 'Yes, I suppose it generally is.'

'Poor Mrs Foxe,' Mary Amberley went on. 'I imagine there was a minimum of geniality there.'

'Did you know her husband?' he asked.

'Only as a child. One grown-up seems as boring as another then. But my mother's often talked to me about him. Thoroughly beastly. And thoroughly virtuous. God preserve me from a virtuous beast! The vicious ones are bad enough; but at least they're never beastly on principle. They're inconsistent: so they're sometimes nice by mistake. Whereas the virtuous ones – they never forget; they're beastly all the time. Poor woman! She had a dog's life, I'm afraid. But she seems to be getting it back on her son all right.'

'But she adores Brian,' he protested. 'And Brian adores her.'

'That's exactly what I was saying. All the love she never got from her husband, all the love she never gave him – it's being poured out on that miserable boy.'

'He isn't miserable.'

'He may not know it, perhaps. Not yet. But you wait!' Then, after a little pause, 'You're lucky,' Mrs Amberley went on. 'A great deal luckier than you know.'

CHAPTER SEVENTEEN

May 26th 1934

Literature for peace – of what kind? One can concentrate on economics: trade barriers, disorganized currency, impediments in the way of migration, private interests bent on making profits at all costs. And so on. One can concentrate on politics : danger of the concept of the sovereign state, as a wholly immoral being having interests irreconcilable with those of other sovereign states. One can propose political and economic remedies – trade agreements, international arbitration, collective security. Sensible prescriptions following sound diagnosis. But has the diagnosis gone far enough, and will the patient follow the treatment prescribed?

This question came up in the course of today's discussion with Miller. Answer in the negative. The patient can't follow the treatment prescribed, for a good reason : there is no patient. States and Nations don't exist as such. There are only people. Sets of people living in certain areas, having certain allegiances. Nations won't change their national policies unless and until people change their private policies. All governments, even Hitler's, even Stalin's, even Mussolini's, are representative. Today's national behaviour – a large-scale projection of today's individual behaviour. Or rather, to be more accurate, a large-scale projection of the individual's secret wishes and intentions. For we should all like to behave a good deal worse than our conscience and respect for public opinion allow. One of the great attractions of patriotism – it fulfils our worst wishes. In the person of our nation we are able, vicariously, to bully and cheat. Bully and cheat, what's more, with a feeling that we're profoundly virtuous. Sweet and decorous to murder, lie, torture for the sake of the fatherland. Good international policies are projections of individual good intentions and benevolent wishes, and must be of the same kind as good inter-personal policies. Pacifist propaganda must be aimed at people as well as their governments ; must start simultaneously at the periphery and the centre.

Empirical facts :

One. We are all capable of love for other human beings.

Two. We impose limitations on that love.

Three. We can transcend all these limitations – *if we choose to*. (It is a matter of observation that anyone who so desires can overcome personal dislike, class feeling, national hatred, colour prejudice. Not easy; but it can be done, if we have the will and know how to carry out our good intentions.)

Four. Love expressing itself in good treatment breeds love. Hate expressing itself in bad treatment breeds hate.

In the light of these facts, it's obvious what interpersonal, inter-class and international policies should be. But, again, knowledge cuts little ice. We all know; we almost all fail to do. It is a question, as usual, of the best methods of implementing intentions. Among other things, peace propaganda must be a set of instructions in the art of modifying character.

> I see
> The lost are like this, and their scourge to be,
> As I am mine, their sweating selves; but worse.

Hell is the incapacity to be other than the creature one finds oneself ordinarily behaving as.

On the way home from Miller's, dived into the public lavatory at Marble Arch, and there ran into Beppo Bowles deep in conversation with one of those flannel-trousered, hatless young men who look like undergraduates and are, I suppose, very junior clerks or shop assistants. On B.'s face, what a mingling of elation and anxiety. Happy, drunk with thrilling anticipation, and at the same time horribly anxious and afraid. He might be turned down – unspeakable humiliation! He might not be turned down – appalling dangers! Frustration of desire, if there was failure, cruel blow to pride, wound to the very root of personality. And, if success, fear (through all the triumph) of blackmail and police court. Poor wretch! He was horribly embarrassed at the sight of me. I just nodded and hurried past. B.'s hell – an underground lavatory with rows of urinals stretching to infinity in all directions and a boy at each. Beppo walking up and down the rows, for ever – his sweating self, but worse.

CHAPTER EIGHTEEN
December 8th 1926

MORE guests kept arriving – young people mostly, friends of Joyce and Helen. Dutifully, they crossed the drawing-room to the far corner where Mrs Amberley was sitting between Beppo

Bowles and Anthony, said good evening, then hurried off to dance.

'They put one in one's middle-aged place all right,' said Anthony, but either Mrs Amberley preferred not to hear the remark, or else she was genuinely absorbed in what Beppo was saying with such loud and fizzling enthusiasm about Berlin – the most amusing place in Europe nowadays! Where else would you find, for example, those special tarts for masochists? In top-boots; yes, genuine top-boots! And the Museum of Sexology: such photographs and wax models – almost too *trompe-l'œil* – such astounding objects in horn from Japan, such strange and ingenious tailoring for exhibitionists! And all those delicious little Lesbian bars, all those cabarets where the boys were dressed up as women ...

'There's Mark Staithes,' said Mrs Amberley, interrupting him, and waved to a shortish, broad-shouldered man who had just entered the drawing-room. 'I forget,' she said, turning to Anthony, 'whether you know him.'

'Only for the last thirty years,' he answered, finding once again a certain malicious pleasure in insisting, to the point of exaggeration, on his vanished youth. If he were no longer young, then Mary had ceased to be young nine years ago.

'But with long gaps,' he qualified. 'During the war and then afterwards, for all that time he was in Mexico. And I've hardly had more than a glimpse of him since he came back. I'm delighted to have this chance ...'

'He's a queer fish,' said Mary Amberley, thinking of the time, just after his return from Mexico, some eighteen months before, when he had first come to her house. His appearance, his manner, as of some savage and fanatical hermit, had violently attracted her. She had tried all her seductions upon him – without the smallest effect. He had ignored them – but so completely and absolutely that she felt no ill-will towards him for the rebuff, convinced, as she was, that in fact there hadn't been any rebuff, merely a display of symptoms, either, she diagnosed judicially, of impotence, or else, less probably (though of course one never knew, one *never* knew), of homosexuality. 'A queer fish,' she repeated, and decided that she'd take the next opportunity of asking Beppo about the homosexuality. He would be sure to know. They always did know about one another. Then, waving again, 'Come and sit with us, Mark,' she called through the noise of the gramophone.

Staithes crossed the room, drew up a chair and sat down. His hair had retreated from his forehead, and above the ears was already grey. The brown face – that fanatical hermit's face which Mary Amberley had found so strangely attractive – was deeply lined. No smooth obliterating layer of fat obscured its inner structure. Under the skin each strip of muscle in the cheek and jaw seemed to stand out distinct and separate like the muscles in those lime-wood statues of flayed human beings that were made for Renaissance anatomy rooms. When he smiled – and each time that happened it was as though the flayed statue had come to life and were expressing its agony – one could follow the whole mechanism of the excruciating grimace; the upward and outward pull of the zygomaticus major, the sideways tug of the risorius, the contraction of the great sphincters round the eyelids.

'Am I interrupting?' he asked, looking with sharp, inquisitorial movements from one to the other.

'Beppo was telling us about Berlin,' said Mrs Amberley.

'I popped over to get away from the General Strike,' Beppo explained.

'Naturally,' said Staithes, and his face twitched in the anguish of amused contempt.

'Such a heavenly place!' Beppo exploded irrepressibly.

'You feel like Lord Haldane about it? Your spiritual home?'

'Carnal,' Anthony amended.

Only too happy to plead guilty, Beppo giggled. 'Yes, those transvestists!' he had to admit rapturously.

'I was over there this winter,' said Staithes. 'On business. But of course one has to pay one's tribute to pleasure too. That night life . . .'

'Didn't you find it amusing?'

'Oh, passionately.'

'You see!' Beppo was triumphant.

'One of the creatures came and sat at my table,' Staithes went on. 'I danced with it. It looked like a woman.'

'You simply can't tell them apart,' Beppo cried excitedly, as though he were taking personal credit for the fact.

'When we'd finished dancing, it painted its face a bit and we drank a little beer. Then it showed me some indecent photographs. That rather surgical, anti-aphrodisiac kind – you know. Damping. Perhaps that was why the conversation flagged. Anyhow, there were uncomfortable silences. Neither it nor I seemed to know what to say next. We were becalmed.' He threw out his two thin and knotted hands horizontally, as though sliding them across an absolutely flat surface. 'Utterly becalmed. Until, suddenly, the creature did a most remarkable thing. One of its regular gambits, no doubt; but never having had it played on me before, I was impressed. 'Would you like to see something?' it said. I said yes, and immediately it began to poke and pull at something under its blouse. 'Now, look!' it said at last. I looked. It smiled triumphantly, like a man playing the ace of trumps – or rather playing two aces of trumps; for what it plunked down on the table was a pair. A pair of superb artificial breasts, made of pink rubber sponge.'

'But how revolting!' cried Mrs Amberley, while Anthony laughed and Beppo's round face took on an expression of pained distress. 'How revolting!' she repeated.

'Yes, but how satisfactory!' Staithes insisted, making that crooked and agonized grimace that passed with him for a smile. 'It's so good when things happen as they ought to happen – artistically, symbolically. Two rubber breasts between the beer mugs – that's what vice ought to be. And when that was what it actually *was* – well, it felt as though something had clicked into place. Inevitably, beautifully. Yes, *beautifully*,' he repeated. 'Beautifully revolting.'

'All the same,' Beppo insisted, 'you must admit there's a lot to be said for a town where that sort of thing can happen. In public,' he added earnestly, 'in *public*, mind you. It's the most tolerant in the world, the German Government. You've got to admit that.'

'Oh, I do,' said Staithes. 'It tolerates everybody. Not only girls in boiled shirts and boys with rubber breasts, but also monarchists, fascists, Junkers, Krupps. Communists too, I'm thankful to say. All its enemies of every colour.'

'I think that's rather fine,' said Mrs Amberley.

'Very fine indeed, until its enemies rise up and destroy it. I only hope the communists will get in first.'

'But seeing that they're tolerated, why should its enemies want to destroy it?'

'Why not? *They* don't believe in tolerance. Quite rightly,' he added.

'You're barbarous,' Beppo protested.

'As one should be if one lives in the Dark Ages. You people – you're survivors from the Age of the Antonines.' He looked from one to the other, smiling his flayed smile, and shook his head. 'Imagining you're still in the first volume of Gibbon. Whereas we're well on in the third.'

'Do you mean to say . . .? But, good heavens,' Mrs Amberley interrupted herself, 'there's Gerry!'

At her words, at the sight of Gerry Watchett himself, fox-trotting in from the back drawing-room with Helen, Anthony took out his pocket-book and quickly examined its contents. 'Thank God!' he said. 'Only two pounds.' Gerry had caught him with ten the previous month and, on the strength of a most improbably distressing story, borrowed them all. He ought to have disbelieved the story, of course, ought to have withheld the loan. Ten pounds were more than he could afford. He had said so, but had lacked the firmness to persist in his refusal. It had taken more than a fortnight of strict economy to make up that lost money. Economizing was an unpleasant process; but to say no and to go on saying it in the teeth of Gerry's impor-tunities and reproaches would have been still more unpleasant. He was always ready to sacrifice his rights to his conveniences. People though him disinterested, and he would have liked, he did his best, to accept their diagnosis of his character. But aware-ness of the real state of affairs kept breaking through. When it did, he accepted self-knowledge with a laugh. He was laughing now. 'Only two,' he repeated. 'Luckily I can afford . . .'

He broke off. Behind Mary's back, Beppo had tapped him on the shoulder, was making significant grimaces. Anthony turned and saw that she was still staring intently and with knitted brows at the new arrivals.

'He told me he wasn't coming this evening,' she said, almost as though she were speaking to herself. Then, through the music, 'Gerry!' she called sharply in a voice that had suddenly lost all its charm – a voice that reminded Anthony only too plainly of those distasteful scenes in which, long since, he had played his part. So that was it, he said to himself, and felt sorry for poor Mary.

Gerry Watchett turned, and with the expression of one who refers to some excellent shared joke gave her a quick smile and even a hint of a wink, then looked down again to go on talking to his partner.

Mrs Amberley flushed with sudden anger. Grinning at her like that! It was intolerable. Intolerable too – but how typical! – to appear like this, unannounced, out of the blue – casually dancing with another woman, as though it were the most natural thing in the .world. This time, it was true, the other woman was only Helen; but that was merely because he hadn't found anyone else to dance with, anyone worse. 'The beast!' she thought, as she followed him round the room with her eyes. Then, making an effort, she looked away, she forced herself to pay attention to what was going on around her.

'. . . a country like this,' Mark Staithes was saying, 'a country where a quarter of the population's genuinely bourgeois and another quarter passionately longs to be.'

'You're exaggerating,' Anthony protested.

'Not a bit. What does the Labour Party poll at an election? A third of the votes. I'm generously assuming it might some day poll half of them. The rest's bourgeois. Either naturally bourgeois by interest and fear, or else artificially, by snobbery and imagination. It's childish to think you can get what you want by constitutional methods.'

'And what about unconstitutional ones?'

'There's a chance.'

'Not much of a chance,' said Anthony. 'Not against the new weapons.'

'Oh, I know,' said Mark Staithes, 'I know. *If* they use their strength, the middle classes can obviously win. They could win, most likely, even without tanks and planes – just because they're potentially better soldiers than the proletariat.'

'Better soldiers?' Beppo protested, thinking of those guardsmen friends of his.

'Because of their education. A bourgeois gets anything from ten to sixteen years of training – most of it, what's more, in a boarding school; that's to say, in barracks. Whereas a workman's child lives at home and doesn't get more than six or seven years at his day school. Sixteen years of obedience and *esprit de corps*. No wonder that Waterloo was won on the playing fields of Eton. If they'll use only half their resources – use them ruthlessly – the game's theirs.'

'You think they won't use their resources?'

Mark shrugged his shoulders. 'Certainly the German republicans don't seem ready to use theirs. And think of what happened here, during the Strike. Even the majority of industrialists were ready to compromise.'

'For the simple reason,' Anthony put in, 'that you can't be a successful industrialist unless you have the compromising habit. A business isn't run by faith; it's run by haggling.'

'Anyhow,' Mark went on, 'the fact remains that the available resources weren't used. That's what allows one to hope that a revolution might succeed. Provided it were carried out very quickly. For, of course, once they realized they were seriously in danger, they'd forget their scruples. But they might hesitate long enough, I think, to make a revolution possible. Even a few hours of compunction would be sufficient. Yes, in spite of tanks, there's still a chance of success. But you must be prepared to take a chance. Not like the imbeciles of the T.U.C. Or the rank and file of the Unions, for that matter. As full of scruples as the bourgeoisie. It's the hang-over of evangelical Christianity. You've no idea what a lot of preaching and hymn-singing there was during the General Strike. I was flabbergasted. But it's good to know the worst. Perhaps the younger generation ...' He shook his head. 'But I don't feel certain even of them. Methodism may be decaying. But look at those spiritualist chapels that are sprouting up all over the industrial areas ! Like toadstools.'

*

The next time he passed, Gerry called her name; but Mary Amberley refused to acknowledge his greeting. Turning coldly away she pretended to be interested only in what Anthony was saying.

'Ass of a woman!' thought Gerry, as he looked at her averted face. Then, aloud, 'What do you say to putting on this record another time?' he asked his partner.

Helen nodded ecstatically.

The music of the spheres, the beatific vision ... But why should heaven be a monopoly of ear or eye? The muscles as they move, they too have their paradise. Heaven is not only an illumination and a harmony; it is also a dance.

'Half a tick,' said Gerry, when they were opposite the gramophone.

Helen stood there as he wound up the machine, quite still, her arms hanging limp at her sides. Her eyes were closed; she was shutting the world away from her, shutting herself out of existence. In this still vacancy between two heavens of motion, existence was without a point.

The music stopped for a moment; then began again in the middle of a bar. Behind her closed eyelids, she was aware that Gerry had moved, was standing over her, very near; then his arm encircled her body.

'Onward, Christian soldiers!' he said; and they stepped out once more into the music, into the heaven of harmoniously moving muscles.

*

There had been a silence. Determined not to pay any attention to that beast, Mrs Amberley turned to Staithes. 'And those scents of yours?' she asked with an assumption of bright, amused interest.

'Flourishing,' he answered. 'I've had to order three new stills and take on more labour.'

Mrs Amberley smiled at him and shook her head. 'You of all people!' she said. 'It seems peculiarly ridiculous that *you* should be a scent-manufacturer.'

'Why?'

'The most unfrivolous of men,' she went on, 'the least gallant, the most implacable misogynist!' (Either impotent or homosexual – there couldn't be a doubt; and, after his story about Berlin, almost certainly impotent, she thought.)

With a smile of excruciated mockery, 'But hasn't it occurred to you,' Staithes asked, 'that those might be reasons for being a scent-maker?'

'Reasons?'

'A way of expressing one's lack of gallantry.' In point of fact, it was entirely by chance that he had gone into the scent business. His eye had been caught by an advertisement in *The Times*, a small factory for sale very cheap. ... Just luck. But now, after the event, it heightened his self-esteem to say that he had chosen the profession deliberately, in order to express his contempt for the women for whom he catered. The lie, which he had willed and by this time half believed to be the truth, placed him in a position of superiority to all women in general and, at this moment, to Mary Amberley in particular. Leaning forward, he took Mary's hand, raised it as though he were about to kiss it, but, instead, only sniffed at the skin – then let it fall again. 'For example,' he said, 'there's civet in the stuff you've scented yourself with.'

'Well, why not?'

'Oh, no reason at all,' said Staithes, 'no reason at all, if you happen to have a taste for the excrement of polecats.'

Mrs Amberley made a grimace of disgust.

'In Abyssinia,' he went on, 'they have civet farms. Twice a week, you take a stick and go and poke the cats until they're thoroughly angry and frightened. That's when they secrete their stuff. Like children wetting their knickers when they're afraid. Then you catch them with a pair of tongs, so that they can't bite, and scrape out the contents of the little pouch attached to their genital organs. You do it with an egg-spoon and the stuff's a kind of yellow grease, rather like ear-wax. Stinks like hell when it's undiluted. We get it in London packed in buffalo horns. Huge cornucopias full of dark brown stinking ear-wax. At a hundred and seventeen shillings the ounce, what's more. That's one of the reasons why your scent costs you so much. The poor can't afford to smear themselves with cat's mess. They have to be content with plain iso-eugenol and phenyl acetic aldehyde.'

*

Colin and Joyce had stopped dancing and were sitting on the landing outside the drawing-room door. Alone. It was Colin's opportunity for releasing some of the righteous indignation that had been accumulating within him, ever since dinner-time.

'I must say, Joyce,' he began, 'some of your mother's guests ...'

Joyce looked at him with eyes in which there was anxiety as well as adoration. 'Yes, I know,' she apologized. 'I know,' and was abjectly in a hurry to agree with him about Beppo's degeneracy and Anthony Beavis's cynicism. Then, seeing that he was enjoying his indignation and that she herself rather profited than suffered by it, she even volunteered the information that that man who had come in last and was sitting with her mother was a Bolshevik. Yes, Mark Staithes was a Bolshevik.

The phrase that Colin had been meditating all the evening found utterance. 'I may be stupid and all that,' he said with an assumption of humility that cloaked an overweening self-satisfaction in what he regarded as the quite extraordinary quality of his ordinariness; 'I may be ignorant and badly educated; but at least' (his tone changed, he was proudly giving expression to his consciousness of being uniquely average), 'at least I know – well, I do know what's *done*. I mean, if one's a *gentleman*.' He underlined the words to make them sound slightly comic and so prove that he had a sense of humour. To speak seriously of what one took seriously – this, precisely, was one of the things that wasn't done. That touch of humour proved more cogently than any emphasis could do, any emotional trembling of the voice, that he *did* take these things seriously – as a uniquely average gentleman must take them. And of course Joyce understood that he did. She glanced at him worshippingly and pressed his hand.

*

Dancing, dancing ... Oh, if only, thought Helen, one could go on dancing for ever! If only one didn't have to spend all that time doing other things! Wrong things, mostly, stupid things, things one was sorry for after they were done. Dancing, she lost her life in order to save it; lost her identity and became something greater than herself; lost perplexities and self-hatreds in a bright harmonious certitude; lost her bad character and was made perfect; lost the regretted past, the apprehended future, and gained a timeless present of consummate happiness. She who could not paint, could not write, could not even sing in tune, became while she danced an artist; no, more than an artist; became a god, the creator of a new heaven and a new earth, a creator rejoicing in his creation and finding it good.

' "Yes, sir, she's my baby. No, sir ..." ' Gerry broke off his humming. 'I won sixty pounds at poker last night,' he said. 'Pretty good, eh?'

She smiled up at him and nodded in a rapturous silence. Good, good – everything was wonderfully good.

*

'And I can't tell you,' Staithes was saying, 'how intensely I enjoy those advertisements.' The muscles in his face were working as though for an anatomical demonstration. 'The ones about bad breath and body odours.'

'Hideous!' Mrs Amberley shuddered. 'Hideous! There's only one Victorian convention I appreciate, and that's the convention of not speaking about those things.'

'Which is precisely why it's such fun to speak about them,' said Staithes, beaming at her between contracted sphincters. 'Forcing humans to be fully, *verbally* conscious of their own and other people's disgustingness. That's the beauty of this kind of advertising. It shakes them into awareness.'

'And into buying,' put in Anthony. 'You're forgetting the profits.'

Staithes shrugged his shoulders. 'They're incidental,' he said; and it was obvious, Anthony reflected, as he watched him, it was obvious that the man was telling the truth. For him, the profits *were* incidental. Breaking down your protective convention,' he went on, turning again to Mary, 'that's the real fun. Leaving you defenceless against the full consciousness of the fact that you can't do without your fellow humans, and that, when you're with them, they make you sick.'

CHAPTER NINETEEN

July 7th 1912

MRS FOXE was looking through her engagement book. The succession of committee meetings, of district visitings, of afternoons at the cripples' playroom, darkened the pages. And in between whiles there would be calls, and tea at the vicarage and luncheon-parties in London. And yet (she knew it in advance) the total effect of the coming summer would be one of emptiness. However tightly crammed with activity, time always seemed strangely empty when Brian was away. In other years there had been a wedge of well-filled time each summer. But this July, after only a week or two at home, Brian was going to Germany. To learn the language. It was essential. She knew that he had to go; she earnestly wanted him to go. All the same, when the moment actually came for his departure, it was painful. She wished she could be frankly selfish and keep him at home.

'This time tomorrow,' she said, when Brian came into the room, 'you'll be driving across London to Liverpool Street.'

He nodded without speaking and, laying a hand on her shoulder, bent down and kissed her.

Mrs Foxe looked up at him and smiled. Then, forgetting for a moment that she had vowed not to say anything to him about her feelings, 'It'll be a sadly empty summer, I'm afraid,' she said; and immediately reproached herself for having brought that expression of distress to his face; reproached herself even while, with a part of her being, she rejoiced to find him so responsibly loving, so sensitively concerned with her feelings. 'Unless you fill it with your letters,' she added by way of qualification. 'You will write, won't you?'

'Of c-c-c . . . N-naturally, I'll wr-write.'

Mrs Foxe proposed a walk; or what about a little drive in the dogcart? Embarrassed, Brian looked at his watch.

'But I'm l-lunching with the Th-Thursleys,' he answered uncomfortably. 'There w-wouldn't be much t-t-t . . . much leisure' (how he hated these ridiculous circumlocutions!) 'for a drive.'

'But how silly of me!' cried Mrs Foxe. 'I'd quite forgotten your lunch.' It was true that she had forgotten; and this sudden, fresh realization that for long hours, on this last day, she would have to do without him was like a wound. She made an effort to prevent any sign of the pain she felt from appearing on her face or sounding in her voice. 'But there'll be time at least for a stroll in the garden, won't there?'

They walked out through the French window and down the long green alley between the herbaceous borders. It was a sunless day, but warm, almost sultry. Under the grey sky the flowers took on a brilliance that seemed somehow almost unnatural. Still silent, they turned at the end of the alley and walked back again.

'I'm glad it's Joan,' said Mrs Foxe at last; 'and I'm glad you care so much. Though in a way it's a pity you met her when you did. Because, I'm afraid, it'll be such a weary long time before you'll be able to get married.'

Brian nodded without speaking.

'It'll be a testing time,' she went on. 'Difficult; not altogether happy perhaps. All the same' (and her voice vibrated movingly), 'I'm glad it happened, I'm *glad*,' she repeated. 'Because I believe in love.' She believed in it, as the poor believe in a heaven of posthumous comfort and glory, because she had never known it. She had respected her husband, admired him for his achievements, had liked him for what was likeable in him, and, maternally, had pitied him for his weaknesses. But there had been no transfiguring passion, and his carnal approach had always remained for her an outrage, hardly supportable. She had never loved him. That was why her belief in love's reality was so strong. Love had to exist in order that the unfavourable balance of her own personal experience might be at least vicariously redressed. Besides, there were the attestations of the poets; it *did* exist and was wonderful, holy, a revelation. 'It's a kind of special grace,' she went on, 'sent by God to help us, to make us stronger and better, to deliver us from evil. Saying no to the worst is easy when one has said yes to the best.'

Easy, Brian was thinking in the ensuing silence, even when one hasn't said yes to the best. The woman who had come and sat at their table in the Café-Concert, when Anthony and he were learning French at Grenoble, two years before – it hadn't been difficult to resist *that* temptation.

'*Tu as l'air bien vicieux,*' she had said to him in the first entr'acte; and to Anthony, '*Il doit être terrible avec les femmes, hein?*' Then she had suggested that they should come home with her. '*Tous les deux, j'ai une petite amie. Nous nous amuserons bien gentiment. On vous fera voir des choses drôles. Toi qui es si vicieux – ça t'amusera.*'

No, that certainly hadn't been difficult to resist, even though he had never set eyes on Joan at the time. The real temptations were not the worst, but the best. At Grenoble, it had been the best in literature. *Et son ventre, et ses seins, ces grappes de ma vigne. . . . Elle se coula à mon côté, m'appela des noms les plus tendres at des noms les plus effroyablement grossiers, qui glissaient sur ses lèvres en suaves murmures. Puis elle se tût et commença à me donner ces baisers qu'elle savait. . . .* The creations of the best stylists had proved to be far more dangerously attractive, far less easily resistible than the sordid realities of the Café-Concert. And now that he had said yes to the best possible reality, the appeal of the worst was even less effective, had ceased altogether to be anything remotely resembling a temptation. Such temptation as there was came once more from the best. It had been impossible to desire the low, vulgar, half-animal creature of the Café-Concert. But Joan was beautiful, Joan was refined, Joan shared his interests – and precisely for those reasons was desirable. Just because she was the best (and this for him was the paradox that it was so painful and bewildering to live through), he desired her in the wrong way, physically. . . .

Do you remember those lines of Meredith's?' said Mrs Foxe, breaking the silence. Meredith was one of her favourite authors. 'From the *Woods*,' she specified, affectionately abbreviating the title of the poem almost to a nickname. And she quoted:

> 'Love, the great volcano, flings
> Fires of lower earth to sky.

Love's a kind of philosopher's stone,' she went on. 'Not only does it deliver us; it also transforms. Dross into gold. Earth into heaven.'

Brian nodded affirmatively. And yet, he was thinking, those voluptuous and faceless bodies created by the stylists had actually come to assume Joan's features. In spite of love, or just because of it, the succubi now had a name, a personality.

The stable clock struck twelve; and at the first stroke there was a noiseless explosion of doves, like snowflakes whirling up against the clotted darkness of the elms beyond.

'The beauty of it!' said Mrs Foxe with a kind of muted intensity.

But suppose, it suddenly occurred to Brian, suppose she were suddenly left with no money at all? And if Joan were as poor as that wretched woman at Grenoble, as hopelessly without an alternative resource?

Slowly the last bell note expired, and one by one the whirling doves dropped back on to their turreted cote above the clock.

'Perhaps,' said Mrs Foxe, 'you ought to be starting if you're going to get there punctually.'

Brian knew how reluctant his mother was to let him go; and this display of generosity produced in him a sense of guilt and, along with it (since he did not want to feel guilty), a certain resentment. 'B-but I d-don't need an hour,' he said almost angrily, 'to c-cycle three m-miles.'

A moment later he was feeling ashamed of himself for the note of irritation in his voice, and for the rest of the time he was with her he showed himself more than ordinarily affectionate.

At half past twelve he took his bicycle and rode over to the Thursleys'. The maid opened the nineteenth-century Gothic front door and he stepped into a faint smell of steamed pudding flavoured with cabbage. As usual. The vicarage always smelt of steamed pudding and cabbage. It was a symptom, he had discovered, of poverty and, as such, gave him a feeling of moral discomfort, as though he had done something wrong and were suffering from an uneasy conscience.

He was ushered into the drawing-room. Behaving as if he were some very distinguished old lady, Mrs Thursley rose from her writing-table and advanced to meet him. 'Ah, dear Brian!' she cried. Her professionally Christian smile was pearly with the flash of false teeth. 'So *nice* to see you!' She took and held his hand. 'And your dear mother – how's she? Sad because you're going to Germany, I'm sure. We're all sad, if it comes to that. You've got such a gift for making people miss you,' she continued in the same complimentary strain, while Brian blushed and fidgeted in an agony of discomfort. Saying nice things to people's faces, particularly to the faces of the rich, the influential, the potentially useful, was a habit with Mrs Thursley. A Christian habit she would have called it, if she had been pressed for an explanation. Loving one's neighbour; seeing the good in everybody; creating an atmosphere of sympathy and trust. But below the level of the avowal, almost below the level of consciousness, she knew that most people were greedy for flattery, however outrageous, and were prepared, in one way or another, to pay for it.

'Ah, but here's Joan,' she cried, interrupting her praise of him, and added, in a tone that was charged with sprightly meaning, 'You won't want to go on talking with her tiresome old mother – will he, Joanie?'

The two young people looked at one another in a speechless embarrassment.

The door suddenly flew open and Mr Thursley hurried into the room. 'Look at this!' he cried in a voice that trembled with rage, and held out a glass ink-pot. 'How do you expect me to do my work with an eighth of an inch of sediment? Dipping, dipping, dipping the whole morning. Never able to write more than two words at a time. . . .'

'Here's Brian, Daddy,' said Joan in the hope, which she knew in advance was vain, that the stranger's presence might shame him into silence.

His pointed nose still white with rage, Mr Thursley glared at Brian, shook hands and, turning away, at once went on with his angry complaint. 'It's always like that in this house. How can one be expected to do serious work?'

'Oh, God,' Joan inwardly prayed, 'make him stop, make him shut up.'

'As if he couldn't fill the pot himself!' Brian was thinking. 'Why doesn't she tell him so?'

But it was impossible for Mrs Thursley to say or even think anything of the kind. He had his sermons, his articles in the *Guardian*, his studies in Neo-Platonism. How could he be expected to fill his own ink-pot? For her as well as for him it was obvious, it had become, after these five and twenty years of abjectly given and unreflectingly accepted slavery, completely axiomatic that he couldn't do such a thing. Besides, if she were to suggest in any way that he wasn't perfectly right, his anger would become still more violent. Goodness only knew what he mightn't do or say – in front of Brian! It would be awful. She began to make excuses for the empty ink-pot. Abject excuses on her own behalf, on Joan's, on her servants'. Her tone was at once deprecatory and soothing; she spoke as though she were dealing with a mixture between Jehovah and a very savage dog that might bite at any moment.

The gong – the Thursleys had a gong that would have been audible from end to end of a ducal mansion – rumbled up to a thunderous fortissimo that reduced even the vicar to silence. But as the sound ebbed, he began again.

'It's not as though I asked for very much,' he said.

'He'll be quieter when he's had something to eat,' Mrs Thursley thought, and led the way into the dining-room, followed by Joan. Brian wanted the vicar to precede him; but even in his righteous anger Mr Thursley remembered his good manners. Laying his hand on Brian's shoulder, he propelled him towards the door, keeping up all the time a long-range bombardment of his wife.

'Only a little quiet, only the simplest material conditions for doing my work. The barest minimum. But I don't get it. The house is as noisy as a railway station, and my ink-pot's neglected till I have nothing but a little black mud to write with.'

Under the bombardment, Mrs Thursley walked as though shrunken and with bowed head. But Joan, Brian noticed, had gone stiff; her body was rigid and ungraceful with excess of tension.

In the dining-room they found the two boys, Joan's younger brothers, already standing behind their chairs. At the sight of them, Mr Thursley reverted from his ink-pot to the noise in the house. 'Like a railway station,' he repeated, and the righteous indignation flared up in him with renewed intensity. 'George and Arthur have been rushing up and down the stairs and round the garden the whole morning. Why can't you keep them in order?'

They were all at their places now; Mrs Thursley at one end of the table, her husband at the other; the two boys on the left; Joan and Brian on her right. They stood there, waiting for the vicar to say grace.

'Like hooligans,' said Mr Thursley; the flames of wrath ran through him; he was filled with a tingling warmth, horribly delicious. 'Like savages.'

Making an effort, he dropped his long cleft chin on his chest and was silent. His nose was still deathly pale with anger; like marine animals in an aquarium, the nostrils contracted and expanded in a pulse of regular but fluttering movement. In his right hand he still held the ink-pot.

'*Benedictus benedicat, per Jesum Christum Dominum nostrum,*' he said at last in his praying voice, which was deep, with the suspicion of a tremolo, and charged with transcendental significance.

With the noise of pent-up movement suddenly released, they all sat down.

'Screaming and howling,' said Mr Thursley, reverting from the tone of piety to his original shrill harshness. 'How am I expected to do my work?' With an indignant bang, he put the ink-pot down on the table in front of him, then unfolded his napkin.

At the other end of the table Mrs Thursley was cutting up the mock duck with extraordinary rapidity.

'Pass that to your father,' she said to the nearest boy. It was essential to get him eating as soon as possible.

A second or two later the parlour-maid was offering Mr Thursley the vegetable. Her apron and cap were stiff with starch and she was as well drilled as a guardsman. The vegetable dishes were hideous, but had been expensive; the spoons were of heavy Victorian silver. With them, the vicar helped himself first to boiled potatoes, then to cabbage, mashed and moulded into damp green bricks.

Still indulging himself in the luxury of anger, 'Women simply don't understand what serious work is,' Mr Thursley went on; then started eating.

When she had helped the others to their mock duck, Mrs Thursley ventured a remark. 'Brian's just off to Germany,' she said.

Mr Thursley looked up, chewing his food very rapidly with his front teeth, like a rabbit. 'What part of Germany?' he asked, darting a sharp inquisitorial look at Brian. His nose had flushed again to its normal colour.

'M-marburg.'

'Where there's the university?'

Brian nodded.

Startlingly, with a noise like coke being poured down a

chute, Mr Thursley burst out laughing. 'Don't take to beer-drinking with the students,' he said.

The storm was over. In part out of the thankfulness of her heart, in part to make her husband feel that she had found his joke irresistible, Mrs Thursley also laughed. 'Oh, no,' she cried, don't take to *that* !'

Brian smiled and shook his head.

'Water or soda-water?' the parlour-maid asked confidentially, creaking with starch and whalebone as she bent over him.

'W-water, please.'

After lunch, when the vicar had returned to his study, Mrs Thursley suggested, in her bright, embarrassingly significant way, that the two young people should go for a walk. The ogival front door slammed behind them. Like a prisoner at last restored to liberty, Joan drew a deep breath.

The sky was still overcast, and beneath the low ceiling of grey cloud the air was soft and as though limp with fatigue, as though weary with the burden of too much summer. In the woods, into which they turned from the high-road, the stillness was oppressive, like the intentional silence of sentient beings, pregnant with unavowed thoughts and hidden feelings. An invisible tree-creeper started to sing; but it was as if the clear bright sound were coming from some other time and place. They walked on hand in hand; and between them was the silence of the wood and at the same time the deeper, denser, more secret silence of their own unexpressed emotions. The silence of the complaints she was too loyal to utter and the pity that, unless she complained, it would, he felt, be insulting for him to put into words; her longing for the comfort of his arms and those desires he did not wish to feel.

Their path led them between great coverts of rhododendrons, and suddenly they were in a narrow cleft, hemmed in by high walls of the impenetrable, black-green foliage. It was a solitude within a solitude, the image of their own private silence visibly hollowed out of the greater stillness of the wood.

'Almost f-frightening,' he whispered, as they stood there listening – listening (for there was nothing else for them to hear) to their own heart-beats and each other's breathing and all the words that hung unspoken between them.

All at once, she could bear it no longer, 'When I think of what it'll be like at home ...' The complaint had uttered itself, against her will. 'Oh, I wish you weren't going, Brian!'

Brian looked at her and, at the sight of those trembling lips, those eyes bright with tears, he felt himself as it were disintegrated by tenderness and pity. Stammering her name, he put his arm about her. Joan stood for a little while quite still, her head bent, her forehead resting on his shoulder. The touch of her hair was electric against his lips, he breathed its perfume. All at once, as though waking from sleep, she stirred into motion and, drawing a little away from him, looked up into his face. Her regard had a desperate, almost inhuman fixity.

'Darling,' he whispered.

Joan's only answer was to shake her head.

But why? What was she denying, what implication of his endearment was she saying no to? 'But J-joan ... ?' There was a note of anxiety in his voice.

Still she did not answer; only looked at him and once more slowly shook her head. How many negations were expressed in that single movement! The refusal to complain; the denial for herself of the possibility of happiness; the sad insistence that all her love and all his availed nothing against the pain of absence; the resolution not to exploit his pity, not to elicit, however much she longed for it, another, a more passionate avowal. ...

Suddenly, he took her face between his hands and, stooping, kissed her on the mouth.

But this was what she had resolved not to extort from him, this was the gesture that could avail nothing against her inevitable unhappiness! For a second or two she stiffened her body in resistance, tried to shake her head again, tried to draw back. Then, vanquished by a longing stronger than herself, she was limp in his arms; the shut, resisting lips parted and were soft under his kisses; her eyelids closed, and there was nothing left in the world but his mouth and the thin hard body pressed against her own.

Fingers stirred the hair above the nape of her neck, slid round to the throat and dropped to her breast. The strength went out of her, she felt herself sinking deeper and deeper into that mysterious other world, behind her eyelids, into the sightless universe of touch.

Then, without warning, as though in precipitate obedience to some inaudible word of command, he broke away from her. For an instant she thought she was going to fall; but the strength came back to her knees, just in time. She swayed unsteadily, then recovered her balance, and with it the consciousness of the outrage he had inflicted upon her. She had leaned upon him with her whole being, soul as well as body, and he had allowed her to fall, had withdrawn his lips and arms and chest and left her suddenly cold and horribly exposed, defenceless and as if naked. She opened hurt, reproachful eyes and saw him standing there pale and strangely furtive; he met her glance for a moment, then averted his face.

Her resentful sense of outrage gave place to anxiety. 'What is it, Brian?'

He looked at her for a moment, then turned away again. 'Perhaps we'd better go home,' he said in a low voice.

*

It was a day late in September. Under a pale blue sky the distances were mournful, were exquisitely tender with faint mist. The world seemed remote and unactual, like a memory or an ideal.

The train came to a standstill. Brian waved to the solitary porter, but he himself, nevertheless, got out with the heaviest of the suit-cases. By straining his muscles he found that he was able to relieve his conscience of some of the burden that the ability to buy a poor man's services tended, increasingly as he grew older, to impose upon it.

The porter came running up and almost snatched the bag out of Brian's hand. He too had his conscience. 'You leave that to me, sir,' he said, almost indignantly.

'T-two more in the c-c-c ... inside,' he emended, long after the porter had stepped into the unpronounceable compartment to collect the remaining pieces. 'Sh-shall I give a hand?' he offered. The man was old – forty years older than himself, Brian calculated; white-haired and wrinked, but called him 'sir', but carried his bags and would be grateful for a shilling. 'Sh-shall I ...?'

The old porter did not even answer, but swung the suit-cases down from the rack, taking evident pride in his well-directed strength.

A touch on his shoulder made Brian turn sharply round. The person who had touched him was Joan.

'In the king's name!' she said; but the laughter behind her words was forced, and there was an expression in her eyes of anxiety – the accumulated anxiety of weeks of bewildered speculation. All those queer, unhappy letters he had written from Germany – they had left her painfully uncertain what to think, how to feel, what to expect of him when he came back. In his letters, it was true, he had reproached only himself – with a violence for whose intensity she was unable to account. But to the extent that she was responsible for what had happened in the wood (and of course she was partly responsible; why not? what was so wrong with just a kiss?), she felt that the reproaches were also addressed to her. And if he reproached her, could he still love her? What did he really feel about her, about himself, about their relations to one another? It was because she simply couldn't wait an unnecessary minute for the answer that she had come, surreptitiously, to meet him at the station.

Brian stood there speechless; he had not expected to see her so soon, and was almost dismayed at thus finding himself, without preparation, in her presence. Automatically, he held out his hand. Joan took it and pressed it in her own, hard, hard, as if hoping to force the reality of her love upon him; but even while doing so, she swayed away from him in her apprehension, her embarrassed uncertainty of what he might have become, swayed away as she would have done from a stranger.

The grace of that shy, uneasy movement touched him as poignantly as it had touched him at their first meeting. It was the grace, in spite of the embarrassment that the movement expressed, of a young tree in the wind. That was how he thought of it then. And now it had happened again; and the beauty of the gesture was again a revelation, but more poignant than it had been the first time, because of its implication that he was once again an alien; but an alien, against whose renewed strangeness the pressure on his hand protested, almost violently.

Her face, as she looked up into his, seemed to waver; and suddenly that artificial brightness was quenched in profound apprehension.

'Aren't you glad to see me, Brian?' she asked.

Her words broke a spell; he was able to smile again, able to speak. 'G-glad?' he repeated; and, for answer, kissed her hand. 'But I didn't th-think you'd be here. It almost g-gave me a fright.'

His expression reassured her. During those first seconds of silence, his still, petrified face had seemed the face of an enemy. Now, by that smile, he was transfigured, was once more the old Brian she had loved; so sensitive, so kind and good; and so beautiful in his goodness, beautiful in spite of that long, queer face, that lanky body, those loose, untidily moving limbs.

Noisily, the train started, gathered speed and was gone. The old porter walked away to fetch a barrow. They were alone at the end of the long platform.

'I thought you didn't love me,' she said after a long silence.

'But, J-joan!' he protested. They smiled at one another; then, after a moment, he looked away. Not love her? he was thinking. But the trouble was that he loved her too much, loved her in a bad way, even though she was the best.

'I thought you were angry with me.'

'But why sh-should I be?' His face was still averted.

'You know why.'

'I wasn't a-angry with *you*.'

'But it was my fault.'

Brian shook his head. 'It w-wasn't.'

'It was,' she insisted.

At the thought of what his sensations had been as he held her there, in the dark cleft between the rhododendron coverts, he shook his head a second time, more emphatically.

The old porter was there again with his barrow and his comments on the weather, his scraps of news and gossip. They followed him, playing for his benefit their parts as supernumerary characters in the local drama.

When they were almost at the gate, Joan laid a hand on Brian's arm. 'It's all right, isn't it?' Their eyes met. 'I'm allowed to be happy?'

173

He smiled without speaking and nodded.

In the dogcart on the way to the house he kept remembering the sudden brightening of her face in response to that voiceless gesture of his. And all he could do to repay her for so much love was to ... He thought of the rhododendron coverts again and was overcome with shame.

When she learned from Brian that Joan had been at the station, Mrs Foxe felt a sharp pang of resentment. By what right? Before his own mother ... And besides, what bad faith! For Joan had accepted her invitation to come to lunch the day after Brian's return. Which meant that she had tacitly admitted Mrs Foxe's exclusive right to him on the day itself. But here she was, stealing surreptitiously to the station to catch him as he stepped out of the train. It was almost dishonest.

Mrs Foxe's passion of indignant jealousy lasted only a few seconds; its very intensity accelerated her recognition of its wrongness, its unworthiness. No sign of what she felt had appeared on her face, and it was with a smile of amused indulgence that she listened to Brian's vaguely stammered account of the meeting. Then, with a strong effort of the will, she not only shut off the expression of her emotion, but even excluded the emotion itself from her consciousness. All that, as it seemed, an impersonal regard for right conduct justified her in still feeling was a certain regretful disapproval of Joan's – how should she put it? – disingenuousness. For the girl to have stolen that march upon her was not quite right.

Not quite right; but still very understandable, she now went on to reflect, very excusable. When one's in love ... And Joan's was an impulsive, emotional character. Which had its fortunate side, Mrs Foxe reflected. The impulses were as strong towards right as towards wrong. If one could canalize that deep and powerful stream of life within her, if one could make the right appeal to what was best in her, if one could confirm her in those fine generous aspirations of hers – why, she would be a splendid person. Splendid, Mrs Foxe insisted to herself.

'Well,' she said next day, when Joan came over to lunch, 'I hear you caught our migrant on the wing before he'd even had time to settle.' The tone was playful, there was a charming smile on Mrs Foxe's face. But Joan blushed guiltily.

'You didn't mind, did you?' she asked.

'Mind?' Mrs Foxe repeated. 'But, my dear, why should I? I only thought we'd agreed on today. But, of course, if you felt you absolutely couldn't wait ...'

'I'm sorry,' said Joan. But something that was almost hatred mounted hot within her.

Mrs Foxe laid her hand affectionately on the girl's shoulder. 'Let's stroll out into the garden,' she suggested, 'and see if Brian's anywhere about.'

CHAPTER TWENTY

December 8th 1926

TIPTOEING out of the back drawing-room, Hugh Ledwidge had hoped to find the refreshment of a little solitude; but on the landing he was caught by Joyce and Colin. And Colin, it appeared, was tremendously keen on natives, had always been anxious to talk to a professional ethnologist about his experiences on shikar. For nearly half an hour he had to listen, while the young man poured out his illiterate nonsense about India and Uganda. An immense fatigue overwhelmed him. His one desire was to escape, to get away from this parrot house of stupid chatter, back to delicious silence and a book.

They left him, thank God, at last, and drawing a deep breath, he braced himself for the final ordeal of leave-taking. That saying good-bye at the end of an evening was one of the things Hugh most intensely disliked. To have to expose yourself yet once more to personal contact, to be compelled, weary as you were and thirsty for solitude, to grin again and gibber and make yet another effort of hypocrisy – how odious that could be! Particularly with Mary Amberley. There were evenings when the woman simply wouldn't allow you to say good-bye but clung to you desperately, as though she were drowning. Questions, confidences, scabrous discussions of people's love-affairs – anything to keep you a few minutes longer. She seemed to regard each successive departure of a guest as the death of a fragment of her own being. His heart sank as he made his way across the room towards her. 'Damned woman!' he thought, and positively hated her; hated her, as well as for all the other reasons, because Helen was still dancing with that groom; and now with a fresh access of malevolence, because, as he suddenly perceived through the mists of his dim sight, Staithes and that man Beavis were sitting with her. All his insane thoughts about the plot came rushing back into his mind. They had been talking about him, him and the fire escape, him on the football field, him when they threw the slippers over the partition of his cubicle. For a moment, he thought of turning back and slipping out of the house without a word. But they had seen him coming, they would suspect the reason of his flight, they would laugh all the louder. His common sense returned to him, it was all nonsense, there was no plot. How could there be a plot? And even if Beavis did remember, what reason had he to talk? But all the same, all the same ... Squaring his narrow shoulders, Hugh Ledwidge marched resolutely towards the anticipated ambush.

To his immense relief, Mary Amberley let him go almost without a protest. 'Must you be off, Hugh? So soon?' That was all. She seemed to be absent, thinking of something else.

Beppo fizzled amiably; Staithes merely nodded; and now it was Beavis's turn. Was that smile of his what it seemed to be – just vaguely and conventionally friendly? Or did it carry hidden significances, did it secretly imply derisive reminders of those past shames? Hugh turned and hurried away. Why on earth, he wondered, did one ever go to these idiotic parties? Kept on going, what was more, again and again, when one knew it was all utterly pointless and boring. ...

Mark Staithes turned to Anthony. 'You realize who that is?' he asked.

'Who? Ledwidge? Is he anyone special?'

Staithes explained.

'Goggler!' Anthony laughed. 'Why of course. Poor Goggler! How fiendish we were to him!'

'That's why I've always pretended I didn't know who he was,' said Staithes, and smiled an anatomical smile of pity and contempt. 'I think it would be charitable,' he added, 'if you did the same.' Protecting Hugh Ledwidge gave him genuine pleasure.

Utterly pointless and boring – yes, and humiliating, Hugh was thinking, humiliating as well. For there was always some humiliation. A Beavis smiling; a Gerry Watchett, like an insolent groom ...

There was a hurrying of feet on the stairs behind him. 'Hugh! Hugh!' He started almost guiltily and turned round. 'Why were you slinking away without saying good night to me?'

Essaying a joke, 'You seemed so busy,' he began, twinkling up at Helen through his spectacles; then fell silent in sudden astonishment, almost in awe.

She was standing there, three steps above him, one hand on the banister, the fingers of the other splayed out against the opposite wall, leaning forward as though on the brink of flight. But what had happened to her, what miracle? The flushed face that hung over him seemed to shine with an inward illumination. This was not Helen, but some supernatural creature. In the presence of such unearthly beauty, he blushed for the ignoble irrelevance of his waggery, his knowing look.

'Busy?' she echoed. 'But I was only dancing.' And it was as though some ingenuous and unconscious Moses had said to his bedazzled Israelites: 'I was only talking to Jehovah.' 'You had no excuse,' she went on. Then quickly, as though a new and curious idea had suddenly occurred to her, 'Or were you cross with me for some reason?' she added in another tone.

He began by shaking his head; but felt impelled, on second thoughts, to try to explain a little. 'Not cross,' he distinguished, 'just ... just a bit unsociable.'

The light behind her face seemed to leap up in a quivering rush of intenser flame. Unsociable! That was really too exquisitely funny! The dancing had made her perfect, had transformed earth into heaven. At the idea that one could be (preposterous word!) unsociable, that one could feel anything but an overflowing love for everyone and everything, she could only laugh.

'You *are* funny, Hugh!'

'I'm glad you think so.' His tone was offended. He had turned away his head.

The silk of her dress rustled sharply; a little gust of perfume was cool on his cheek – and she was standing only one step above him, very close. 'You're not hurt because I said you were funny?' she asked.

He lifted his eyes again and found her face on a level with his own. Mollified by that expression of genuine solicitude he shook his head.

'I didn't mean funny in the horrid way,' she explained. 'I meant . . . well, you know: nicely funny. Funny, but a darling.'

In threateningly personal circumstances, a well-timed foolery is a sure defence. Smiling, Hugh raised his right hand to his heart. '*Je suis pénétré de reconnaissance*', was what he was going to say by way of acknowledgement for that 'darling'. The courtly jape, the mock-heroic gesture were his immediate and automatic reaction to her words. '*Je suis pénétré . . .*'

But Helen gave him no time to take cover behind his *dix-huitième* waggery. For she followed up her words by laying her two hands on his shoulders and kissing him on the mouth.

For a moment he was almost annihilated with surprise and confusion and a kind of suffocating, chaotic joy.

Helen drew back a little and looked at him. He had gone very pale – looked as though he had seen a ghost. She smiled – for he was funnier than ever – then bent forward and kissed him again.

The first time she had kissed him, it had been out of the fullness of the life that was in her, because she was made perfect in a perfect world. But his scared face was so absurdly comic that the sight of it somehow transformed this fullness of perfect life into a kind of mischievous wantonness. The second time she kissed him, it was for fun; for fun and, at the same time, out of curiosity. It was an experiment, made in the spirit of hilarious scientific inquiry. She was a vivisector – licensed by perfection, justified by happiness. Besides, Hugh had an extraordinarily nice mouth. She had never kissed such full soft lips before; the experience had been startlingly pleasurable. It was not only that she wanted to see, scientifically, what the absurd creature would do next; she also wanted to feel once more that cool resilience against her mouth, to experience that strange creeping of pleasure that tingled out from her lips and ran, quick and almost unbearable, like moths, along the surface of her body.

'You were so sweet to take all that trouble,' she said by way of justification for the second kiss. The moths had crept again, deliciously, had settled with an electric tremor of vibrating wings on her breasts. 'All that trouble about my education.'

But 'Helen!' was all that he could whisper; and, before he had time to think, he had put his arms about her and kissed her.

His mouth, for the third time; and those hurrying moths along the skin ... But, oh, how quickly he drew away!

'Helen!' he repeated.

They looked at one another; and now that he had had the time to think, Hugh found himself all of a sudden horribly embarrassed. His hands dropped furtively from her body. He didn't know what to say to her – or, rather, knew, but couldn't bring himself to say it. His heart was beating with a painful violence. 'I love you, I want you,' he was crying, he was positively shouting, from behind his embarrassed silence. But no word was uttered. He smiled at her rather foolishly, and dropped his eyes – the eyes, he now reflected, that must look so hideous, like a fish's eyes, through the thick lenses of his spectacles.

'How funny he is,' Helen thought. But her scientific laughter had died down. His shyness was infectious. To put an end to the uncomfortable situation, 'I shall read all those books,' she said. 'And that reminds me, you must give me the list.'

Grateful to her for supplying him with a subject about which it was possible to talk, he looked up at her again – for a moment only, because of those fish-eyes, goggling. 'I'll fill in the gaps and send it you,' he said. Then, after a second or two, he realized that in his improvidence he had exhausted the preciously impersonal topic of the books in a single sentence. The silence persisted, distressingly; and at last, in despair, because there was nothing else to say, he decided to say good night. Trying to charge his voice with an infinity of loving significance, 'Good night, Helen,' he said. The words were intended to be as eloquent as a whole speech. But would she hear the eloquence, would she understand the depths of his implied meaning? He bent forward and kissed her again, quickly, very lightly, a kiss of tenderly respectful devotion.

But he had not reckoned with Helen. The embarrassment that had momentarily clouded her wanton perfection had evaporated at the touch of his lips; she was once more the laughing vivisector.

'Kiss me again, Hugh,' she said. And when he obeyed, she would not let him go; but kept his mouth pressed to hers, second after second . . .

The noise of voices and music became suddenly louder; somebody had opened the drawing-room door.

'Good night, Hugh,' she whispered against his lips; then loosed her hold and ran up the stairs two at a time.

*

Looking after her, as she ran out of the room to say good night to old Ledwidge, Gerry had smiled to himself complacently. Pink in the face; with shining eyes. As though she'd drunk a bottle of champagne. Absolutely buffy with the dancing. It was fun when they lost their heads like that; lost them so enthusiastically, so ungrudgingly, so completely. Not keeping anything back, but chucking it all out of the window, so to speak. Most girls were so damned avaricious and calculating. They'd only lose half their heads and carefully keep the other half to play the outraged virgin with. Mean little bitches! But with Helen you felt that the engine was all out. She stepped on the gas and didn't care what was in the way. He liked that sort of thing, and liked it not only because he hoped to profit by the lost head, but also disinterestedly, because he couldn't help admiring people who let themselves go and didn't care two hoots about the consequences. There was something fine and generous and spirited about such people. He was like that himself, when he could afford it. Guts: that was what she'd got. And the makings of a temperament, he was thinking with an inward satisfaction, when a touch on his arm from behind made him suddenly start. His surprise turned almost instantaneously to anger. There was nothing he hated more than to be taken unawares, off his guard. He turned sharply round and, seeing that the person who had touched him was Mary

Amberley, tried to readjust his face. Vainly; the hard resentful eyes belied his smile.

But Mary was herself too angry to notice the signs of his annoyance. 'I want to talk to you, Gerry,' she said in a low voice that she tried to keep level and unemotional, but that trembled in spite of all her efforts.

'Christ!' he thought; 'a scene', and felt angrier than ever with the tiresome woman. 'Talk away,' he said aloud; and, with an offensive air of detachment, he took out his cigarette-case, opened and proffered it.

'Not here,' she said.

Gerry pretended not to understand her. 'Sorry. I thought you didn't mind people smoking here.'

'Fool!' Her anger broke out with sudden violence. Then, catching him by the sleeve, 'Come!' she commanded, and almost dragged him to the door.

Running upstairs, Helen was in time to see her mother and Gerry mounting from the drawing-room landing towards the higher floors of the tall house. 'I shall have to find somebody else to dance with,' was all she thought; and a moment later she had found little Peter Quinn and was gliding away once more into paradise.

'Talk of floaters!' said Anthony as their hostess left the room with Gerry Watchett. 'I didn't realize that Gerry was the present incumbent. . . .'

Beppo nodded. 'Poor Mary!' he sighed.

'On the contrary,' said Staithes, 'rich Mary! She'll be poor later.'

'And nothing can be done about it?' asked Anthony.

'She'd hate you if you tried.'

Anthony shook her head. 'These dismal compulsions! Like cuckoos in August. Like stags in October.'

'She showed symptoms of having a compulsion about me,' said Staithes. 'Just after I first met her, it was. But I soon cured her of that. And then that ruffian Watchett turned up.'

'Fascinating, the way these aristocrats can behave!' Anthony's tone was one of scientific enthusiasm.

Staithes's flayed face twisted itself into a grimace of contempt.

'Just a coarse, vulgar gangster,' he said. 'How on earth you ever put up with him at Oxford, I simply cannot imagine.' In fact, of course, he was busily imagining that Anthony had done it out of mere ignoble toadyism.

'Just snobbery,' said Anthony, depriving the other of half his pleasure by the easy confession. 'But, then, I insist, people like Gerry are an essential part of any liberal education. There was something really rather magnificent about him when he was rich. A certain detached and disinterested recklessness. Now . . .' He raised his hand and let it fall again. 'Just a gangster – you're quite right. But that's the fascinating thing – the ease with which aristocrats turn into gangsters. Very comprehensible, when you come to think of it. Here's a man brought up to believe that he has a divine right to the best of everything. And so long as he gets his rights it's all *noblesse oblige* and honour and all the rest of it. Inextricably mixed up with insolence, of course; but genuinely there. Now, take away his income; the oddest things are liable to happen. Providence intended you to have the best of everything; therefore intended you to have the means for procuring the best of everything; therefore, when the means don't come to you legitimately, justifies you in getting them illegitimately. In the past, our Gerry could have gone in for banditry or simony. He'd have made an admirable *condottiere*, an almost perfect cardinal. But nowadays the church and the army are too respectable, too professional. They've no place for amateurs. The impoverished nobleman finds himself driven into business. Selling cars. Touting stocks and shares. Promoting dubious companies. To the accompaniment, of course, if he's presentable, of a judicious prostitution of his body. If he has the luck to be born with a gift of the gab, he can make a good living out of the politer forms of blackmail and sycophancy – as a gossip writer. *Noblesse oblige*; but so does poverty. And when they both oblige simultaneously – well, we of the middle classes had better start counting the silver. Instead of which . . .' He shrugged his shoulders. 'Poor Mary!'

*

Upstairs, in the bedroom, the torrent of Mary's reproaches and abuse streamed on, unceasingly. Gerry did not even look at her.

Averted, he seemed absorbed in the contemplation of the Pascin hanging over the mantelpiece. The painting showed two women lying foreshortened on a bed, naked.

'I like this picture,' he said with deliberate irrelevance, when Mrs Amberley had paused for breath. 'You can see that the man who painted it had just finished making love to those girls. Both of them. At the same time,' he added.

Mary Amberley went very pale; her lips trembled, her nostrils fluttered as though with a separate and uncontrollable life of their own.

'You haven't even been listening to me,' she cried. 'Oh, you're awful, you're horrible!' The torrent began to flow again, more vehemently than ever.

Still turning his back to her, Gerry went on looking at the Pascin nudes; then at last, blowing out a final cloud of tobacco-smoke, he threw the stump of his cigarette into the fireplace and turned round.

'When you've quite done,' he said in a tired voice, 'we may as well go to bed.' And after a little pause, while, unable to speak, she glared furiously in his face, 'Seeing that that's what you really want,' he added, and, smiling ironically, advanced across the room towards her. When he was quite near her, he halted and held out his hands invitingly. They were large hands, immaculately kept, but coarse, insensitive, brutal. 'Hideous hands,' Mary thought as she looked at them, 'odious hands!' All the more odious now, because it was by their very ugliness and brutality that she had first been attracted, was even at this very moment being attracted, shamefully, in spite of all the reasons she had for hating him. 'Well, aren't you coming?' he asked in the same bored, derisive tone.

For an answer, she hit out at his face. But he was too quick for her, caught the flying hand in mid-air and, when she tried to bring the other into play, caught that too. She was helpless in his grasp.

Still smiling down at her, and without a word, he pushed her backwards, step by step, towards the bed.

'Beast!' she kept repeating, 'beast!' and struggled, vainly, and found an obscure pleasure in her helplessness. He pushed her against the end of the low divan, further and further, inexorably,

and at last she lost her balance and fell back across the counterpane – (fell back, while, with one knee on the edge of the bed, he bent over her, still smiling the same derisive smile). 'Beast, beast!' But in fact, as she secretly admitted to herself – and the consciousness was intoxicating in its shamefulness – in fact, she really *wanted* to be treated as he was treating her – like a prostitute, like an animal; and in her own house, what was more, with her guests all waiting for her, and the door unlocked, and her daughters wondering where she was, perhaps at this very moment coming up the stairs to look for her. Yes, she really wanted it. Still struggling, she gave herself up to the knowledge, to the direct physical intuition that this intolerable degradation was the accomplishment of an old desire, was a revelation marvellous as well as horrible, was the Apocalypse, the Apocalypse at once angel and beast, plague, lamb and whore in a single divine, revolting, overwhelming experience. . . .

*

'Civilization and sexuality,' Anthony was saying: 'there's a definite correlation. The higher the one, the intenser the other.'

'My word,' said Beppo, fizzling with pleasure, 'we *must* be civilized!'

'Civilization means food and literature all round. Beefsteaks and fiction magazines for all. First-class proteins for the body, fourth-class love-stories for the spirit. And this in a safe urban world, where there are no risks, no physical fatigues. In a town like this, for example, one can live for years at a time without being made aware that there's such a thing as nature. Everything's man-made and punctual and convenient. But people can have too much of convenience; they want excitement, they want risks and surprises. Where are they going to find them under our dispensation? In money-making, in politics, in occasional war, in sport, and finally in sex. But most people can't be speculators or active politicians; and war's getting to be too much of a good thing; and the more elaborate and dangerous sports are only for the rich. So that sex is all that's left. As material civilization rises, the intensity and importance of sexuality also rises. Must rise, inevitably. And since at the same time food and literature have increased the amount of available appetite . . .' He shrugged his shoulders. 'Well, you see!'

Beppo was charmed. 'You explain it all,' he cried. '*Tout comprendre c'est tout pardonner.*' He felt delightedly, that Anthony's argument gave, not only absolution, but also a plenary indulgence – to everyone (for Beppo unselfishly wanted everyone to be as happy as he was) and for everything, everything, from the ravishing barmen at Toulon to those top-booted tarts (so definitely not for him) on the Kurfürstendamm.

Staithes said nothing. If social progress, he was thinking, just meant greater piggishness for more people, why then – then, what?

'Do you remember that remark of Dr Johnson's?' Anthony began again with a note of elation in his voice. It had suddenly come to him, an unexpected gift from his memory to his discursive reason – come to enrich the pattern of his thinking, to fill out his argument and extend its scope. His voice reflected the sudden triumphant pleasure that he felt. 'How does it go? "A man is seldom so innocently employed as when he is making money." Something like that. Admirable!' He laughed aloud. 'The innocence of those who grind the faces of the poor, but refrain from pinching the bottoms of their neighbours' wives! The innocence of Ford, the innocence of Rockefeller! The nineteenth century was the Age of Innocence – that sort of innocence. With the result that we're now almost ready to say that a man is seldom more innocently employed than when making love.'

There was a silence. Staithes looked at his watch. 'Time one was getting out of here,' he said. 'But the problem,' he added, turning round in his chair to scan the room, 'the problem is one's hostess.'

They got up, and while Beppo hurried off to greet a couple of young acquaintances on the other side of the room, Staithes and Anthony made their way to the door.

'The problem,' Staithes kept repeating, 'the problem . . .'

On the landing, however, they met Mrs Amberley and Gerry coming down the stairs.

'We were looking for you,' said Anthony. 'To say good night.'

'So soon?' cried Mary with a sudden access of anxiety.

But they were firm. A couple of minutes later the three of

them, Staithes, Gerry Watchett, and Anthony, were walking up the street together.

It was Gerry who broke the silence. 'These old hags,' he said in a tone of meditative rancour, and shook his head. Then more cheerfully. 'What about a game of poker?' he suggested. But Anthony didn't know how, and Mark Staithes didn't desire, to play poker; he had to go off alone in search of more congenial company.

'Good riddance,' said Mark. 'And now what about coming to my rooms for an hour?'

*

It was the most important thing, Hugh Ledwidge felt as he walked home, the most important and also the most extraordinary, most incredible thing that had ever happened to him. So beautiful, so young. 'Fashioned so slenderly.' (If only she had thrown herself into the Thames and he had rescued her! 'Helen! My poor child!' And, 'Hugh!' she would have murmured gratefully. 'Hugh ...') But even without the suicide it had been astonishing enough. Her mouth against his. Oh, why hadn't he shown more courage, more presence of mind? All the things he might have said to her, the gestures he ought to have made! And yet, in a certain sense, it was better that he should have behaved as he did – stupidly, timidly, ineptly. Better, because it proved more conclusively that she cared for him; because it gave a higher value to her action, so young, so pure – and yet spontaneously, under no compulsion of his, in the teeth, indeed, of what had almost been his resistance, she had stepped down, had laid her hands on his shoulders, had kissed him. Kissed him in spite of everything, he repeated to himself with a kind of astonished triumph that mingled strangely with his sense of shame, his conviction of weakness and futility; in spite of everything. *Non più andraï,* he hummed to himself as he walked along; then, as though the dank London night were a morning on the downs in spring, broke out into unequivocal singing.

> *Delle belle turbando il riposo,*
> *Narcissetto, Adoncino d'amor. ...*

At home, he sat down at once to his desk and began to write to her.

Helen, Helen. .... If I repeat the syllables too often, they lose their sense, become just a noise in my silent room – terrifying in their meaninglessness. But if I say the name just two or three times, very softly, how rich it becomes, how full! Charged with echoes and reminders. Not so much, for me, of the original Greek Helen. I can't feel that she was ever anything but a mature woman – never anything but married to Menelaus and eloping with Paris. Never really young, as you are – exquisitely, exquisitely, like a flower. No, it's more Poe's Helen I catch sight of through the name. The beauty that carries the traveller back to his own native shore – takes him home. Not to the obvious, worldly home of the passions. No ; to that further, rarer, lovelier home, beyond and above them. Beyond and above ; and yet implying, yet including, even while transcending, the passions ...

It was a long letter ; but he was in time, running out, to catch the midnight post. The sense of triumph with which he returned this second time was almost unalloyed. Momentarily, he had forgotten his shyness, his humiliating cowardice ; he remembered only that consciousness of soaring power that had filled him while he wrote his letter. Exalted above his ordinary self, he forgot, when undressing, to put his truss away in the chest of drawers, so that Mrs Brinton shouldn't see it when she came in with his early tea in the morning. In bed, he lay for a long time thinking tenderly, paternally, poetically, thinking at the same time with desire, but a desire so lingeringly gentle that lasciviousness assumed the quality of prayer, thinking of Helen's exquisite youthfulness, fashioned so slenderly, and her innocence, her slender innocence, and those unexpected, those extraordinary kisses.

CHAPTER TWENTY-ONE

August 31st 1933

HELEN rang the bell, then listened. In the silence behind the closed door, nothing stirred. She had come straight from the station after a night in the train ; it was not yet ten ; her mother would still be asleep. She rang again ; then, after a pause, once more. Heavily asleep – unless, of course, she had stayed out all night. Where? And with whom? Remembering that horrible Russian she had met at her mother's flat the last time she was in Paris, Helen frowned. She rang a fourth time, a fifth. From within the apartment there was suddenly an answering sound of movement. Helen sighed, partly with relief that her mother had only been asleep, partly in apprehension of what the coming minutes or hours held in store. The door opened at last, opened on a twilight that smelt of cats and ether and stale food; and there, in dirty pink pyjamas, her dyed orange hair dishevelled, and still blinking, still strangely swollen with sleep, stood her mother. For a second the face was a mask, bloated and middle-aged, of stupefied incomprehension; then, in a flash, it came back to life, almost back to youth, with a sudden smile of genuine delight.

'But what fun!' cried Mrs Amberley. 'Darling, I'm so glad.'

If she hadn't known – by how bitter an experience! – that this mood of gaiety and affectionateness would inevitably be followed by, at the best, a spiteful despondency, at the worst, by a fit of insanely violent anger, Helen would have been touched by the warmth of her mother's greeting. As it was, she merely suffered herself to be kissed and, her face still set and stony, stepped across the threshold into the horribly familiar nightmare of her mother's life.

This time, she found, the nightmare had a comic element.

'It's all because of that beastly old *femme de ménage*,' Mrs Amberley explained as they stood there in the smelly little lobby. 'She was stealing my stockings. So I had to lock the bedroom door when I went out. And then somehow I lost the key. You know what I am,' she added complacently, boasting by force of habit of that absent-mindedness of which she had always been so proud. 'Hopeless, I'm afraid.' She shook her head and smiled that crooked little smile of hers, conspiratorially. 'When I got home, I had to smash that panel.' She pointed to the oblong aperture in the lower half of the door. 'You should have seen me, banging away with the flat-iron!' Her voice was richly vibrant with laughter. 'Luckily it was like matchwood. Cheap and nasty to a degree. Like everything in this beastly place.'

'And you crawled through?' Helen asked.

'Like this.' And going down on her hands and knees, Mrs

Amberley pushed her head through the hole, turned sideways so as to admit an arm and shoulder, then, with surprising agility, pulled and pushed with a hand beyond and feet on the hither side of the door, till only her legs remained in the lobby. First one, then the other, the legs were withdrawn, and an instant later, as though from a dog-kennel, Mrs Amberley's face emerged, a little flushed, through the aperture.

'You see,' she said. 'It's as easy as winking. And the beauty of it is that old Madame Roger's much too fat. No possible chance of her getting through. I don't have to worry about my stockings any more.'

'Do you mean to say she never goes into your bedroom?'

Mrs Amberley shook her head. 'Not since I lost the key; and that was three weeks ago, at least.' Her tone was one of triumph.

'But who makes the bed and does the cleaning?'

'Well ...' There was a moment's hesitation. 'Why, I do, of course,' the other replied a little irritably.

'You?'

'Why not?' From her kennel door, Mrs Amberley looked up almost defiantly into her daughter's face. There was a long silence; then, simultaneously, both of them burst out laughing.

Still smiling, 'Let's have a look,' said Helen, and went down on all fours. The stony face had softened into life; she felt an inward warmth. Her mother had been so absurd, peering up like that out of her kennel, so childishly ridiculous, that suddenly she was able to love her again. To love her while she laughed at her, just because she could laugh at her.

Mrs Amberley withdrew her head. 'Of course it *is* a bit untidy,' she admitted rather anxiously, as Helen wriggled through the hole in the door. Still kneeling, she pushed some dirty linen and the remains of yesterday's lunch under the bed.

On her feet again, inside the bedroom, Helen looked round. It was filthier even than she had expected – much filthier. She made an effort to go on smiling; but the muscles of her face refused to obey her.

*

Three days later Helen was on her way back to London. Opening the English newspaper she had bought at the Gare du Nord, she read, with an equal absence of interest, about the depression, the test match, the Nazis, the New Deal. Sighing, she turned the page. Printed very large, the words, 'An Exquisite First Novel,' caught her eye. And below, in small letters, 'The Invisible Lover. By Hugh Ledwidge. Reviewed by Catesby Rudge.' Helen folded back the page to make it more manageable and read with an intense and fixed attention.

Just another book, I thought, like all the rest. And I was on the point of throwing it aside, unread. But luckily something – some mystic intuition, I suppose – made me change my mind. I opened the book. I turned over the pages, glancing at a sentence here and there. And the sentences, I found, were gems – jewels of wrought crystal. I decided to read the book. That was at nine in the evening. And at midnight I was still reading, spellbound. It was nearly two before I got to bed – my mind in a whirl of enthusiasm for this masterpiece I had just read.

How shall I describe the book to you? I might call it a fantasy. And as far as it goes, that description holds good. *The Invisible Lover* is a fantasy. But a fantasy that is poignant as well as airy; profound as well as intriguing and light; fraught with tears as well as with smiles; at once subtly humorous and of a high, Galahad-like spirituality. It is full of a kind of broken-hearted fun, and its laughter is dewy with tears. And throughout runs a vein of naïve and child-like purity, infinitely refreshing in a world full of Freudians and sex-novelists and all their wearisome ilk. This fantasy of the invisible but ever present, ever watchful, ever adoring lover and his child-beloved has an almost celestial innocence. If I wanted to describe the book in a single phrase, I should say that it was the story of Dante and Beatrice told by Hans Andersen. ...

Falling into her memories of Hugh's few ignominious attempts to make love to her, the words produced in Helen's mind a kind of violent chemical reaction. She burst out laughing; and since the ridiculous phrases went echoing on, since the grotesque memories kept renewing themselves with ever heightened intensity and in ever fuller, more painfully squalid detail, the laughter continued, irrepressibly. The story of Dante and Beatrice told by Hans Andersen! Tears of hysterical merriment ran down her cheeks; she was breathless, and the muscles of her throat were contracted in a kind of agonizing cramp. But still she went on laughing – was utterly unable to stop; it was as though she were possessed by a demon. Luckily, she was alone in the compartment. People would have taken her for a mad-woman.

In the cab, on the way to Hugh's flat – *her* flat too, in spite of Dante and Beatrice and Hans Andersen – she wondered whether he'd have gone to bed already, and just how upset he'd be to see her. She hadn't warned him of her arrival; he would be unprepared to receive her, unbraced against the shock of her grossly physical presence. Poor old Hugh! she thought with a derisive pity. Enjoying his private and invisible fun, like Dante with his phantom, and then having to suffer the trampling intrusion of Signora Alighieri! But tonight, she realized, as she stood at last before the door of the flat, looking in her bag for the latch-key, that invisible solitude of his had already been invaded. Somebody was playing the piano; there was a sound of laughter and voices. Hugh must be having a party. And all at once Helen saw herself making a dramatic entrance like Banquo's ghost, and was delighted by the vision. The reading of that article had momentarily transposed her entire being into the key of laughter. Everything was a vast, extravagant, savage joke – or if it wasn't already, should be made so. It was with a tingling sense of excited anticipation that she opened the door and silently slipped into the hall. An assortment of strange hats hung on the pegs, lay on the chairs – a couple of rich hats, she noticed, very new and shapely, and the rest deformed, and ancient; hats, one could see, of the intellectual poor. There were some letters on the marble-topped table; she bent down by mere force of habit to look at them, and found that one was addressed to her – from Anthony, she recognized; and that too was a joke. Did he seriously imagine that she would read his letters? Enormous ass! She popped the envelope unopened into her bag, then tiptoed along the passage to her room. How tidy it was! How dead! Like a family vault under dust-sheets. She took off her coat and hat, washed, combed her hair, made up her face, then, as silently as she had come, crept back to the hall and stood at the door of the sitting-room, trying to guess by the sound of their voices who were the guests. Beppo Bowles, for one; that giggle, those squeaks and fizzlings were unmistakable. And Mark Staithes. And then a voice she wasn't sure of, and another, very soft and confidential, that must be old Croyland's. And who

was that ridiculous foreigner who spoke so slowly and ponder-
ously, all on one note? She stood there at the door for a long
minute, then very gently turned the handle, drew the door
gradually open, and without a sound edged into the room.
Nobody had noticed her. Mark Staithes was seated at the piano,
with Beppo, a Beppo fatter than ever, she noticed, and balder
and more nervously agitated, and – yes, beard and all! – old
Croyland, standing one on either side of him, leaning on the
instrument and looking down at him while he spoke. Hugh
was on the sofa near the fireplace, with the owner of the voice
she hadn't recognized, but who turned out to be Caldwell, the
publisher – the publisher, of course, of *The Invisible Lover*, she
reflected, and had great difficulty in checking another uprush
of mirth. With them was a young man she had never seen before
– a young man with very pale flaxen hair and a ruddy open face
that wore at the moment an expression of almost child-like
seriousness. His, it was evident, had been the foreign accent –
German, she supposed.

But now the moment had come.

'Good evening,' she called, and stepped forward.

They were all startled; but as for poor Hugh – he jumped as
though someone had fired a cannon in his ear. And after the
first fright, what an expression of appalled dismay! Irresistibly
comic!

'Well, Hugh,' she said.

He looked up into her laughing face, unable to speak. Ever
since the first laudatory notices of his book had begun to come
in, he had been feeling so strong, so blissfully secure. And now
here was Helen – come to humiliate him, come to bear shameful
witness against him.

'I didn't expect,' he managed to mumble incoherently. 'I
mean, why did you ...?'

But Caldwell, who had a reputation for after-dinner speaking
to keep up, interrupted him. Raising the glass he was holding,
'To the Muse,' he called out. 'The Muse and also – I don't think
it's an indiscretion if I say so – also the heroine of our masterpiece.' Charmed by the felicity of his own phrasing, he beamed
at Helen; then, turning to Hugh with a gesture of affectionate
proprietorship, he patted him on the shoulder. 'You must drink

too, old man. It's not a compliment to you – not this time.' And he uttered a rich chuckle.

Hugh did as he was told and, averting his eyes, took a gulp of whisky-and-soda.

'Thank you, thank you,' cried Helen. The laughter was seething within her, like water in a kettle. She gave one hand to Caldwell and the other to Hugh. 'I can't tell you how thrilled I was,' she went on. 'Dante and Beatrice by Hans Andersen – it sounds too delicious.'

Blushing, Hugh tried to protest. 'That frightful article ...'

Cutting him short, 'But why did you keep it up your sleeve?' she asked.

Yes why, why? Hugh was thinking; and that he had been mad to publish the book without first showing it to Helen. He had always wanted to show it to her – and always, at the last moment, found the task too difficult, too embarrassing. But the desire to publish had remained with him, had grown stronger, until at last, senselessly, he had taken the manuscript to Caldwell and, after its acceptance, arranged with him that it should appear while Helen was out of the country. As though that would prevent her knowing anything about it! Madness, madness! And the proof that he had been mad was her presence here tonight, with that strange wild smile on her face, that brightness in the eyes. An uncalculating recklessness was one of the child-beloved's most characteristic and engaging traits; she was a celestial *enfant terrible*. But in the real Helen this recklessness seemed almost fiendish. She was capable of doing anything, absolutely anything.

'Why *did* you?' she insisted.

He made a vague apologetic noise.

'You ought to have told me you were Dante Andersen. I'd have tried to live up to you. Beatrice and the Little Match Girl rolled into one. Good evening, Beppo! and Mark!' They had come over from the piano to greet her. 'And, Mr Croyland, how are you?'

Mr Croyland gave a perfect performance of an old gentleman greeting a lovely young woman – benevolently, yet with a touch of playfulness, an attenuated echo of gallantry.

'Such an unexpected enchantment,' he breathed in the soft,

deliberately ecstatic voice he ordinarily reserved for describing *quattrocento* paintings or for addressing the celebrated or the very rich. Then, with a gesture that beautifully expressed an impulsive outburst of affection, Mr Croyland sandwiched her hand between both of his. They were very pale, soft hands, almost gruesomely small and dainty. By comparison, it seemed to Helen that her own brown hand was like a peasant's. Mr Croyland's silvery and prophetic beard parted in a smile that ought to have been the gracious confirmation of his words and gestures, but which, with its incongruous width and the sudden ferocity of all its large and yellowing teeth, seemed instead to deny all reality to the old gentleman's exquisite refinement of manner. That smile belonged to the Mr Croyland who had traded so profitably in the Old Masters; the little white hands and their affectionate gestures, the soft, ecstatic voice and its heartfelt words, were the property of that other, that ethereal Croyland who only cared about Art.

Helen disengaged her hand. 'Did you ever see those china mugs, Mr Croyland,' she asked, 'you who know Italy so well? The ones they sell at Montecatini for drinking the purgative waters out of? White, with an inscription in golden letters: *Io son Beatrice che ti faccio andare.*'

'But what an outrage!' Mr Croyland exclaimed, and lifted his small hands in horror.

'But it's the sort of joke I really enjoy. Particularly now that Beatrice is really me ...' Becoming aware that the flaxen-haired young man was standing at attention about a yard to the west of her, evidently trying to attract her notice, Helen interrupted herself and turned towards him, holding out her hand.

The young man took it, bowed stiffly from the waist and, saying 'Giesebrecht', firmly squeezed it.

Laughing (it was another joke), Helen answered, 'Ledwidge'; then, as an afterthought, '*geboren* Amberley.'

Nonplussed by this unexpected gambit, the young man bowed again in silence.

Staithes intervened to explain that Giesebrecht was his dis-covery. A refugee from Germany. Not because of his nose, he added as (taking pity on poor old Hugh) he drew her con-fidentially out of the group assembled round the sofa; not because of his nose – because of his politics. Aryan, but communist – ardently and all along the line.

'He believes that as soon as all incomes are equalized, men will stop being cruel. Also that all power will automatically find itself in the hands of the best people. And he's absolutely convinced that nobody who obtains power will be capable of even wishing to abuse it.' Staithes shook his head. 'One doesn't know whether to admire and envy or to thank God for not having made one such an ass. And to complicate matters, he's such a thoroughly good ass. An ass with the moral qualities of a saint. Which is why he's such an admirable propagandist. Saintliness is almost as good as sex-appeal.' He pulled up a chair for Helen, and himself sat down again at the piano and began to play the first few bars of Beethoven's *Für Elise*; then broke off and, turning back to her, 'The trouble,' he resumed, 'is that *nothing* works. Not faith, not intelligence, not saintliness, not even villainy – nothing. Faith's just organized and directed stupidity. It may remove a mountain or two by dint of mere obstinate butting; but it's blinkered, it can't see that if you move the mountains, you don't destroy them, you merely shove them from one place to another. You need intelligence to see that; but intelligence isn't much good because people can't feel enthusiastic about it; it's at the mercy of the first Hitler or Mussolini that comes along – of anyone who can rouse enthusiasm; and one can rouse enthusiasm for *any* cause however idiotic and criminal.'

Helen was looking across the room. 'I suppose his hair's naturally that colour?' she said, more to herself than to her companion. Then, turning back to Staithes, 'And what about saintliness?' she asked.

'Well, look at history,' he answered.

'I don't know any.'

'Of course not. But I take it that you've heard of someone called Jesus? And occasionally, no doubt, you read the papers? Well, put two and two together, the morning's news and the saint, and draw your own conclusions.'

Helen nodded. 'I've drawn them.'

'If saintliness were enough to save the world,' he went on, 'then obviously the world would have been saved long ago.

Dozens of times. But saintliness can exist without intelligence. And though it's attractive, it isn't more attractive than lots of other things – good food, for example, comfort, going to bed with people, bullying, feeling superior.'

Laughing (for this also was laughable), 'It looks,' said Helen, 'as if there were nothing to do but throw up everything and become an invisible lover.' She helped herself to a sandwich and a tumbler of white wine from the tray.

The group at the other end of the room had disintegrated, and Beppo and Mr Croyland were drifting back towards the piano. Staithes smiled at them and, picking up the thread of the argument that Helen's arrival had interrupted, 'Alternatively,' he said, 'one might become an aesthete.'

'You use the word as though it were an insult,' Beppo protested with the emphatic peevishness that had grown upon him with age. Life was treating him badly – making him balder, making him stouter, making young men more and more reluctant to treat him as their contemporary, making sexual successes increasingly difficult of achievement, making that young German of Staithes's behave almost rudely to him. 'Why should one be ashamed of living for beauty?'

The thought of Beppo living for beauty – living for it with his bulging waistcoat and the tight wide seat of his check trousers and his bald crown and Florentine page's curls – almost made Helen choke over her wine.

From the depths of his armchair, '"Glory be to God for *dappled* things",' murmured Mr Croyland. 'I've been re-reading Father Hopkins lately. So poignant! Like a *dagger*. "What lovely behaviour of silk-sack clouds!"' He sighed, he pensively shook his head. 'They're among the things that wound one with their loveliness. Wound and yet sustain, make life liveable.'

There was a cathedral silence.

Then, making an effort to keep the laughter out of her voice, 'Be an angel, Beppo,' said Helen, 'and give me some more of that hock.'

Mr Croyland sat remote, behind half-closed eyelids, the inhabitant of a higher universe.

When the clinking of the glasses had subsided, '"Ripeness is all",' he quoted. '"That sober certainty of waking bliss."

Waking,' he insisted. 'Piercingly conscious. And then, of course, there are pictures – the Watteaus at Dresden, and Bellini's *Transfiguration*, and those Raphael portraits at the Pitti. Buttresses to shore up the soul. And certain philosophies, too. Zarathustra, the Symposium.' He waved his little hand. 'One would be lost without them – lost!'

'And, with them, I take it, you're saved?' said Mark from his seat at the piano; and, without waiting for an answer, 'I wish *I* were,' he went on. 'But there seems to be so little substance in it all. Even in the little that's intrinsically substantial. For of course most thinking has never been anything but silly. And as for Art, as for literature – well, look at the museums and the libraries. *Look* at them! Ninety-nine per cent of nonsense and mere rubbish.'

'But the Greeks,' Mr Croyland protested, 'the Florentines, the Chinese ...' He sketched in the air an exquisitely graceful gesture, as though he were running his fingers over the flanks of a Sung jar, round the cup-shaped navel of a High Renaissance water-nymph. Subtly, with what was meant to be the expression of a Luini madonna, he smiled; but always, through the opening fur, his large yellow teeth showed ferociously, rapaciously – even when he talked about the Schifanoia frescoes, even when he whispered, as though it were an Orphic secret, the name of Vermeer of Delft.

But nonsense, Staithes insisted, almost invariably nonsense and rubbish. And most of what wasn't nonsense or rubbish was only just ordinarily good. 'Like what you or I could do with a little practice,' he explained. 'And if one knows oneself – the miserable inept little self that can yet accomplish such feats – well, really, one can't be bothered to take the feats very seriously.'

Mr Croyland, it was evident from his frown, didn't think of his own self in quite this spirit.

'Not but what one can enjoy the stuff for all kinds of irrevelant reasons,' Staithes admitted. 'For its ingenuity, for example, if one's in any way a technician or an interpreter. Steady progressions in the bass, for example, while the right hand is modulating apparently at random. Invariably delightful! But then, so's carpentry. No; ultimately it isn't interesting, that ordinarily good stuff. However great the accomplishment or the talent. Ultimately it's without value; it differs from the bad only in degree. Composing like Brahms, for example – what is it, after all, but a vastly more elaborate and intellectual way of composing like Meyerbeer? Whereas the best Beethoven is as far beyond the best Brahms as it's beyond the worst Meyerbeer. There's a difference in kind. One's in another world.'

'Another world,' echoed Mr Croyland in a religious whisper. 'But that's just what I've been trying to get you to admit. With the highest art one enters another world.'

Beppo fizzled with emphatic agreement.

'A world, Mr Croyland insisted, 'of gods and angels.'

'Don't forget the invisible lovers,' said Helen, who was finding, as she drank her white wine, that everything was becoming more and more uproariously amusing.

Mr Croyland ignored the interruption. 'A next world,' he went on. 'The great artists carry you up to *heaven*.'

'But they never allow you to stay there,' Mark Staithes objected. 'They give you just a taste of the next world, then let you fall back, flop, into the mud. Marvellous while it lasts. But the time's so short. And even while they've actually got me in heaven, I catch myself asking: Is that all? Isn't there anything more, anything futher? The other world isn't other enough. Even *Macbeth*, even the Mass in D, even the El Greco *Assumption*.' He shook his head. 'They used to satisfy me. They used to be an escape and a support. But now ... now I find myself wanting something more, something heavenlier, something less human. Yes, less human,' he repeated. Then the flayed face twisted itself up into an agonized smile. 'I feel rather like Nurse Cavell about it,' he added. 'Painting, music, literature, thought – they're not enough.'

'What is enough, then?' asked Beppo. 'Politics? Science? Moneymaking?'

Staithes shook his head after every suggestion.

'But what else is there?' asked Beppo.

Still anatomically smiling, Mark looked at him for a moment in silence, then said, 'Nothing – absolutely nothing.'

'Speak for yourself,' said Mr Croyland. 'They're enough

for me.' He dropped his eyelids once more and retired into spiritual fastnesses.

Looking at him, Staithes was moved by the sudden angry desire to puncture the old gentleman's balloon-like complacency – to rip a hole in that great bag of cultural gas, by means of which Mr Croyland contrived to hoist his squalid traffickings sky-high into the rarefied air of pure aesthetics. 'And what about death? You find them adequate against death?' he insisted in a tone that had suddenly become brutally inquisitorial. He paused, and for a moment the old man was enveloped in a horribly significant silence – the silence of those who in the presence of a victim or an incurable tactfully ignore the impending doom. 'Adequate against life, for that matter,' Mark Staithes went on, relenting; 'against life in any of its more unpleasant or dangerous aspects.'

'Such as dogs falling on one out of aeroplanes!' Helen burst out laughing.

'But what *are* you talking about?' cried Beppo.

'Father Hopkins won't keep dogs off,' she went on breathlessly 'I agree with *you*, Mark. A good umbrella, any day ...'

Mr Croyland rose to his feet. 'I must go to bed,' he said. 'And so should you, my dear.' The little white hand upon her shoulder was benevolent, almost apostolic. 'You're tired after your journey.'

'You mean, you think I'm drunk,' Helen answered, wiping her eyes. 'Well, perhaps you're right. Gosh,' she added, 'how nice it is to laugh for a change!'

When Mr Croyland was gone, and Beppo with him, Staithes turned towards her. 'You're in a queer state, Helen.'

'I'm amused,' she explained.

'What by?'

'By everything. But it began with Dante; Dante and Hans Andersen. If you'd been married to Hugh, you'd know why *that* was so extraordinarily funny. Imagine Europa if the bull had turned out after all to be Narcissus!'

'I don't think you'd better talk so loud,' said Staithes, looking across the room to where, with an expression on his face of hopeless misery, Hugh was pretending to listen to an animated discussion between Caldwell and the young German.

Helen also looked round for a moment; then turned back with a careless shrug of the shoulders. 'If *he* says he's invisible, why shouldn't *I* say I'm inaudible?' Her eyes brightened again with laughter. 'I shall write a book called *The Inaudible Mistress*. A woman who says exactly what she thinks about her lovers while they're making love to her. But they can't hear her. Not a word.' She emptied her glass and refilled it.

'And what does she say about them?'

'The truth, of course. Nothing but the truth. That the romantic Don Juan is just a crook. Only I'm afraid that in reality she wouldn't find that out till afterwards. Still, one might be allowed a bit of poetic licence – make the *esprit d'escalier* happen at the same time as the romantic affair. The moonlight, and "My darling", and "I adore you", and those extraordinary sensations – and at the same moment "You're nothing but a sneakthief, nothing but a low blackguardly swindler". And then there'd be the spiritual lover – Hans Dante, in fact.' She shook her head. 'Talk of Krafft-Ebing!'

'But what does she say to him?'

'What indeed!' Helen took a gulp of wine. 'Luckily she's inaudible. We'd better skip that chapter and come straight to the epicurean sage. With the sage, she doesn't have to be quite so obscure. "You think you're a man, because you happen not to be impotent". That's what she says to him. "But in fact you're not a man. You're sub-human. In spite of your sageness – because of it even. Worse than the crook in some ways." And then, bang, like a sign from heaven, down comes the dog!'

'But what dog?'

'Why, the dog Father Hopkins can't protect you from. The sort of dog that bursts like a bomb when you drop it out of an aeroplane. Bang!' The laughing excitement seethed and bubbled within her, seeking expression, seeking an outlet; and the only possible assuagement was through some kind of outrage, some violence publicly done to her own and other people's feelings. 'It almost fell on Anthony and me,' she went on, finding a strange relief in speaking thus openly and hilariously about the unmentionable event. 'On the roof of his house it was. And we had no clothes on. Like the Garden of

Eden. And then, out of the blue, down came that dog – and exploded, I tell you, literally exploded.' She threw out her hands in a violent gesture. 'Dog's blood from head to foot. We were drenched – but *drenched*! In spite of which this imbecile goes and writes me a letter.' She opened her bag and produced it. 'Imagining I'd read it, I suppose. As though nothing had happened, as though we were still in the Garden of Eden. I always told him he was a fool. There!' She handed the letter to Staithes. 'You open it and see what the idiot has to say. Something witty, no doubt; something airy and casual; humorously wondering why I took it into my funny little head to go away.' Then, noticing that Mark was still holding the letter unopened. 'But why don't you read it?' she asked.

'Do you really want me to?'

'Of course. Read it aloud. Read it with expression.' She rolled the *r* derisively.

'Very well, then.' He tore open the envelope and unfolded the thin sheets. '"I went to look for you at the hotel,"' he read out slowly, frowning over the small and hurried script. '"You were gone – and it was like a kind of death."'

'Ass!' commented Helen.

'"It's probably too late, probably useless; but I feel I must try to tell you in this letter some of the things I meant to say to you, yesterday evening, in words. In one way it's easier – for I'm inept when it comes to establishing a purely *personal* contact with another human being. But in another way, it's much more difficult; for these written words will be just words and no more, will come to you, floating in a void, unsupported, without the life of my physical presence."'

Helen gave a snort of contemptuous laughter. 'As though *that* would have been a recommendation!' She drank some more wine.

'"Well, what I wanted to tell you,"' Staithes read on, '"was this: that suddenly (it was like a conversion, like an inspiration) while you were kneeling there yesterday on the roof, after that horrible thing had happened . . ."'

'He means the dog,' said Helen. 'Why can't he say so?'

'". . . suddenly I realized . . ."' Mark Staithes broke off. 'Look here,' he said, 'I really can't go on.'

'Why not? I insist on you going on,' she cried excitedly.

He shook his head. 'I've got no right!'

'But I've given you the right.'

'Yes, I know. But he hasn't.'

'What has he got to do with it? Now that I've received the letter ...'

'But it's a love-letter.'

'A love-letter?' Helen repeated incredulously, then burst out laughing. 'That's too good!' she cried. 'That's really sublime! Here, give it to me.' She snatched the letter out of his hand. 'Where are we? Ah, here! "... kneeling on the roof after that horrible thing had happened, suddenly I realized that I'd been living a kind of outrageous lie towards you!"' She declaimed the words rhetorically and to the accompaniment of florid gesticulations. '"I realized that in spite of all the elaborate pretence that it was just a kind of detached irresponsible amusement, I really loved you." He really lo-o-oved me,' she repeated, drawing the word into a grotesque caricature of itself. 'Isn't that wonderful? He really lo-o-oved me.' Then, turning round in her chair, 'Hugh!' she called across the room.

'Helen, be quiet!'

But the desire, the need to consummate the outrage was urgent within her.

She shook off the restraining hand that Staithes had laid on her arm, shouted Hugh's name again and, when they all turned towards her, 'I just wanted to tell you he really lo-o-oved me,' she said, waving the letter.

'Oh, for God's sake shut up!'

'I certainly won't shut up,' she retorted, turning back to Mark. 'Why shouldn't I tell Hugh the good news? He'll be delighted, seeing how much he lo-o-oves me himself. Don't you, Hughie?' She swung back again, and her face was flushed and brilliant with excitement. 'Don't you?' Hugh made no answer, but sat there pale and speechless, looking at the floor.

'Of course you do,' she answered for him. 'In spite of all appearances to the contrary. Or rather,' she emended, uttering a little laugh, 'in spite of all disappearances – seeing that it was always invisible, that love of yours. Oh yes, Hughie darling, definitely invisible.. But still ... still, in spite of all disappearances to the contrary, you do lo-o-ove me, don't you? Don't you?' she insisted, trying to force him to answer her, 'don't you?'

Hugh rose to his feet and, without speaking a word, almost ran out of the room.

'Hugh!' Caldwell shouted after him, 'Hugh!' There was no answer. Caldwell looked round at the others. 'I think perhaps one ought to see that he's all right,' he said, with the maternal solicitude of a publisher who sees a first-rate literary property rushing perhaps towards suicide. 'One never knows.' And jumping up he hurried after Hugh. The door slammed.

There was a moment's silence. Then, startlingly, Helen broke into laughter. 'Don't be alarmed, Herr Giesebrecht,' she said, turning to the young German. 'It's just a little bit of English family life. *Die Familie im Wohnzimmer*, as we used to learn at school. *Was tut die Mutter? Die mutter spielt Klavier. Und was tut der Vater? Der Vater sitzt in einem Lehnstuhl und raucht seine Pfeife*. Just that, Herr Giesebrecht, no more, Just a typical bourgeois family.'

'Bourgeois,' the young man repeated, and nodded gravely. 'You say better than you know.'

'Do I?'

'You are a wictim,' he went on, very slowly, and separating word from word, 'a wictim of capitalist society. It is full of wices ...'

Helen threw back her head and laughed again more loudly than before; then, controlling herself with an effort, 'You mustn't think I'm laughing at you,' she gasped. 'I think you're being sweet to me – extraordinarily decent. And probably you're quite right about capitalist society. Only somehow at this particular moment – I don't know why – it seemed rather ... rather...' The laughter broke out once more. 'I'm sorry.'

'We must be going,' said Mark, and rose from his chair. The young German also got up and came across the room towards them. 'Good night, Helen.'

'Good night, Mark. Good night, Mr Giesebrecht. Come and see me again, will you? I'll behave better next time.'

He returned her smile and bowed. 'I will come whenever you wish,' he said.

CHAPTER TWENTY-TWO

December 8th 1926

MARK lived in a dingy house off the Fulham Road. Dark brown brick with terra-cotta trimmings; and, within, patterned linoleum; bits of red Axminster carpet; wallpapers of ochre sprinkled with bunches of cornflowers, of green, with crimson roses; fumed oak chairs and tables; rep curtains; bamboo stands supporting glazed blue pots. The hideousness, Anthony reflected, was so complete, so absolutely unrelieved, that it could only have been intentional. Mark must deliberately have chosen the ugliest surroundings he could find. To punish himself, no doubt – but why, for what offence?

'Some beer?'

Anthony nodded.

The other opened a bottle, filled a single glass; but himself did not drink.

'You still play, I see,' said Anthony, pointing in the direction of the upright piano.

'A little,' Mark had to admit. 'It's a consolation.'

The fact that the Matthew Passion, for example, the Hammer-klavier Sonata, had had human authors was a source of hope. It was just conceivable that humanity might some day and somehow be made a little more John-Sebastian-like. If there were no Well-Tempered Clavichord, why should one bother even to wish for revolutionary change?

'Turning one kind of common humanity into common humanity of a slightly different kind – well, if that's all that revolution can do, the game isn't worth the candle.'

Anthony protested. For a sociologist it was the most fascinating of all games.

'To watch or to play?'

'To watch, of course.'

A spectacle bottomlessly comic in its grotesqueness, endlessly varied. But looking closely, one could detect the uniformities under the diversity, the fixed rules of the endlessly shifting game.

'A revolution to transform common humanity into common humanity of another variety. You will find it horrifying. But that's just what I'd like to live long enough to see. Theory being put to the test of practice. To detect, after your catastrophic reform of everything, the same old uniformities working themselves out in a slightly different way – I can't imagine anything more satisfying. Like logically inferring the existence of a new planet and then discovering it with a telescope. As for producing more John Sebastians . . .' He shrugged his shoulders. 'You might as well imagine that revolution will increase the number of Siamese twins.'

That was the chief difference between literature and life. In books, the proportion of exceptional to commonplace people is high; in reality, very low.

'Books are opium,' said Mark.

'Precisely. That's why it's doubtful if there'll ever be such a thing as proletarian literature. Even proletarian books will deal with exceptional proletarians. And exceptional proletarians are no more proletarian than exceptional bourgeois are bourgeois. Life's so ordinary that literature has to deal with the exceptional. Exceptional talent, power, social position, wealth. Hence those geniuses of fiction, those leaders and dukes and millionaires. People who are completely conditioned by circumstances – one can be desperately sorry for them; but one can't find their lives very dramatic. Drama begins where there's freedom of choice. And freedom of choice begins when social or psychological conditions are exceptional. That's why the inhabitants of imaginative literature have always been recruited from the pages of *Who's Who*.'

'But do you really think that people with money or power are free?'

'Freer than the poor, at any rate. Less completely conditioned by matter and other people's wills.'

Mark shook his head. 'You don't know my father,' he said. 'Or my disgusting brothers.'

At Bulstrode, Anthony remembered, it was always, 'My pater says . . .' or 'My frater at Cambridge . . .'

'The whole vile brood of Staitheses,' Mark went on.

He described the Staithes who was now a Knight Commander

of St Michael and St George and a Permanent Under-Secretary. Pleased as Punch with it all, and serenely conscious of his own extraordinary merits, adoring himself for being such a great man.

'As though there were any real difficulty in getting where he's got! Anything in the least creditable about that kind of piddling little conquest!' Mark made a flayed grimace of contemptuous disgust. 'He thinks he's a marvel.'

And the other Staitheses, the Staitheses of the younger generation – they also thought that they were marvels. There was one of them at Delhi, heroically occupied in bullying Indians who couldn't stand up for themselves. And the other was on the Stock Exchange and highly successful. Successful as what? As a cunning exploiter of ignorance and greed and the insanity of gamblers and misers. And on top of everything the man prided himself on being an amorist, a professional Don Juan.

(Why the poor devil shouldn't be allowed to have a bit of fun, Anthony was unable, as he sipped his beer, to imagine.)

One of the boys! One of the dogs! A dog among bitches – what a triumph!

'And you call them free,' Mark concluded. 'But how can a climber be free? He's tied to his ladder.'

'But social ladders,' Anthony objected, 'become broader as they rise. At the bottom, you can only just get your foot on to them. At the top the rungs are twenty yards across.'

'Well, perhaps it's a wider perch than the bank clerk's,' Mark admitted. 'But not wide enough for me. And not high enough; above all, not clean enough.'

The rage they had been in when he enlisted during the war as a private! Feeling that he'd let the family down. The creatures were incapable of seeing that, if you had the choice, it was more decent to elect to be a private than a staff lieutenant.

'Turds to the core,' he said. 'So they can't think anything but turdish thoughts. And above all, they can't conceive of anyone else thinking differently. Turd calls to turd; and, when it's answered by non-turd, it's utterly at a loss.'

And when the war was over, there was that job his father had taken such pains to find for him in the City – with Lazarus and Coit, no less! – just waiting for him to step into the moment he was demobilized. A job with almost unlimited prospects for a young man with brains and energy – for a Staithes, in a word. 'A five-figure income by the time you're fifty,' his father had insisted almost lyrically, and had been really hurt and grieved, as well as mortally offended, furiously angry, when Mark replied that he had no intention of taking it.

' "But why not?" the poor old turd kept asking. "Why not?" And simply couldn't see that it was just because it was so good that I couldn't take his job. So unfairly good! So ignobly good! He just couldn't see it. According to his ideas, I ought to have rushed at it, headlong, like all the Gadarene swine rolled into one. Instead of which I returned him his cow-pat and went to Mexico – to look after a coffee *finca*.'

'But did you know anything about coffee?'

'Of course not. That was one of the attractions of the job.' He smiled. 'When I did know something about it, I came back to see if there was anything doing here.'

'And is there anything doing?'

The other shrugged his shoulders. God only knew. One joined the Party, one distributed literature, one financed pressure-groups out of the profits on synthetic carnations, one addressed meetings and wrote articles. And perhaps it was all quite useless. Perhaps, on the contrary, the auspicious moment might some day present itself . . .

'And then what?' asked Anthony.

'Ah, that's the question. It'll be all right at the beginning. Revolution's delightful in the preliminary stages. So long as it's a question of getting rid of the people at the top. But afterwards, if the thing's a success – what then? More wireless sets, more chocolates, more beauty parlours, more girls with better contraceptives.' He shook his head. 'The moment you give people the chance to be piggish, they take it – thankfully. That freedom you were talking about just now, the freedom at the top of the social ladder – it's just the licence to be a pig; or alternatively a prig, a self-satisfied pharisee like my father. Or else both at once, like my precious brother. Pig and prig simultaneously. In Russia they haven't yet had the chance to be pigs. Circumstances have forced them to be ascetics. But suppose their economic experiment succeeds; suppose a time comes when they're all prosperous – what's to prevent them turning into Babbitts? Millions and millions of soft, piggish Babbitts, ruled by a small minority of ambitious Staitheses.'

Anthony smiled. 'A new phase of the game played according to the old unchanging rules.'

'I'm horribly afraid you're right,' said the other. 'It's orthodox Marxism, of course. Behaviour and modes of thoughts are the outcome of economic circumstances. Reproduce Babbitt's circumstances and you can't help reproducing his manners and customs. Christ!' He rose, walked to the piano and, drawing up a chair, sat down in front of it, 'Let's try to get *that* taste out of our mouths.' He held his large bony hands poised for a moment above the keyboard; then began to play Bach's Toccata and Fugue in D. They were in another universe, a world where Babbitts and Staitheses didn't exist, were inconceivable.

Mark had played for only a minute or two when the door opened and an elderly woman, thin and horse-faced, in a brown silk dress and wearing round her neck an old diseased brown fur, entered the room. She walked on tiptoe, acting in elaborate pantomime the very personification of silence, but in the process produced an extraordinary volume and variety of disturbing noises – creaking of shoes, rustling of silk, glassy clinkings of bead necklaces, jingling of the silver objects suspended by little chains from the waist. Mark went on playing without turning his head. Embarrassed, Anthony rose and bowed. The horse-faced creature waved him back to his place, and cautiously, in a final prolonged explosion of noise, sat down on the sofa.

'Exquisite!' she cried when the final chord had been struck. 'Play us some more, Mark.'

But Mark got up, shaking his head. 'I want to introduce you to Miss Pendle,' he said to Anthony; and to the old woman, 'Anthony Beavis was at Bulstrode with me,' he explained.

Anthony took her hand. She gave him a smile. The teeth, which were false ones and badly fitting, were improbably too white and bright. 'So you were at Bulstrode with Mark!' she cried. 'Isn't that extraordinary!'

'Extraordinary that we should still be on speaking terms?' said Mark.

'No, no,' said Miss Pendle, and with a playfulness that

Anthony found positively ghoulish, gave him a little slap on the arm. 'You know exactly what I mean. He always was like that, Mr Beavis, even when he was a boy – do you remember?'

Anthony duly nodded assent.

'So sharp and sarcastic! Even before you knew him at Bulstrode. Shocking!' She flashed her false teeth at Mark in a sparkle of loving mock-reprobation. 'He was my first pupil, you know,' she went on confidentially. 'And I was his first teacher.'

Anthony rose gallantly to the occasion. 'Let me congratulate Mark,' he said, 'and condole with you.'

Miss Pendle looked at Mark. 'Do you think I need his condolences?' she asked, almost archly, like a young girl, coquettishly fishing for compliments.

Mark did not answer, only smiled and shrugged his shoulders. 'I'll go and make some tea,' he said. 'You'd like tea, wouldn't you Penny?' Miss Pendle nodded, and he rose and left the room.

Anthony was wondering rather uncomfortably what he should say to this disquietingly human old hag, when Miss Pendle turned towards him. 'He's wonderful, Mark is; really wonderful.' The false teeth flashed, the words came gushingly with an incongruously un-equine vehemence. Anthony felt himself writhing with an embarrassed distaste. 'Nobody knows how kind he is,' she went on. 'He doesn't like it told; but I don't mind – I want people to know.' She nodded so emphatically that the beads of her necklace rattled. 'I was ill last year,' she went on. Her savings had gone, she couldn't get another job. In despair, she had written to some of her old employers, Sir Michael Staithes among them. 'Sir Michael sent me five pounds,' she said. 'That kept me going for a bit. Then I had to write again. He said he couldn't do anything more. But he mentioned the matter to Mark. And what do you think Mark did?' She looked at Anthony in silence, a horse transfigured, with an expression at once of tenderness and triumph and her red-lidded brown eyes full of tears.

'What did he do?' asked Anthony.

'He came to me where I was staying – I had a room in Camberwell then – he came and he took me away with him.

Straight away, the moment I could get my things packed up, and brought me here. I've kept house for him ever since. What do you think of that, Mr Beavis?' she asked. Her voice trembled and she had to wipe her eyes; but she was still triumphant. 'What do you think of that?'

Anthony really didn't know what to think of it; but said, meanwhile, that it was wonderful.

'Wonderful,' the horse repeated, approvingly. 'That's exactly what it is. But you mustn't tell him I told you. He'd be furious with me. He's like that text in the Gospel about not letting your left hand know what your right hand is doing. That's what he's like.' She gave her eyes a final wipe and blew her nose. 'There, I hear him coming,' she said, and, before Anthony could intervene, had jumped up, darted across the room in a storm of rustlings and rattlings, and opened the door. Mark entered, carrying a tray with the tea-things and a plate of mixed biscuits.

Miss Pendle poured out, said she oughtn't to eat anything at this time of night, but, all the same, took a round biscuit with pink sugar icing on it

'Now, tell me what sort of a boy young Master Mark was at Bulstrode,' she said in that playful way of hers. 'Up to all kind of mischief, I'll be bound!' She took another bite at her biscuit.

'He bullied me a good deal,' said Anthony.

Miss Pendle interrupted her quick nibbling to laugh aloud. 'You naughty boy!' she said to Mark; then the jaws started to work again.

'Being so good at football, he had the right to bully me.'

'Yes, you were captain of the eleven, weren't you?'

'I forget,' said Mark.

'He forgets!' Miss Pendle repeated, looking triumphantly at Anthony. 'That's typical of him. He forgets!' She helped herself to a second biscuit, pushing aside the plain ones to select another with icing on it, and began to nibble once more with the intense and concentrated passion of those whose only sensual pleasures have been the pleasures of the palate.

When she had gone to bed, the two men sat down again by the fire. There was a long silence.

'She's rather touching,' said Anthony at last.

For some time Mark made no comment. Then, 'A bit too touching,' he brought out.

Anthony looked into his face and saw there a demonstration of the anatomy of sardonic irony. There was another silence. The clock, which was supported by two draped nymphs in gilded bronze, ticked from its place among the imitation Dresden figures that thronged the shelves of the elaborate overmantel. Hideous on purpose, Anthony said to himself, as his eye took in the details of each separate outrage on good taste. And the poor old horse – was she merely the largest, the most monstrous of the knick-knacks? 'I'm surprised,' he said aloud, 'that you don't wear a hair-shirt. Or perhaps you do?' he added.

CHAPTER TWENTY-THREE

June 1st 1934

TONIGHT, at dinner with Mark, saw Helen, for the first time since my return from America.

Consider the meaning of a face. A face can be a symbol, signifying matter which would require volumes for its exposition in successive detail. A vast sum, for the person on whom it acts as a symbol, of feelings and thoughts, of remembered sensations, impressions, judgements, experiences – all rendered synthetically and simultaneously, at a single glance. As she came into the restaurant, it was like the drowning man's instantaneous vision of life. A futile, bad, unsatisfactory life; and a vision charged with regret. All those wrong choices, those opportunities irrevocably missed! And that sad face was not only a symbol, indirectly expressive of *my* history; it was also a directly expressive emblem of hers. A history for whose saddening and embittering quality I was at least in part responsible. If I had accepted the love she wanted to give me, if I had consented to love (for I *could* have loved) in return ... But I preferred to be *free*, for the sake of my *work* – in other words, to remain enslaved in a world where there could be no question of freedom, for the sake of my amusements. I insisted on irresponsible sensuality, rather than love. Insisted, in other words, on her becoming a means to the end of my detached, physical satisfaction and, conversely, of course, on my becoming a means to hers.

Curious how irrelevant appears the fact of having been, technically, 'lovers'! It doesn't qualify her indifference or my feeling. There's a maxim of La Rochefoucauld's about women forgetting the favours they have accorded to past lovers. I used to like it for being cynical; but really it's just a bald statement of the fact that something that's meant to be irrelevant, *i.e.* sensuality, *is* irrelevant. Into my present complex of thoughts, feelings, and memories, physical desire, I find, enters hardly at all. In spite of the fact that my memories are of intense and complete satisfactions. Surprising, the extent to which eroticism is a matter of choice and focus. I don't think much in erotic terms now; but very easily could, if I wished to. Choose to consider individuals in their capacity as potential givers and receivers of pleasure, focus attention on sensual satisfactions: eroticism will become immensely important and great quantities of energy will be directed along erotic channels. Choose a different conception of the individual, another focal range: energy will flow elsewhere and eroticism seem relatively unimportant.

Spent a good part of the evening arguing about peace and social justice. Mark, as sarcastically disagreeable as he knew how to be about Miller and what he called my neo-Jesus avatar. 'If the swine want to rip one another's guts out, let them; anyhow, you can't prevent them. Swine will be swine.' But may become human, I insisted. *Homo non nascitur, fit.* Or rather makes himself out of the ready-made elements and potentialities of man with which he's born.

Helen's was the usual communist argument – no peace or social justice without a preliminary 'liquidation' of capitalists, liberals, and so forth. As though you could use violent, unjust means and achieve peace and justice! Means determine ends; and must be like the ends proposed. Means intrinsically different from the ends proposed achieve ends like themselves, not like those they were meant to achieve. Violence and war will produce a peace and a social organization having the potentialities of more violence and war. The war to end war resulted, as usual, in a peace essentially like war; the revolution to achieve communism, in a hierarchical state where a minority rules by police methods à la Metternich–Hitler–Mussolini, and where the power to oppress in virtue of being rich is replaced by the power to oppress in virtue of being a member of the oligarchy. Peace and social justice, only obtainable by means that are just and pacific. And people will behave justly and pacifically only if they have trained themselves as individuals to do so, even in circumstances where it would be easier to behave violently and unjustly. And the training must be simultaneously physical and mental. Knowledge of how to use the self and of what the self should be used for. Neo-Ignatius and neo-Sandow was Mark's verdict.

Put Mark into a cab and walked, as the night was beautiful, all the way from Soho to Chelsea. Theatres were closing. Helen brightened suddenly to a mood of malevolent high spirits. Commenting in a ringing voice on passers-by. As though we were at the Zoo. Embarrassing, but funny and acute, as when she pointed to the rich young men in top-hats trying to look like the De Reszke Aristocrat, or opening and shutting cigarette-cases in the style of Gerald du Maurier; to the women trying to look like Vogue, or expensive advertisements (for winter cruises or fur coats), head in air, eyelids dropped superciliously – or slouching like screen vamps, with their stomachs stuck out, as though expecting twins. The pitiable models on which people form themselves! Once it was the Imitation of Christ – now of Hollywood.

Were silent when we had left the crowds. Then Helen asked if I were happy. I said, yes – though didn't know if happiness was the right word. More substantial, more complete, more interested, more aware. If not happy exactly, at any rate having greater potentialities for happiness. Another silence. Then, 'I thought I could never see you again, because of that dog. Then Ekki came, and the dog was quite irrelevant. And now he's gone, it's still irrelevant. For another reason. Everything's irrelevant, for that matter. Except communism.' But that was an afterthought – an expression of piety, uttered by force of habit. I said our ends were the same, the means adopted, different. For her, end justified means; for me, means the end. Perhaps, I said, one day she would see the importance of the means.

June 3rd 1934

At today's lesson with Miller found myself suddenly a step forward in my grasp of the theory and practice of the technique. To learn proper use one must first inhibit all improper uses of the self. Refuse to be hurried into gaining ends by the equivalent (in personal, psycho-physiological terms) of violent revolution; inhibit this tendency, concentrate on the means whereby the end is to be achieved; then act. This process entails knowing good and bad use – knowing them apart. By the 'feel'. Increased awareness and increased power of control result. Awareness and control: trivialities take on new significance. Indeed, nothing is trivial any more or negligible. Cleaning teeth, putting on shoes – such processes are reduced by habits of bad use to a kind of tiresome non-existence. Become conscious, inhibit, cease to be a greedy end-gainer, concentrate on means: tiresome non-existence turns into absorbingly interesting reality.' In Evans-Wentz's last book on Tibet I find among 'The Precepts of the Gurus' the injunction: 'Constantly retain alertness of consciousness in walking, in sitting, in eating, in sleeping.' An injunction, like most injunctions, unaccompanied by instructions as to the right way of carrying it out. Here, practical instructions accompany injunctions; one is taught how to become aware. And not only that. Also how to perform rightly, instead of wrongly, the activities of which there is awareness. Nor is this all. Awareness and power of control are transferable. Skill acquired in getting to know the muscular aspect of mind – body can be carried over into the exploration of other aspects. There is increasing ability to detect one's motives for any given piece of behaviour, to assess correctly the quality of a feeling, the real significance of a thought. Also, one becomes more clearly and consistently conscious of what's going on in the outside world, and the judgement associated with that heightened consciousness is improved. Control also is transferred. Acquire the art of inhibiting muscular bad use and you acquire thereby the art of inhibiting more complicated trains of behaviour. Not only this : there is prevention as well as cure. Given proper correlation, many occasions for behaving undesirably just don't arise. There is an end, for example, of neurotic anxieties and depressions – whatever the previous history. For note; most infantile and adolescent histories are disastrous : yet only some individuals develop serious neurosis. Those, precisely, in whom use of the self is particularly bad. They succumb because resistance is poor. In practice, neurosis is always associated with some kind of wrong use. (Note the typically bad physical posture of neurotics and lunatics. The stooping back, the muscular tension, the sunken head.) Re-educate. Give back correct physical use. You remove a keystone of the arch constituting the neurotic personality. The neurotic personality collapses. And in its place is built up a personality in which all the habits of physical use are correct. But correct use entails – since body – mind is indivisible except in thought – correct mental use. Most of us are slightly neurotic. Even slight neurosis provides endless occasions for bad behaviour. Teaching of right use gets rid of neurosis – therefore of many occasions for bad behaviour. Hitherto preventive ethics has been thought of as external to individuals. Social and economic reforms carried out with a view to eliminating occasions for bad behaviour. This is important. But not nearly enough. Belief that it is enough makes the social-reform conception of progress nonsensical. The knowledge that it is nonsensical has always given me pleasure. Sticking pins in large, highly inflated balloons – one of the most delightful of amusements. But a bit childish ; and after a time it palls. So how satisfactory to find that there seems to be a way of making sense of the nonsense. A method of achieving progress from within as well as from without. Progress, not only as a citizen, a machine-minder and machine-user, but also as a human being.

Prevention is good ; but can't eliminate the necessity for cure. The power to cure bad behaviour seems essentially similar to the power to cure bad coordination. One learns this last when learning the proper use of self. There is a transference. The power to inhibit and control. It becomes easier to inhibit undesirable impulses. Easier to follow as well as see and approve the better. Easier to put good intentions into practice and be patient, good-tempered, kind, unrapacious, chaste.

CHAPTER TWENTY-FOUR

June 23rd and July 5th 1927

She couldn't afford it; but that didn't matter. Mrs Amberley was used to doing things she couldn't afford. It was really so simple; you just sold a little War Loan, and there you were. There you were with your motor tour in Italy, your nudes by Pascin, your account at Fortnum and Mason. And there, finally, you were in Berkshire, in the most adorable little old house, smelling of pot-pourri, with towering lime trees on the lawn and the downs at your back door, stretching away mile after mile in smooth green nakedness under the sky. She couldn't afford it; but it was so beautiful, so perfect. And after all, what were a hundred and fifty pounds of War Loan? How much did they bring in? About five pounds a year, when the taxes had been paid. And what were five pounds a year? Nothing. Absolutely nothing. And besides, Gerry was going to re-invest her money for her. Her capital might have shrunk; but her income would soon start growing. Next year she would be able to afford it; and so, in anticipation of that happy time, here she was, sitting under the lime trees on the lawn with her guests around her.

Propped up on one elbow, Helen was lying on a rug behind her mother's chair. She was paying no attention to what was being said. The country was so exquisitely beautiful that one really couldn't listen to old Anthony holding forth about the place of machines in history; no, the only thing one could do in such heavenly circumstances was to play with the kitten. What the kitten liked best, she found, was the rug game. You pushed a twig under the corner of the rug, very slowly, till the end reappeared again on the other side, like the head of an animal cautiously peeping out from its burrow. A little way, very suspiciously; and then with a jerk you withdrew it. The animal had taken fright and scuttled back to cover. Then, plucking up its courage, out it came once more, went nosing to the right and left between the grass stems, then retired to finish its meal safely under the rug. Long seconds passed; and suddenly out it popped like a jack-in-the-box, as though it were trying to catch any impending danger unaware, and was back again in a flash. Then once more, very doubtfully and reluctantly – impelled only by brute necessity and against its better judgement – it emerged into the open, conscious, you felt, of being the predestined victim, foreknowing its dreadful fate. And all this time the tabby kitten was following its comings and goings with a bright expressionless ferocity. Each time the twig retired under the rug, he came creeping, with an infinity of precautions, a few inches nearer. Nearer, nearer, and now the moment had come for him to crouch for the final, decisive spring. The green eyes stared with an absurd baleful-ness; the tiny body was so heavily overcharged with a tigerish intensity of purpose that, not the tail only, but the whole hindquarters shook under the emotional pressure. Overhead, meanwhile, the lime trees rustled in a faint wind, the round dapplings of golden light moved noiselessly back and forth across the grass. On the other side of the lawn the herbaceous borders blazed in the sunshine as though they were on fire, and beyond them lay the downs like huge animals, fast asleep, with the indigo shadows of clouds creeping across their flanks. It was all so beautiful, so heavenly, that every now and then Helen simply couldn't stand it any longer, but had to drop the twig and catch up the kitten, and rub her cheek against the silky fur, and whisper meaningless words to him in baby language, and hold him up with ridiculously dangling paws in front of her face, so that their noses almost touched, and stare into those blankly bright green eyes, till at last the helpless little beast began to mew so pathetically that she had to let him go again. 'Poor darling!' she murmured repentantly. 'Did I torture him?' But the torturing had served its purpose; the painful excess of her happiness had overflowed, as it were, and left her at ease, the heavenly beauty was once more support-able. She picked up the twig. Forgivingly, for he had already forgotten everything, the kitten started the game all over again.

The ringing of a bicycle bell made her look up. It was the postman riding up the drive with the afternoon delivery. Helen scrambled to her feet and, taking the kitten with her, walked quickly but, she hoped, inconspicuously towards the house. At the door she met the parlour-maid coming out with the letters. There were two for her. The first she opened was from Joyce, from Aldershot. (She had to smile as she read the address at the head of the paper. 'Joyce is now living at *A-a*ldershot,' her mother would say, lingering over the first syllable of the name with a kind of hollow emphasis and in a tone of slightly shocked incredulity, as though it were really inconceivable that any daughter of hers should find herself at such a place. 'At *A-a*ldershot, my dear.' And she managed to endow that military suburb with the fabulous strangeness of Tibet, the horror and remoteness of darkest Liberia. 'Living at *A-a-a*ldershot – as a mem-sahib.')

Just a line [Helen read, still smiling] to thank you for your sweet letter. I am rather worried by what you say about Mother's taking so many sleeping draughts. They *can't* be good for her. Colin thinks she ought to take more healthy *exercise*. Perhaps you might suggest riding. I have been having riding lessons lately, and it is really *lovely* once you are used to it. We are now quite settled in, and you have no idea how adorable our little house looks now. Colin and I worked like niggers to get things straight, and I must say the results are worth all the trouble. I had to pay a lot of nerve-racking calls; but everybody has been *very* nice to me and I feel quite at home now. Colin sends his love. – Yours,   JOYCE

The other letter – and that was why she had gone to meet the postman – was from Hugh Ledwidge. If the letters had been brought to Mrs Amberley on the lawn; if she had sorted them out, in public ... Helen flushed with imagined shame and anger at the thought of what her mother might have said about that letter from Hugh. In spite of all the people sitting round; or rather because of them. When they were alone, Helen generally got off with a teasing word. But when other people were there, Mrs Amberley would feel inspired by her audience to launch out into elaborate descriptions and commentaries. 'Hugh and Helen,' she would explain, 'they're a mixture between Socrates and Alcibiades and Don Quixote and Dulcinea.' There were moments when she hated her mother. 'It's a case,' said the remembered voice, 'a case of : I could not love thee, dear, so much, loved I not ethnology more.' Helen had had to suffer a great deal on account of those letters.

She tore open the envelope.

Midsummer Day, Helen. But you're too young, I expect, to think much about the significance of special days. You've only been in the world for about seven thousand days altogether; and one has got to have lived through at least ten thousand before one begins to realize that there aren't an indefinite number of them and that you can't do exactly what you want with them. I've been here more than thirteen thousand days, and the end's visible, the boundless possibilities have narrowed down. One must cut according to one's cloth; and one's cloth is not only exiguous; it's also of one special kind – and generally of poor quality at that. When one's young, one thinks one can tailor one's time into all sorts of splendid and fantastic garments – shakoes and chasubles and Ph.D. gowns; Nijinsky's tights and Rimbaud's slate-blue trousers and Garibaldi's red shirt. But by the time you've lived ten thousand days, you begin to realize that you'll be lucky if you succeed in cutting one decent workaday suit out of the time at your disposal. It's a depressing realization; and Midsummer is one of the days that brings it home. The longest day. One of the sixty or seventy longest days of one's five and twenty thousand. And what have I done with this longest day – longest of so few, of so uniform, of so shoddy? The catalogue of my occupations would be humiliatingly absurd and pointless. The only creditable and, in any profound sense of the word, reasonable thing I've done is to think a little about you, Helen, and write this letter. . . .

'Any interesting letters?' asked Mrs Amberley when her daughter came out again from the house.

'Only a note from Joyce.'

'From our mem-sahib?'

Helen nodded.

'She's living at A-aldershot, you know,' said Mary Amberley to the assembled company. 'At A-a-aldershot,' she insisted, dragging out the first syllable, till the place became ludicrously unreal and the fact that Joyce lived there, a fantastic and slightly indecent myth.

'You can thank your stars that *you* aren't living at Aldershot,' said Anthony. 'After all, you ought to be. A general's daughter.'

For the first moment Mary was put out by his interruption; she had looked forward to developing her fantastic variations on the theme of Aldershot. But her good humour returned as she perceived the richer opportunity with which he had provided her. 'Yes, I know,' she cried eagerly. 'A general's daughter. And do you realize that, but for the grace of God, I might at this moment be a colonel's wife? I was within an ace of marrying a soldier. Within an ace, I tell you. The most ravishingly beautiful creature. But ivory,' she rapped her forehead, 'solid ivory. It was lucky he was such a crashing bore. If he'd been the tiniest bit brighter, I'd have gone out to India with him. And then what? It's unimaginable.'

'Unimaginable!' Beppo repeated, with a little squirt of laughter.

'On the contrary,' said Anthony, 'perfectly imaginable. The club every evening between six and eight; parties at government house; adultery in the hot weather, polo in the cold; incessant bother with the Indian servants; permanent money difficulties and domestic scenes; occasional touches of malaria and dysentery; the monthly parcel of second-hand novels from The Times Book Club; and all the time the inexorable advance of age – twice as fast as in England. If you've ever been to India, nothing's more easy to imagine.'

'And you think all that would have happened to *me*?' asked Mary.

'What else *could* have happened? You don't imagine you'd have gone about buying Pascins in Quetta?'

Mary laughed.

'Or reading Max Jacob in Rawalpindi? You'd have been a mem-sahib like all the other mem-sahibs. A bit more bored and discontented than most of them, perhaps. But still a mem-sahib.'

'I suppose so,' she agreed. 'But is one so hopelessly at the mercy of circumstances?'

He nodded.

'You don't think I'd have escaped?'

'I can't see why.'

'But that means there isn't really any such thing as me. *Me*,' she repeated, laying a hand on her breast. 'I don't really exist.'

'No, of course you don't. Not in that absolute sense. You're a chemical compound, not an element.'

'But if one doesn't really exist, one wonders why ...' she hesitated.

'Why one makes such a fuss about things,' Anthony suggested. 'All that howling and hurrahing and gnashing of teeth. About the adventures of a self that isn't really a self – just the result of a lot of accidents. And of course,' he went on, 'once you start wondering, you see at once that there *is* no reason for making such a fuss. And then you don't make a fuss – that is, if you're sensible. Like me,' he added, smiling.

There was a silence. 'You don't make a fuss,' Mrs Amberley repeated to herself, and thought of Gerry Watchett. 'You don't make a fuss.' But how was it possible not to make a fuss, when he was so stupid, so selfish, so brutal, and at the same time so excruciatingly desirable – like water in the desert, like sleep after insomnia? She hated him; but the thought that in a few days he would be there, staying in the house, sent a prickling sensation of warmth through her body. She shut her eyes and drew a deep breath.

Still carrying the kitten, like a furry baby, in her arms, Helen had walked away across the lawn. She wanted to be alone, out of ear-shot of that laughter, those jarringly irrelevant voices. 'Seven thousand days,' she repeated again and again. And it was not only the declining sun that made everything seem so solemnly and richly beautiful; it was also the thought of the passing days, of human limitations, of the final unescapable dissolution. 'Seven thousand days,' she said aloud, 'seven thousand days.' The tears came into her eyes; she pressed the sleeping kitten more closely to her breast.

*

Savernake, the White Horse, Oxford; and in between whiles the roar and screech of Gerry's Bugatti, the rush of the wind, the swerves and bumps, the sickening but at the same time delicious terrors of excessive speed. And now they were back again. After an age, it seemed; and at the same time it was as though they had never been away. The car came to a halt; but Helen made no move to alight.

'What's the matter?' Gerry asked. 'Why don't you get out?'

'It seems so terribly final,' she said with a sigh. 'Like breaking a spell. Like stepping out of the magic circle.'

'Magic?' he repeated questioningly. 'What kind? White or black?'

Helen laughed. 'Piebald. Absolutely heavenly and absolutely awful. You know, Gerry, you ought to be put in jail, the way you drive. Or in a lunatic asylum. Crazy and criminal. But I adored it,' she added, as she opened the door and stepped out.

'Good!' was all he answered, while he gave her a smile that was as studiedly unamorous as he could make it. He threw the car into gear and, in a stink of burnt castor oil, shot off round the house, towards the garage.

Charming! he was thinking. And how wise he had been to take that jolly, honest-to-God, big-brother line with her! Ground bait. Getting the game accustomed to you. She'd soon be eating out of his hand. The real trouble, of course, was Mary. Tiresome bitch! he thought, with a sudden passion of loathing. Jealous, suspicious, interfering. Behaving as though he were her private property. And greedy, insatiable. Perpetually thrusting herself upon him – thrusting that ageing body of hers. His face, as he manoeuvred the car into the garage, was puckered into the folds of distaste. But thank God, he went on to reflect, she'd got this chill on the liver, or whatever it was. That ought to keep her quiet for a bit, keep her out of the way.

Without troubling to take off her coat, and completely forgetting her mother's illness and for the moment her very existence, Helen crossed the hall and, almost running, burst into the kitchen.

'Where's Tompy, Mrs Weeks?' she demanded of the cook. The effect of the sunshine and the country and Gerry's Bugatti had been such that it was now absolutely essential to her that she should take the kitten in her arms. Immediately. 'I must have Tompy,' she insisted. And by the way of excuse and explanation, 'I didn't have time to see him this morning,' she added; 'we started in such a hurry.'

'Tompy doesn't seem to be well, Miss Helen.' Mrs Weeks put away her sewing.

'Not well?'

'I put him in here,' Mrs Weeks went on, getting up from her Windsor chair and leading the way to the scullery. 'It's cooler. He seemed to feel the heat so. As though he was feverish like. I'm sure I don't know what's the matter with him,' she concluded in a tone half of complaint, half of sympathy. She was sorry for Tompy. But she was also sorry for herself because Tompy had given her all this trouble.

The kitten was lying in the shadow, under the sink. Crouching down beside the basket, Helen stretched out her hand to take him; then, with a little exclamation of horror, withdrew it, as though from the contact of something repellent.

'But what *has* happened to him?' she cried.

The little cat's tabby coat had lost all its smoothness, all its silky lustre, and was matted into damp uneven tufts. The eyes were shut and gummy with a yellow discharge. A running at the nose had slimed the beautifully patterned fur of the face. The absurd lovely little Tompy she had played with only yesterday, the comic and exquisite Tompy she had held up, pathetically helpless, in one hand, had rubbed her face against, had stared into the eyes of, was gone, and in his place lay a limp unclean little rag of living refuse. Like those kidneys, it suddenly occurred to her with a qualm of disgust; and at once she felt ashamed of herself for having had the thought, for having, in that first gesture of recoil, automatically acted upon the thought even before she had consciously had it.

'How beastly I am!' she thought. 'Absolutely beastly!'

Tompy was sick, miserable, dying perhaps. And she had been too squeamish even to touch him. Making an effort to overcome her distaste, she reached out once more, picked up the little cat, and with the fingers of her free hand caressed (with what a sickening reluctance!) the dank bedraggled fur. The tears came into her eyes, overflowed, ran down her cheeks.

'It's too awful, it's too awful,' she repeated in a breaking voice. Poor little Tompy! Beautiful, adorable, funny little Tompy! Murdered – no; worse than murdered: reduced to a

223

squalid little lump of dirt; for no reason, just senselessly; and on this day of all days, this heavenly day with the clouds over the White Horse, the sunshine between the leaves in Savernake forest. And now, to make it worse, she was disgusted by the poor little beast, couldn't bear to touch him, as though he were one of those filthy kidneys – she, who had pretended to love him, who did love him, she insisted to herself. But it was no good her holding him like this and stroking him; it made no difference to what she was really feeling. She might perform the gesture of overcoming her disgust; but the disgust was still there. In spite of the love.

She lifted a streaming face to Mrs Weeks. 'What *shall* we do?'

Mrs Weeks shook her head. 'I never found there was much you *could* do,' she said. 'Not for cats.'

'But there must be something.'

'Nothing except leave them alone,' insisted Mrs Weeks, with a pessimism evidently reinforced by her determination not to be bothered. Then, touched by the spectacle of Helen's misery, 'He'll be all right, dear,' she added consolingly. 'There's no need to cry. Just let him sleep it off.'

Footsteps sounded on the flagstones of the stable yard, and through the open window came the notes of 'Yes, sir, she's my baby,' whistled slightly out of tune. Helen straightened herself up from her crouching position and, leaning out, 'Gerry!' she called; then added, in response to his expression of surprised commiseration, 'Something awful has happened.'

In his large powerful hands Tompy seemed more miserably tiny than ever. But how gentle he was, and how efficient! Watching him, as he swabbed the little cat's eyes, as he wiped away the slime from the nostrils, Helen was amazed by the delicate precision of his movements. She herself, she reflected with a heightened sense of her own shameful ineptitude, had been incapable of doing anything except stroke Tompy's fur and feel disgusted. Hopeless, quite hopeless! And when he asked for her help in getting Tompy to swallow half an aspirin tablet crushed in milk, she bungled everything and spilt the medicine.

'Perhaps I can do it better by myself,' he said, and took the spoon from her. The cup of her humiliation was full. ...

*

Mary Amberley was indignant. Here she was, feverish and in pain, worrying herself, what was more, into higher fever, worse pain, with the thought of Gerry's dangerous driving. And here was Helen, casually strolling into her room after having been in the house for more than two hours – more than two hours without having had the common decency to come and see how she was, more than two hours while her mother – her mother, mind you! – had lain there, in an agony of distress, thinking that they must have had an accident.

'But Tompy was dying,' Helen explained. 'He's dead now.' Her face was very pale, her eyes red with tears.

'Well, if you prefer a wretched cat to your mother ...'

'Besides, you were asleep. If you hadn't been asleep, you'd have heard the car coming back.'

'Now you're begrudging me my sleep,' said Mrs Amberley bitterly. 'Aren't I to be allowed a moment's respite from pain? Besides,' she added, 'I wasn't asleep. I was delirious. I've been delirious several times today. Of course I didn't hear the car.' Her eyes fell on the bottle of Somnifaine standing on the table by her bed, and the suspicion that Helen might also have noticed it made her still more angry. 'I always knew you were selfish,' she went on. 'But I must say I didn't think you'd be quite as bad as this.'

At another time Helen would have flared up in angry self-defence, or else, convicted of guilt, would have burst out crying. But today she was feeling too miserable to be able to shed any more tears, too much subdued by shame and unhappiness to resent even the most flagrant injustice. Her silence exasperated Mrs Amberley still further.

'I always used to think,' she resumed, 'that you were only selfish from thoughtlessness. But now I see that it's heartlessness. Plain heartlessness. Here am I – having sacrificed the best years of my life to you; and what do I get in return?' Her voice trembled as she asked the question. She was convinced of the reality of that sacrifice, profoundly moved by the thought of its extent, its martyr-like enormity. 'The most cynical indifference.

225

I might die in a ditch; but you wouldn't care. You'd be much more upset about your cat. And now go away,' she almost shouted, 'go away! I *know* my temperature's gone up. Go away.'

*

After a lonely dinner – for Helen was keeping her room on the plea of a headache – Gerry went up to sit with Mrs Amberley. He was particularly charming that evening, and so affectionately solicitous that Mary forgot all her accumulated grounds of complaint and fell in love with him all over again, and for another set of reasons – not because he was so handsome, so easily and insolently dominating, such a ruthless and accomplished lover, but because he was kind, thoughtful, and affectionate, was everything, in a word, she had previously known he wasn't.

Half past ten struck. He rose from his chair. 'Time for your spot of shut-eye.'

Mary protested; he was firm – for her own good.

Thirty drops were the normal dose of Somnifaine; but he measured out forty-five, so as to make quite sure of her sleeping, made her drink, then tucked her up ('like an old Nanny,' she cried laughing with pleasure, as he busied himself round the bed) and, after kissing her good night with an almost material tenderness, turned out the light and left her.

The clock of the village church sounded eleven – how sadly, Helen thought as she listened to the strokes of the distant bell, how lonelily ! It was as though she were listening to the voice of her own spirit, reverberated in some mysterious way from the walls of the enclosing night. One, two, three, four ... Each sweet, cracked note seemed more hopelessly mournful, seemed to rise from the depths of a more extreme solitude, than the last. Tompy had died, and she hadn't even been capable of giving him a spoonful of milk and crushed aspirin, hadn't had the strength to overcome her disgust.

Selfish and heartless : her mother was quite right. But lonely as well as selfish, all alone among the senseless malignities that had murdered poor little Tompy; and her heartlessness spoke with the despairing voice of that bell; night was empty and enormous all around.

'Helen!'

She started and turned her head. The room was impenetrably black.

'It's me,' Gerry's voice continued. 'I was so worried about you. Are you feeling better?'

Her first surprise and alarm had given place to a feeling of resentment that he should intrude upon the privacy of her unhappiness. 'You needn't have bothered,' she said coldly. 'I'm quite all right.'

Enclosed in his faint aura of Turkish tobacco, of peppermint-flavoured tooth-paste and bay rum, he approached invisibly. Through the blanket, a groping hand touched her shin; then the springs creaked and tilted under his weight as he sat down on the edge of the bed.

'Felt a bit responsible,' he went on. 'All that looping the loop!' The tone of his voice implied the unseen smile, suggested a whimsical and affectionate twinkling of hidden eyes.

She made no comment; there was a long silence. A bad start, Gerry thought, and frowned to himself in the darkness; then began again on another tack.

'I can't help thinking of that miserable little Tompy,' he said in a different voice. 'Extraordinary how upsetting it is when an animal gets ill like that. It seems frightfully *unfair*.'

In a few minutes she was crying, and he had an excuse to console her.

Gently, as he had handled Tompy, and with all the tenderness that had so much touched Mrs Amberley, he stroked her hair, and later, when the sobs began to subside, drew the fingers of his other hand along her bare arm. Again and again, with the patient regularity of a nurse lulling her charge to sleep; again and again ... Three hundred times at least, he was thinking, before he risked any gesture that could possibly be interpreted as amorous. Three hundred times; and even then the caresses would have to deviate by insensible degrees, as though by a series of accidents, till gradually, unintentionally, the hand that was now on her arm would come at last to be brushing, with the same maternal persistence, against her breast, while the fingers that came and went methodically among the curls would have strayed to the ear, and from the ear across the cheek to the lips, and would linger there lightly, chastely, but charged with the stuff of kisses, proxies, and forerunners of the mouth that would ultimately come down on hers, through the darkness, for the reward of its long patience.

May 20th 1931

IT was another 'knock'. Fitzimmons, Jefferies, Jack Johnson, Carpentier, Dempsey, Gene Tunney – the champions came and went; but the metaphor in which Mr Beavis described his successive bereavements remained unaltered.

Yes, a hard knock. And yet, it seemed to Anthony, there was a note almost of triumph in his father's reminiscences, over the luncheon table, of Uncle James as a schoolboy.

'Poor James ... such curly hair he had then ... *nos et mutamur*.' The commiseration and regret were mingled with a certain satisfaction – the satisfaction of an old man who finds himself still alive, still able to attend the funerals of his contemporaries, his juniors.

'Two years,' he insisted. 'There was the best part of two years between James and me. I was Beavis major at school.'

He shook his head mournfully; but the old, tired eyes had brightened with an irrepressible light. 'Poor James!' He sighed. 'We hadn't seen one another much these last years. Not since his conversion. How *did* he do it? It beats me. A Catholic – he of all people ...'

Anthony said nothing. But after all, he was thinking, it wasn't so surprising. The poor old thing had grown up as a Bradlaugh atheist. Ought to have been blissfully happy, parading his cosmic defiance, his unyielding despair. But he had had the bad luck to be a homosexual at a time when one couldn't avow it even to oneself. Ingrowing pederasty – it had poisoned his whole life. Had turned that metaphysical and delightfully Pickwickian despair into real, common or garden misery. Misery and neurasthenia; the old man had been half mad, really. (Which hadn't prevented him from being a first-rate actuary.) Then, during the war, the clouds had lifted. One could be kind to wounded soldiers – be kind *pro patria* and with a blameless conscience. Anthony remembered Uncle James's visits to him in hospital. He had come almost every day. Loaded with gifts for a dozen adopted nephews as well as for the real one. On his thin, melancholy face there had been, in those days, a perpetual smile. But happiness never lasts. The armistice had come; and, after those four years in paradise, hell had seemed blacker than ever. In 1923 he had turned papist. It was only to be expected.

But Mr Beavis simply couldn't understand. The idea of James surrounded by Jesuits, James bobbing up and down at Mass, James going to Lourdes with his inoperable tumour, James dying with all the consolations of religion – it filled him with horrified amazement.

'And yet,' said Anthony, 'I admire the way they usher you out of life. Dying – it's apt to be an animal process. More exclusively animal even than sea-sickness.' He was silent for a moment, thinking of poor Uncle James's last and most physiological hour. The heavy, snoring breath, the mouth cavernously gaping, the scrabbling of the hands.

'How wise the Church has been to turn it into a ceremonial!'

'Charades,' said Mr Beavis contemptously.

'But good charades,' Anthony insisted. 'A work of art. In itself, the event's like a rough channel crossing – only rather worse. But they manage to turn it into something rather fine and significant. Chiefly for the spectator, of course. But perhaps also significant for the actor.'

There was a silence. The maid changed the plates and brought in the sweet. 'Some apple tart?' Pauline questioned, as she cut the crust.

'Apple pie, my dear.' Mr Beavis's tone was severe. 'When will you learn that a tart's uncovered? A thing with a roof is a pie.'

They helped themselves to cream and sugar.

'By the way,' said Pauline suddenly, 'had you heard about Mrs Foxe?' Anthony and Mr Beavis shook their heads. 'Maggie Clark told me yesterday. She's had a stroke.'

'Dear, dear,' said Mr Beavis. Then, reflectively, 'Curious the way people pass out of one's life,' he added. 'After being very much in it. I don't believe I've seen Mrs Foxe half a dozen times in the last twenty years. And yet before that . . .'

'She had no sense of humour,' said Pauline, by the way of explanation.

Mr Beavis turned to Anthony. 'I don't suppose you've . . . well, "kept up" with her very closely, not since that poor boy of hers died.'

Anthony shook his head, without speaking. It was not agreeable to be reminded of all that he had done to avoid keeping up with Mrs Foxe. Those long affectionate letters she had written to him during the first year of the war – letters which he had answered more and more briefly, perfunctorily, conventionally; and at last hadn't answered at all; hadn't even read. Hadn't even read, and yet – moved by some superstitious compunction – had never thrown away. At least a dozen of the blue envelopes, addressed in the large, clear, flowing writing, were still lying unopened in one of the drawers of his desk. Their presence there was, in some obscure, inexplicable way, a salve to his conscience. Not an entirely effective salve. His father's question had made him feel uncomfortable; he hastened to change the subject.

'And what have you been delving into recently?' he asked, in the sort of playfully archaic language that his father himself might have used.

Mr Beavis chuckled and begun to describe his researches into modern American slang. Such savoury locutions! Such an Elizabethan wealth of new coinages and original metaphors! Horse feathers, dish the dope, button up your face – delicious! 'And how would you like to be called a fever frau?' he asked his younger daughter, Diana, who had sat in silence, severely aloof, throughout the meal. 'Or worse, a cinch pushover, my dear? Or I might say that you had a dame complex, Anthony. Or refer regretfully to your habit of smooching the sex jobs.' He twinkled with pleasure.

'It's like so much Chinese,' said Pauline from the other end of the table. Across her round placid face mirth radiated out in concentric waves of soft pink flesh; the succession of her chins shook like jelly. 'He thinks he's the cat's pyjamas, your father does.' She reached out, helped herself to a couple of chocolate creams from the silver bowl on the table in front of her and popped one of them into her mouth. 'The cat's pyjamas,' she repeated indistinctly and heaved with renewed laughter.

Mr Beavis, who had been working himself up to the necessary pitch of naughtiness, leaned forward and asked Anthony, in a confidential whisper, 'What would you do if the fever frau had the misfortune to be storked?'

They were darlings, Diana was thinking; that went without saying. But how silly they could be, how inexpressibly *silly*! All the same, Anthony had no right to criticize them; and under that excessive politeness of his he obviously was criticizing them, the wretch! She felt quite indignant. Nobody had a right to criticize them except herself and possibly her sister. She tried to think of something unpleasant to say to Anthony; but he had given her no opening and she had no gift for epigram. She had to be content with silently frowning. And anyhow it was time to go back to the lab.

Getting up, 'I must go,' she said in her curt, abrupt way. 'I absolutely forbid you to eat all those sweets,' she added, as she bent down to kiss her mother. 'Doctor's orders.'

'You're not a doctor yet, darling.'

'No, but I shall be next year.'

Tranquilly Pauline poked the second chocolate cream into her mouth. 'And next year, perhaps, I'll stop eating sweets,' she said.

Anthony left a few minutes later. Walking through South Kensington, he found his thoughts harking back to Mrs Foxe. Had the stroke, he wondered, been a bad one? Was she paralysed? He had been so anxious to prevent his father from talking about her, that there had been no time for Pauline to say. He pictured her lying helpless, half dead, and was horrified to find himself feeling, along with sympathy, a certain satisfaction, a certain sense of relief. For, after all, she was the chief witness for the prosecution, the person who could testify most damningly against him. Dead, or only half dead, she was out of court; and, in her absence, there was no longer any case against him. With part of his being he was glad of Pauline's news. Shamefully glad. He tried to think of something else, and, meanwhile,

boarded a bus so as to reach more quickly the haven of the
London Library.

He spent nearly three hours there, looking up references to
the history of the Anabaptists, then walked home to his rooms
in Bloomsbury. He was expecting Gladys that evening before
dinner. The girl had been a bit tiresome recently; but still ...
He smiled to himself with anticipatory pleasure.

She was due at six; but at a quarter past she had not yet come.
Nor yet at half past. Nor yet at seven. Nor yet at half past
seven. At eight, he was looking at those blue envelopes, post-
marked in 1914 and 1915 and addressed in Mrs Foxe's writing
– looking at them and wondering, in self-questioning despondency that had succeeded his first impatience and rage, whether
he should open them. He was still wondering, when the telephone bell rang, and there was Mark Staithes asking him if
by any chance he was free for dinner. A little party had formed
itself at the last moment. Pitchley would be there, and his wife,
the psychologist, and that Indian politician, Sen, and Helen
Ledwidge ... Anthony put the letters back in their drawer and
hurried out of the house.

CHAPTER TWENTY-SIX

September 5th 1933

I t was after two o'clock. Anthony lay on his back staring up
into the darkness. Sleep, it seemed, deliberately refused to come,
was being withheld by someone else, some malignant alien
inhabiting his own body. Outside, in the pine trees the cicadas
harped incessantly on the theme of their existence; and at long
intervals a sound of cock-crowing would swell up out of the
darkness, louder and nearer, until all the birds in the surround-
ing gardens were shouting defiance back and forth, peal answering peal. And then for no reason, first one, then another fell
silent and the outburst died away fainter and fainter into the
increasing distance – right across France, he fancied as he
strained his ears after the receding sound, in a hurrying wave
of ragged crowing. Hundreds of miles, perhaps. And then

somewhere, the wave would turn and roll back again as swiftly as it had come. Back from the North Sea, perhaps; over the battlefields; round the fringes of Paris and from bird to distant bird through the forests; then across the plains of Beauce; up and down the hills of Burgundy and, like another aerial river of sound, headlong down the valley of the Rhône; past Valence, past Orange and Avignon, past Arles and Aix and across the bare hills of Provence; until here it was again, an hour after its previous passage, flowing tumultuously shrill across the cicadas' loud, unremitting equivalent of silence.

He was reminded suddenly of a passage in Lawrence's *The Man who Died*, and, thankful of an excuse to interrupt for a little his vain pursuit of sleep, he turned on the light and went downstairs to look for the book. Yes, here it was. 'As he came out, the young cock crowed. It was a diminished, pinched cry, but there was that in the voice of the bird stronger than chagrin. It was the necessity to live and even to cry out the triumph of life. The man who had died stood and watched the cock who had escaped and been caught, ruffling himself up, rising forward on his toes, throwing up his head, and parting his beak in another challenge from life to death. The brave sounds rang out, and though they were diminished by the cord round the bird's leg, they were not cut off. The man who had died looked nakedly on life, and saw a vast resoluteness everywhere flinging itself up in the stormy or subtle wave crests, foam-tips emerging out of the blue invisible, a black orange cock or the green flame-tongues out of the extremes of the fig tree. They came forth, these things and creatures of spring, glowing with desire and assertion. They came like crests of foam, out of the blue flood of the invisible desire, out of the vast invisible sea of strength, and they came coloured and tangible, evanescent, yet deathless in their coming. The man who had died looked on the great swing into existence of things that had not died, but he saw no longer their tremulous desire to exist and to be. He heard instead their ringing, ringing, defiant challenge to all other things existing. . . .'

Anthony read on till he had finished the story of the man who had died and come to life again, the man who was himself the escaped cock; then put away the book and went back to bed. The foam on the waves of that invisible sea of desire and strength. But life, life as such, he protested inwardly – it was not enough. How could one be content with the namelessness of mere energy, with the less than individuality of a power, that for all its mysterious divineness, was yet unconscious, beneath good and evil? The cicadas sounded incessantly, and again, at about four, the tide of cock-crowing came sweeping across the land and passed on out of hearing, towards Italy.

Life irrepressibly living itself out. But there were emblems, he reflected, more vividly impressive than the crowing cock or the young leaves breaking out from the winter fig tree's bone-white skeleton. He remembered that film he had seen of the fertilization of a rabbit's ovum. Spermatozoa, a span long on the screen, ferociously struggling towards their goal – the moon-like sphere of the egg. Countless, aimed from every side, their *flagella* in frantic vibration. And now the foremost had reached their objective, were burrowing into it, thrusting through the outer wall of living matter, tearing away in their violent haste whole cells that floated off and were lost. And at last one of the invaders had penetrated to the quick of the nucleus, the act of fertilization was consummated; and suddenly the hitherto passive sphere stirred into movement. There was a violent spasm of contraction; its smooth rounded surface became corrugated and in some way resistant to the other sperms that vainly threw themselves upon it. And then the egg began to divide, bending in its walls upon itself till they met in the centre, and there were two cells instead of one; then, as the two cells repeated the process, four cells; then eight, then sixteen. And within the cells the granules of protoplasm were in continuous motion, like peas in a boiling pot, but self-activated, moving by their own energy.

In comparison with these minute fragments of living matter, the crowing cock, the cicadas endlessly repeating the proclamation of their existence, were only feebly alive. Life under the microscope seemed far more vehement and irrepressible than in the larger world. Consolingly and at the same time appallingly irrepressible. For, yes, it was also appalling, the awful unconsciousness of that unconquerable, crawling desire! And, oh, the horror of that display of sub-mental passion, of violent and impersonal egotism! Intolerable, unless one could think of it only as raw material and available energy.

Yes, raw material and a stream of energy. Impressive for their quantity, their duration. But qualitatively they were only potentially valuable : would become valuable only when made up into something else, only when used to serve an ulterior purpose. For Lawrence, the animal purpose had seemed sufficient and satisfactory. The cock, crowing, fighting, mating – anonymously; and man anonymous like the cock. Better such mindless anonymity, he had insisted, than the squalid relationships of human beings advanced half-way to consciousness, still only partially civilized.

But Lawrence had never looked through a microscope, never seen biological energy in its basic undifferentiated state. He hadn't wanted to look, had disapproved on principle of microscopes, fearing what they might reveal; and had been right to fear. Those depths beneath depths of namelessness, crawling irrepressibly – they would have horrified him. He had insisted that the raw material should be worked up – but worked only to a certain pitch and no further; the primal crawling energy should be used for the relatively higher purposes of animal existence, but for no existence beyond the animal. Arbitrarily, illogically. For the other, ulterior purposes and organizations existed and were not to be ignored. Moving through space and time, the human animal discovered them on his path, unequivocally present and real.

Thinking and the pursuit of knowledge – these were purposes for which he himself had used the energy that crawled under the microscope, that crowed defiantly in the darkness. Thought as an end, knowledge as an end. And now it had become suddenly manifest that they were only means – as definitely raw material as life itself. Raw material – and he divined, he *knew*, what the finished product would have to be; and with part of his being he revolted against the knowledge. What, set about trying to turn his raw material of life, thought, knowledge into *that* – at his time of life, and he a civilized human being! The mere idea was ridiculous. One of those absurd hang-overs from Christianity – like his father's terror of the more disreputable realities of existence, like the hymn-singing

235

of workmen during the General Strike. The headaches, the hiccups of yesterday's religion. But with another part of his mind he was miserably thinking that he would never succeed in bringing about the transformation of his raw material into the finished product; that he didn't know how or where to begin; that he was afraid of making a fool of himself; that he lacked the necessary courage, patience, strength of mind.

At about seven, when behind the shutters the sun was already high above the horizon, he dropped off into a heavy sleep, and woke with a start three hours later to see Mark Staithes standing besides his bed and peering at him, smiling, an amused and inquisitive gargoyle, through the mosquito net.

'Mark?' he questioned in astonishment. 'What on earth . . . ?'

'Bridal!' said Mark, poking the muslin net. 'Positively *première communion*! I've been watching you sleeping.'

'For long?'

'Oh, don't worry,' he said, replying not to the spoken, but to the unspoken question implied by Anthony's tone of annoyance. 'You don't give yourself away in your sleep. On the contrary, you take other people in. I've never seen anyone look so innocent as you did under that veil. Like the infant Samuel. Too sweet!'

Reminded of Helen's use of the same word on the morning of the catastrophe, Anthony frowned. Then, after a silence, 'What have you come for?' he asked.

'To stay with you.'

'You weren't asked.'

'That remains to be seen,' said Mark.

'What do you mean?'

'I mean, you may discover it after the event.'

'Discover what?'

'That you wanted to ask me. Without knowing that you wanted it.'

'What makes you think that?'

Mark drew up a chair and sat down before answering. 'I saw Helen the night she got back to London.'

'Did you?' Anthony's tone was as blankly inexpressive as he could make it. 'Where?' he added.

'At Hugh's. Hugh was giving a party. There were some uncomfortable moments.'

'Why?'

'Well, because she wanted them to be uncomfortable. She was in a queer state, you know.'

'Did she tell you why?'

Mark nodded. 'She even made me read your letter. The begining of it, at least. I wouldn't go on.'

'Helen made you read my letter?'

'Aloud. She insisted. But, as I say, she was in a very queer state.' There was a long silence. 'That's why I came here,' he added at last.

'Thinking that I'd be glad to see you?' the other asked in an ironical tone.

'Thinking that you'd be glad to see me,' Mark answered gravely.

After another silence, 'Well, perhaps you're not altogether wrong,' said Anthony. 'In a way, of course, I simply hate the sight of you.' He smiled at Mark. 'Nothing personal intended, mind you. I should hate the sight of anyone just as much. But in another way I'm glad you've come. And this *is* personal. Because I think you're likely – well, likely to have some notion of what's what,' he concluded with a non-committal vagueness. 'If there's anybody who can ...' He was going to say 'help': but the idea of being helped was so repugnant to him, seemed so grotesquely associated with the parson's well-chosen words after a death in the family, with the housemaster's frank, friendly talk about sexual temptations, that he broke off uncomfortably. 'If anybody can make a sensible remark about it all,' he began again, on a different level of expression, 'I think it's you.'

The other nodded without speaking, and thought how typical it was of the man to go on talking about sensible remarks – even now!

'I have a feeling,' Anthony went on slowly, overcoming inward resistances in order to speak, 'a feeling that I'd like to get it over, get things settled. On another basis,' he brought out as though under torture. 'The present one ...' He shook his head. 'I'm a bit bored with it.' Then, perceiving with a sense of shame the ludicrous inappropriateness and the worse than ludicrous falsity of the understatement, 'It won't do,' he

237

added resolutely. 'It's a basis that can't carry more than the weight of a ghost. And in order to use it, I've turned myself into a ghost.' After a pause, 'These last few days,' he went on slowly, 'I've had a queer feeling that I'm really not there, that I haven't been there for years past. Ever since ... well, I don't exactly know when. Since before the war, I suppose.' He could not bring himself to speak of Brian. 'Not there,' he repeated.

'A great many people aren't there,' said Mark. 'Not as people, at any rate. Only as animals and incarnate functions.'

'Animals and incarnate functions,' the other repeated. 'You've said it exactly. But in most cases they have no choice; nonentity is forced on them by circumstance. Whereas I was free to choose – at any rate, so far as anybody is free to choose. If I wasn't there, it was on purpose.'

'And do you mean to say that you've only just discovered the fact that you've never been there?'

Anthony shook his head. 'No, no, I've known it, of course. All the time. But theoretically. In the same way as one knows ... well, for example, that there are birds that live symbiotically with wasps. A curious and interesting fact, but no more. I didn't let it be more. And then I had my justifications. Work: too much personal life would interfere with my work. And the need for freedom: freedom to think, freedom to indulge my passion for knowing about the world. And freedom for its own sake. I wanted to be free, because it was intolerable not to be free.'

'I can understand that,' said Mark, 'provided that there's someone there who can enjoy the freedom. And provided,' he added, 'that that someone makes himself conscious of being free by overcoming the obstacles that stand in the way of freedom. But how can you be free, if there's no "you"?'

'I've always put it the other way round,' said Anthony. 'How can you be free – or rather (for one must think of it impersonally) how can there be freedom – so long as the "you" persists? A "you" has got to be consistent and responsible, has got to make choices and commit itself. But if one gets rid of the "you", one gets rid of responsibility and the need for consistency. One's free as a succession of unconditioned, uncommitted states without past or future, except in so far as one can't voluntarily get rid of one's memories and anticipations.' After a silence, 'The staggering imbecility of old Socrates!' he went on. 'Imagining that one had only to know the correct line of conduct in order to follow it. One practically always knows it – and more often than not one doesn't follow it. Or perhaps you're not like that,' he added in another tone, looking at Mark through the mosquito net. 'One's inclined to attribute one's own defects to everyone else. Weakness, in my case. Not to mention timidity,' he added with a laugh, that uttered itself automatically, so deeply ingrained was the habit of half withdrawing, as soon as it was spoken, anything in the nature of a personal confidence, of evoking in the listener's mind a doubt as to the seriousness of his intention in speaking; 'timidity, and downright cowardice, and indolence in regard to anything that isn't my work.' He laughed again as though it were all absurd, not worth mentioning. 'One forgets that other people may be different. Tough-minded, firm of purpose. I dare say you always do what you know is right.'

'I always do it,' Mark answered. 'Whether it's right or wrong.' He demonstrated the anatomy of a smile.

Anthony lay back on his pillows, his hands clasped behind his head, his eyes half shut. Then, after a long silence, he turned to Staithes and said abruptly: 'Don't you ever feel that you simply can't be bothered to do what you've decided on? Just now, for example, I found myself wondering all of a sudden why on earth I'd been talking to you like this – why I'd been thinking these things before you came – why I'd been trying to make up my mind to do something. Wondering and feeling that I simply couldn't be bothered. Thinking it would be better just to evade it all and go back to the familiar routine. The quiet life. Even though the quiet life would be fatal. Fatal, mortal, but all the same anything for it.' He shook his head. 'Probably if you hadn't come to shame me into some sort of resolution, that's what I would have done – escaped from it all and gone back to the quiet life.' He laughed. 'And perhaps,' he added, 'I shall do it even now. In spite of you.' He sat up, lifted the mosquito net and stepped out of bed. 'I'm going to have my bath.'

CHAPTER TWENTY-SEVEN

May 27th 1914

Aｎｔｈｏｎｙ came down to breakfast to find his father explaining to the children the etymology of what they were eating. '... merely another form of "pottage". You say "porridge" just as you say – or rather' (he twinkled at them) 'I hope you don't say – "shurrup" for "shut up".'

The two little girls went on stolidly eating.

'Ah, Anthony!' Mr Beavis went on. 'Better late than never. What, no pottage this morning? But you'll have an Aberdeen cutlet, I hope.'

Anthony helped himself to the haddock and sat down in his place.

'Here's a letter for you,' said Mr Beavis, and handed it over. 'Don't I recognize Brian's writing?' Anthony nodded. 'Does he still enjoy his work at Manchester?'

'I think so,' Anthony answered. 'Except, of course, that he does too much. He's at the newspaper till one or two in the morning. And then from lunch to dinner he works at his thesis.'

'Well, it's good to see a young man who has the energy of his ambitions,' said Mr Beavis. 'Because, of course, he needn't work so hard. It's not as if his mother hadn't got the wherewithal.'

The wherewithal so exasperated Anthony that, though he found Brian's action absurd, it was with a cutting severity that he answered his father. 'He won't accept his mother's money,' he said very coldly. 'It's a matter of principle.'

There was a diversion while the children put away their porridge plates and were helped to Aberdeen cutlets. Anthony took the opportunity to start reading his letter.

No news of you for a long time. Here all goes on as usual, or would do, if I were feeling a bit sprightlier. But sleep has been none too good and internal workings not all they might be. Am slowing down, in consequence, on the thesis, as I can't slow down on the paper. All this makes me look forward longingly to our projected fortnight in Langdale. Don't let me down, for heaven's sake. What a bore one's carcass is when it goes in the least wrong! Even when it goes right, for that matter. Such a lot of unmodern inconveniences. I sometimes bitterly resent this physical predestination to scatology and obscenity.

Write soon and let me know how you are, what you've been reading, whether you've met anybody of interest. And will you do me a kindness? Joan's in town now, staying with her aunt and working for the Charity Organization people. Her father didn't want her to go, of course – preferred to have her at home, so that he could tyrannize her. There was a long battle, which he finally lost; she has been in town nearly a month now. For which I'm exceedingly thankful – but at the same time, for various reasons, feel a bit worried. If I could get away for the week-ends, I'd come myself; but I can't. And perhaps, in a certain sense, it's all for the best. In my present mouldy condition I should be rather a skeleton at the feast; and besides, there are certain complications. I can't explain them in a letter; but when you come north in July I'll try. I ought to have asked your advice before this. You're harder in the head than I am. Which is ultimately the reason why I didn't talk to you about the matter – for fear of being thought a fool by you! Such is one's imbecility. But, there, we'll discuss it all later. Meanwhile, will you get in touch with her, take her out to a meal, get her to talk, then write and tell me how you think she's reacting to London, what she feels about life in general, and so forth. It's been a violent transition – from remote country life to London, from cramping poverty to a rich house, from subjection to her father's bad-tempered tyranny to independence. A violent transition; and, though I'm glad of it, I'm a bit nervous as to its effects. But you'll see. – Yours,   B.

Anthony did see that same day. The old shyness, he noticed, as they shook hands in the lobby of the restaurant, was still there – the same embarrassed smile, the same swaying movement of recoil. In face and body she was more of a woman than when he had seen her last, a year before, seemed prettier too – chiefly, no doubt, because she was better dressed.

They passed into the restaurant and sat down. Anthony ordered the food and a bottle of Vouvray, then began to explore the ground.

London – how did she like London?

Adored it.

Even the work?

Not the office part, perhaps. But three times a week she helped at a crèche. 'I love babies.'

241

'Even those horrible little smelly ones?'

Joan was indignant. 'They're adorable. I love the work with them. Besides, it allows me to enjoy all the rest of London with a clear conscience. I feel I've paid for my theatres and dances.'

Shyness broke up her talk, plunged it, as it were, into alternate light and shade. At one moment she would be speaking with difficulty, hardly opening her lips, her voice low and indistinct, her face averted; the next, her timidity was swept aside by an uprush of strong feeling – delight, or some distress, or irrepressible mirth, and she was looking at him with eyes grown suddenly and surprisingly bold; from almost inaudible, her voice had become clear; the strong white teeth flashed between lips parted in a frank expression of feeling. Then suddenly she was as though appalled by her own daring; she became conscious of him as a possible critic. What was he thinking? Had she made a fool of herself? Her voice faltered, the blood rose to her cheeks, she looked down at her plate; and for the next few minutes he would get nothing but short mumbled answers to his questions, nothing but the most perfunctory of nervous laughs in response to his best efforts to amuse her. The food, however, and the wine did their work, and as the meal advanced, she found herself more at ease with him. They began to talk about Brian.

'You ought to prevent him from working so hard,' he said.

'Do you think I don't try?' Then, with something almost like anger in her voice, 'It's his nature,' she went on. 'He's so terribly conscientious.'

'It's your business to make him unconscientious.' He smiled at her, expecting a return in kind. But, instead of that, she frowned; her face took on an expression of resentful misery. 'It's easy for you to talk,' she muttered. There was a silence, while she sat with downcast eyes, sipping her wine.

They could have married, it occurred to him for the first time, if Brian had consented to live on his mother. Why on earth, then, seeing how much he was in love with the girl ...?

With the peach-melba it all came out. 'It's difficult to talk, about,' she said. 'I've hardly mentioned it to anyone. But with you it's different. You've known Brian such a long time; you're his oldest friend. You'll understand. I feel I can tell you about it.'

Curious, but at the same time a little disquieted, he murmured something vaguely polite.

She failed to notice the signs of his embarrassment; for her, at the moment, Anthony was only the heaven-sent opportunity for at last releasing in speech a flood of distressing feelings too long debarred from expression.

'It's that conscientiousness of his. If you only knew ...! Why has he got the idea that there's something wrong about love? The ordinary, happy kind of love, I mean. He thinks it isn't right; he thinks he oughtn't to have those feelings.'

She pushed away her plate, and, leaning forward, her elbows on the table, began to speak in a lower, more intimate tone of the kisses that Brian had given and been ashamed of, and those other kisses that, by way of atonement, he had refused to give.

Anthony listened in astonishment. 'Certain complications' was what Brian had written in his letter; it was putting it mildly. This was just craziness. Tragic – but also grotesque, absurd. It occurred to him that Mary would find the story particularly ludicrous.

'He said he wanted to be worthy of me,' she went on. 'Worthy of love. But all that happened was that it made *me* feel unworthy. Unworthy of everything, in every way. Guilty – feeling I'd done something wrong. And dirty too, if you understand what I mean, as though I'd fallen in the mud. But, Anthony, it isn't wrong, is it?' she questioned. 'I mean, we'd never done anything that wasn't ... well, you know : quite innocent. Why does he say he's unworthy, and make me feel unworthy at the same time? Why does he?' she insisted. There were tears in her eyes.

'He was always rather like that,' said Anthony. 'Perhaps his upbringing ... His mother's a wonderful person,' he added, dropping, as he suddenly realized, while the words were being spoken, into Mrs Foxe's own idiom. 'But perhaps a bit oppressive, just for that reason.'

Joan nodded emphatically, but did not speak.

'It may be she's made him aim a bit too high,' he went on, 'Too high all along the line, if you see what I mean – even when he's not directly following her example. That business of not wanting to take her money, for instance ...'

Joan caught up the subject with passionate eagerness, 'Yes, why *does* he want to be different from everyone else? After all, there are other good people in the world and they don't feel it necessary to do it. Mind you,' she added, looking up sharply into Anthony's face, as if trying to catch and quell any expression of disapproval there, or, worse, of patronizing amusement, 'mind you, I think it's wonderful of him to do it. Wonderful!' she repeated with a kind of defiance. Then, resuming the critical tone which she would not allow Anthony to use, but to which it seemed to her that her own feelings for Brian gave her a right, 'All the same,' she went on, 'I can't see how it would hurt him to take that money. I believe it was mostly his mother's doing.'

Surprised, 'But he told me that Mrs Foxe had tried to insist on his taking it.'

'Oh, she made it *seem* as though she wanted him to take it. We were there for a week-end in May to talk it over. She kept telling him that it wasn't wrong to take the money, and that he ought to think about me and getting married. But then, when Brian and I told her that I'd agreed to his not taking it, she . . .'

Anthony interrupted her. 'But *had* you agreed?'

Joan dropped her eyes. 'In a way,' she said sullenly. Then looking up again with sudden anger, 'How could I help agreeing with him? Seeing that that was what he wanted to do, and would have done, what's more, even if I hadn't agreed. And besides, I've told you, there was something rather splendid and wonderful about it. Of course, I had agreed. But agreeing didn't mean that I really *wanted* him to refuse the money. And that's where her falseness came in – pretending to think that I wanted him to refuse it, and congratulating me and him on what we'd done. Saying we were heroic and all that. And so encouraging him to go on with the idea. It *is* her doing, I tell you. Much more than you think.'

She was silent, and Anthony thought it best to allow the subject to drop. Heaven only knew what she'd say if he allowed her to go on talking about Mrs Foxe. 'Poor Brian,' he said aloud, and added, taking refuge in platitude, 'The best is the enemy of the good.'

'Yes, that's just it!' she cried. 'The enemy of the good. He wants to be perfect – but look at the result! He tortures himself and hurts me. Why should I be made to feel dirty and criminal? Because that's what he's doing. When I've done nothing wrong. Nor has he, for that matter. And yet he wants me to feel the same about him. Dirty and criminal. Why does he make it so difficult for me? As difficult as he possibly can.' Her voice trembled, the tears overflowed. She pulled out her handkerchief and quickly wiped her eyes. 'I'm sorry,' she said. 'I'm making a fool of myself. But if you knew how hard it's been for me! I've loved him so much, I want to go on loving him. But he doesn't seem to want to allow me to. It ought to be so beautiful; but he does his best to make it all seem ugly and horrible.' Then, after a pause, and in a voice that had sunk almost to a whisper, 'I sometimes wonder if I can go on much longer.'

Did it mean, he wondered, that she had already decided to break it off – had already met someone else who was prepared to love her and be loved less tragically, more normally than Brian? No; probably not, he decided. But there was every likelihood that she soon would. In her way (it didn't happen to be exactly the way he liked) she was attractive. There would be no shortage of candidates; and if a satisfactory candidate presented himself, would she be able – whatever she might consciously wish – to refuse?

Joan broke the silence. 'I dream so often of the house we're going to live in,' she said. 'Going from room to room; and it all looks so nice. Such pretty curtains and chair covers. And vases full of flowers.' She sighed; then, after a pause, 'Do you understand his not wanting to take his mother's money?'

Anthony hesitated a moment; then replied noncommittally; 'I understand it; but I don't think I should do it myself.'

She sighed once more. 'That's how I feel too.' She looked at her watch; then gathered up her gloves. 'I shall have to go.' With this return from intimacy to the prosaic world of time and people and appointments, she suddenly woke up again to painful self-consciousness. Had it bored him? Did he think her a fool? She looked into his face, trying to divine his thoughts; then dropped her eyes. 'I'm afraid I've been talking a lot about myself,' she mumbled. 'I don't know why I should burden you . . .'

He protested. 'I only wish I could be of some help.'

Joan raised her face again and gave him a quick smile of gratitude. 'You've done a lot by just listening.'

They left the restaurant and, when he had seen her to her bus, he set off on foot towards the British Museum, wondering, as he went, what sort of letter he ought to write to Brian. Should he wash his hands of the whole business and merely scribble a note to the effect that Joan seemed well and happy? Or should he let out that she had told him everything, and then proceed to expostulate, warn, advise? He passed between the huge columns of the portico into the dim coolness within. A regular sermon, he thought with distaste. If only one could approach the problem as it ought to be approached – as a Rabelaisian joke. But then poor Brian could hardly be expected to see it in that light. Even though it would do him a world of good to think for a change in Rabelaisian terms. Anthony showed his card to the attendant and walked down the corridor to the Reading Room. That was always the trouble, he reflected; you could never influence anybody to be anything except himself, or influence him by any means that he didn't already accept the validity of. He pushed open the door and was under the dome, breathing the faint acrid smell of books. Millions of books. And all those hundreds of thousands of authors, century after century – each convinced he was right, convinced that he knew the essential secret, convinced that he could convince the rest of the world by putting it down in black and white. When in fact, of course, the only people anyone ever convinced were the ones that nature and circumstances had actually or potentially convinced already. And even those weren't wholly to be relied on. Circumstances changed. What convinced in January wouldn't necessarily convince in August. The attendant handed him the book that had been reserved for him, and he walked off to his seat. Mountains of the spirit in interminable birth-pangs; and the result was – what? Well, *si ridiculum murem requiris, circumspice*. Pleased with his invention, he looked about him at his fellow readers – the men like walruses, the dim females, the Indians, emaciated or overblown, the whiskered patriarchs, the youths in spectacles. Heirs to all the ages. Depressing, if you took it seriously; but also irresistibly comic. He sat down and opened his book – De Lancre's *Tableau de l'Inconstance des mauvais anges* – at the place where he had stopped reading the day before. '*Le Diable estoit en forme de bouc, ayant une queue et au dessoubs un visage d'homme noir, où elle fut contrainte le baiser. . . .*' He laughed noiselessly to himself. Another one for Mary, he thought.

At five he rose, left his books at the desk and, from Holborn, took the tube to Gloucester Road. A few minutes later he was at Mary Amberley's front door. The maid opened; he smiled at her familiarly and, assuming the privilege of an intimate of the house, ran upstairs to the drawing-room, unannounced.

'I have a story for you,' he proclaimed, as he crossed the room.

'A coarse story, I hope,' said Mary Amberley from the sofa.

Anthony kissed the hand in that affected style he had recently adopted, and sat down. 'To the coarse,' he said, 'all things are coarse.'

'Yes, how lucky that is !' And with that crooked little smile of hers, that dark glitter between narrowed lids, 'A filthy mind,' she added, 'is a perpetual feast.' The joke was old and not her own; but Anthony's laughter pleased her none the less for that. It was whole-hearted laughter, loud and prolonged – louder and longer than the joke itself warranted. But then it wasn't at the joke that he was really laughing. The joke was hardly more than an excuse; that laughter was his response, not to a single stimulus, but to the whole extraordinary and exciting situation. To be able to talk freely about anything (*anything,* mind you) with a woman, a lady, a genuine 'loaf-kneader', as Mr Beavis, in his moments of etymological waggery, had been known to say, a true-blue English loaf-kneader who was also one's mistress, had also read Mallarmé, was also a friend of Guillaume Apollinaire; and to listen to the loaf-kneader preaching what she practised and casually mentioning beds, water-closets, the physiology of what (for the Saxon words still remained unpronounceable) they were constrained to call *l'amour* – for Anthony, the experience was still, after two years and in spite of Mary's occasional infidelities, an intoxicating mixture of liberation and forbidden fruit, of relief and titillation. In his father's universe, in the world of Pauline and the Aunts, such things were simply not there – but not there with a painfully, glaringly conspicuous absence. Like the hypnotized patient who has been commanded to see the five of clubs as a piece of virgin pasteboard, they deliberately failed to perceive the undesirable things, they were conspiratorially silent about all they had been blind to. The natural functions even of the lower animals had to be ignored; there were silences even about quadrupeds. That goat incident, for example – it was the theme, now, of one of Anthony's choicest anecdotes. Exquisitely comic – but how much more comic now than at the time, nearly two years before he first met Mary, when it had actually happened! Picnicking on that horrible Scheideck Pass, with the Weisshorn hanging over them like an obsession, and a clump of gentians, carefully sought out by Mr Beavis, in the grass at their feet, the family had been visited by a half-grown kid, greedy for the salt of their hard-boiled eggs. Shrinking and a little disgusted under their delight, his two small half-sisters had held out their hands to be licked, while Pauline took a snapshot, and Mr Beavis, whose interest in goats was mainly philological, quoted Theocritus. Pastoral scene! But suddenly the little creature had straddled its legs and, still expressionlessly gazing at the Beavis family through the oblong pupils of its large yellow eyes, had proceeded to make water on the gentians.

'They're not very generous with their butter,' and 'How jolly the dear old Weisshorn is looking today,' Pauline and Mr Beavis brought out almost simultaneously – the one, as she peered into her sandwich, in a tone of complaint, the other, gazing away far-focused, with a note in his voice of a rapture none the less genuinely Wordsworthian for being expressed in terms of a gentlemanly and thoroughly English facetiousness.

In haste and guiltily, the two children swallowed their incipient shriek of startled mirth and averted frozen faces from one another and the outrageous goat. Momentarily compromised the world of Mr Beavis and Pauline and the Aunts had settled down again to respectability.

'And what about your story?' Mrs Amberley inquired, as his laughter subsided.

'You shall hear,' said Anthony, and was silent for a little, lighting a cigarette, while he thought of what he was about to say and the way he meant to say it. He was ambitious about his story, wanted to make it a good one, at once amusing and psychologically profound; a smoking-room story that should also be a library story, a laboratory story. Mary must be made to pay a double tribute of laughter and admiration.

'You know Brian Foxe?' he began.

'Of course.'

'Poor old Brian!' By his tone, by the use of the patronizing adjective, Anthony established his position of superiority, asserted his right, the right of the enlightened and scientific vivisector, to anatomize and examine. Yes, poor old Brian! That maniacal preoccupation of his with chastity! Chastity – the most unnatural of all the sexual perversions, he added parenthetically, out of Rémy de Gourmont. Mary's appreciative smile acted on him like a spur to fresh efforts. Fresh efforts, of course, at Brian's expense. But at the moment, that didn't occur to him.

'But what can you expect,' Mrs Amberley put in, 'with a mother like that? One of those spiritual vampires. A regular St Monica.'

'St Monica by Ary Scheffer,' he found himself over-bidding. Not that there was a trace in Mrs Foxe of that sickly insincerity of Scheffer's saint. But the end of his story-telling, which was to provoke Mary's laughter and admiration, was sufficient justification for any means whatever. Scheffer was an excellent joke, too good a joke to be neglected, even if he were beside the point. And when Mary brought out what was at the moment her favourite phrase and talked of Mrs Foxe's 'uterine reactions', he eagerly seized upon the words and began applying them, not merely to Mrs Foxe, but also to Joan and even (making another joke out of the physical absurdity of the thing) to Brian. Brian's uterine reactions towards chastity in conflict with his own and Joan's uterine reactions towards the common desires – it was a drama. A drama, he explained, whose existence hitherto he had only suspected and inferred. Now there was no more need to guess; he knew. Straight from the horse's mouth. Or rather, straight from the mare's. Poor Joan! The vivisector laid another specimen on the operating table.

'Like early Christians,' was Mrs Amberley's comment, when he had finished.

The virulent contempt in her voice made him suddenly remember, for the first time since he had begun his story, that

Brian was his friend, that Joan had been genuinely unhappy. Too late, he wanted to explain that, in spite of all appearances to the contrary, there was nobody he liked and admired and respected more than Brian. 'You mustn't misunderstand me,' he said to Mary retrospectively and in imagination. 'I'm absolutely devoted to him.' Inside his head, he became eloquent on the subject. But no amount of this interior eloquence could alter the fact that he had betrayed confidences and been malicious without apology or qualifying explanation. At the time, of course, this malice had seemed to him the manifestation of his own psychological acuteness; these betrayed confidences, the indispensable facts without which the acuteness could not have been exercised. But now . . .

He found himself all at once confused and tongue-tied with self-reproach.

'I felt awfully sorry for Joan,' he stammered, trying to make amends. 'Promised I'd do all I could to help the poor girl. But what? That's the question. What?' He exaggerated the note of perplexity. Perplexed, he was justified in betraying Joan's confidences; he had told the story (he now began to assure himself) solely for the sake of asking Mary's advice – the advice of an experienced woman of the world.

But the experienced woman of the world was looking at him in the most disquieting way. Mrs Amberley's eyelids had narrowed over a mocking brilliance; the left-hand corner of her mouth was drawn up ironically. 'The nicest thing about you,' she said judicially, 'is your innocence.'

Her words were so wounding that he forgot in an instant Joan, Brian, his own discreditable behaviour, and could think only of his punctured vanity.

'Thank you,' he said, trying to give her a smile of frank amusement. Innocent – she thought him innocent? After their time in Paris. After those jokes about uterine reactions?

'So deliciously youthful, so touching.'

'I'm glad you think so.' The smile had gone all awry; he felt the blood mounting to his cheeks.

'A girl comes to you.' Mrs Amberley went on, 'and complains because she hasn't been kissed enough. And here you are, solemnly asking what you ought to do to help her! And now you're blushing like a beetroot. Darling, I absolutely adore you!' Laying her hand on his arm, 'Kneel down on the floor here,' she commanded. Rather sheepishly, he obeyed. Mary Amberley looked at him for a little in silence, with the same bright mocking expression in her eyes. Then, softly, 'Shall I show you what you can do to help her?' she asked. 'Shall I show you?'

He nodded without speaking; but still, at arm's length, she smiled inquiringly into his face.

'Or am I a fool to show you?' she asked. 'Won't you learn the lesson too well? Perhaps I shall be jealous?' She shook her head and smiled – a gay and 'civilized' smile. 'No, I don't believe in being jealous.' She took his face between her two hands and, whispering, 'This is how you can help her,' drew him towards her.

Anthony had felt humiliated by her almost contemptuous assumption of the dominant role; but no shame, no resentment could annul his body's consciousness of the familiar creepings of pleasure and desire. He abandoned himself to her kisses.

A clock struck, and immediately, from an upper floor, came the approaching sound of shrill childish voices. Mrs Amberley drew back and, laying a hand over his mouth, pushed him away from her. 'You've got to be domestic,' she said, laughing. 'It's six. I do the fond mother at six.'

Anthony scrambled to his feet and, with the idea of fabricating a little favourable evidence, walked over to the fire and stood there with his elbows on the mantelpiece, looking at a Conder water-colour.

The door burst open, and with a yell like the whistle of an express train a small round child of about five came rushing into the room and fairly hurled herself upon her mother. Another little girl, three or four years older than the first, came hurrying after.

'Helen!' she kept calling, and her face, with its expression of anxious disapproval, was the absurd parody of a governess's face. 'Helen! You mustn't. Tell her she mustn't shout like that, Mummy,' she appealed to Mrs Amberley.

But Mrs Amberley only laughed and ran her fingers through

the little one's thick yellow hair. 'Joyce believes in the Ten Commandments,' she said, turning to Anthony. 'Was born believing in them. Weren't you, darling?' She put an arm round Joyce's shoulder and kissed her. 'Whereas Helen and I . . .' She shook her head, 'Stiff-necked and uncircumcised in heart and ears.'

'Nanny says it's the draught that gives her a stiff neck,' Joyce volunteered, and was indignant when her mother and Anthony, and even, by uncomprehending contagion, little Helen, burst out laughing. 'But it's true!' she cried; and tears of outraged virtue were in her eyes. 'Nanny said so.'

CHAPTER TWENTY-EIGHT
June 25th 1934

THE facility with which one could become a Stiggins in modern dress! A much subtler, and therefore more detestable, more dangerous Stiggins. For of course Stiggins himself was too stupid to be either intrinsically very bad or capable of doing much harm to other people. Whereas if I set my mind to it, heaven knows what I mightn't achieve in the way of lies in the soul. Even with *not* setting my mind to it, I could go far – as I perceived, to my horror, today, when I found myself talking to Purchas and three or four of his young people. Talking about Miller's 'anthropological approach'; talking about peace as a way of life as well as an international policy – the way of life being the condition of any policy that had the least hope of being permanently successful. Talking so clearly, so profoundly, so convincingly. (The poor devils were listening with their tongues hanging out.) Much more convincingly than Purchas himself could have done; that muscular-jocular-Christian style starts by being effective, but soon makes hearers feel that they're being talked down to. What they like is that the speaker should be thoroughly serious, but comprehensible. Which is a trick I happen to possess. There I was, discoursing in a really masterly way about the spiritual life, and taking intense pleasure in that mastery, secretly congratulating myself on being not only so clever, but also so good – when all at once I realized who I was: Stiggins. Talking about the theory of courage, self-sacrifice, patience, without any knowledge of the practice. Talking, moreover, in the presence of people who *had* practised what I was preaching – preaching so effectively that the proper rules were reversed: they were listening to me, not I to them. The discovery of what I was doing came suddenly. I was overcome with shame. And yet – more shameful – went on talking. Not for long, however. A minute or two, and I simply had to stop, apologize, insist that it wasn't my business to talk.

This shows how easy it is to be Stiggins by mistake and unconsciously. But also that unconsciousness is no excuse, and that one's responsible for the mistake, which arises, of course, from the pleasure one takes in being more talented than other people and in dominating them by means of those talents. Why is one unconscious? Because one hasn't ever taken the trouble to examine one's motives; and one doesn't examine one's motives, because one's motives are mostly discreditable. Alternatively, of course, one examines one's motives, but tells oneself lies about them until one comes to believing that they're good. Which is the conviction of the self-conscious Stiggins. I've always condemned showing off and the desire to dominate as vulgar, and imagined myself pretty free of these vulgarities. But in so far as free at all, free, I now perceive, only thanks to the indifference which has kept me away from other people, thanks to the external-economic and internal-intellectual circumstances which made me a sociologist rather than a banker, administrator, engineer, working in direct contact with my fellows. Not to make contacts, I have realized, is wrong; but the moment I make them, I catch myself showing off and trying to dominate. Showing off, to make it worse, as Stiggins would have done, trying to dominate by a purely verbal display of virtues which I don't put into practice. Humiliating to find that one's supposed good qualities are mainly due to circumstances and the bad habit of indifference, which made me shirk occasions for behaving badly – or well, for that matter, seeing that it's very difficult to behave either well or badly except towards other people. More humiliating still to find that when, with an effort of goodwill, one creates the necessary opportunities, one immediately responds to them by behaving badly. Note: meditate on the virtues that are the contraries of vanity, lust for power, hypocrisy.

CHAPTER TWENTY-NINE

May 24th 1931

T H E blinds were up; the sunlight lay bright across the dressing-table. Helen, as usual, was still in bed. The days were so long. Lying in the soft, stupefying warmth of her own body under the quilt, she shortened them with sleep, with vague inconsequent thoughts, with drowsy reading. The book, this morning, was Shelley's poems. 'Warm fragrance,' she read, articulating the words in an audible whisper, 'seemed to fall from her light dress ...' (She saw a long-legged figure in white muslin, with sloping shoulders and breasts high set.)

> ... from her light dress
> And her loose hair; and where some heavy tress
> The air of her own speed has disentwined. ...

(The figure was running now, in square-toed pumps cross-gartered with black ribbon over the white cotton stockings.)

> The sweetness seems to satiate the faint wind;
> And in the soul a wild odour is felt
> Beyond the sense, like fiery dews that melt
> Into the bosom of a frozen bud. ...

The half-opened rose gave place to Mark Staithes's strangely twisted face. Those things he had told her the other night about perfumes. Musk, ambergris ... And Henri Quatre with his bromidrosis of the feet. *Bien vous en prend d'être roi; sans cela on ne vous pourrait souffrir. Vous puez comme charogne.* She made a grimace. Hugh's smell was like sour milk.

A clock struck. Nine, ten, eleven, twelve. Twelve! She felt guilty; then defiantly decided that she would stay in bed for lunch. A remembered voice – it was Cynthia's – sounded reproachfully in her memory. 'You ought to go out more, see more people.' But people, Cynthia's people, were such bores. Behind closed eyelids, she saw her mother rapping the top of her skull : 'Solid ivory, my dear!' Hopelessly stupid, ignorant, tasteless, slow. ' I was brought up above my mental station,' was what she had said to Anthony the other night. 'So that now, if ever I have to be with people as silly and uneducated as myself, it's torture, absolute torture!'

Cynthia was sweet, of course; always had been, ever since they were at school together. But Cynthia's husband – that retriever! And her young men, and the young men's young women! 'My boy friend. My girl friend.' How she loathed the words and, still more, the awful way they spoke them! So coy, such saucy implications of sleeping together! When, in fact, most of them were utterly respectable. In the few cases where they weren't respectable, it seemed even worse – a double hypocrisy. Really sleeping together, and pretending to be only archly pretending to do it. The dreary, upper-class Englishness of it all! And then they were always playing games. 'Ga-ames,' Mrs Amberley drawled out of a pre-morphia past. 'A Dear Old School in every home.' See more of those people, do more of the things they did ... She shook her head.

> Spouse! Sister! Angel! Pilot of the Fate
> Whose course has been so starless ...

Was it all nonsense? Or did it mean something – something marvellous she had never experienced? But, yes, she *had* experienced it.

> For in the fields of Immortality
> My spirit should at first have worshipped thine,
> A divine presence in a place divine. ...

It was humiliating, now, to admit it; but the fact remained that, with Gerry, she had known exactly what those lines signified. A divine presence in a place divine. And it had been the presence in bed of a swindler who was also a virtuoso in the art of love-making. She found a perverse pleasure in insisting, as brutally as she could, upon the grotesque disparity between the facts and what had then been her feelings.

I love thee; yes, I feel
That on the fountain of my heart a seal
Is set, to keep its waters pure and bright
For thee ...

Noiselessly, Helen laughed. The sound of the clock chiming the quarter made her think again of Cynthia's advice. There were also the other people – the people they met when Hugh and she dined with the Museum or the University. 'Those god-fearing people' (her mother spoke again), 'who still go on fearing God even though they've pitched him overboard.' Fearing God on committees. Fearing him in W.E.A. lecture-rooms. Fearing him through interminable discussions of the Planned Society. But Gerry's good looks, Gerry's technique as a lover – how could those be planned out of existence? Or the foetus irrepressibly growing and growing in the womb? 'A coordinated housing scheme for the whole country.' She remembered Frank Ditchling's eager, persuasive voice. He had a turned-up nose, and the large nostrils stared at one like a second pair of eyes, insistently. 'Redistribution of the population ... Satellite towns ... Green belts ... Lifts even in working-class flats ...' She had listened, she had succumbed to the spell of his hypnotic nostrils, and at a time it had seemed splendid, worth dying for. But afterwards ... Well, lifts were very convenient – she wished there were one to her own flat. Parks were nice to walk in. But how would Frank Ditchling's crusade affect any of the serious issues? Coordinated housing wouldn't make her mother any less dirty, any less hopelessly at the mercy of an intoxicated body. And Hugh – would Hugh be any different in a satellite town and with a lift from what he was now, when he walked up four flights of stairs in London? Hugh! She thought, derisively, of his letters – all the delicate, beautiful things he had written – and then of the man as he had been in everyday reality, as a husband. 'Show me how I can help you, Hugh.' Arranging his papers, typing his notes, looking up references for him in the library. But always, his eyes glassy behind glass, he had shaken his head: either he didn't need help, or else she wasn't capable of giving it. 'I want to be a good wife, Hugh.' With her mother's laughter loud in her imagination, it had been difficult to pronounce those words. But she had meant them; she *did* want to be a good wife. Darning socks, making hot milk for him before he went to bed, reading up his subject, being *sérieuse*, in a word, for the first time and profoundly. But Hugh didn't want her to be a good wife, didn't want her, so far as she could see, to be anything. A divine presence in a place divine. But the place was his letters; she was present, so far as he was concerned, only at the other end of the postal system. He didn't even want her in bed – or at any rate not much, not in any ordinary way. Green belts, indeed!

It was all beside the point. For the point was those silences in which Hugh enclosed himself at meals. The point was that martyred expression he put on if ever she came into his study while he was working. The point was the furtive squalor of those approaches in the darkness, the revolting detachment and gentleness of a sensuality, in which the part assigned to her was purely ideal. The point was that expression of dismay, almost of horror and disgust, which she had detected that time, within the first few weeks of their marriage, when she was laid up with the flu. He had shown himself solicitous; and at first she had been touched, had felt grateful. But when she discovered how heroic an effort it cost him to attend upon her sick body, the gratitude had evaporated. In itself, no doubt, the effort was admirable. What she resented, what she couldn't forgive was the fact that an effort had had to be made. She wanted to be accepted as she was, even in fever, even vomiting bile. In that book on mysticism she had read, there was an account of Mme Guyon picking up from the floor a horrible gob of phlegm and spittle and putting it in her mouth – as a test of will. Sick, she had been Hugh's test of will; and, since then, each month had renewed his secret horror of her body. It was an intolerable insult – and would be no less intolerable in one of Ditchling's satellite towns in the planned world those god-fearing atheists were always talking about.

But there was also Fanny Carling. 'The mouse' was Helen's name for her – she was so small, so grey, so silently quick. But a mystical mouse. A mouse with enormous blue eyes that seemed perpetually astonished by what they saw behind the appearances of things. Astonished, but bright at the same time with an inexplicable happiness – a happiness that to Helen seemed almost indecent, but which she envied. 'How does one believe in the things that are obviously false' she had asked, half in malice, half genuinely desirous of learning a valuable secret. 'By living,' the mouse answered. 'If you live in the right way, all these things turn out to be obviously true.' And she went on to talk incomprehensible stuff about the love of God and the love of things and people for the sake of God. 'I don't know what you mean.' 'Only because you don't want to, Helen.' Stupid, maddening answer! 'How do you know what I want?'

Sighing, Helen returned to her book.

> I never was attached to that sect,
> Whose doctrine is, that each one should select
> Out of the crowd a mistress or a friend,

('One of my boy friends . . .')

> And all the rest, though fair and wise, commend
> To cold oblivion, though it is the code
> Of modern morals, and the beaten road
> Which those poor slaves with weary footsteps tread,
> Who travel to their home among the dead
> By the broad highway of the world, and so
> With one chained friend, perhaps a jealous foe,
> The dreariest and the longest journey go.

The dreariest and the longest, she repeated to herself. But it could be as long, she thought, and as dreary with several as with only one – with Bob and Cecil and Quentin as with Hugh.

> True Love in this differs from gold and clay,
> That to divide is not to take away.

'I don't believe it,' she said aloud; and anyhow there hadn't been much love to divide. For poor little Cecil she had never pretended to be more than sorry. And with Quentin it was just – well, just hygiene. As for Bob, he had genuinely cared for her and she, on her side, had done her best to care for him. But under those charming manners of his, under those heroic good looks there was really nothing. And as a lover, how hopelessly clumsy he had been, how barbarous and uncomprehending! She had broken with him after only a few weeks. And perhaps, she went on to think, that was her fate – to lose her heart only to men like Gerry, to be loved only by men like Hugh, and Bob and Cecil. To worship cruelty and meanness, be adored by deficiency.

The telephone bell rang; Helen picked up the receiver.

'Hullo.'

It was the voice of Anthony Beavis that answered. He wanted her to dine with him tomorrow.

'I'd love to,' she said, though she had promised the evening to Quentin.

There was a smile on her face, as she leaned back again on the pillows. An intelligent man, she was thinking. Worth fifty of these wretched little Cecils and Quentins. And amusing, charming, even rather good-looking. How nice he had been to her the other night at Mark's dinner! Had gone out of his way to be nice. Whereas that pretentious ass Pitchley had gone out of his way to be rude and snubbing. She had wondered at the time whether Anthony wasn't rather attracted by her. Had wondered and rather hoped so. Now this invitation gave her reasons, not only for hoping, but for thinking so as well. She hummed to herself; then suddenly energetic, threw back the bed-clothes. She had decided that she would get up for lunch.

CHAPTER THIRTY

July 2nd 1914

So far as Mary Amberley was concerned, that spring and early summer had been extremely dull. Anthony was a charming boy, no doubt. But two years were a long time; he had lost his novelty. And then he was really too much in love. It was pleasant having people in love with you, of course, but not too violently, not if it went on too long. They became a nuisance in that case; they began to imagine that they had rights and that you had duties. Which was intolerable. All the fuss that Anthony had made last winter about that art critic in Paris! Flattering, in a certain sense. Mary had rarely seen anyone so desperately upset. And seeing that the art critic had turned out, on a nearer acquaintance, to be a bit of a bore, she had quite enjoyed the process of letting herself be blackmailed by Anthony's dumb miseries and tears. But the principle was wrong. She didn't want to be loved in that blackmailing way. Particularly if it was a long-drawn blackmail. She liked things to be short and sharp and exciting. Another time, and with anyone who wasn't the art critic, she wouldn't allow Anthony to blackmail her. But the trouble was that, except for Sidney Gattick – and she wasn't really sure if she could tolerate Sidney's voice and manner – there was nobody else in sight. The world was a place where all amusing and exciting things seemed, all of a sudden, to have stopped happening. There was nothing for it but to make them happen. That was why she went on at Anthony about what she called 'Joan's treatment', went on and on with a persistence quite out of proportion to any interest she felt in Joan, or in Brian Foxe, or even in Anthony – went on simply in the hope of creating a little fun out of the boring nothingness of the time.

'How's the treatment advancing?' she asked yet again that afternoon in July.

Anthony replied with a long story, elaborately rehearsed, about his position as Heavy Uncle; and how he was gradually establishing himself, on a more intimate footing, as Big Brother; how from Big Brother, he proposed to develop, almost imperceptibly, into Sentimental Cousin; and from Sentimental Cousin into ...

'The truth being,' said Mrs Amberley, interrupting him, 'that you're doing nothing at all.'

Anthony protested. 'I'm going slow. Using strategy.'

'Strategy!' she echoed contemptuously. 'It's just funk.'

He denied it, but with an irrepressible blush. For of course she was half right. The funk was there. In spite of the two years he had spent as Mary's lover, he still suffered from shyness, still lacked self-confidence in the presence of women. But his timidity was not the only inhibiting force at work. There was also compunction, also affection and loyalty. But of these it would be all but impossible to talk to Mary. She would say that he was only disguising his fear in a variety of creditable fancy dresses, would simply refuse to believe in the genuineness of these other feelings of his. And the trouble was that she would have some justification for the refusal. For, after all, there hadn't been much sign of that compunction, that affection and loyalty, when he originally told her the story. How often since then, in futile outbursts of retrospective anger, he had cursed himself for having done it! And, trying to persuade himself that the responsibility was not exclusively his, had also cursed Mary. Blaming her for not having told him that he was betraying confidences out of mere wantonness and vanity; for not having refused to listen to him.

'The fact of the matter,' Mary went on, implacably, 'is that you haven't got the guts to kiss a woman. You can only put on one of those irresistibly tender and melancholy faces of yours and silently beg to be seduced.'

'What nonsense!' But he was blushing more hotly than ever.

Ignoring the interruption, '*She* won't seduce you, of course,' Mary continued. 'She's too young. Not too young to be tempted, perhaps. Because the thing you go for is the mother instinct, and even a child of three has got that. Even a child of three would feel her little heart wrung for you. Absolutely wr-wrung.' She rolled the *r* derisively. 'But seduction ...' Mrs Amberley shook her head. 'You can't expect that till a good deal later. Certainly not from a girl of twenty.'

'As a matter of fact,' said Anthony, trying to divert her from this painful dissection of his character, 'I've never found Joan particularly attractive. A bit too rustic.' He emphasized the word in Mary's own style. 'Besides, she's really rather childish,' he added, and was instantly made to regret his words; for Mary was down on him again, like a hawk.

'Childish!' she repeated. 'I like that. And what about you? Talk about pots and kettles! The feeding-bottle calling the diaper childish. Though of course,' she went on, returning to the attack at the point where she had broken through before, 'it's only natural that you should complain of her. She *is* too childish for you. Too childish to do the pouncing. Childish enough to expect to be pounced on. Poor girl! she's come to the wrong address. She'll get no more kisses out of you than she gets out of that benighted early Christian of hers. Even though you do profess to be civilized. ...'

She was interrupted by the opening of the door.

'Mr Gattick,' the maid announced.

Large, florid, almost visibly luminous with the inner glow of his self-satisfaction and confidence, Sidney Gattick came striding in. His voice boomed resonantly as he spoke his greetings, inquired after her health. A deep voice, virile as only the voice of an actor-manager playing the part of a strong man can be virile. And his profile, Anthony suddenly perceived – that too was an actor's : too noble to be quite true. And after all, he went on to think, with a contempt born of jealousy and a certain envy of the other's worldly success, what were these barristers but actors? Clever actors, but clever with the cleverness of examination-passers; capable of mugging up a case and forgetting it again the moment it was finished, as one mugged up formal logic or The Acts of the Apostles for Pass Mods or Divvers. No real intelligence, no coherent thinking. Just the examinee's mind lodged in the actor's body and expressing itself in the actor's booming voice. And, for this, society paid the creature five or six thousand pounds a years. And the creature regarded itself as important, wise, a man of note; the creature felt itself in a position to be patronizing. Not that it mattered, Anthony assured himself, being patronized by this hollow, booming mountebank. One could laugh – it was so absurd! But in spite of the absurdity, and even while one laughed, the patronage seemed painfully humiliating. The way, for example, he now acted the distinguished old military man, the bluff country squire, and, patting him on the shoulder, said, 'Well, Anthony my lad!' – it was absolutely intolerable. On this occasion, however, the intolerableness, it seemed to Anthony, was worth putting up with. The man might be a tiresome and pretentious fool; but at least his coming had delivered him from the assaults of Mary. In Gattick's presence she couldn't go on at him about Joan.

But he reckoned without Mary and her boredom, her urgent need to make something amusing and exciting happen. Few things are more exciting than deliberate bad taste, more amusing than the spectacle of someone else's embarrassment. Before Gattick had had time to finish his preliminary boomings, she was back again on the old painful subject.

'When you were Anthony's age,' she began, 'did you always wait for the woman to seduce you?'

'Me?'

She nodded.

Recovering from his surprise, Gattick smiled the knowing smile of an experienced Don Juan and, in his most virile *jeune premier*'s voice, said, 'Of course not.' He laughed complacently. 'On the contrary, I'm afraid I used to rush in where angels fear to tread. Got my face slapped sometimes. But more often, not.' He twinkled scabrously.

'Anthony prefers to sit still,' said Mrs Amberley; 'to sit still and wait for the woman to make the advances.'

'Oh, that's bad, Anthony, that's very bad,' said Gattick; and his voice once more implied the military moustaches, the country gentleman's Harris tweeds.

'Here's a poor girl who wants to be kissed,' Mrs Amberley went on, 'and he simply hasn't got the courage to put an arm round her waist and do it.'

'Nothing to say in your own defence, Anthony?' Gattick asked.

Trying, rather unsuccessfully, to pretend that he didn't care, Anthony shrugged his shoulders. 'Only that it isn't true.'

'What isn't true?' asked Mary.

'That I haven't the courage.'

'But it is true that you haven't done the kissing. Isn't it?' she insisted. 'Isn't it?' And when he had to admit that it was true, 'I'm only drawing the obvious inference from the facts,' she said. 'You're a lawyer, Sidney. Tell me if it's a justifiable inference.'

'Absolutely justifiable,' said Gattick, and the Lord Chancellor himself could not have spoken more weightily. An aura of robes and full-bottomed wigs hung round him. He was justice incarnate.

Anthony opened his mouth to speak, then shut it again. In front of Gattick, and with Mary obstinately determined to be only 'civilized', how could he say what he really felt? And if that were what he really felt, why (the question propounded itself once more), why had he told her the story? And told it in that particular style – as though he were a vivisecting comedian? Vanity, wantonness; and then, of course, the fact that he was in love with her and anxious to please, at any cost, even at the cost of what he really felt. (And at the moment of telling, he was forced to admit he hadn't really felt anything but the desire to be amusing.) But, again, that couldn't be put into words. Gattick didn't know about their affair, mustn't know. And even if Gattick hadn't been there, it would have been difficult, almost impossible, to explain it to Mary. She would laugh at him for being romantic – romantic about Brian, about Joan, even about herself; would think him absurd and ridiculous for making tragic mountains out of a simple amorous mole-hill.

'People will insist,' she used to say, 'on treating the *mons Veneris* as though it were Mount Everest. Too silly!'

When at last he spoke, 'I don't do it,' he confined himself to saying, 'because I don't want to do it.'

'Because you don't dare,' cried Mary.

'I do.'

'You don't!' Her dark eyes shone. She was thoroughly enjoying herself.

Booming, but with a hint of laughter in his ponderousness, the Lord Chancellor let fly once more. 'It's an overwhelming case against you,' he said.

'I'm ready to bet on it,' said Mary. 'Five to one. If you do it within a month, I'll give you five pounds.'

'But I tell you I don't want to,' he persisted.

'No, you can't get out of it like that. A bet's a bet. Five pounds to you if you bring it off within a month from today. And if you don't, you pay me a pound.'

'You're too generous,' said Gattick.

'Only a pound,' she repeated. 'But I shall never speak to you again.'

For a few seconds they looked at one another in silence. Anthony had gone very pale. Close-lipped and crookedly, Mary was smiling; between the half-closed lids, her eyes were bright with malicious laughter.

Why did she have to be so horrible to him, he wondered, so absolutely beastly? He hated her, hated her all the more because of his desire for her, because of the memory of the anticipation of those pleasures, because of her liberating wit and knowledge, because of everything, in a word, that made it inevitable for him to do exactly what she wanted. Even though he knew it was stupid and wrong.

Watching him, Mary saw the rebellious hatred in his eyes, and when at last he dropped them, the sign of her own triumph.

'Never again,' she repeated. 'I mean it.'

*

At home, as Anthony was hanging up his hat in the hall, his father called to him.

'Come and look here, dear boy.'

'Damn!' Anthony said to himself resentfully; it was with an aggrieved expression, which Mr Beavis was much too busy to notice, that he entered his father's study.

'Just having a little fun with the map,' said Mr Beavis, who was sitting at his desk with a sheet of the Swiss ordnance survey spread out before him. He had a passion for maps, a passion due in part to his love of walking, in part to his professional interest in place names. 'Comballas,' he murmured to himself, without looking up from the map. 'Chamossaire. Charming, charming!' Then, turning to Anthony, 'It's a thousand pities,' he said, 'that your conscience won't allow you to take a holiday and come along with us.'

Anthony, who had made his work for the research fellowship an excuse for staying in England with Mary, gravely nodded. 'One really can't do any serious reading at high altitudes,' he said.

'So far as I can see,' said Mr Beavis, who had turned back to his map, 'we ought to have the jolliest walks and scrambles all round les Diablerets. And what a delicious name *that* is!' he added parenthetically. 'Up the Col du Pillon, for example.' He ran his finger sinuously along the windings of a road. 'Can you see, by the way!' Perfunctorily, Anthony bent a little closer. 'No, you can't,' Mr Beavis went on. 'I cover it all up with my hand.' He straightened himself up and dipped first into one pocket, then into another. 'Where on earth,' he said, frowning; then suddenly, as his most daring philological joke came to his mind, he changed the frown into a sly smile. 'Where on earth is my teeny weeny penis. Or, to be accurate, my teeny weeny *weeny* ...'

Anthony was so taken aback that he could only return a blank embarrassed stare to the knowing twinkle his father gaily shot at him.

'My pencil,' Mr Beavis was forced to explain. '*Penecillus*: diminutive of *peniculus*: double diminutive of *penis*; which as you know,' he went on, at last producing the teeny weeny *weeny* from his inside left breast pocket, 'originally meant a tail. And now let's attack the Pillon again.' Lowering the point of the pencil to the map, he traced out the zigzags. 'And when we're at the top of the Col,' he continued, 'we bear north-north-west round the flank of Mont Fornettaz until . . .'

It was the first time, Anthony was thinking that his father had ever, in his presence, made any allusion to the physiology of sex.

CHAPTER THIRTY-ONE

September 6th 1933

'DEATH,' said Mark Staithes. 'It's the only thing we haven't succeeded in completely vulgarizing. Not from any lack of the desire to do so, of course. We're like dogs on an acropolis. Trotting round with inexhaustible bladders and only too anxious to lift a leg against every statue. And mostly we succeed. Art, religion, heroism, love – we've left our visiting-card on all of them. But death – death remains out of reach. We haven't been able to defile *that* statue. Not yet, at any rate. But progress is still progressing.' He demonstrated the anatomy of a smile. The larger hopes, the proliferating futures . . .' The bony hands went out in a lavish gesture. 'One day, no doubt, some genius of the kennel will manage to climb up and deposit a well-aimed tribute bang in the middle of the statue's face. But luckily progress hasn't yet got so far. Death still remains.'

'It remains,' Anthony repeated. 'But the smoke-screen is pretty thick. We manage to forget it most of the time.'

'But not all the time. It remains, unexorcizably. Intact. Indeed,' Mark qualified, 'more than intact. We have bigger and better smoke-screens than our fathers had. But behind the smoke the enemy is more formidable. Death's grown, I should say, now that that the consolations and hopes have been taken away. Grown to be almost as large as it was when people seriously believed in hell. Because, if you're a busy film-going, newspaper-reading, football-watching, chocolate-eating modern, then death *is* hell. Every time the smoke-screen thins out a bit, people catch a glimpse and are terrified. I find that a very consoling thought.' He smiled again. 'It makes up for a great deal. Even for those busy little dogs on the acropolis.' There was a silence. Then, in another tone, 'It's a comfort,' he resumed, 'to think that death remains faithful. Everything else may have gone; but death remains faithful,' he repeated. 'If we choose to risk our lives, we can risk them as completely as ever we did.' He rose, took a turn or two about the room; then, coming to a halt in front of Anthony's chair, 'That's what I really came to see you about,' he said.

'What?'

'About this business of risking one's life. I've been feeling as though I were stuck. Bogged to the neck in civilized humanity.' He made the grimace of one who encounters a foul smell. 'There seemed to be only one way out. Taking risks again. It would be like a whiff of fresh air. I thought perhaps that you too . . .' He left the sentence unfinished.

'I've never taken a risk,' said Anthony, after a pause. 'Only had one taken for me once,' he added, remembering the bumpkin with the hand-grenade.

'Isn't that a reason for beginning?'

'The trouble,' said Anthony, frowning to himself, 'the trouble is that I've always been a coward. A moral one, certainly. Perhaps also a physical one – I don't know. I've never really had an opportunity of finding out.'

'I should have thought that that was a still more cogent reason.'

'Perhaps.'

'If it's a case of changing the basis of one's life, wouldn't it be best to change it with a bang?'

'Bang into a corpse?'

'No, no. Just a risk; not suicide. It's merely dangerous, the business I'm thinking of. No more.' He sat down again. 'I had a letter the other day,' he began. 'From an old friend of mine in Mexico. A man I worked with on the coffee *finca*. Jorge Fuentes, by name. A remarkable creature, in his way.'

He outlined Don Jorge's history. Besieged by the revolutionaries on his estate in the valley of Oaxaca. Most of the other landowners had fled. He was one of the only men who put up a resistance. At first he had had his two brothers to help him. But they were killed, one at long range, the other by machetes in an ambush among the cactuses. He had carried on the fight single-handed. Then, one day when he was out riding round the fields, a dozen of them managed to break into the house. He had come home to find the bodies of his wife and their two little boys lying mangled in the courtyard. After that, the place seemed no longer worth defending. He stayed long enough to shoot three of the murderers, then abandoned his patrimony and went to work for other men. It was during this period that Mark had known him. Now he possessed his own house again and some land; acted as agent for most of the planters on the Pacific coast of Oaxaca state; recruited their labour for them in the mountain villages, and was the only man the Indians trusted, the only one who didn't try to swindle them. Recently, however, there had been trouble. Don Jorge had gone into politics, become the leader of a party, made enemies and hardly less dangerous friends. He was in opposition now; the state governor was persecuting him and his allies. A bad man, according to Don Jorge; corrupt, unjust – unpopular too. It shouldn't be difficult to get rid of him. Some of the troops would certainly come over. But before he started, Don Jorge wanted to know if there was any prospect of Mark's being in the neighbourhood of Oaxaca in the immediate future.

'Poor old Jorge! He has a most touching belief in the soundness of my judgement.' Mark laughed. Thus to understate Don Jorge's faith in him, thus to withhold the reasons of that faith, sent a glow of satisfaction running through his body. He might have told Anthony of that occasion when the old ass had gone and let himself be caught by bandits, and of the way he had been rescued. A good story, and creditable to himself. But not to tell it gave him more pleasure than telling it would have done. 'True, it's better than *his* judgement,' Mark went on. 'But that isn't saying much. Don Jorge's brave – brave as a lion; but fool-hardy. No sense of reality. He'll make a mess of his *coup d'état.*'

'Unless you are there to help him, I take it. And do you propose to be there?'

Mark nodded. 'I've written him that I'll start as soon as I can settle my affairs in England. It occurred to me that you ...' Again he left the sentence unfinished and looked inquiringly at Anthony.

'Do you think it's a good cause?' Anthony asked at last.

The other laughed. 'As good as any other Mexican politician's cause,' he answered.

'Is that good enough?'

'For my purpose. And anyhow, what is a good cause? Tyranny under commissars, tyranny under *Gauleiters* – it doesn't seem to make much difference. A drill-sergeant is always a drill-sergeant, whatever the colour of his shirt.'

'Revolution for revolution's sake, then?'

'No, for mine. For the sake of every man who takes part in the thing. For every man can get as much fun out of it as I can.'

'I expect it would be good for me,' Anthony brought out after a pause.

'I'm sure it would be.'

'Though I'm devilishly frightened – even at this distance.'

'That'll make it all the more interesting.'

Anthony drew a deep breath. 'All right,' he said at last. 'I'll come with you.' Then vehemently, 'It's the most stupid, senseless idea I've ever heard of,' he concluded. 'So, as I've always been so clever and sensible ...' He broke off and, laughing, reached for his pipe and the tin of tobacco.

CHAPTER THIRTY-TWO

July 29th 1934

WITH Helen today to hear Miller speaking at Tower Hill, during the dinner hour. A big crowd. He spoke well – the right mixture of arguments, jokes, emotional appeal. The theme, peace. Peace everywhere or no peace at all. International peace not achievable unless a translation into policy of inter-individual relations. Militarists at home, in factory, and office, towards inferiors and rivals, cannot logically expect governments which represent them to behave as pacifists. Hypocrisy and stupidity of those who advocate peace between states, while conducting private wars in business or the family. Meanwhile, there was much heckling by communists in the crowd. How can anything be achieved without revolution? Without liquidating the individuals and classes standing in the way of social progress? And so on. Answer (always with extraordinary good humour and wit): means determine ends. Violence and coercion produce a post-revolutionary society, not communistic but (like the Russian) hierarchical, ruled by an oligarchy using secret police methods. And all the rest.

After about a quarter of an hour, an angry young heckler climbed on to the little wall, where Miller was standing, and threatened to knock him off if he didn't stop. 'Come on then, Archibald.' The crowd laughed; the young man grew still angrier, advanced, clenched, squared up. 'Get down, you old bastard, or else . . .' Miller stood quite still, smiling, hands by side, saying, All right; he had no objection to being knocked off. The attacker made sparring movements, brought a fist to within an inch of Miller's nose. The old man didn't budge, showed no sign of fear or anger. The other drew back the hand, but instead of bringing it into Miller's face, hit him on the chest. Pretty hard. Miller staggered, lost his balance and fell off the wall into the crowd. Apologized to the people he'd fallen on, laughed, got up again on to the wall. Repetition of the performance. Again the young man threatened the face, but again, when Miller didn't lift his hands, or show either fear or anger, hit him on the chest. Miller went down and again climbed up. Got another blow. Came up once more. This time the man screwed himself up to hitting the face, but only with the flat of his hand. Miller straightened his head and went on smiling. 'Three shots a penny, Archibald.' The man let out at the body and knocked him off the wall. Up again. Miller looked at his watch. 'Another ten minutes before you need go back to work, Archibald. Come on.' But this time the man could only bring himself to shake his fist and call Miller a bloodsucking old reactionary. Then turned and walked off along the wall, pursued by derisive laughter, jokes, and whistlings from the crowd. Miller went on with his speech.

Helen's reaction was curious. Distress at the spectacle of the young man's brutality towards the old. But at the same time anger with Miller for allowing himself to be knocked about without resistance. The reason for this anger? Obscure; but I think she resented Miller's success. Resented the fact that the young man had been reduced, psychologically, to impotence. Resented the demonstration that there was an alternative to terrorism and a non-violent means of combating it. 'It's only a trick,' she said. Not a very easy trick, I insisted; and that I certainly couldn't perform it. 'Anyone could learn it, if he tried.' 'Possibly; wouldn't it be a good thing if we all tried?' 'No. I think it's stupid.' Why? She found it hard to answer. 'Because it's unnatural,' was the reason she managed to formulate at last – and proceeded to develop it in terms of a kind of egalitarian philosophy. 'I want to be like other people. To have the same feelings and interests. I don't want to make myself different. Just an ordinary person; not somebody who's proud of having learnt a difficult trick. Like that old Miller of yours.' I point out that we'd all learnt such difficult tricks as driving cars, working in offices, reading and writing, crossing the street. Why shouldn't we all learn this other difficult trick? A trick, potentially, so much more useful. If all were to learn it, then one could afford to be like other people, one could share all their feelings in safety, with the certainty that one would be sharing something good, not bad. But Helen wasn't to be persuaded. And when I suggested that we should join the old man for a late lunch, she refused. Said she didn't want to know him. That the young man had been quite right; Miller was a reactionary. Disguising himself in a shroud of talk about economic justice; but underneath just a tory agent. His insistence that changes in social organization weren't enough, but that they must be accompanied by, must spring from a change in personal relations – what was that but a plea for conservatism? 'I think he's pernicious,' she said. 'And I think you're pernicious.' But she consented to have lunch with me. Which showed how little stock she set on my powers to shake her convictions! Arguments – I might have lots of good arguments; to those she was impervious. But

Miller's action had got between the joints of her armour. He acted his doctrine, didn't rest content with talking it. Her confidence that I couldn't get between the joints, as he had done, was extremely insulting. The more so as I knew it was justified.

Perseverance, courage, endurance. All, fruits of love. Love goodness enough, and indifference and slackness are inconceivable. Courage comes as to the mother defending her child; and at the same time there is no fear of the opponent, who is loved, whatever he may do, because of the potentialities for goodness in him. As for pain, fatigue, disapproval – they are borne cheerfully, because they seem of no consequence by comparison with the goodness loved and pursued. Enormous gulf separating me from this state! The fact that Helen was not afraid of my perniciousness (as being only theoretical), while dreading Miller's (because his life was the same as his argument), was a painful reminder of the existence of this gulf.

CHAPTER THIRTY-THREE

July 18th 1914

THE curtain rose, and before them was Venice, green in the moonlight, with Iago and Roderigo talking together in the deserted street.

'Light, I say! Light!' Brabantio called from his window. And in an instant the street was thronged, there was a clanking of weapons and armour, torches and lanterns burned yellow in the green darkness. . . .

'Horribly vulgar scenery, I'm afraid,' said Anthony as the curtain fell after the first scene.

Joan looked at him in surprise. 'Was it?' Then : 'Yes, I suppose it was,' she added, hypocritically paying the tribute of philistinism to taste. In reality, she had thought it too lovely. 'You know,' she confessed, 'this is only the fifth time I've ever been in a theatre.'

'Only the fifth time?' he repeated incredulously.

But here was another street and more armed men and Iago

again bluff and hearty, and Othello himself, dignified like a king, commanding in every word and gesture; and when Brabantio came in with all his men, and the torchlight glittering on the spears and halberds, how heroically serene! 'Keep up your bright swords, for the dew will rust them.' A kind of anguish ran up and down her spine as she listened, as she saw the dark hand lifted, as the sword-points dropped, under his irresistible compulsion, towards the ground.

'He speaks the lines all right,' Anthony admitted.

The council chamber was rich with tapestry; the red-robed senators came and went. And here was Othello again. Still kingly, but with a kingliness that expressed itself, not in commands, this time, not in the lifting of a hand, but on a higher plane than that of the real world – in the calm, majestic music of the record of his wooing.

> Wherein of antres vast and deserts idle,
> Rough quarries, rocks and hills whose heads touch heaven,
> It was my hint to speak. . . .

Her lips moved as she repeated the familiar words after him – familiar but transfigured by the voice, the bearing of the speaker, the setting, so that, though she knew them by heart, they seemed completely new. And here was Desdemona, so young, so beautiful, with her neck and her bare shoulders rising frail and slender out of the heavy magnificence of her dress. Sumptuous brocade, and beneath it, the lovely irrelevance of a girl's body; beneath the splendid words, a girl's voice.

> You are the Lord of duty,
> I am hitherto your daughter; but here's my husband.

She felt again that creeping anguish along her spine. And now they were all gone, Othello, Desdemona, senators, soldiers, all the beauty, all the nobleness – leaving only Iago and Roderigo whispering together in the empty room. 'When she is sated of his body, she will find the error of her choice.' And then that fearful soliloquy. Evil, deliberate, and conscious of itself. . . .

The applause, the lights of the entr'acte were a sacrilegious irrelevance; and when Anthony offered to buy her a box of chocolates she refused almost indignantly.

'Do you think there really are people like Iago?' she asked.

He shook his head. 'Men don't tell themselves that the wrong they're doing is wrong. Either they do it without thinking. Or else they invent reasons for believing it's right. Iago's a bad man who passes other people's judgements of him upon himself.'

The lights went down again. They were in Cyprus. Under a blazing sun, Desdemona's arrival; then Othello's – and oh, the protective tenderness of his love!

The sun had set. In cavernous twilight, between stone walls, the drinking, the quarrel, the rasping of sword on sword, and Othello again, kingly and commanding, imposing silence, calling them all to obedience. Kingly and commanding for the last time. For in the scenes that followed, how terrible it was to watch the great soldier, the holder of high office, the civilized Venetian, breaking down, under Iago's disintegrating touches, breaking down into the African, into the savage, into the uncontrolled and primordial beast! 'Handkerchief – confessions – handkerchief! ... Noses, ears, and lips! Is it possible?' And then the determination to kill. 'Do it not with poison, strangle her in bed, even the bed she hath contaminated.' And afterwards the horrible outburst of his anger against Desdemona, the blow delivered in public; and in the humiliating privacy of the locked room, that colloquy between the kneeling girl and an Othello, momentarily sane again, but sane with the base, ignoble sanity of Iago, cynically knowing only the worst, believing in the possibility only of what was basest.

> I cry you mercy then;
> I took you for that cunning whore of Venice
> That married with Othello.

There was a hideous note of derision in his voice, an undertone of horrible obscene laughter. Irrepressibly, she began to tremble.

'I can't bear it,' she whispered to Anthony between the scenes. 'Knowing what's going to happen. It's too awful. I simply can't bear it.'

Her face was pale, she spoke with a violent intensity of feeling.

'Well, let's go,' he suggested. 'At once.'

She shook her head. 'No, no. I must see it to the end. *Must*.'

'But if you can't bear it . . . ?'

'You mustn't ask me to explain. Not now.'

The curtain rose again.

> My mother had a maid call'd Barbara;
> She was in love, and he she lov'd prov'd mad
> And did forsake her; she had a song of 'willow'.

Her heart was beating heavily; she felt sick with anticipation. In an almost childish voice, sweet, but thin and untrained, Desdemona began to sing.

> The poor soul sat sighing by a sycamore tree,
> Sing all a green willow.

The vision wavered before Joan's eyes, became indistinct; the tears rolled down her cheeks.

It was over at last; they were out in the street again.

Joan drew a deep breath. 'I feel I'd like to go for a long walk,' she said. 'Miles and miles without stopping.'

'Well, you can't,' he said shortly 'Not in those clothes.'

Joan looked at him with an expression of pained astonishment. 'You're angry with me,' she said.

Blushing, he did his best to smile it off. 'Angry? Why on earth should I be angry?' But she was right, of course. He *was* angry – angry with everyone and everything that entered into the present insufferable situation: with Mary for having pushed him into it; with himself for having allowed her to push him in; with Joan for being the subject of that monstrous bet; with Brian because he was ultimately responsible for the whole thing; with Shakespeare, even, and the actors and this jostling crowd. . . .

'Don't be cross,' she pleaded. 'It's been such a lovely evening. If you knew how marvellous it's made me feel! But I have to be so careful with the marvellousness. Like carrying a cup that's full to the brim. The slightest jolt – and down it goes. Let me carry it safely home.'

Her words made him feel very embarrassed, almost guilty. He laughed nervously. 'Don't you think you can carry it home safely in a hansom?' he asked.

Her face lit up with pleasure at the suggestion. He waved his hand; the cab drew up in front of them. They climbed in and closed the door upon themselves. The driver jerked his reins. The old horse walked a few steps, then, at the crack of the whip, broke reluctantly into a very slow trot. Along Coventry Street, through the glare of the Circus, into Piccadilly. Above the spire of St James's the dilute blackness of the sky was flushed with a coppery glow. Reflected in the polished darkness of the roadway, the long recession of the lamps seemed inexpressibly mournful, like a reminder of death. But here were the trees of the Green Park – bright wherever the lamplight struck upwards into the leaves with an earthly, a more than spring-like freshness. There was life as well as death.

Joan sat in silence, holding firm within herself the fragile cup of that strange happiness that was also and at the same time intensest sadness. Desdemona was dead, Othello was dead, and the lamps retreating for ever down their narrowing vistas were symbols of the same destiny. And yet the melancholy of these converging parallels and the pain of the tragedy were as essential constituents of her present joy as her delight in the splendour of the poetry, as her pleasure in the significant and almost allegorical beauty of those illumined leaves. For this joy of hers was not one particular emotion exclusive of all others; it was all emotions – a state, so to speak, of general and undifferentiated movedness. The overtones and aftertones of horror, of delight, of pity and laughter – all lingered harmoniously in her mind. She sat there, behind the slowly trotting horse, serene, but with a serenity that contained the potentiality of every passion. Sadness, delight, fear, mirth – they were all there at once, impossibly conjoined within her mind. She cherished the precarious miracle.

A hansom, he was thinking – it was the classical opportunity. They were already at Hyde Park Corner; by this time he ought at least to have been holding her hand. But she sat there like a statue, staring at nothing in another world. She would feel outraged if he were to call her roughly back to reality.

'I shall have to invent a story for Mary,' he decided. But it wouldn't be easy; Mary had an extraordinary talent for detecting lies.

Reined in, the old horse gingerly checked itself, came to a halt. They had arrived. Oh, too soon, Joan thought, too soon.

She would have liked to drive on like this for ever, nursing in silence her incommunicable joy. It was with a sigh that she stepped on to the pavement.

'Aunt Fanny said you were to come and say good night to her if she was still up.'

That meant that the last chance of doing it had gone, he reflected, as he followed her up the steps and into the dimly lighted hall.

'Aunt Fanny,' Joan called softly as she opened the drawing-room door. But there was no answer; the room was dark.

'Gone to bed?'

She turned back towards him and nodded affirmatively. They stood there for a moment in silence.

'I shall have to go,' he said at last.

'It was a wonderful evening, Anthony. Simply wonderful.'

'I'm glad you enjoyed it.' Behind his smile, he was thinking with apprehension that that last chance had not yet disappeared.

'It was more than enjoying,' she said. 'It was . . . I don't know how to say what it was.' She smiled at him, added 'Good night,' and held out her hand.

Anthony took it, said good night in his turn; then, suddenly deciding that it was now or never, stepped closer, laid an arm round her shoulder and kissed her.

The suddenness of his decision and his embarrassment imparted to his movements a clumsy abruptness indistinguishable from that which would have been the result of a violent impulse irrepressibly breaking through restraints. His lips touched her cheek first of all, then found her mouth. She made as if to withdraw, to avert her face; but the movement was checked almost before it was begun. Her mouth came back to his, drawn irresistibly. All the diffuse and indefinite emotion that had accumulated within her during the evening suddenly crystallized, as it were, round her surprise and the evidence of his desire and this almost excruciating pleasure that, from her lips, invaded her whole body and took possession of her mind. The astonishment and anger of the first second were swallowed up in an apocalypse of new sensations. It was as though a quiet darkness were violently illuminated, as though the relaxed dumb strings of an instrument had been wound up and were vibrating ever more shrilly and piercingly, until at last the brightness and the tension annihilated themselves in their own excess. She felt herself becoming empty; enormous spaces opened up within her, gulfs of darkness.

Anthony felt her body droop limp and heavy in his arms. So heavy indeed, and with so unexpected a weight, that he almost lost his balance. He staggered, then braced himself and held her up more closely.

'What is it, Joan?'

She did not answer, but leaned her forehead against his shoulder. He could feel that if he were now to let her go, she would fall. Perhaps she was ill. He would have to call for help – wake up the aunt – explain what had happened. . . . Wondering desperately what to do, he looked about him. The lamp in the hall projected through the open door of the drawing-room a strip of light that revealed the end of a sofa covered with yellow chintz. Still holding her up with one arm about her shoulders, he bent down and slid the other behind her knees; then, with an effort (for she was heavier than he had imagined), lifted her off her feet, carried her along the narrow path of illumination that led into the darkness, and lowered her as gently as her weight would allow him on to the sofa.

Kneeling on the floor beside her, 'Are you feeling better now?' he asked.

Joan drew a deep breath, passed a hand across her forehead, then opened her eyes and looked at him, but only for a moment; overcome by an access of timidity and shame, she covered her face with her hands. 'I'm so sorry,' she whispered. 'I don't know what happened. I felt so faint all of a sudden.' She was silent for a little; the lamps were alight again, the stretched wires were vibrating – but tolerably, not to excess. She parted her hands once more and turned towards him, shyly smiling.

With eyes that had grown accustomed to the faint light, he looked anxiously into her face. Thank God, she seemed to be all right. He wouldn't have to call the aunt. His feeling of relief was so profound that he took her hand and pressed it tenderly.

'You're not cross with me, Anthony?'

'Why should I be?'

'Well, you have every right. Fainting like that . . .' Her face felt naked and exposed; withdrawing her hand from his grasp, she once more hid her shame. Fainting like that ... The recollection humiliated her. Thinking of that sudden, silent, violent gesture of his, 'He loves me,' she said to herself. And Brian? But Brian's absence seemed to have been raised to a higher power. He was not there with an unprecedented intensity, not there to the point of never having been there. All that was really there was this living presence beside her – the presence of desire, the presence of hands and mouth, the presence, potential but waiting, waiting to actualize itself again, of those kisses. She felt her breasts lift, though she was unaware of having taken a deep breath; it was as though someone else had drawn it. 'He loves me,' she repeated; it was a justification. She dropped her hands from her face, looked at him for a moment, then reached out and, whispering his name, drew his head down towards her.

*

'Well, what's the result?' Mary called from the sofa as he entered. By the gloomy expression on Anthony's face she judged that it was she who had won the bet; and this annoyed her. She felt suddenly very angry with him – doubly and trebly angry; because he was so spiritless; because he hadn't cared enough for her to win his bet in spite of the spiritlessness; because he was forcing upon her a gesture which she didn't in the least want to make. After a day's motoring with him in the country she had come to the conclusion that Sidney Gattick was absolutely insufferable. By contrast, Anthony seemed the most charming of men. She didn't want to banish him, even temporarily. But her threat had been solemn and explicit; if she didn't carry it out, at least in part, all her authority was gone. And now the wretch was forcing her to keep her word. In a tone of angry reproach, 'You've been a coward and lost,' she said. 'I can see it.'

He shook his head. 'No, I've won.'

Mary regarded him doubtfully. 'I believe you're lying.'

'I'm not.' He sat down beside her on the sofa.

'Well, then, why do you look so glum? It's not very flattering to me.'

'Why on earth did you make me do it?' he burst out. 'It was idiotic.' It had also been wrong; but Mary would only laugh if he said that. 'I always knew it was idiotic. But you insisted.' His voice was shrill with a complaining resentment. 'And now God knows where I've landed myself.' Where he'd landed Joan and Brian, for that matter. 'God knows.'

'But explain,' cried Mary Amberley, 'explain! Don't talk like a minor prophet.' Her eyes were bright with laughing curiosity. She divined some delightfully involved and fantastic situation. 'Explain,' she repeated.

'Well, I did what you told me,' he answered sullenly.

'Hero!'

'There's nothing funny about it.'

'What! did you get your face slapped?'

Anthony frowned angrily and shook his head.

'Then how *did* she take it?'

'That's just the trouble: she took it seriously.'

'Seriously?' Mary questioned. 'You mean, she threatened to tell papa?'

'I mean, she thought I was in love with her. She wants to break it off with Brian.'

Mrs Amberley threw back her head and gave utterance to a peal of her clear, richly vibrant laughter.

Anthony felt outraged. 'It's not a joke.'

'That's where you make your mistake.' Mary wiped her eyes and took a deep breath. 'It's one of the best jokes I ever heard. But what do you propose to do?'

'I shall have to tell her it's all a mistake.'

'That'll be an admirable scene!'

He shook his head. 'I shall write a letter.'

'Courageous, as usual!' She patted his knee. 'But now I want to hear the details. How was it that you let her go as far as she did? To the point of thinking you were in love with her. To the point of wanting to break it off with Brian. Couldn't you nip it in the bud?'

'It was difficult,' he muttered, avoiding her inquisitive eye. 'The situation . . . well, it got a bit out of control.'

'You mean, you lost your head?'

'If you like to put it that way,' he admitted reluctantly, thinking what a fool he had been, what an utter fool. He ought, of course, to have retreated when she turned towards him in the darkness; he ought to have refused her kisses, to have made it quite clear that his own had been light-hearted and without significance. But instead of that he had accepted them: out of laziness and cowardice, because it had been too much of an effort to make the necessary and necessarily difficult explanation; out of a certain weak and misplaced kindness of heart, because it would have hurt and humiliated her if he had said no – and to inflict a suffering he could actually witness was profoundly distasteful to him. And having accepted, he had enjoyed her kisses, had returned them with a fervour which *he* knew to be the result only of a detached, a momentary sensuality, but which Joan, it was obvious now (and he had known it even at the time), would inevitably regard as being roused specifically by herself, as having her for its special and irreplaceable object. An impartial observer would say that he had done his best, had gone out of his way, to create the greatest possible amount of misunderstanding in the shortest possible time.

'How do you propose to get out of it?' Mary asked.

He hated her for putting the question that was tormenting him. 'I shall write her a letter,' he said. As though *that* were an answer!

'And what will Brian say about it?'

'I'm going to stay with him tomorrow,' he replied irrelevantly. 'In the Lakes.'

'Like Wö-ödsworth,' said Mary. 'What fun that'll be! And what exactly do you propose to tell him about Joan?' she went on inexorably.

'Oh, I shall explain.'

'But suppose Joan explains first – in a different way?'

He shook his head. 'I told her I didn't want her to write to Brian before I'd talked to him.'

'And you think she'll do what you ask?'

'Why shouldn't she?'

Mary shrugged her shoulders and looked at him, smiling crookedly, her eyes bright between narrowed eyelids. 'Why should she, if it comes to that?'

CHAPTER THIRTY-FOUR

March 3rd 1928

'Reorganization . . .' 'Readjustment . . .' 'Writing down of capital values in the light of existing trade conditions . . .' Anthony lifted his eyes from the printed page. Propped up on her pillows, Mary Amberley was staring at him, he found, with an embarrassing intentness.

'Well?' she asked, leaning forward. Hennaed to an impossible orange, a lock of tousled hair fell drunkenly across her forehead. Her bed-jacket opened as she moved; under soiled lace, the breasts swung heavily towards him. 'What does it mean?'

'It means that they're politely going bankrupt on you.'

'Going bankrupt?'

'Paying you six and eightpence in the pound.'

'But Gerry told me they were doing so well,' she protested in a tone of angry complaint.

'Gerry doesn't know everything,' he charitably explained.

But, of course, the ruffian had known only too well; had known, had acted on his knowledge, had been duly paid by the people who wanted to unload their shares before the crash came. 'Why don't you ask *him* about it?' he said aloud, and in a tone that implied some of the resentment he felt at having been dragged, this very evening of his return from New York, into the entanglements of Mary's squalid tragedy. Everyone else, he supposed, had fled from her since she'd started taking that morphia; alone of all the friends, having been out of England for half a year, he had had as yet no opportunity and been given no reason to flee. Absence had preserved their friendship, as though in cold storage, in the state it was in before he left. When she had asked him urgently to come and see her, he had no excuse to refuse. Besides, people exaggerated; she couldn't be as bad as they made out.

'Why don't you ask *him*?' he repeated irritably.

'He's gone to Canada.'

'Oh, he's gone to Canada.'

There was a silence. He laid the paper down on the coverlet.

Mrs Amberley picked it up and re-read it – for the hundredth time, in the absurd and desperate hope that there might, this hundredth time, be something new in it, something different.

Anthony looked at her. The lamp on the bed-table lit up the profile she presented to him with a ruthlessly revealing brilliance. How hollow the cheeks were! And those lines round the mouth, those discoloured pouches of skin beneath the eyes! Remembering how she looked when he had seen her last, that time in Berkshire, only the previous summer, Anthony was appalled. The drug had aged her twenty years in half as many months. And it was not only her body that had been ravaged; the morphia had also changed her character, transformed her into someone else, someone (there had been no exaggeration at all) much worse. That engaging absence of mind, for example, that vagueness, of which, as of yet another feminine allurement, she always used to be so irritatingly vain, had now degenerated into almost an idiot's indifference. She forgot, she wasn't aware; above all, she didn't care, she couldn't any longer be bothered. Grotesquely dyed (in the hope, he supposed, of regaining some of the attractiveness which she could not help noticing that she had lost), the hair was greasy and uncombed. A smear of red paint, clumsily laid on, enlarged her lower lip into an asymmetrical shapelessness. A cigarette-end had burned a round hole in the eiderdown, and the feathers fluttered up like snow-flakes each time she moved. The pillows were smudged with rouge and yolk of egg. There was a brown stain of coffee on the turned-back sheet. Between her body and the wall, the tray on which her dinner had been brought up stood precariously tilted. Still stained with gravy, a knife had slipped on to the counterpane.

With a sudden movement, Mrs Amberley crumpled up the paper and threw it from her. 'That beast!' she cried, in a voice that trembled with rage. 'That beast! He absolutely forced me to put my money into this. And now look what's happened!' The tears overflowed, carrying the black of her painted eyelashes in long sooty trickles down her cheeks.

'He did it on purpose,' she went on through her angry sobbing. 'Just in order to harm me. He's a sadist, really. He likes hurting people. He does it for pleasure.'

'For profit,' Anthony almost said; but checked himself. She

seemed to derive some consolation from the thought that she had been swindled, not from vulgarly commercial motives, but gratuitously, because of a fiendishness allied to and springing from the passion of love. It would be unkind to deprive her of that illusion. Let the poor woman think the thoughts she found least painfully humiliating. Besides, the less she was contradicted and diverted, the sooner, it might be hoped, would she stop. Prudently as well as considerately, he contented himself with a non-committal nod.

'When I think of all I did for that man!' Mrs Amberley burst out. But while she recited her incoherent catalogue of generosities and kindnesses, Anthony could not help thinking of what the man had done for her; above all, of the terms in which Gerry was accustomed to describe what he had done. Gross, extravagantly cynical terms. Terms of an incredible blackguardism. One was startled, one was set free into sudden laughter; and one was ashamed that such inadmissible brutalities should contain any element of liberating truth. And yet they *were* true.

'All the most intelligent people in London,' Mrs Amberley was sobbing. 'He met them all at my house.'

'These old hags!' Gerry Watchett's voice sounded clearly in Anthony's memory. 'They'll do anything to get it, absolutely anything.'

'Not that he ever appreciated them,' she went on. 'He was too stupid for that, too barbarous.'

'Not a bad old bitch really, if she gets enough of it to keep her quiet. The problem is to give her enough. It's uphill work, I can tell you.'

The tone changed from anger to self-pity. 'But what shall I do?' she wailed. 'What *can* I do? Without a penny. Living on charity.'

He tried to reassure her. There was still something. Quite a decent little sum, really. She would never starve. If she lived carefully, if she economized ...

'But I shall have to give up this house,' she interrupted, and, when he agreed that of course she would have to give up, broke out into new and louder lamentations. Giving up the house was worse than being penniless and living on charity – worse, because more conceivable, a contingency nearer to the

284

realities of her actual life. Without her pictures, without her furniture, how could she live? She was made physically ill by ugliness. And then small rooms – she developed claustrophobia in small rooms. And how could she possibly manage without her books? How did he expect her to work, when she was poor? For of course she was going to work; had already planned to write a critical study of the modern French novel. Yes, how *did* he expect her to do that, if he deprived her of her books?

Anthony stirred impatiently in his chair. 'I don't expect you to do anything,' he said. 'I'm simply telling you what you'll find you've got to do.'

There was a long silence. Then, with a little smile that she tried to make ingratiating and appealing, 'Now you're angry with me,' she said.

'Not in the least. I'm merely asking you to face the facts.' He rose, and feeling himself in danger of being inextricably entangled in Mary's misfortune, symbolically asserted his right to be free by walking restlessly up and down the room. 'I ought to talk to her about the morphia,' he was thinking; 'try to persuade her to go into a home and get cured. For her own sake. For the sake of poor Helen.' But he knew Mary. She'd start to protest, she'd scream, she'd fly into a rage. It would be like a public-house brawl. Or worse, much worse, he thought with a shudder, she'd repent, she'd make promises, she'd melt into tears. He would find himself her only friend, her moral support for life. In the end, he said nothing. 'It wouldn't do any good,' he assured himself. 'It never does do any good with these morphia cases.' 'One's got to come to terms with reality,' he said aloud. Meaningless platitude – but what else was there to say?

Unexpectedly, with a submissive alacrity that he found positively disquieting, she agreed with him. Oh, absolutely agreed! It was no use crying over spilt milk. No use building castles in the air. What was needed was a plan – lots of plans – serious, practical, sensible plans for the new life. She smiled at him with an air of connivance, as though they were a pair of conspirators.

Reluctantly, and with mistrust, he accepted her invitation to sit on the edge of the bed. The plans unfolded themselves – serious to a degree. A little flat in Hampstead. Or else a tiny house in one of those slummy streets off the King's Road, Chelsea. She could still give an occasional party, very cheaply. The real friends would come, in spite of the cheapness – wouldn't they? she insisted with rather a pathetic anxiety to be reassured.

'Of course,' he had to say; though it wasn't the cheapness that would put them off; it was the dirt, the squalor, the morphia, this sickening smell of ether on the breath.

'One can have bottle parties,' she was saying. 'It'll be fun!' Her face brightened. 'What sort of bottle will you bring, Anthony?' And before he could answer, 'We shall get *in*finitely tight with all those mixed drinks,' she went on. '*In*finitely ...' A moment later she had begun to tell him about the advances that George Wyvern had taken it into his head to make to her these days. Rather embarrassing, in the circumstances – seeing that Sally Wyvern was also ... well! She smiled that enigmatic smile of hers, close-lipped and between half-shut eyelids. And what was really *too* extraordinary, even old Hugh Ledwidge had recently shown signs ...

Anthony listened in astonishment. Those pathetically few real friends had been transformed, as though by magic, into positively a host of eager lovers. Did she seriously believe in her own inventions? But anyhow, he went on to think, it didn't seem to matter whether she believed in them or not. Even unbelieved, these fictions evidently had power to raise her spirits, to restore her, at least for the moment, to a state of cheerful self-confidence.

'That time in Paris,' she was saying intimately. 'Do you remember?'

But this was awful!

'The Hôtel des Saints-Pères.' Her voice deepened and vibrated with a subterranean laughter.

Anthony nodded without raising his head. She had obviously wanted him to echo her hint of significant mirth to take up the scabrous reference to that old joke of theirs about the Holy Fathers and their own amusements under that high ecclesiastical patronage. In their private language, 'doing a slight Holy Father', or, yet more idiomatically, 'doing Holiers', had signified 'making love'. He frowned, feeling suddenly very angry. How did she dare ...?

The seconds passed. Making a desperate effort to fill the icy gulf of his silence. 'We had a lot of fun,' said Mary in a tone of sentimental reminiscence.

'A lot,' he repeated, as unemphatically as possible.

Suddenly she took his hand. 'Dear Anthony !'

'Oh, God,' he thought, and tried, as politely as might be, to withdraw. But the clasp of those hot dry fingers never relaxed.

'We were fools to quarrel,' she went on. 'Or rather, *I* was a fool.'

'Not at all,' he said politely.

'That stupid bet,' she shook her head. 'And Sidney . . .'

'You did what you wanted to do.'

'I did what I didn't want to do,' she answered quickly. 'One's always doing things one doesn't want – stupidly, out of sheer perversity. One chooses the worse just because it is the worse. Hyperion to a satyr – and *therefore* the satyr.'

'But for certain purposes,' he couldn't resist saying, 'the satyr may be more satisfactory.'

Ignoring his words, Mary sighed and shut her eyes.

'Doing what one doesn't want,' she repeated, as though to herself. 'Always doing what one doesn't want.' She released his hand, and, clasping her own behind her head, leaned back against the pillows in the attitude, the known and familiar attitude, that in the Hôtel des Saints-Pères had been so delicious in its graceful indolence, so wildly exciting because of that white round throat stretched back like a victim's, those proffered breasts, lifted and taut beneath the lace. But today the lace was soiled and torn, the breasts hung tired under their own weight, the victim throat was no more a smooth column of white flesh, but a withered, wrinkled, hollow between starting tendons.

She opened her eyes, and, with a start, he recognized the look she gave him as the same, identically the same look, at once swooning and cynical, humorous and languidly abandoned, as had invited him, irresistibly then, in Paris, fifteen years ago. It was the look of 1913 in the face of 1928 – painfully out of its context. He stared at her for a second or two, appalled; then managed to break the silence.

'I shall have to go.'

But before he could rise, Mrs Amberley had quickly leaned forward and laid her hands on his shoulders.

'No, don't go. You mustn't go.' She tried to repeat that laughingly voluptuous invitation, but could not prevent a profound anxiety from showing in her eyes.

Anthony shook his head and, in spite of that sickening smell of ether, did his best to smile as he lied about the supper-party he had promised to join at eleven. Gently, but with a firm and decided movement, he lifted her confining hands and stood up by the side of the bed.

'Good night, dear Mary!' The tone of his voice was warm; he could afford to be affectionate, now. '*Bon courage!*' he squeezed her hands; then, bending down, kissed first one, then the other. Now that he was on his feet, and with the road to freedom clear before him, he felt at liberty to plunge into almost any emotional extravagance. But, instead of taking the cue, Mary Amberley returned him a look that had now become fixed and as though stony with unwavering misery. The mask he had adjusted to be so radiant with whimsical affectionateness seemed all of a sudden horribly out of keeping with the real situation. He could feel its irrelevance, physically, in the muscles of his face. Fool, hypocrite, coward! But it was almost at a run that he made towards the door and hurried down the stairs.

'If a woman,' Helen was reading in the Encyclopedia, 'administers to herself any poison or other noxious thing, or unlawfully uses any instrument or other means to procure her own miscarriage, she is guilty of . . .' The sound of Anthony's feet on the stairs caught her ear. She rose, and quickly walked to the door and out on to the landing.

'Well?' She smiled no greeting in answer to his, simulated no pleasure at seeing him. The face she lifted was as tragically naked of all the conventional grimaces as her mother's had been.

'But what's the matter, Helen?' he was startled into exclaiming. She looked at him for a few seconds in silence, then shook her head and began to ask him about those shares, the whole financial position.

Obviously, he was thinking as he answered her questions, one would expect her to find it all very upsetting. But upsetting to this point – he looked at her again : no – one wouldn't have expected that. It wasn't as if the girl had ever had a wild devotion for her mother. In the teeth of Mary's ferocious egotism, how could she? And after all, it was nearly a year since the wretched woman had started on her morphia. One would think that by this time the horror would have lost some of its intensity. And yet he had never seen an unhappier face. Such youth, such freshness – it wasn't right that they should be associated with an expression of so intense a despair. The sight of her made him feel somehow guilty – guiltily responsible. But when he made another gesture of inquiring sympathy, she only shook her head again and turned away.

'You'd better go,' she said.

Anthony hesitated a moment, then went. After all, she wanted him to go. Still feeling guilty, but with a sense of profound relief, he closed the front door behind him, and, drawing a deep breath, set off towards the Underground station.

Helen went back to her volume of the Encyclopedia '... to procure her own miscarriage, she is guilty of felony. The punishment for this offence is penal servitude for life, or not less than three years, or imprisonment for not more than two years. If the child is born alive ...' But they didn't say which the proper poisons were, nor what sort of instruments you had to use, and how. Only this stupid nonsense about penal servitude. Yet another loophole of escape had closed against her. It was as though the whole world had conspired to shut her in with her own impossibly appalling secret.

Melodiously, the clock in the back drawing-room struck eleven. Helen rose, put the heavy volume back in its place, and went upstairs to her mother's room.

With an unwontedly careful precision of movement, Mrs Amberley was engaged, when her daughter entered, in filling a hypodermic syringe from a little glass ampoule. She started as the door opened, looked up, made a movement as if to hide syringe and ampoule under the bedclothes, then, fearful of spilling any of the precious liquor, checked herself in the midst of her gesture.

'Go away!' she called angrily. 'Why do you come in without knocking? I won't have you coming in my room without knocking,' she repeated more shrilly, glad of the excuse she had discovered for her fury.

Helen stood for a second or two in the doorway, quite still, as if incredulous of the evidence of her own eyes; then hurried across the room.

'Give those things to me,' she said, holding out her hand.

Mrs Amberley shrank back towards the wall. 'Go away!' she shouted.

'But you promised ...'

'I didn't.'

'You did, Mummy.'

'I did not. And, anyhow, I shall do what I like.'

Without speaking, Helen reached out and caught her mother by the wrist. Mrs Amberley screamed so loudly that, fearful lest the servants should come down to see what was the matter, Helen relaxed her grip.

Mrs Amberley stopped screaming; but the look she turned on Helen was terrifying in its malevolence. 'If you make me spill any of this,' she said in a voice that trembled with rage, 'I shall kill you. Kill you,' she repeated.

They looked at one another for a moment without speaking. It was Helen who broke the silence. 'You'd like to kill me,' she said slowly, 'because I don't let you kill yourself.' She shrugged her shoulders. 'Well, I suppose if you really *want* to kill yourself ...' She left the sentence unfinished.

Mrs Amberley stared at her in silence. 'If you really want ...' She remembered the words she had spoken to Anthony only a few minutes since, and suddenly the tears ran down her cheeks. She was overwhelmed with self-pity. 'Do you think I *want* to do this?' she said brokenly. 'I hate it. I absolutely hate it. But I can't help it.'

Sitting down on the edge of the bed, Helen put her arm round her mother's shoulders. 'Mummy darling!' she implored. 'Don't cry. It'll be all right.' She was profoundly moved.

'It's all Gerry's fault,' Mrs Amberley cried; and without noticing the little shuddering start Helen gave, 'everything's his fault,' she went on. 'Everything. I always knew he was a beast. Even when I cared for him most.'

As though her mother had suddenly become a stranger whom it was not right to be touching so intimately, Helen withdrew her encircling arm. 'You *cared* for him?' she whispered incredulously. 'In *that* way?'

Answering quite a different question, parrying a reproach that had never been made. 'I couldn't help it,' Mrs Amberley replied. 'It was like *this*.' She made a little movement with the hand that held the hypodermic syringe.

'You mean,' said Helen, speaking very slowly, and as though overcoming an almost invisible reluctance, 'you mean he was ... he was your lover?'

The strangeness of the tone aroused Mrs Amberley, for the first time since their conversation had begun, to something like a consciousness of her daughter's real personal existence. Turning, she looked at Helen with an expression of astonishment. 'You didn't know?' Confronted by that extraordinary pallor, those uncontrollably trembling lips, the older woman was seized with a sudden compunction. 'But, darling, I'm sorry. I didn't imagine ... You're still so young; you don't understand. You can't ... But where are you going? Come back! Helen!'

The door slammed. Mrs Amberley made a move to follow her daughter, then thought better of it, and, instead, resumed the interrupted task of filling her hypodermic syringe.

CHAPTER THIRTY-FIVE

August 4th 1934

Returned depressed from an evening with Helen and half a a dozen of her young political friends. Such a passion for 'liquidating' the people who don't agree with them! And such a sincere conviction that liquidation is necessary!

Revolting – but only to be expected. Regard the problem of reform exclusively as a matter of politics and economics, and you *must* approve and practise liquidation.

Consider recent history. Industrialism has grown *pari passu* with population. Now, where markets are expanding, the two besetting problems of all industrial societies solve themselves. New inventions may create technological unemployment; but expanding markets cure it as it's made. Each individual may possess inadequate purchasing power; but the total number of individuals is steadily rising. Many small purchasing powers do as much as fewer big ones.

Our population is now stationary, will soon decline. Shrinkage instead of expansion of markets. Therefore, no more automatic solution of the economic problems. Birth control necessitates the use of coordinating political intelligence. There must be a large-scale plan. Otherwise the machine won't work. In other words, politicians will have to be about twenty times as intelligent as heretofore. Will the supply of intelligence be equal to the demand?

And of course, intelligence, as Miller's always insisting, isn't isolated. The act of intelligently planning modifies the emotions of the planners. Consider English politics. We've made plenty of reforms – without ever accepting the principles underlying them. (Compare the king's titles with his present position. Compare our protestations that we'll never have anything to do with socialism with the realities of state control.) There are no large-scale plans in English politics, and hardly any thinking in terms of first principles. With what results? Among others, that English politics have been on the whole very good-natured. The reason is simple. Deal with practical problems as they arise and without reference to first principles; politics are a matter of higgling. Now higglers lose tempers, but don't normally regard one another as fiends in human form. But this is precisely what men of principle and systematic planners can't help doing. A principle is, by definition, *right*; a plan *for the good of the people*. Axioms from which it logically follows that those who disagree with you and won't help to realize your plan are enemies of goodness and humanity. No longer men and women, but personifications of evil, fiends incarnate. Killing men and women is wrong; but killing fiends is a duty. Hence the Holy Office, hence Robespierre and the Ogpu. Men with strong religious and revolutionary faith, men with well-thought-out plans for improving the lot of their fellows, whether in this world or the next, have been more systematically and cold-bloodedly cruel than any others. Thinking in terms of first principles entails acting with machine-guns. A government with a comprehensive plan for the betterment of society is a government that uses torture. *Per contra*, if you never consider principles and have no plan, but deal with situations as they arise, piecemeal, you can afford to have unarmed policemen, liberty of speech, and *habeas corpus*. Admirable. But what happens when an industrial society learns (*a*) how to make technological advances at a constantly accelerating speed, and (*b*) to prevent conception? Answer: it must either plan itself in accordance with general political and economic principles, or else break down. But governments with principles and plans have generally been tyrannies making use of police spies and terrorism. Must we resign ourselves to slavery and torture for the sake of coordination?

Breakdown on the one hand, Inquisition and Ogpu rule on the other. A real dilemma, if the plan is mainly economic and political. But think in terms of individual men, women, and children, not of States, Religions, Economic Systems, and suchlike abstractions: there is then a hope of passing between the horns. For if you begin by considering concrete people, you see at once that freedom from coercion is a necessary condition of their developing into full-grown human beings; that the form of economic prosperity which consists in possessing unnecessary objects doesn't make for individual well-being; that a leisure filled with passive amusements is not a blessing; that the conveniences of urban life are bought at a high physiological and mental price; that an education which allows you to use yourself wrongly is almost valueless; that a social organization resulting in individuals being forced, every few years, to go out and murder another must be wrong. And so on. Whereas if you start from the State, the Faith, the Economic System, there is a complete transvaluation of values. Individuals must murder one another, because the interests of the Nation demand it; must be educated to think of ends and disregard means, because the schoolmasters are there and don't know of any other method; must live in towns, must have leisure to read the newspapers and go to the movies, must be encouraged to buy things they don't need, because the industrial system exists and has to be kept going; must be coerced and enslaved, because otherwise they might think for themselves and give trouble to their rulers.

The sabbath was made for man. But man now behaves like

the Pharisees and insists that he is made for all the things –
science, industry, nation, money, religion, schools – which were
really made for him. Why? Because he is so little aware of his
own interests as a human being that he feels irresistibly tempted
to sacrifice himself to these idols. There is no remedy except to
become aware of one's interests as a human being, and, having
become aware, to learn to act on that awareness. Which means
learning to use the self and learning to direct the mind. It's
almost wearisome, the way one always comes back to the same
point. Wouldn't it be nice, for a change, if there were another
way out of our difficulties! A short cut. A method requiring no
greater personal effort than recording a vote or ordering some
'enemy of society' to be shot. A salvation from outside, like a
dose of calomel.

CHAPTER THIRTY-SIX

July 19th 1914

IN the train going north, Anthony thought of what was in store
for him. Within the next two days, or at the outside three, Brian
would have to be told about what had happened, and a letter
would have to be written to Joan. In what words? And what
excuses should he make for himself? Should he tell the whole
truth about his bet with Mary? For himself, the truth had
certain advantages; if he told it, he could throw most of the
blame for what had happened on Mary – but at the risk, he went
on to think, of seeming miserably feeble. And that was not the
only disadvantage; for Joan, the truth would be intolerably
humiliating. However much blame he threw on Mary, the insult
to Joan would remain. If only he could tell the truth to Brian
and something else to Joan!

But that wasn't possible. They would have to be told the same
story, and, for Joan's sake, a story that wasn't true. But what
story? Which explanation of the facts would throw least dis-
credit upon himself and inflict the least humiliation on Joan?
On the whole, he decided the best thing to say would be that he
had lost his head – been carried away by a sudden impulse, an
impulse that he had subsequently seen the madness of and

regretted. It was somebody else who had kissed her : that was what he would write to Joan. Somebody else – but not *too* else. She wouldn't like it if she were made to feel that it was a mere momentary baboon who had behaved like that in the unlighted drawing-room. The person who had kissed her would have to be partially himself. Enough himself to have been all the time very fond of her, profoundly sorry for her; but someone else to the extent of allowing the circumstances of the evening to transform the affection and sympathy into – what? Love? Desire? No, he would have to avoid saying anything so specific; would have to talk about confusions, temporary insanities spoiling a relationship which had been so fine, and so forth. Meanwhile he could only say that he was sorry and ashamed; that he felt, more strongly than ever now, that Brian was the only man who was worthy of her, that the difficulties that had arisen between herself and Brian were only temporary and would soon ... And all the rest.

Yes, the letter ought to be fairly easy. The trouble was that he would be expected to follow it by interviews and explanations; that he would have to bear reproaches, listen to confidences, perhaps defend himself against declarations of passion. And in the interval there would be Brian to talk to – and with Brian the thing would begin with those interviews; and the more he thought about those interviews, the harder did he find it to foresee the part that Brian would play in them. Anthony imagined himself trying to make it clear that he wasn't in love, that Joan had only momentarily lost her head as he had lost his, that nothing had changed, and that all Brian had to do was to go and kiss her himself. But would he succeed in making Brian believe him? The man being what he was, it seemed to him probable – seemed more probable the more he thought about it – that he would fail. Brian was the sort of man who would imagine that one couldn't kiss a woman under any compulsion less urgent than the deepest, most heart-felt love. He would be told that Joan had been kissed and had returned the kisses; and no amount of talk about lost heads would persuade him that it wasn't a serious matter of love at its intensest pitch. And then, Anthony speculated, what would the man do then? He'd be hurt, of course, he'd feel betrayed : but the chances were that there'd be no recriminations. No, something much worse might happen. Brian would probably take all the blame on himself; would renounce all his rights, would refuse to believe it when Anthony swore that he wasn't in love and that it had all been a kind of bad joke; would insist, just because it would be so agonizing a sacrifice, that Joan should go to the man she really loved and who really loved her. And then, suppose that, on her side, Joan agreed! And it was probable, Anthony thought with dismay as he remembered her response to his kisses, it was almost certain even, that she would do so. Appalling prospect! He couldn't face it. And why should he face it, after all? He could borrow on his securities – enough to get out of the country and stay away; for six months, for a year if necessary. And while the midlands streamed past the window, he leaned back with closed eyes, picturing himself in Italy or, if Italy wasn't far enough from England, in Greece, in Egypt, even in India, Malaya, Java. With Mary; for of course Mary would have to come too, at least for part of the time. She could dump the children with some relation; and Egypt, he reflected, practical in his day-dreaming, Egypt in the off-season was quite cheap, and this war scare of course was nothing. Was Luxor as impressive as it looked in the photographs? And the Parthenon? And Paestum? And what of the tropics? In imagination he sailed from island to island in the Aegean; smoked hashish in the slums of Cairo, ate bhang in Benares; did a slight Joseph Conrad in the East Indies, a slight Loti even, in spite of the chromolithograph style, among the copper-coloured girls and the gardenias, and, though he still found it impossible to like the man as much as Mary did, a slight Gauguin in the South Seas. These future and hypothetical escapes were escapes also here and now, so that for a long time in his corner of the compartment he quite forgot the reason for his projected flight into the exotic. The memory of what had happened, the apprehensive anticipation of what was going to happen, returned only with the realization that the train was crossing Shap Fell, and that in less than an hour he would be talking to Brian on the platform at Ambleside. All the old questions propounded themselves with more desperate urgency. What should he say? How? On what occasion? And what would be Brian's response?

What Joan's when she got his letter? Horrible questions! But why had he put himself in the position of having to provide or receive the answers to them? What a fool he had been not to take flight at once! By this time he could have been at Venice, in Calabria, on a ship in the Mediterranean. Beyond the reach of letters. Secure and happy in complete ignorance of the results of his actions. And free. Instead of which he had stupidly stayed where he was and consented to be made the slave of the circumstances his folly had created. But even now, at the eleventh hour, it wasn't too late. He could get out at the next station, make his way back to London, raise a little money and be off within twenty-four hours. But when the train stopped at Kendal, he made no move. The taking of so sudden and momentous a decision was something from which he shrank. He hated suffering, and looked forward with dread to what the next few days and weeks held in store for him. But his fear of suffering was less than his fear of action. He found it easier to accept passively what came than to make a decisive choice and act upon it.

As the train rolled on again, he thought of all the reasons why it had been right for him not to take that decision. Brian was counting on him, would be so disturbed by his non-arrival that he might easily rush down to London to find out what had happened, see Joan and learn everything, at once. And how should he explain things to his father? Besides, there was no reason to think that Mary would come with him; she had made her arrangements for the summer and wouldn't, perhaps couldn't, alter them. And while he was away, heaven only knew what rivals would present themselves. Besides flight would be cowardly, he went on to assure himself, and immediately afterwards was reflecting that he could probably escape from his difficulties just as effectively if he stayed in England. A little tact, a bit of passive resistance . . .

Brian was waiting on the platform when the train drew in, and at the sight of him Anthony felt a sudden pang of pitying distress. For between the man and his clothes there was a startling and painful incongruousness. The rough homespun jacket and breeches, the stockings, the nailed boots, the bulging rucksack were emblems of energy and rustic good health. But the Brian who wore these emblems was the living denial of their significance. The long face was emaciated and sallow. The nose seemed larger than in the past, the eye-sockets deeper, the cheek-bones more prominent. And when he spoke, he stammered more uncontrollably than ever.

'But what *is* the matter with you?' cried Anthony, laying a hand on his friend's shoulder. 'You look wretched.'

Half touched by this display of a genuine solicitude (it was extraordinary, he reflected, how charming Anthony could unexpectedly be), half annoyed by having been, as he felt, found out, Brian shook his head and mumbled something about being a bit tired and in need of a rest.

But his idea of a rest, it turned out, was to walk twenty miles a day up and down the steepest hills he could find.

Anthony looked at him disapprovingly. 'You ought to be out in a deck-chair,' he said, but could see, as he spoke, that his advice was unwelcome. With Brian it was a kind of dogma that taking violent exercise in mountain scenery was intrinsically good. Good, because of Wordsworth; because, in his mother's version of Christianity, landscape took the place of revelation.

'I l-like w-walking,' Brian insisted. 'S-saw a d-dipper yesterday. The p-place is f-full of nice b-birds.'

In his distress at finding his friend so ill, Anthony had forgotten all about Joan and the events of the last days; but those birds (those bö-öds, those piddle-warblers) reminded him violently of what had happened. Feeling suddenly ashamed, as though he had been caught in some unworthy display of hypocrisy, Anthony withdrew his hand from Brian's shoulder. They made their way in silence along the platform and out into the street. There they halted for a discussion. Brian wanted to send the luggage by the carrier and walk to their cottage in Langdale. Anthony proposed that they should take a car.

'You've no business to walk a step further today,' he said; then, when the other protested that he hadn't taken enough exercise, changed ground and insisted that it was he who was tired after the journey, and that anyhow he couldn't walk because he was wearing unsuitable clothes and shoes. After a final plea to be allowed to walk back to Langdale by himself,

Brian was overruled and submitted to the car. They drove away.

Breaking a long silence, 'Have you seen J-joan lately?' Brian asked.

The other nodded without speaking.

'How w-was she?'

'Quite well,' Anthony found himself replying in the brightly vague tone in which one answers questions about the health of those in whom one takes no particular interest. The lie – for it was a lie by omission – had come to him of its own accord. By means of it, his mind had defended itself against Brian's question as automatically and promptly as his body, by blinking, by lifting an arm, by starting back, would have defended itself against an advancing fist. But the words were no sooner spoken than he regretted their brevity and the casualness with which they had been uttered, than he felt that he ought at once to qualify them with additional information, in another and more serious tone. He ought to rush in immediately, and without further delay make a clean breast of everything. But time passed; he could not bring himself to speak; and within a few seconds he had begun already to dignify his cowardice with the name of consideration, he was already assuring himself that it would be wrong, Brian's health being what it was, to speak out at once, that the truly friendly thing was to wait and choose an occasion, tomorrow perhaps or the day after, when Brian was in a better state to receive the news.

'You d-don't think she was w-worrying?' Brian went on. 'I m-mean ab-bout all this delay in our g-getting married?'

'Well, of course,' Anthony admitted, 'she's not altogether happy about it.'

Brian shook his head. 'N-nor am I. But I th-think it's r-right; and I th-think in the l-long r-run she'll see it was r-right.' Then, after a silence, 'If only one were a-absolutely certain,' he said. 'S-sometimes I w-wonder if it isn't a k-kind of s-selfishness.'

'What is?'

'St-sticking to p-principles, reg-gardless of p-people. P-people – o-other p-people, I mean – p-perhaps they're m-more imp-portant e-even than what one kn-knows is a r-right p-principle. But if you d-don't st-stick to your p-principles ...' he hesitated, turned a puzzled and unhappy face towards Anthony, then looked away again: 'well, where are you?' he concluded despairingly.

'The sabbath is made for man,' said Anthony; and thought resentfully what a fool Brian had been not to take whatever money he could get and marry out of hand. If Joan had been safely married, there would have been no confidences, no bet, no kiss, and none of the appalling consequences of kissing. And then, of course, there was poor Joan. He went on to feel what was almost righteous indignation against Brian for not having grasped the fundamental Christian principle that the sabbath is made for man, not man for the sabbath. But was it made for man, an intrusive voice suddenly began asking, to the extent of man's having the right, for a bet, to disturb the equilibrium of another person's feelings, to break up a long-established relationship, to betray a friend?

Brian meanwhile was thinking of the occasion, a couple of months before, when he and Joan had talked over the matter with his mother.

'You still think, 'she had asked, 'that you oughtn't to take the money?' and went on, when he told her that his opinions hadn't changed, to set forth all the reasons why it wouldn't be wrong for him to take it. The system might be unjust, and it might be one's duty to alter it; but meanwhile one could use one's financial advantages to help the individual victims of the system, to forward the cause of desirable reform.

'That's what I've always felt about it,' his mother concluded.

And had been right, he insisted; and that he didn't dream of criticizing what she had done, of even thinking it criticizable. But that was because her circumstances had been so different from his. A man, he had opportunities to make his own living such as she had never had. Besides, she had been left with responsibilities; whereas he . . .

'But what about Joan?' she interrupted, laying her hand affectionately, as she spoke, on Joan's arm. 'Isn't she a responsibility?'

He dropped his eyes and, feeling that it was not for him to answer the question, said nothing.

There were long seconds of an uncomfortably expectant

silence, while he wondered whether Joan would speak and what, if she didn't, he should say and do.

Then, to his relief, 'After all,' Joan brought out at last in a curiously flat and muffled voice, 'Brian was a child then. But I'm grown up, I'm responsible for myself. And I'm able to understand his reasons.'

He raised his head and looked at her with a smile of gratitude. But her face was cold and as though remote; she met his eyes for only a moment, then looked away.

'You understand his reasons?' his mother questioned.

Joan nodded.

'And you approve them?'

She hesitated for a moment, then nodded again. 'If Brian thinks it's right,' she began, and broke off.

His mother looked from one to the other. 'I think you're a pair of rather heroic young people,' she said, and the tone of her voice, so beautiful, so richly vibrant with emotion, imparted to the words a heightened significance. He felt that he had been confirmed in his judgement.

But later, he remembered with a pained perplexity, later, when Joan and he were alone together and he tried to thank her for what she had done, she turned on him with a bitterly resentful anger.

'You love your own ideas more than you love me. Much more.'

Brian sighed and, shaking himself out of his long distraction, looked at the trees by the side of the road, at the mountains so sumptuously shadowed and illumined by the late afternoon sunlight, at the marbly island of clouds in the sky – looked at them, saw that they were beautiful, and found their beauty hopelessly irrelevant.

'I wish to G-god,' he said, 'I knew what to d-do,'

So did Anthony, though he did not say so.

CHAPTER THIRTY-SEVEN

Autumn 1933

I⊤ took longer than Mark expected to dispose of his business, and at moments, during the long weeks that preceded their departure, the temptation to throw up the whole ridiculous enterprise and scuttle back into the delicious other-world of Mediterranean sunshine and abstract ideas became, for Anthony, almost irresistible.

'What are you really going for?' he asked resentfully.

'Fun,' was all the answer that Mark condescended to give.

'And your Don Jorge,' Anthony insisted. 'What does he hope to achieve by this little revolution of his?'

'His own greater glory.'

'But the peasants, the Indians?'

'They'll be exactly where they were before, where they always will be : underneath.'

'And yet you think it's worth while to go and help this Jorge of yours?'

'Worth while for me.' Mark smiled anatomically. 'And worth while for you. Very much worth while for you,' he insisted.

'But not for the peons, I gather.'

'It never is. What did the French peons get out of their revolution? Or our friends, the Russians, for that matter? A few years of pleasant intoxication. Then the same old treadmill. Gilded, perhaps; repainted. But in essentials the old machine.'

'And you expect me to come along with you for fun?' The thought of the Mediterranean and his books heightened Anthony's indignation. 'It's crazy, it's abominable.'

'In other words,' said Mark, 'you're afraid. Well, why not? But if you are, for God's sake say so. Have the courage of your cowardice.'

How he had hated Mark for telling him the home truths he knew so well! If it hadn't been for Mr Beavis, and that interview with Helen, and finally Beppo Bowles, perhaps he *would* have had the courage of his cowardice. But they made it impossible for him to withdraw. There was his father, first of all, still deep in the connubial burrow, among the petticoats and the etymologies and the smell of red-haired women – but agitated, as Anthony had never seen him before, hurt, indignant, bitterly resentful. The presidency of the Philological Society, which ought, without any question, to have come to him, had gone instead to Jenkins. Jenkins, if you please ! A mere ignorant popularizer, the very antithesis of a real scholar. A charlatan, a philological confidence trickster, positively (to use an American colloquialism) a 'crook'.

Jenkins's election had taken Mr Beavis long strides towards death. From being a man much younger than his years, he had suddenly come to look his age. An old man; and tired into the bargain, eroded from within.

'I'm worried,' Pauline had confided to Anthony. 'He's making himself ill. And for something so childish, really. I can't make him see that it doesn't matter. Or rather I can't make him *feel* it. Because he sees it all right, but goes on worrying all the same.'

Even in the deepest sensual burrow, Anthony reflected as he walked back to his rooms, even in the snuggest of intellectual other-worlds, fate could find one out. And suddenly he perceived that, having spent all his life trying to react away from the standards of his father's universe, he had succeeded only in becoming precisely what his father was – a man in a burrow. With this small difference, that in his case the burrow happened to be intermittently adulterous instead of connubial all the time; and that the ideas were about societies and not words. For the moment, he was out of his burrow – had been chased out, as though by ferrets. But it would be easy and was already a temptation to return. To return and be snug, be safe. No, not safe; that was the point. At any moment a Jenkins might be elected to some presidency or other, and then, defenceless in one's burrow of thought and sensuality, one would be at the mercy of any childish passion that might arise. Outside, perhaps, one might learn to defend oneself against such contingencies. He decided to go with Mark.

But in the succeeding days the temptation kept coming back. In spite of the spectacle of Mr Beavis's self-destroying childishness, the quiet life seemed immensely attractive. 'Mark's mad,' he kept assuring himself. 'We're doing something stupid and wrong. And after all, my sociology is important. It'll help people to think clearly.' Wasn't it (ridiculous word!) a 'duty' to go on with it? But then, more than six weeks after his return to London, he saw Helen and Beppo Bowles – saw them in the course of a single afternoon. The meeting with Helen was a chance one. It was in the French Room at the National Gallery. Anthony was stooping to look closely into Cézanne's *Mont Sainte Victoire*, when he became aware that two other visitors had halted just behind him. He shifted a little to one side, so as to let them see the picture, and continued his meticulous examination of the brushwork.

A few seconds passed; then, very slowly and with a foreign accent, a man's voice said: 'See now here how the nineteenth-century petit bourgeois tried to escape from industrialism. Why must he paint such landscapes, so romantic? Because he will forget the new methods of production. Because he will not think of the proletariat. That is why.'

'Yes, I suppose that is the reason,' said another voice.

With a start, Anthony recognized it as Helen's. 'What shall I do?' he was wondering, when the voice spoke again.

'Why, it's Anthony!' A hand touched his arm.

He straightened himself up and turned towards her, making the gestures and noises appropriate to delighted astonishment. That face, which he had last seen alternately stony and bright with mockery, then in the rapt agony of pleasure, then dabbled with blood and pitiably disintegrated by a grief extreme beyond expression, finally hard as it had been at first, harder, more rigidly a stone – that face was now beautifully alive, and tender, illuminated from within by a kind of secure joy. She looked at him without the least trace of embarrassment. It was as though the past had been completely abolished, as though, for her, only the present existed and were real.

'This is Ekki Giesebrecht,' she said.

The fair-haired young man beside her bent stiffly forwards as they shook hands.

'He had to escape from Germany,' she was explaining. 'They would have killed him for his politics.'

It was not jealousy that he felt as he looked from one glad

face to the other – not jealousy, but an unhappiness so acute that it was like a physical pain. A pain that endured and that was not in the least diminished by the solemn absurdity of the little lecture which Helen now delivered on art as a manifestation of class interests. Listening, he could laugh to himself, he could reflect with amusement on love's fantastic by-products in matters of taste, political opinions, religious beliefs. But behind the laughter, beneath the ironical reflections, that pain of unhappiness persisted.

He refused her invitation to have tea with them.

'I've promised to go and see Beppo,' he exclaimed.

'Give him my love,' she said, and went on to ask if, since his return, he had met Hugh.

Anthony shook his head.

'We're parting company, you know.'

Making an effort to smile, 'All good wishes for the divorce,' he said, and hurried away.

Walking through the smoky dimness of the afternoon, he thought of that softly radiant face of hers, and felt, along with the pain of unhappiness, a renewal of that other, profounder pain of dissatisfaction with himself. Since his arrival in London he had led his ordinary London life – the lunches with men of learning and affairs, the dinners where women kept the conversation more gossipy and amusing – and the easy, meaningless successes, which his talents and a certain natural charm always allowed him to score at such gatherings, had made him all but completely forget his dissatisfaction, had masked the pain of it, as a drug will mask neuralgia or toothache. This meeting with Helen had instantaneously neutralized the soothing drug and left him defenceless against a pain no whit diminished by the temporary anodyne – rather, indeed, intensified by it. For the realization that he had permitted himself to be soothed by an opiate of such poor quality was a new cause for dissatisfaction added to the old. And then to think that he had been seriously considering the idea of returning to the old quiet life ! So quietly squalid, so quietly inhuman and, for all the expense of thought it entailed, so quietly mad. Mark's enterprise might be stupid and even disgraceful; but, however bad, it was still preferable to that quietude of work and occasional detached sensuality beside the Mediterranean.

Standing at the door of Beppo's flat, he heard the sound of voices – Beppo's and another man's. He rang the bell. Time passed. The door remained unopened. The voices talked on, inarticulately, but with shrill squeaks on Beppo's side and, on that of the stranger, a crescendo of gruff barks which proclaimed that they were quarrelling. He rang again. There were a few more squeaks and shouts; then the sound of hurrying feet. The door was flung open, and there stood Beppo. The face was flushed, the bald crown shiny with perspiration. Behind him, very upright and soldierly in his carriage, appeared a rather coarsely handsome young man, with a small moustache and carefully oiled wavy brown hair, dressed in a blue serge suit of extreme and somehow improbable smartness.

'Come in,' said Beppo rather breathlessly.

'Am I disturbing you?'

'No, no. My friend was just going – this is Mr Simpson, by the way – just going.'

'Was he?' asked the young man in a significant voice and with a Nottinghamshire accent. 'I hadn't known he was.'

'Perhaps *I*'d better go,' Anthony suggested.

'No, please don't, please don't.' There was a note in Beppo's voice of almost desperate appeal.

The young man laughed. 'He wants protection – that's what it is. Thinks he's going to be blackmailed. And I could if I wanted to.' He looked at Anthony with knowing, insolent eyes. 'But I don't want to.' He assumed an expression that was meant to be one of lofty moral indignation. 'I wouldn't do it for a thousand pounds. It's a skunk's game, that's what I say.' From being loftily general, the moral indignation came down to earth and focused itself on Beppo. 'But a man's got no business to be mean,' he went on. 'That's a skunk's game too.' He pointed an accusing finger. 'A mean, dirty swine. That's what *you* are. I've said it before, and I say it again. And I don't care who hears me. Because I can prove it. Yes, and you know I can. A mean dirty swine.'

'All right, all right,' Beppo cried, in the tone of one who makes unconditional surrender. Catching Anthony by the arm, 'Go into the sitting-room, will you,' he begged.

Anthony did as he was told. Outside in the hall, a few almost whispered sentences were exchanged. Then, after a silence, the front door slammed, and Beppo, pale and distracted, entered the room. With one hand he was wiping his forehead; but it was only after he had sat down that he noticed what he was holding in the other. The fat white fingers were closed round his wallet. Embarrassed, he put the compromising object away in his breast pocket. Then, fizzling explosively in misery as he fizzled in mirth, 'It's only money that they're after,' he burst out like an opened ginger-beer bottle. 'You've seen it. Why should I try to hide it? Only money.' And he rambled on, popping, squeaking, fizzling in almost incoherent denunciation of 'them', and commiseration for himself. Yes, he was doubly to be pitied – pitied for what he had to suffer because of 'their' mercenary attitude, when the thing *he* was looking for was love for love's and adventure for adventure's sake; pitied also for that growing incapacity to find the least satisfaction in any amorous experience that was not wholly new. Increasingly, repetition was becoming the enemy. Repetition killed what he called the *frisson*. Unspeakable tragedy. He, who so longed for tenderness, for understanding, for companionship, was debarred from ever getting what he wanted. To have an affair with somebody of one's own class, somebody one could talk to, had come to be out of the question. But how could there be real tenderness without the sensual relationship? With 'them', the relationship was possible, was wildly desirable. But tenderness could no more flourish without communication than it could flourish without sensuality. And sensuality entirely divorced from communication and tenderness seemed now to be possible only under the stimulus of a constant change of object. There had to be another of 'them' each time. For that he was to be pitied; but the situation had its romantic side. Or at any rate might have it – used to have it. Nowadays, Beppo complained, 'they' had changed, were becoming mercenary, frankly rapacious, mere prostitutes.

'You saw just now,' he said, 'the sordidness of it, the lowness!' His misery bubbled over as though under an inner pressure of carbonic acid gas. In his agitation he heaved himself out of his chair and began to walk up and down the room, exposing to Anthony's eyes, now the bulging waistcoat, the lavish tie from Sulka's, the face with its pendant of chins, the bald and shining crown, now the broad seat of pale check trousers, the black jacket rising pear-like to narrow shoulders, and below the central baldness that fuzz of pale brown hair, like a Florentine page's, above the collar. 'And I'm *not* mean. God knows, I've got plenty of other faults, but not that. Why can't they understand that it isn't meanness, that it's a wish to ... to ...' he hesitated, 'well, to keep the thing on a human basis? A basis at least of romance, of adventure. Instead of that, they make these awful, humiliating scenes. Refusing to understand, absolutely refusing.'

He continued to walk up and down the room in silence. Anthony made no comment, but wondered inwardly how far poor old Beppo knew the truth or whether he too refused to understand – refused to understand that, to 'them', his ageing and unpalatable person could hardly be expected to seem romantic, that the only charm which remained to him, outside a certain good taste, and a facile intelligence which 'they' were not in a position to appreciate, was his money. Did he know all this? Yes, of course he did; it was unavoidable. He knew it quite well and refused to understand. 'Like me,' Anthony said to himself.

That evening he telephoned to Mark to tell him definitely that he could book their passages.

CHAPTER THIRTY-EIGHT

August 10th 1934

TODAY Helen talked again about Miller. Talked with a kind of resentful vehemence. (Certain memories, certain trains of thought are like the aching tooth one must always be touching just to make sure it still hurts.) Non-violence : this time, it was not only a mere trick, insignificant; it was also wrong. If you're convinced people are wicked, you've no right not to try to make them behave decently. Agreed : but how are you most likely to succeed? By violence? But violence may make people assume

the forms of good behaviour for the moment; it won't produce
the reality of genuine and permanent behaviour. She accused
me of shirking real issues, taking refuge in vague idealism. It
all boiled down at last to her vengeful hatred for the Nazis.
Peace all round, except for Nazis and, by contagion, fascists.
These should be punished, painfully exterminated – like rats.
(Note that we're all ninety-nine per cent pacifists. Sermon on
Mount, provided we're allowed to play Tamburlane or Napoleon in our particular one per cent of selected cases. Peace,
perfect peace, so long as we can have the war that suits us.
Result: everyone is the predestined victim of somebody else's
exceptionally permissible war. Ninety-nine per cent pacifism is
merely another name for militarism. If there's to be peace, there
must be hundred per cent pacifism.)

We exchanged a lot of arguments; then, for some time, said
nothing. Finally, she began to talk about Giesebrecht. Executed
after God only knew what tortures. 'Can you be surprised if I
feel like this about the Nazis?' Not surprised at all – any more
than by the Nazis themselves. Surprising would have been
tolerance on their part, forgiveness on hers. 'But the person who
might have forgiven vanished when Ekki vanished. I was good
while he was with me. Now I'm bad. If he were still here I
might be able to forgive them for taking him away. But that's
an impossible condition. I can't ever forgive.' (There were
answers to that, of course. But it didn't seem to me that I had
any right, being what I am, acting as I still do, to make them.)
She went on to describe what he had been to her. Someone she
didn't have to be ashamed of loving, as she had had to be
ashamed of loving Gerry. Someone she had been able to love
with her whole being – 'not just occasionally and with part of
me, on a roof; or just for fun, in a studio, before dinner.' And
she came back to the same point – that Ekki had made her kind,
truthful, unselfish, as well as happy. 'I was somebody else while
I was with him. Or perhaps I was myself – for the first time.'
Then, 'Do you remember how you laughed at me that time on
the roof, when I talked about my real self?' Did I not remember! I hadn't even been real enough, at that moment, to perceive
my own remoteness from reality. Afterwards, when I saw her

crying, when I knew that I'd been deliberately refusing to love her, I did perceive it.

After a silence, 'At the beginning I believe I could have loved you almost as much as I loved Ekki.'

And I'd done my best, of course, to prevent her.

Her voice brightened with malicious derision. Like her mother's. 'Extraordinary how funny a tragedy is, when you look at it from the wrong side!' Then, still smiling, 'Do you imagine you care for me now? Lo-ove me, in a word?'

Not only imagined; did really.

She held up a hand, like a policeman. 'No film stuff here. I'd have to throw you out if you began that game. Which I don't want to do. Because, oddly enough, I really like you. In spite of everything. I never thought I should. Not after that dog. But I do.' That painful brightness came back into her face. 'All the things I thought I should never do again! Such as eating a square meal; but I was doing it after three days. And wanting to make love. That seemed inconceivably sacrilegious. And yet within three or four months it was occurring to me. I was having dreams about it. And one of these days, I suppose, I shall actually be doing it. Doing it "without any obligation", as they say when they send you the vacuum-cleaner on approval. Exactly as I did before.' She laughed again. 'Most probably with you, Anthony. Till the next dog comes down. Would you be ready to begin again?'

Not on the old basis. I'd want to give more, receive more.

'It takes two to give and receive.' Then she switched the conversation on to another line; who was I having an affair with at the moment? and when I answered: with nobody, asked whether it wasn't difficult and disagreeable to be continent, and why I should want to imitate Mark Staithes. Tried to explain that I wasn't imitating Mark, that Mark's asceticism was undertaken for its own sake and above all for *his*, that he might feel himself more separate, more intensely himself, in a better position to look down on other people. Whereas what I was trying to do was to avoid occasions for emphasizing individual separateness through sensuality. Hate, anger, ambition explicitly deny human unity; lust and greed do the same indirectly and by implication – by insisting exclusively on particular individual experiences and, in the case of lust, using other people merely as a means for obtaining such experiences. Less dangerously so than malevolence and the passions for superiority, prestige, social position, lust is still incompatible with pacifism; can be made compatible only when it ceases to be an end in itself and becomes a means towards the unification through love of two separate individuals. Such particular union, a paradigm of union in general.

CHAPTER THIRTY-NINE

March 25th 1928

WHEN Helen kept her eyes closed, the red darkness behind the lids came wildly and chaotically to life. Like a railway station, it seemed, full of hurrying people, loud with voices; and the colours glowed, the forms stood sharply out, jewelled, with the more than real definition of forms and colours under limelight. It was as though the fever had assembled a crowd inside her head, had lighted lamps and turned on the gramophone. On the unnaturally brilliant stage the images came and went on their own initiative and in ferocious disregard of Helen's own wishes. Came and went, talked, gesticulated, acted out their elaborate, insane dramas, unceasingly, without mercy on her fatigue, without consideration for her longing to be at rest and alone. Sometimes, in the hope that the outer world would eclipse this scurrying lunacy within, she opened her eyes. But the light hurt her; and in spite of those bunched roses on the wallpaper, in spite of the white counterpane and the knobs at the end of the bedstead, in spite of the looking-glass, the hair-brushes, the bottle of eau-de-Cologne, those images on the other side of her eyes went on living that private life of theirs, undisturbed. A vehement and crazy life – now utterly irrelevant, like a story invented by somebody else, then all at once agonizingly to the point, agonizingly *hers*.

This morning, for example, this afternoon (which was it? time was at once endless and non-existent: but at any rate it was just after Mme Bonifay had been in to see her – stinking, stinking of garlic and dirty linen), there had been a huge hall, with statues. Gilded statues. She recognized Voltaire, fifty feet high, and there was one of those Chinese camels, but enormous. People were standing in groups, beautifully placed, like people on the stage. Indeed, they *were* on the stage. Acting a play of intrigue, a play with love scenes and revolvers. How bright the spotlights were! how clearly and emphatically they spoke the lines! Each word a bell, each figure a shining lamp.

'Hands up ... I love you ... If she falls into the trap ...' And yet who were they, what were they saying? And now for some extraordinary reason they were talking about arithmetic. Sixty-six yards of linoleum at three and eleven a yard. And the woman with the revolver was suddenly Miss Cosmas. There was no Voltaire, no gilded camel. Only the blackboard. Miss Cosmas had always hated her because she was so bad at maths, had always been odious and unfair. 'At three and eleven,' Miss Cosmas shouted, 'at three and eleven.' But Mme Bonifay's number was eleven, and Helen was walking once again along the rue de la Tombe-Issoire, feeling more and more sick with apprehension at every step. Walking slowlier and slowlier in the hope of never getting there. But the houses came rushing down towards her, like the walls of the moving staircases in the Underground. Came rushing towards her, and then, when number eleven drew level, stopped dead, noiselessly. 'Mme Bonifay. Sage Femme de Ière Classe.' She stood looking at the words, just as she had stood in reality, two days before; then walked on, just as she had walked on then. Only one more minute, she pleaded with herself, till she got over her nervousness, till she felt less sick. Walked up the street again, and was in the garden with her grandmother and Hugh Ledwidge. It was a walled garden with a pine wood at one end of it. And a man came running out of the wood, a man with some awful kind of skin disease on his face. Red blotches and scabs and scurf. Horrible! But all her grandmother said was, 'God spat in his face,' and everyone laughed. But in the middle of the wood, when she went on, stood a bed, and immediately, some-how, she was lying on it, looking at a lot more people in another play, in the same play, perhaps. Bright under the spotlights, with voices like bells in her ears; but incomprehensible, unrecognizable. And Gerry was there, sitting on the edge of her bed, kissing her, stroking her shoulders, her breasts. 'But, Gerry, you mustn't! All those people – they can see us. Gerry, don't!' But when she tried to push him away, he was like a block of granite, immovable; and all the time his hands, his lips were releasing soft moths of quick and fluttering pleasure under her skin; and the shame, the dismay at being seen by all those people, let loose at the same time a special physical anguish of its own – a finer-footed, wildlier-fluttering sensation that was no longer a moth, but some huge beetle, revolting to the touch, and yet revoltingly delicious. 'Don't, Gerry, don't!' And suddenly she remembered everything – that night after the kitten had died, and all the other nights, and then the first signs, the growing anxiety, and the day she had telephoned to him and been told that he'd gone to Canada, and finally the money, and that evening when her mother ... 'I hate you!' she cried : but as she managed with a last violent effort to push him away, she felt a stab of pain so excruciating that for a moment she forgot her delirium and was wholly at the mercy of immediate, physical reality. Slowly the pain died down; the other-world of fever closed in on her again. And it wasn't Gerry any more, it was Mme Bonifay. Mme Bonifay with that thing in her hand. *Je vous ferai un peu mal.* And it wasn't the bed or the pine wood but the couch in Mme Bonifay's sitting-room. She clenched her teeth, just as she had clenched them then. Only this time it was worse, because she knew what was going to happen. And under the limelight the people were still there, acting their play. And lying there on the couch she herself was part of the play, outside, and at last was no longer herself, but someone else, someone in a bathing dress, with enormous breasts, like Lady Knipe's. And what was there to prevent *her* breasts from getting to be like that? Bell-clear, but incomprehensible, the actors discussed the nightmarish possibility. The possibility of Helen with enormous breasts, of Helen with thick rolls of fat round her hips, of Helen with creases in her thighs, of Helen with rows and rows of children – howling all the time; and that disgusting smell of curdled milk; and their diapers. And here, all of a sudden, was Joyce wheeling the pram along the streets of Aldershot. Taking the baby out. Feeding him. Half horrified, half fascinated, she watched him clinging, sucking. Flattened against the breast, the little frog face wore an expression of determined greed that gradually relaxed, as the stomach filled, to one of sleepy, imbecile ecstasy. But the hands – those were fully human, those were little miracles of the most delicate elegance. Lovely, exquisite little hands! Irresistible little hands! She took the baby from Joyce, she pressed him close against her body, she bent her head so as to be able to kiss those adorable little fingers. But the thing she held in her arms was the dying kitten, was those kidneys at the butcher's, was that horrible thing which she had opened her eyes to see Mme Bonifay nonchalantly picking up and carrying away in a tin basin to the kitchen.

*

The surgeon had been called in time, and Helen now was out of all danger. Reassured, Mme Bonifay had resumed the motherly and Rabelaisian good humour that was natural to her.

It was almost with a wink that she now talked of the operation that had saved Helen's life. '*Ton petit curetage,*' she would say with a kind of jovial archness, as though she were talking of some illicit pleasure. For Helen, every tone of that fat, jolly voice was yet another insult, yet a further humiliation. The fever had left her; her present weakness was lucid; she inhabited the real world once more. Turning her head, she could see herself reflected in the wardrobe mirror. It gave her a certain satisfaction to see how thin she was, how pale, what blue transparent shadows there were under the eyes, and the eyes themselves, how lifelessly without lustre. She could have powdered herself now, painted her lips a little, and rouged her cheeks, brushed back the gloss into her dull untidy hair; but, perversely, she preferred her sick pallor and dishevelment. 'Like the kitten,' she kept thinking. Reduced to a dirty little rag of limp flesh, transformed from the bright living creature into something repellent, into the likeness of kidneys, of that unspeakable thing that Mme Bonifay . . . She shuddered. And now *ton petit curetage* – in the same tone as *ton petit amoureux*. It was horrible, the final humiliation. She loathed the beastly woman, but at the same time was glad that she was so awful. That cheerful gross vulgarity was somehow appropriate – in keeping with all the rest. But when Mme Bonifay had left the room she would start crying, silently, in an agony of self-pity.

Returning unexpectedly, Mme Bonifay found her, that second morning after the *petit curetage*, with the tears streaming down her face. Genuinely distressed, she offered comfort. But the comfort smelt, as usual, of onions. Physically disgusted as well as resentful of the intrusion upon the privacy of her unhappiness, Helen turned aside, and when Mme Bonifay tried to force consolation upon her, she shook her head and told her to go away. Mme Bonifay hesitated for a moment, then obeyed, but with a Parthian insult in the form of a tenderly suggestive remark about the letter she had brought and which she now laid on Helen's pillow. From *him*, without a doubt. A good heart, in spite of everything ...

The letter, it turned out, was from Hugh. 'A holiday in Paris!' he wrote. 'From my dingy little kennel among the bric-à-brac, how I envy you, Helen! Paris in high summer. Gaily beautiful, as this place of hazy distances can never be. London's always mournful, even in the sunshine. One pines for the clear, unequivocal brilliance of the Paris summer. How I wish I were there! Selfishly, first of all, for the pleasure of being with you and out of London and the Museum. And then unselfishly, for your sake – because it worries me, the thought of your being all alone in Paris. Theoretically, with all my head, I know that nothing is likely to happen to you. But all the same – I'd like to be there, protective, but invisible, so that you wouldn't be aware of me, never feel my devotion as an importunity, but so that you should always have the confidence that comes from being two instead of one. Not, alas, that I should be a very good second in a tight corner. (How I hate myself sometimes for my shameful inadequacy!) But better, perhaps, than nobody. And I'd never encroach, never trespass or interfere. I'd be non-existent; except when you needed me. My reward would be just being in your neighbourhood, just seeing and hearing you – the reward of someone who comes out of a dusty place into a garden, and looks at the flowering trees, and listens to the fountains.

'I've never told you before (was afraid you'd laugh – and you may laugh; I don't mind : for after all it's *your* laughter), but the truth is that I sit sometimes, spinning stories to myself – stories in which I'm always with you, as I've told you I'd like to be with you now in Paris. Watching over you, keeping you from harm, and in return being refreshed by your loveliness, and warmed by your fire, and dazzled by your bright purity ...'

Angrily, as though the irony in it had been intentional, Helen threw the letter aside. But an hour later she had picked it up again and was re-reading it from the beginning. After all, it was comforting to know that there was somebody who cared.

CHAPTER FORTY

September 11th 1934

WITH Miller to see a show of scientific films. Development of the sea urchin. Fertilization, cell division, growth. A renewal of last year's almost nightmarish vision of a more-than-Bergsonian life force, of an ultimate Dark God, much darker, stranger, and more violent than any that Lawrence imagined. Raw material that, on its own inhuman plane, is already a perfectly finished product. A picture of earthworms followed. Week-long hermaphroditic love-making, worm to worm, within a tube of slime. Then an incredibly beautiful film showing the life-history of the blow-fly. The eggs. The grubs on their piece of decaying meat. Snow-white, like a flock of sheep on a meadow. Hurrying away from light. Then, after five days of growth, descending to the earth, burrowing, making a cocoon. In twelve more days, the fly emerges. Fantastic process of resurrection ! An organ in the head is inflated like a balloon. Blown up so large, that the walls of the cocoon are split. The fly wriggles out. Positively now, instead of negatively phototropic, as it was as a grub. (Minor and incidental miracle !) Burrowing upwards, towards the light. At the surface, you see it literally pumping up its soft, wet body with air, smoothing out its crumpled wings by forcing blood into the veins. Astonishing and moving spectacle.

I put the question to Miller : what will be the influence of the spread of knowledge such as this? Knowledge of a world incomparably more improbable and more beautiful than the imaginings of any myth-maker. A world, only a few years ago, completely unknown to all but a handful of people. What the effects of its general discovery by all? Miller laughed. 'It will have exactly as much or as little effect as people want it to have. Those who prefer to think about sex and money will go on thinking about sex and money. However loudly the movies proclaim the glory of God.' Persistence of the ingenuous notion that the response to favourable circumstances is inevitably and automatically good. Raw material, once again, to be worked up. One goes on believing in automatic progress, because one *wants* to cherish this stupidity : it's so consoling. Consoling, because it puts the whole responsibility for everything you do or fail to do on somebody or something other than yourself.

CHAPTER FORTY-ONE

December 1933

At Colon they drove in a cab, at evening, along an esplanade. Whitish, like a vast fish's eye, the sea lay as though dead. Against a picture postcard sunset the immoderately tall thin palms were the emblems of a resigned hopelessness, and in the nostrils the hot air was like a vapour of wool. They swam for a little in the warm fish-eye, then returned through the deepening night to the town.

For the rich there were, after dinner, cabaret shows with expensive drinks and genuinely white prostitutes at ten dollars. For the poor, in the back streets, the mulatto women sat at doors that opened directly on to lighted bedrooms.

'If one were really conscientious,' said Anthony, as they walked back late that night to the hotel, 'I suppose one would have to go and infect oneself with syphilis.'

The smell of sweat, the smell of alcohol, the smells of sewage and decay and cheap perfumes; then, next morning, the Canal, the great locks, the ship climbing up from one ocean and down again to the other. A more than human achievement that made it possible, Mark explained, smiling anatomically, to transport whores and whisky by water instead of overland from Colon to Panama.

Their ship headed northwards. Once every couple of days they would call at a little port to pick up cargo. From among the bananas at San José, a spider, large as a fist and woolly, made its way into their cabin. Off Champerico, where the lighters came out loaded with bags of coffee, an Indian fell into the sea and was drowned.

At night, it was not the ship that seemed to move, but the stars. They mounted slowly, slantwise, hung at the top of their trajectory, then swooped downwards, travelled tentatively to the right and back to the left, then, beginning all over again, mounted once more towards the zenith.

'Rather sickening,' was Anthony's verdict, 'but beautiful.'

An improvement on the ordinary celestial mechanics. One could lie there and look at them indefinitely.

There was a note of grim satisfaction in Staithes's voice as he replied that in two days' time they would be at Puerto San Felipe.

Puerto San Felipe was a village of huts, with some wooden sheds, near the water, for storing coffee. Don Jorge's agent at the port helped them through the customs. A pure Spaniard, half dead with tropical diseases, but still elaborately courteous. 'My house is yours,' he assured them, as they climbed the steep path towards his bungalow, 'my house is yours.'

Orchids hung from the veranda, and, among them, cages full of incessantly screaming green parakeets.

An emaciated woman, prematurely old and tired, hopelessly tired, beyond the limit of her strength, came shuffling out of the house to welcome them, to apologize in advance for her hospitality. Puerto San Felipe was a small place, lacked commodities; and besides, she explained, the child was not well, not at all well. Mark asked her what was the matter. She looked at him with eyes expressionless with fatigue, and answered vaguely that it was fever; fever and a pain in the head.

They went with her into the house, and were shown a little girl lying on a camp-bed, restlessly turning her head from side to side, as if seeking, but always vainly, some cool place on which to rest her cheek, some position in which she might find relief from pain. The room was full of flies, and a smell of fried fish came from the kitchen. Looking at the child, Anthony suddenly found himself remembering Helen, that day on the roof – turning and turning her head in the torture of pleasure.

'I suppose it must be mastoid,' Mark was saying. 'Or meningitis, perhaps.'

As he spoke, the child lifted thin arms from under the sheet and, clasping her head between her hands, began to roll still more violently from side to side, and at last broke out into a paroxysm of screaming.

In immediate response, the noise of the parakeets on the veranda swelled up, shriek after shriek, to a deafening maximum of intensity.

'Quiet, quiet,' the mother kept repeating, wheedlingly at first, then with a growing insistence, begging, exhorting, commanding the child to stop crying, to feel less pain. The screaming continued, the head went on rolling from side to side.

Tortured by pleasure, tortured by pain. At the mercy of one's skin and mucus, at the mercy of those thin threads of nerve.

'Quiet, quiet,' the woman repeated almost angrily. She bent over the bed and, by main force, dragged down the child's lifted arms; then, holding the two thin wrists in one hand, laid the other on the head in an effort to hold it unmoving on the pillows. Still screaming, the little girl struggled under the constraint. The woman's bony hand tightened round the wrists, rested more heavily on the forehead. If she could forcefully restrain the manifestations of pain, perhaps the pain itself would cease, perhaps the child would stop that screaming, would sit up perhaps, smiling, and be well again.

'Quiet, quiet,' she commanded between clenched teeth.

With a violent effort the child released her arms from the grasp of those claw-like fingers; the hands flew once more to the head. Before the woman could snatch them away again, Mark touched her on the arm. She looked round at him.

'Better to leave her,' he was saying.

Obediently she straightened herself up and walked away towards the door that gave on to the veranda. They followed her. There was nothing whatever that they could do.

'*Mi casa es suya.*'

Thank God, it wasn't. The child's screams had subsided; but the frying fish, the parakeets among the orchids ... Politely, Mark refused the invitation to an early luncheon. They walked out again into the oppressive sunshine. The *mozos* had loaded their baggage on to the pack-mules, and the riding animals stood in the shade of a tree, ready saddled. They buckled on enormous spurs and mounted.

The track wound up and up from the coast, through a jungle silvery and brownish pink with drought. Sitting bolt upright on his high-backed saddle, Mark read *Timon of Athens* from his pocket edition of the Tragedies. Each time he turned a page, he gave his mule the spur; and for a few yards she would climb a little more quickly, then revert to the old, slow pace.

In the hotel at Tapatlan, where they spent the night, Anthony was bitten for the first time in his life by bed bugs, and the next morning it was an attack of dysentery. ... On the fourth day he was well enough to go out and see the sights. The last earthquake had almost wrecked the church. A dense black fruitage of bats hung, like ripe plums, from the rafters; an Indian boy, ragged and bare-footed, was sweeping up the droppings; from the altars the baroque saints flapped and gesticulated in a frozen paroxysm of devotion. They walked out again into the market-place, where, secret and as though ambushed within their dark shawls, the brown Indian women squatted in the dust before their little piles of fruit and withering vegetables. The meat on the butcher's stall was covered with a crust of flies. Rhythmically shaking their long ears the donkeys passed, on small quick hoofs, noiseless in the dust. The women came and went in silence, carrying kerosene tins of water on their heads. From under hat brims, dark eyes regarded the strangers with an inscrutably reptilian glitter that seemed devoid of all curiosity, all interest, any awareness even of their presence.

'I'm tired,' Anthony announced. They had not walked very far; but at Tapatlan, it was an immense fatigue even to be living and conscious. 'When I die,' he went on after a silence, 'this is the part of hell I shall be sent to. I recognize it instantly.'

The bar of the hotel was in a dim crypt-like room with a vaulted ceiling supported at the centre by a pier of masonry, inordinately thick for its height, to resist the earthquake shocks. 'The Saxon ossuary,' Mark called it; and here, while he went to their room to fetch a handkerchief, he left Anthony installed in a cane chair.

Propped against the bar, a smartly dressed young Mexican in riding-breeches and an enormous felt hat was boasting to the proprietress about the alligators he had shot in the swamps at the mouth of the Coppalita, of his firmness in dealing with the Indians who had come to pick the coffee on his estate, of the money he expected to make when he sold his crop.

'A bit tight,' Anthony reflected, listening and looking on from his chair; and was enjoying the performance, when the young man turned, and, bowing with the grave formality of one who is so drunk that he must do everything with a conscious deliberation, asked if the foreign cavalier would take a glass of *tequila* with him.

Fatigue had made Anthony's Spanish more halting than usual. His efforts to explain that he had not been well, that it would not be good for him to drink alcohol, landed him very soon in incoherence. The young man listened, fixing him all the time with dark eyes, bright like the Indians', but, unlike theirs, comprehensibly expressive – European eyes, in which it was possible to read an intense and passionate interest, a focused awareness. Anthony mumbled on, and all at once those eyes took on a new and dangerous glitter; an expression of anger distorted the handsome face, the knuckles of the strong rapacious hands went white under a sudden pressure. The young man stepped forward menacingly.

'*Usted me desprecia*,' he shouted.

His movement, the violence of his tone, startled Anthony into a kind of panic alarm. He scrambled to his feet and, edging behind his chair, began to explain in a voice that he had meant to be calmly conciliatory, but which, in spite of all his efforts to keep it grave and steady, trembled into a breathless shrillness, that he hadn't dreamed of despising anyone, that it was merely a question of – he fumbled for the medical explanation and could find nothing better than a pain in the stomach – merely a question of *un dolor en mi estómago*.

For some reason the word *estómago* seemed to the young man the final, most outrageous insult. He bellowed something incomprehensible, but evidently abusive; his hand went back to his hip-pocket and, as the proprietress screamed for help, came forward again, holding a revolver.

'Don't, don't!' Anthony cried out, without knowing what he was saying; then, with extraordinary agility, darted out of his corner to take shelter behind the massive pillar at the centre of the room.

For a second the young man was out of sight. But suppose he were to creep up on tiptoe. Anthony imagined the revolver suddenly coming round the pillar into his face; or else from behind – he would feel the muzzle pressed against his back, would hear the ghastly explosion, and then ... A fear so intense that it was like the most excruciating physical pain possessed him entirely; his heart beat more violently than ever, he felt as though he were going to be sick. Overcoming terror by a greater terror, he stuck out his head to the left. The young man was standing only two yards away, staring with a ferocious fixity at the pillar. Anthony saw him jerk into movement, and with a despairing shout for help jumped to the right, looked out again and jumped back to the left; then once more to the right.

'I can't go on,' he was thinking. 'I can't do it much longer.' The thought of that pistol coming unexpectedly round the pillar forced him to look out yet again.

The young man moved, and he darted precipitately to the left.

The noise of the revolver going off – that was what he dreaded most. The horrible noise, sudden and annihilating like the noise of that other explosion years before. His eyelids had stiffened and were irrepressibly trembling, ready to blink, in anticipation of the horrifying event. The lashes flickered before his eyes, and it was through a kind of mist that, peering out, he saw the door open and Mark moving swiftly across the room, Mark catching the young man by the wrist ... The pistol went off; reverberated from the walls and ceiling, the report was catastrophically loud. Anthony uttered a great cry, as though he had been wounded, and, shutting his eyes, flattened himself against the pillar. Conscious only of nausea and that pain in the genitals, those gripings of the bowels, he waited, reduced to a mere quivering embodiment of fearful anticipation, for the next explosion. Waited for what seemed hours. Dim voices parleyed incomprehensibly. Then a touch on his shoulder made him start. He shouted, 'No, don't,' and lifting eyelids that still twitched with the desirable blink, saw Mark Staithes, demonstrating muscle by muscle a smile of friendly amusement.

'All clear,' he said, 'you can come out.'

Feeling profoundly ashamed and humiliated, Anthony followed him into the open. The young Mexican was at the bar again and already drinking. As they approached, he turned and with outstretched arms came to meet them. '*Hombre*,' he said to Anthony, as he took him affectionately by the hand, '*hombre!*'

Anthony felt more abjectly humiliated than ever.

CHAPTER FORTY-TWO

September 15th 1934

HAVE built up during the last few days a meditation on a phrase of William Penn's. 'Force may subdue, but Love gains; and he who forgives first wins the laurel.'

'Force may subdue.' I visualize men using force. First, hand to hand. With fists, knives, truncheons, whips. Weals, red or livid across flesh. Lacerations, bruises, the broken bone sticking in jags through the skin, faces horribly swollen and bleeding. Then try to imagine, in my own body, the pain of a crushed finger, of blows with a stick or lash across the face, the searing touch of red-hot iron. All the short-range brutalities and tortures.

Then, force from a distance. Machine-gun bullets, high explosive, gases, choking or blistering fire.

Force, finally, in the shape of economic coercion. Starved children, pot-bellied and with arms and legs like sticks. Women old at thirty. And those living corpses, standing in silence at the street corners in Durham or South Wales, shuffling in silence through the mud.

Yes, force may subdue. Subdue in death, subdue by wounds, subdue through starvation and terror. Vision of frightened faces, of abject gestures of servility. The manager at his desk, hectoring. The clerk cringing under the threat of dismissal. Force – the act of violently denying man's ultimate unity with man.

'Force may subdue, but Love gains.' I rehearse the history of Penn himself among the Redskins. Remember how Miller used to allay the suspicious hostility of the Indians in the mountain villages. Think of Pennell on the North-West Frontier; of the Quakers during the Russian famine; of Elizabeth Fry and Damien.

Next I consider the translations of love into terms of politics. Campbell-Bannerman's insistence that reparation should be made in South Africa – in the teeth of the protests, the Cassandra-like prophesyings of such 'sane and practical men' as Arthur Balfour. Love gains even in the clumsy, distorted form of a good political constitution. 'He who forgives first wins the laurel.' In South Africa, the English forgave those whom they had wronged – which is only less difficult than forgiving those by whom one has been wronged – and so secured a prize which they couldn't have won by continued coercion. No prize has been won since the last war, because no combatant has yet forgiven those by whom he has been wronged or those he has wronged.

Consistently applied to any situation, love always gains. It is an empirically determined fact. Love is the best policy. The best not only in regard to those loved, but also in regard to the one who loves. For love is self-energizing. Produces the means whereby its policy can be carried out. In order to go on loving, one needs patience, courage, endurance. But the process of loving generates these means to its own continuance. Love gains because, for the sake of that which is loved, the lover is patient and brave.

And what is loved? Goodness and the potentialities for goodness in all human beings – even those most busily engaged in refusing to actualize those potentialities for goodness in relation to the lover himself. If sufficiently great, love can cast out the fear even of malevolently active enemies.

I end by holding the thought of goodness, still, as it were, before the eyes of my mind. Goodness, immanent in its potentialities, transcendent as a realized ideal; conceivable in its perfections, but also susceptible of being realized in practice, of being embodied at least partially in any situation in which we may find ourselves. 'The thought of goodness' – it is the wrong phrase. For in reality it is a whole system of thoughts and sentiments. It is this whole system that I hold, quite still, perceived simultaneously in its entirety – hold it without words, without images, undiscursively, as a single, simple entity. Hold it – then at last must retreat again, back into words, back at last (but refreshed, but made more conscious, but replenished, as it were) into ordinary life.

September 17th 1934

Was called in by Helen to help entertain her sister and brother-in-law, back on leave from India. Had to put on evening clothes – the first time this year – because Colin could not allow himself to be seen in a theatre or at the Savoy Grill in anything but a white tie. A depressing evening. Joyce sickly and gaunt before her time. Colin furtively interested in plumper, fresher bodies. She, jealous and nagging; he resentful at being tied to her and the children, blaming her for the strictness of his own code, which doesn't allow him to be the libertine he would like to be. Each chronically impatient with the other. Every now and then an outburst of bad temper, an exchange of angry or spiteful words. Colin had other grievances as well. England, it seemed, didn't show sufficient respect to the officer and gent. Cabmen were impertinent, the lower classes jostled him in the streets. 'They call this a white man's country.' (This, after the second 'quick one' in the bar of the theatre, between the acts.) 'It isn't. Give me Poona every time.'

Reflect that we all have our Poonas, bolt-holes from un-pleasant reality. The danger, as Miller is always insisting, of meditation becoming such a bolt-hole. Quietism can be mere self-indulgence. Charismata like masturbations. Masturbations, however, that are dignified, by the amateur mystics who practise them, with all the most sacred names of religion and philosophy. 'The contemplative life.' It can be made a kind of high-brow substitute for Marlene Dietrich : a subject for erotic musings in the twilight. Meditation – valuable, not as a pleasurable end; only as a means for effecting desirable changes in the personality and mode of existence. To live contemplatively is not to live in some deliciously voluptuous or flattering Poona; it is to live in London, but to live there in a non-cockney style.

CHAPTER FORTY-THREE

July 20th and 21st 1914

THE right, the auspicious moment for telling Brian the truth – or at any rate as much of the truth as it was expedient for him to know – never seemed to present itself. That first evening had been ruled out in advance – because Anthony felt that he must treat himself to a respite, because poor Brian was looking so ill and tired. At supper and after it, Anthony kept the conversation as entertainingly impersonal as he could make it. He talked about Sorel's *Réflexions sur la violence* – uncomfortable reading for Fabians! And had Brian seen how effectively his beloved Bergson had been punctured by Julien Benda? And what about Lascelles Abercrombie's blank verse? And the latest Gilbert Cannan? Next morning they set out for a walk on the Langdale Pikes. Both were out of training; but in spite of shortened breath and bumping heart, Brian pressed on with a kind of Spartan determination that to Anthony seemed at first absurd, then exasperating. When they got home, late in the afternoon, they were both thoroughly tired; but Anthony was also resent-ful. Rest and a meal did something to change his mood; but he still found it impossible to behave towards Brian except as a man, forgiving indeed, but still on his dignity; and dignity was

326

obviously quite incompatible with the telling of this particular truth. They spent a silent evening – Anthony reading, the other restlessly prowling about the room, as though on the watch for an occasion to speak – an occasion which Anthony's air of intense preoccupation was deliberately intended not to give him.

In bed the next morning Anthony found himself startled broad awake by the uncomfortable thought that time was passing, and passing not only for himself but also for Joan and Brian. Joan's impatience might get the better of her promise not to write to Brian; besides, the longer he postponed the inevitable explanation with Brian, the worse Brian would think of him.

Inventing a blistered heel for the occasion, he let Brian go out by himself, and having watched him indomitably striding away up the steep slope behind the cottage, sat down to write his letter to Joan. To try to write it, rather; for every one of the drafts he produced displayed one or other of two faults, and each of the two faults exposed him, he realized, to a particular danger : the danger that, if he insisted too much on the esteem and affection which had prepared him to lose his head on that accursed evening, she would reply that so much esteem and affection accompanied by head-losing amounted to love, and were his justification (since love was supposed to justify everything) for betraying Brian; and the other danger that, if he insisted too exclusively on the head-losing and temporary insanity, she would feel insulted and complain to Brian, to Mrs Foxe, to her relations, raise a regular hue and cry against him as a cad, a seducer, and heaven only knew what else. After the expense of three hours and a dozen sheets of paper, the best of his efforts seemed to him too unsatisfactory to send off. He put it angrily aside, and, in his mood of exasperation, dashed off a violent letter of abuse to Mary. Damned woman! She was responsible for everything. 'Deliberate malice ...' 'Shameless exploitation of my love for you ...' 'Treating me as though I were some sort of animal you could torment for your private amusement ...' The phrases flowed from his pen. 'This is good-bye,' he concluded, and, with half his mind, believed in what he was dramatically writing. 'I never want to see you again. *Never.*' But a quarrel, the other half of his mind was reflecting, can always be made up : he would give her this lesson : then, perhaps, if she behaved well, if he felt he simply couldn't do without her ... He sealed up the letter, and at once walked briskly to the village to post it. This act of decision did something to restore his self-esteem. On his way home he made up his mind, quite definitely this time, that he would have his talk with Brian that evening, and then, in the light of his knowledge of Brian's attitude, re-write the letter to Joan the following morning.

Brian was back at six, triumphing in the fact that he had walked further and climbed to the tops of more mountains than on any previous occasion in his life, but looking, in spite of his exultations, completely exhausted. At the sight of that face he had known so long, that face now so tragically worn and emaciated beneath the transfiguration of the smile, Anthony felt an intenser renewal of the first evening's emotions – of anxious solicitude for an old friend, of distressed sympathy with a human being's suffering – and along with these an excruciating sense of guilt towards the friend, of responsibility for the human being. Instant confession might have relieved his pain, might have allowed him at the same time to express his feelings; but he hesitated; he was silent; and in a few seconds, by an almost instantaneous process of psychological chemistry, the sympathy and the solicitude had combined with the sense of guilt to form a kind of anger. Yes, he was positively angry with Brian for looking so tired, for being already so miserable, for going to be so much more miserable the moment he was told the truth.

'You're mad to overtire yourself like this,' he said gruffly, and drove him into the house to take a rest before supper.

After the meal they went out on to the strip of terraced lawn in front of the cottage and spreading out a rug, lay down and looked up into a sky green at their arrival with the last trace of summer twilight, then gradually and ever more deeply blue.

The time, thought Anthony, with a certain sinking of the heart, had come, irrevocably; and through a long silence he prepared himself to begin, trying out in his mind one opening gambit after another; hesitating between the abrupt and precipitate clean-breast-of-it-all and more devious strategy that would prepare the victim for the final shock.

But before he had decided which was the best approach to his confession, the other broke out all at once into stammering speech. He too, it was evident, had been waiting for an opportunity to ease his mind, and instead of acting the penitent, as he had intended, Anthony found himself (to the relief of a part of his mind, to the dismay and embarrassment of the inhabitant of a deeper layer of consciousness) suddenly called upon to play the part of confessor and director of conscience; called upon to listen all over again to the story that Joan had already told him – the story that, adorned with St Monicas and uterine reactions, he had so joyfully passed on to Mary Amberley. He had to hear how humiliating, how painful his friend found it to be unable to gain the mastery of his body, to banish all the low desires unworthy of the love he felt for Joan. Or perhaps, Brian had qualified, citing Meredith's great volcano flinging fires of earth to sky, perhaps not unworthy when circumstances should have allowed them to take their place in the complex whole of a perfect marriage; but unworthy at that moment when it was not yet possible for them to find their legitimate expression, unworthy in so far as they were to defy the authority of the conscious mind.

'I've had to r-run away,' he explained, 'h-had to remove my b-body to a safe d-distance. B-because I wasn't able to c-c-c . . .'; 'control' would not come; he had to be satisfied with another less expressive word; 'to m-manage myself with my w-will. One's ash-shamed of being so weak,' Brian concluded.

Anthony nodded. Weak in making up one's mind to kiss, and no less weak when it came to interrupting a momentarily agreeable experience – though there had been something more than weakness there, something positive, a perverse revelling in an action known to be stupid, dangerous, wrong.

'But if one *kn-knows* one c-can't overc-come it,' Brian was saying, 'I s-suppose it's b-best to r-run away. B-better than l-letting it g-get one into av-voidable trouble.'

'Yes, I agree,' said Anthony, wondering why he hadn't followed his impulse and turned back at Kendal.

'And not only one's-self, but o-other people. G-getting *th-them* into trouble t-too.' There was a long silence; then, slowly and laboriously, he set out to explain that the lovely, the splendid thing about Joan was her naturalness. She had the strength of natural things and their spontaneity; she was warm, like nature, and generous and profoundly innocent. She had the qualities of a summer landscape, of a flowering tree, of a water-bird darting bright-eyed and glossy between the rushes. This naturalness was what he had chiefly loved in her, because it was the complementary opposite of his own scrupulousness and intellectualism. But it was this same naturalness that had made it all but impossible for Joan to understand why he had found her presence so dangerous, why he had felt it necessary to keep away from her. She had been hurt by his witholding of himself, had thought it was because he didn't love her; whereas the truth was ...

The truth was, Anthony said to himself, finding a kind of consolation, a renewal of his sense of superiority, in the derisive cynicism of his thoughts, the truth was that she was thirsty for kisses, that at his first caress her whole body revealed itself a shuddering and palpitating protest against the continence that had been imposed on it.

'The t-truth,' Brian was laboriously saying, 'is that I l-love her m-more than I e-ever did. Unspeakably much.' He was silent once more for a little; then, looking up at Anthony, 'What shall I d-do?' he asked.

Still in his critical mood, Anthony scored, with the grossness of his unspoken answer, another private triumph – as short-lived however, as it was easy; for his first thought was succeeded almost instantaneously by the disquieting realization that he was being faced by a choice : either to tell Brian what had happened between himself and Joan; or else to make some anodyne and non-committal reply to his question, and postpone the telling of the truth till later on. By omission, the anodyne reply would be a monstrous falsehood; and when at last he came to tell the truth, this lie and all the other lies implied in more than two days of silence or irrelevant chatter would inevitably be remembered against him. But to tell the truth at once, in this particular context, would be especially painful – and painful, he went on to think, not only to himself but also, and above all, to Brian. After what Brian had been saying this evening, to blurt out a plain account of what had happened would be sheer cruelty and deliberate insult.

'What o-ought I to d-do?' Brian was insisting.

'I think,' Anthony answered softly, 'I think you ought to come to terms with reality.'

He had made this decision – or rather, as he preferred to put it when, later on, in the privacy of his bedroom, he thought of the events of the evening, the decision had made itself. Looking back, he felt that he had had nothing to do with the matter.

CHAPTER FORTY-FOUR

September 21st 1934

REMARKS by St Teresa. 'Let us look at our own faults, and not at other people's. We ought not to insist on everyone following our footsteps, or to take upon ourselves to give instructions in spirituality when, perhaps, we do not even know what it is. Zeal for the good of souls, though given us by God, may often lead us astray.' To which add this. 'It is a great grace of God to practise self-examination, but too much is as bad as too little, as they say; believe me, by God's help, we shall accomplish more by contemplating the divinity than by keeping our eyes fixed on ourselves.' God may or may not exist. But there is the empirical fact that contemplation of the divinity – of goodness in its most unqualified form – is a method of realizing that goodness to some slight degree in one's life, and results, often, in an experience as if of help towards that realization of goodness, help from some being other than one's ordinary self and immensely superior to it. Christian God and the Buddhist's primal Mind – interpretations of concrete experiences, the Buddhist being the rationalization of a state further removed from the normal than the Christian. Christians, of course, have often experienced that state and found great difficulties in explaining it in orthodox terms. Both conceptions are legitimate – just as both macroscopical and microscopical views of matter are legitimate. We look at the universe with a certain kind of physico-mental apparatus. That apparatus can respond only to certain stimuli. Within relatively narrow limits, it is adjustable. The nature of the facts which each of us perceives as primary and given

331

depends on the nature of the individual instrument and on the adjustment we have been brought up, or deliberately chosen, to give it. From these data one can draw inferences. Which may be logically sound or unsound. Any philosophy is intellectually legitimate if, one, it starts from facts which, for the philosopher, are data and if, two, the logical construction based on these facts is sound. But an intellectually is not the same as a morally legitimate philosophy. We can adjust our instrument deliberately, by an act of the will. This means that we can will modifications in the personal experiences which underlie our philosophy, the data from which we argue. Problem : to build really solid logical bridges between given facts and philosophical inferences. All but insoluble. No bullet-proof arguments for any of the main cosmological theories. What, then, shall we do? Stick, so far as possible, to the empirical facts – always remembering that these are modifiable by anyone who chooses to modify the perceiving mechanism. So that one can see, for example, either irremediable senselessness and turpitude, or else actualizable potentialities for good – whichever one likes; it is a question of choice.

CHAPTER FORTY-FIVE

April 14th 1928

Happiness inexpressible – that was what her letter should have brought him. But Hugh's face, as he walked – walked instead of having his lunch – up and down the long gallery of the Ethnographical Collection, was a mask of perplexity and distress. The words of Helen's letter repeated themselves in his memory. 'Nobody cares a pin whether I'm alive or dead.'

From the Mexican case the symbol of death in crystal and that other skull inlaid with turquoise stared out at him as he passed. 'Nobody cares ...' It should have been his opportunity. He had dreamt of her unhappiness – in an agony of commiseration, but also with hope. Unhappy, she would turn to him. 'Nobody cares ...'

'Nobody except you.' His exultant pride and pleasure in those

332

words had been tempered, as he read on, by the realization that she didn't really understand *how* he cared, didn't appreciate the exact quality of his feeling. 'My mother?' she had written. 'But, after all, ever since she started taking that horrible stuff, she's somebody else – always was somebody else really, even when she was well (though of course not *so* else). Just as I was always somebody else, if it comes to that. She expected a daughter; but I was always selfish and irresponsible. Just as she was. Somebody else. How could she care? You're not selfish, Hugh. You're …' But it wasn't a question merely of selfishness or unselfishness, he began to protest, with all the painted faces of the Peruvian vases staring down from the right with an unwinking intensity of frozen life. It was a question of something different, something deeper and more spiritual. On his left the trophies of the Papuan head-hunters hung shrivelled, but fantastically painted, like the heads of decapitated clowns. The skulls from the Torres Straits had been given round shining eyes of mother-of-pearl. Yes, more spiritual, Hugh insisted, thinking of what he had written about her – lyrically, lyrically! – and of that subtle analysis of his own emotions. The unselfishness was there, but melted down, as it were, in contemplation, refined into something aesthetic. Unselfishness in a picture. Unselfishness by Watteau, by Cima da Conegliano. And she herself, the object of his contemplative and aesthetic unselfishness – she too, in his imaginings, in the accumulating pages of his manuscript, had possessed the quality of a picture or a piece of music; something that it would be sufficient happiness merely to look at for ever, to listen to; perhaps, occasionally, to touch, as though she were a statue, to caress with an almost imperceptible tenderness. And sometimes in those imaginings she was cold, was unhappy – nobody cared a pin – and she asked to be comforted and made warm, she crept into his arms, into those unselfish, contemplative, impalpable arms of his, and lay there safely, but naked, lay there a picture, virginal, ideal, but melting, melting … Feathered like an ambassador in full dress uniform, with the beak of a bird, the teeth of a shark, this wooden mask had once made its wearer feel, as he danced, that he was more than human, akin to the gods. 'You've said you'd like to be always with me. Well, I've

333

been thinking about it a lot recently, and I believe that that's what I'd like too. Dear Hugh, I'm not in love with you; but I like you more than anyone else. I think you're nicer, kinder, gentler, less selfish. And surely that's a good enough foundation to build on.' The words, when he read them first, had filled him with a kind of panic; and it was with the same protesting agitation that he now walked between New Caledonia and the Solomon Islands. In the belly of a wooden bonito fish the Melanesian widow opened a little door, and there, like a chamberpot, was her husband's skull. But it was always spiritually and aesthetically that he had wanted to be with her. Hadn't she been able to understand that? Surely he had made it clear enough? 'If you still want it, there I am – I want it too.' It was terrible, he was thinking, terrible! She was forcing a decision on him, making it impossible for him to say no by assuming that he had already said yes. He felt himself hemmed in, driven into a corner. Marriage? But he would have to change his whole way of life. The flat wouldn't be large enough. She'd want to eat meat at night. Mrs Barton would give notice. Of the spears on his left some were tipped with obsidian, some with the spines of sting-rays, some with human bone. 'You probably think I'm a fool, and flighty and irresponsible; and it's true, I have been up till now. I'm hopeless. But I wasn't born hopeless – I was made it, because of the kind of life I've lived. Now I want to be something else, and I know I *can* be something else. *Sérieuse*. A good wife and all that, ridiculous and embarrassing as it sounds when one puts it down on paper. But I refuse to be ashamed of goodness any longer. I absolutely refuse.' That irresponsibility, he was thinking, was one of the loveliest and most moving things about her. It separated her from the common world, it promoted her out of vulgar humanity. He didn't want her to be responsible and a good wife. He wanted her to be like Ariel, like the delicate creature in his own manuscript, a being of another order, beyond good and evil. Meanwhile he had walked into Africa. The image of a Negress holding her long pointed breasts in her two hands glistened darkly from behind the confining glass. Her belly was tattooed, her navel projected in a little cone. The spears in the next case were headed with iron. Like Ariel, he repeated to himself, like those Watteaus at Dresden, like Debussy. For resonator, this xylophone had, not the usual gourd, but a human skull, and there were skulls festooned along the ivory fetish horns, thighbones around the sacrificial drum from Ashanti. She was spoiling everything, he said to himself resentfully. And suddenly, lifting his eyes, he saw that she was there, hurrying along the narrow passage between the cases to meet him.

'You?' he managed to whisper.

But Helen was too much perturbed to see the look of dismay, the pallor, and then the guilty blush, too intensely preoccupied with her own thoughts to hear the note of startled apprehension in his voice.

'I'm sorry,' she said breathlessly, as she took his hand. 'I didn't mean to come and pester you here. But you don't know what it's been like this morning at home.' She shook her head; her lips trembled. 'Mother's been like a madwoman. I can't tell you.... You're the only person, Hugh ...'

Clumsily, he tried to console her. But the reality was profoundly different from his imagination of her unhappiness. The imagination had always been his delicious opportunity; the reality was the menace of an unavoidable doom. Desperately, he tried the effect of changing the subject. These things from Benin were rather interesting. The ivory leopard, spotted with disks of copper inlay. The Negro warriors, in bronze, with their leaf-shaped spears and swords, and the heads of their enemies hanging from their belts. The Europeans, bearded and aquiline, in their high sixteenth-century morions and baggy hose, their matchlocks in their hands, and the cross hanging round their necks. Comic, he remarked, parenthetically, that the only thing these blackamoors ever got out of Christianity should have been the art of crucifying people. The punitive expedition in 1897 found the place full of crosses. And this beautiful head of the young girl with her tapering Phrygian cap of coral beads ...

'Look at this,' Helen suddenly interrupted; and, pulling up her sleeve, she showed him two red semicircular marks on the skin of her forearm a few inches above the wrist. 'That's where she bit me, when I tried to make her go back to bed.'

Hugh was startled into pitying indignation. 'But it's awful!' he cried. 'It's too awful.' He took her hand. 'My poor child!'

335

They stood for a moment in silence. Then, suddenly, his pity was shot through by the realization that the thing had happened. There could be no escape now. He found himself thinking again of Mrs Barton. If she were to give notice, what would he do?

CHAPTER FORTY-SIX

October 30th 1934

Mark, at dinner, said he'd been re-reading *Anna Karenina*. Found it good, as novels go. But complained of the profound untruthfulness of even the best imaginative literature. And he began to catalogue its omissions. Almost total neglect of those small physiological events that decide whether day-to-day living shall have a pleasant or unpleasant tone. Excretion, for example, with its power to make or mar the day. Digestion. And, for the heroines of novel and drama, menstruation. Then the small illnesses – catarrh, rheumatism, headache, eyestrain. The chronic physical disabilities – ramifying out (as in the case of deformity or impotence) into luxuriant insanities. And conversely the sudden accessions, from unknown visceral and muscular sources, of more than ordinary health. No mention, next, of the part played by mere sensations in producing happiness. Hot bath, for example, taste of bacon, feel of fur, smell of freesias. In life, an empty cigarette-case may cause more distress than the absence of a lover; never in books. Almost equally complete omission of the small distractions that fill the greater part of human lives. Reading the papers; looking into shops; exchanging gossip; with all the varieties of day-dreaming, from lying in bed, imagining what one would do if one had the right lover, income, face, social position, to sitting at the picture palace passively accepting ready-made day-dreams from Hollywood.

Lying by omission turns inevitably into positive lying. The implications of literature are that human beings are controlled, if not by reason, at least by comprehensible, well-organized, avowable sentiments. Whereas the facts are quite different. Sometimes the sentiments come in, sometimes they don't. All for love, or the world well lost; but love may be the title of nobility given to an inordinate liking for a particular person's smell or texture, a lunatic desire for the repetition of a sensation produced by some particular dexterity. Or consider those cases (seldom published, but how numerous, as anyone in a position to know can tell!), those cases of the eminent statesmen, churchmen, lawyers, captains of industry – seemingly so sane, demonstrably so intelligent, publicly so high-principled; but, in private, under irresistible compulsion towards brandy, towards young men, towards little girls in trains, towards exhibitionism, towards gambling or hoarding, towards bullying, towards being whipped, towards all the innumerable, crazy perversions of the lust for money and power and position on the one hand, for sexual pleasure on the other. Mere tics and tropisms, lunatic and unavowable cravings – these play as much part in human life as the organized and recognized sentiments. And imaginative literature suppresses the fact. Propagates an enormous lie about the nature of men and women.

'Rightly, no doubt. Because, if human beings were shown what they're really like, they'd either kill one another as vermin, or hang themselves. But meanwhile, I really can't be bothered to read any more imaginative literature. Lies don't interest me. However poetically they may be expressed. They're just a bore.'

Agreed with Mark that imaginative literature wasn't doing its duty. That it was essential to know everything – and to know it, not merely through scientific textbooks, but also in a form that would have power to bring the facts home to the whole mind, not merely to the intellect. A complete expression (in terms of imaginative literature) leading to complete knowledge (with the whole mind) of the complete truth: indispensable preliminary condition of any remedial action, any serious attempt at the construction of a genuinely human being. Construction from within, by training in proper use of the self – training, simultaneously physical and mental. Construction, at the same time, from without, by means of social and economic arrangements devised in the light of a complete knowledge of the individual, and of the way in which the individual can modify himself.

Mark only laughed, and said I reminded him of the men who go round from house to house selling electric washing-machines.

November 4th 1934

Very good meeting in Newcastle with Miller and Purchas. Large and enthusiastic crowds – predominantly of the dispossessed. Note the significant fact that pacifism is in inverse ratio, generally, to prosperity. The greater the poverty, the longer the unemployment, the more whole-hearted the determination not to fight again, and the more complete the scepticism about the conventional idols, Empire, National Honour, and the like. A negative attitude closely correlated with bad economic conditions. Therefore not to be relied on. Such pacifism is without autonomous life. At the mercy, first of all, of anyone who comes along with money – and threats of war would lead to a vast increase of employment. At the mercy, in the second place, of anyone who comes along with an alluring positive doctrine – however crazy and criminal its positiveness may be. The mind abhors a vacuum. Negative pacifism and scepticism about existing institutions are just holes in the mind, emptinesses waiting to be filled. Fascism or communism have sufficient positive content to act as fillers. Someone with the talents of Hitler may suddenly appear. The negative void will be pumped full in a twinkling. These disillusioned pacifist sceptics will be transformed overnight into drilled fanatics of nationalism, class war, or whatever it may be. Question : have we time to fill the vacuum with positive pacifism? Or, having the time, have we the ability?

CHAPTER FORTY-SEVEN

January 10th and 11th 1934

OSTENSIBLY, Don Jorge's telegram was an order for the immediate sale of six hundred bags of coffee. In fact, it announced that the moment had come, and that he was urgently expecting them.

Mark looked at his companion with an expression that was frankly hostile. 'Those blasted guts of yours!' he said.

Anthony protested that he was all right again.

'You're not fit to do the journey.'

'Yes, I am.'

'You're not,' Mark repeated with a solicitude that was at the same time a passionate resentment. 'Three days on a mule across these damned mountains. It's too much for anyone in your condition.'

Piqued by the other's words, and afraid, if he agreed with Mark, of seeming unwilling to face the difficulties and dangers that lay in front of them, Anthony insisted obstinately that he was fit for anything. Wishing to believe it, Mark soon allowed himself to be persuaded. An answer was dispatched to Don Jorge – the six hundred bags were being sold immediately; he might expect to hear further details on Friday – and after lunch, in the blazing heat of the early afternoon, they set out for the *finca*, lying high in the mountains above Tapatlan, where one of Don Jorge's friends would put them up for the night. Mark produced his pocket Shakespeare once again and, for four hours, they spurred their reluctant beasts, up and up, between dusty maize stubbles, and, above the fields, through a dry leafless scrub that gave place at last to the green darkness and golden lights of coffee plantations under their towering shade trees. Up and up, while Mark read the whole of *Hamlet* and two acts of *Troilus and Cressida*, and Anthony sat wondering, in a mist of fatigue, how much longer he could stand it. But at last, as night was falling, they reached their destination.

At four the next morning they were in the saddle again. Under the trees there was a double night of starless shadow; but the mules picked their way along the windings of the track with a reassuring certainty. From time to time they rode under invisible lemon trees, and in the darkness the scent of the flowers was like the brief and inenarrable revelation of something more than earthly – a moment's ecstasy, and then, as the mules advanced, hoof after hoof, up the stony path, the fading of the supernatural presence, the return to a common life symbolically represented by the smell of leather and sweat.

The sun rose, and a little later they emerged from the cultivated forest of the coffee plantations into an upland country of bare rocks and pine woods. Almost level, the track went winding in and out along the buttressed and indented flank of a mountain. To the left, the ground fell steeply away into valleys still dark with shadow. Far off, through air made hazy by the dry season's dust and the smoke of forest fires, a dim whiteness high up in the sky was the Pacific.

Mark went on reading *Troilus and Cressida*.

A descent so steep that they had to dismount and lead their animals brought them in another hour to the banks of a river. They forded it, and, in the blistering sunshine, began to climb the slope beyond. There was no shade, and the vast bald hills were the colour of dust and burnt grass. Nothing stirred, not even a lizard among the stones. There was no sight or sound of life. Hopelessly empty, the chaos of tumbled mountains seemed to stretch away interminably. It was as though they had ridden across the frontier of the world out into nothingness, into an infinite expanse of hot and dusty negation.

At eleven they halted for a meal, and an hour later, with the sun almost perpendicularly above them, were off once more. The path climbed, dropped fifteen hundred feet into a ravine and climbed again. By three o'clock Anthony was so tired that he could scarcely think or even see. The landscape seemed to advance and retreat before his eyes, turned black sometimes and faded away altogether. He heard voices, and, in his mind, his thoughts began to lead a life of their own – a life that was autonomous in its mad and maddening irrelevance. Image succeeded image in a phantasmagoria that it was beyond his power to exorcize. It was as though he were possessed, as though he were being forced to lead someone else's life and think with another person's mind. But the sweat that poured like water off his face and soaked through his shirt and cotton riding-breeches, the intolerable aching of loins and thighs – these were his own. His own and excruciating, intolerable. He was tempted to groan, even to burst into tears. But through the other person's delirium he remembered his assurances to Mark, his confident promise that he wouldn't be tired. He shook his head and rode on – rode on through the illusory world of alien fancy and half-seen, vanishing landscape, rode on through the hideous reality of his pain and fatigue.

Mark's voice startled him out of his stupor.

'Are you all right?'

Looking up, and, with an effort, focusing his eyes, he saw that Mark had halted and was waiting at the turn of the track just above him. Fifty yards further up the slope the *mozo* was riding behind the baggage-mule.

'*Mula-a-a!*' came the long-drawn shout, and along with it the dull thump of a stick on mule-skin.

'Sorry,' Anthony mumbled, 'I must have dropped behind.'

'You're sure you're all right?'

He nodded.

'There's less than an hour to go,' said Mark. 'Stick it out if you can.' In the shadow of the enormous straw hat, his worn face twisted itself into a smile of encouragement.

Touched, Anthony smiled back and, to reassure him, tried to make a joke about the hardness of the wooden saddles on which they were riding.

Mark laughed. 'If we get through intact,' he said, 'we'll dedicate a pair of silver buttocks to St James of Compostella.'

He jerked the reins and gave his mule the spur. The animal started up the slope; then, in a slither of rolling stones, stumbled and fell forward on its knees.

Anthony had shut his eyes to rest them a moment from the glare. At the noise he opened them again and saw Mark lying face downwards on the ground and the mule heaving itself, in a series of violent spasms of movement, to its feet. The landscape snapped back into solidity, the moving images fell still. Forgetting the pain in his back and legs, Anthony swung himself down from the saddle and ran up the path. As he approached, Mark rolled over and raised himself to a sitting position.

'Hurt?' Anthony asked.

The other shook his head, but did not speak.

'You're bleeding.'

The breeches were torn at the left knee, and a red stain was creeping down the leg. Anthony shouted to the *mozo* to come back with the baggage-mule; then, kneeling down, opened his penknife, slid the blade into the rent and sawed a long jagged slit in the tough material.

'You're spoiling my bags,' Mark said, speaking for the first time.

Anthony did not answer, only tore away a wide panel of the stuff.

The whole knee-cap and the upper part of the skin were skinless red flesh, grey, where the blood was not oozing, with dust and grit. On the inner side of the knee was a deep cut that bled profusely.

Anthony frowned, and, as though the pain were his own, caught his lower lip between his teeth. A pang of physical disgust mingled with his horrified sympathy. He shuddered.

Mark had leaned forward to look at the damaged knee. 'Messy,' was his comment.

Anthony nodded without speaking, unscrewed the stopper of his water-bottle, and, wetting his handkerchief, began to wash the dirt out of the wounds. His emotion disappeared; he was wholly absorbed in his immediate task. Nothing was important any more except to wash this grit away without hurting Mark in the process.

By this time, the *mozo* had come back with the baggage-mule and was standing beside them in silence, looking down with expressionless black eyes on what was happening.

'I expect he thinks we're making an unnecessary fuss,' said Mark, and made an attempt to smile.

Anthony rose to his feet, ordered the *mozo* to untie the mule's load, and, from one of the canvas bundles, pulled out the medicine-chest.

Under the sting of the disinfectant Mark gave vent to an explosive burst of laughter. 'No humanitarian nonsense about iodine,' he said. 'The good old-fashioned idea of hurting you for your own good. Like Jehovah. Christ!' He laughed again as Anthony swabbed another patch of raw flesh. Then, when the knee was bandaged, 'Give me a hand,' he went on. Anthony helped him to his feet, and he took a few steps up the path and back again. 'Seems all right.' He bent down to look at the forelegs of his mule. They were hardly scratched. 'Nothing to prevent us pushing on at once,' he concluded.

They helped him to mount, and, spurring with his uninjured leg, he set off at a brisk pace up the hill. For the rest of the way he was, for Anthony, mostly a straight and rigid back, but sometimes also, at the zigzags of the path, a profile, marbly in its fixed pallor – the statue of a stoic, flayed, but still alive and silently supporting his agony.

In less than the appointed hour – for Mark had chosen to keep up a pace that set the mules blowing and sweating in the afternoon heat – they rode into San Cristobal el Alto. The thirty or forty Indian *ranchos* of which the village consisted were built on a narrow ridge between plunging gulfs, beyond which, on either side, the mountains stretched away chaotically, range after range, into the haze.

Seeing distinguished travellers, the village shopkeeper hurried out on to the *plaza* to offer them accommodation for the night. Mark listened to him, nodded and made a movement to dismount; then, wincing, let himself fall back into the saddle.

Without turning his head, 'You'll have to get me off this blasted mule,' he called in a loud, angry voice.

Anthony and the *mozo* helped him down; but, once on the ground, he refused any further assistance.

'I can walk by myself,' he said curtly, frowning while he spoke, as though, in offering an arm, Anthony had meant to insult him.

Their quarters for the night turned out to be a wooden shed, half-full of coffee bags and hides. After inspecting the place, Mark limped out again to look at the thatched lean-to, where the mules were to be stabled; then suggested a walk round the village, 'to see the sights,' he explained.

Walking, it was evident, hurt him so much that he could not trust himself to speak. It was in silence that they crossed the little *plaza*, in silence that they visited the church, the school, the *cabildo*, the village prison. In silence, and one behind the other. For if they walked abreast, Anthony had reflected, he would be able to see Mark's face, and Mark would feel that he was being spied upon. Whereas if he walked in front it would be an insult, a challenge to Mark to quicken his pace. Deliberately, Anthony lagged behind, silent, like an Indian wife trailing through the dust after her husband.

It was nearly half an hour before Mark felt that he had tortured himself sufficiently.

'So much for the sights,' he said grimly. 'Let's go and have something to eat.'

The night was piercingly cold, the bed merely a board of wood. It was from a restless and unrefreshing sleep that Anthony was roused next morning.

'Wake!' Mark was shouting to him. 'Wake!'

Anthony sat up, startled, and saw Mark, in the other wooden bed, propped on his elbow and looking across at him with angry eyes.

'Time to get away,' the harsh voice continued. 'It's after six.'

Suddenly remembering yesterday's accident, 'How's the knee?' Anthony asked.

'Just the same.'

'Did you sleep?'

'No, of course not,' Mark answered irritably. Then looking away. 'I can't manage to get out of bed,' he added. 'The thing's gone stiff on me.'

Anthony pulled on his boots and, having opened the door of the shed to admit the light, came and sat down on the edge of Mark's bed.

'We'd better put on a clean dressing,' he said, and began to untie the bandage.

The lint had stuck to the raw flesh. Anthony pulled it cautiously, then let it go. 'I'll see if they can give me some warm water at the shop,' he said.

Mark uttered a snort of laughter, and taking a corner of the lint between his thumb and forefinger, gave a violent jerk. The square of pink fabric came away in his hand.

'Don't!' Anthony had cried out, wincing as though the pain were his. The other only smiled at him contemptuously. 'You've made it bleed again,' he added, in another tone, finding a medical justification for his outburst. But in point of fact, that trickle of fresh blood was not the thing that disturbed him most when he bent down to look at what Mark had uncovered. The whole knee was horribly swollen and almost black with bruises, and round the edges of the newly opened wound the flesh was yellow with pus.

'You can't possibly go with your knee in this state,' he said.

'That's for me to decide,' Mark answered, and added, after a moment. 'After all, *you* did it the day before yesterday.'

The words implied a contemptuous disparagement. 'If a poor creature like you can overcome pain, then surely I ...' That was what they meant to say. But the insult, Anthony realized, was unintended. It sprang from the depths of an arrogance that was almost childlike in its single-minded intensity. There was something touching and absurd about such ingenuousness. Besides, there was the poor fellow's knee. This was not the time to resent insults.

'I was practically well,' he argued in a conciliatory tone. 'You've got a leg that's ready to go septic at any moment.'

Mark frowned. 'Once I'm on my mule I shall be all right,' he insisted. 'It's just a bit stiff and bruised; that's all. Besides,' he added, in contradiction of what he had said before, 'there'll be a doctor at Miajutla. The quicker I get this thing into his hands, the better.'

'You'll make it ten times worse on the way. If you waited here a day or two ...'

'Don Jorge would think I was leaving him in the lurch.'

'Damn Don Jorge! Send him a telegram.'

'The line doesn't go through this place. I asked.'

'Send the *mozo*, then.'

Mark shook his head. 'I wouldn't trust him.'

'Why not?'

'He'll get drunk at the first opportunity.'

'In other words, you don't want to send him.'

'Besides, it would be too late,' Mark went on. 'Don Jorge will be moving in a day or two.'

'And do you imagine you'll be able to move with him?'

'I mean to be there,' said Mark.

'You can't.'

'I tell you, I mean to be there. I'm not going to let him down.' His voice was cold and harsh with restrained anger. 'And now help me up,' he commanded.

'I won't.'

The two men looked at one another in silence. Then, making an effort to control himself, Mark shrugged his shoulders.

'All right, then,' he said, 'I'll call the *mozo*. And if you're afraid of going on to Miajutla,' he continued in a tone of savage contempt, 'you can ride back to Tapatlan. I'll go on by myself.'

345

Then, turning towards the open door, 'Juan,' he shouted. 'Juan!'

Anthony surrendered. 'Have it your own way. If you really want to be mad ...' He left the sentence unfinished. 'But I take no responsibility.'

'You weren't asked to,' Mark answered. Anthony got up and went to fetch the medicine-chest. He swabbed the wounds and applied the new dressing in silence; then, while he was trying to bandage, 'Suppose we stopped quarrelling,' he said. 'Wouldn't that make things easier?'

For a few seconds Mark remained hostile and averted; then looked up and twisted his face into a reconciliatory smile of friendliness. 'Peace,' he said, nodding affirmatively. 'We'll make peace.'

But he had reckoned without the pain. It began, agonizingly, when he addressed himself to the task of getting out of bed. For it turned out to be impossible for him, even with Anthony's assistance, to get out of bed without bending his wounded knee; and to bend it was torture. When at last he was on his feet beside the bed, he was pale and the expression of his face hardened to a kind of ferocity.

'All right?' Anthony questioned.

Mark nodded and, as though the other had become his worst enemy, limped out of the shed without giving him a glance.

The torture began again when the time came for mounting, and was renewed with every step the mule advanced. As on the previous day, Mark took the lead. At the head of the cavalcade, he proved his superiority and at the same time put himself out of range of inquisitive eyes. The air was still cold; but from time to time, Anthony noticed, he took out his handkerchief and wiped his face, as if he were sweating. Each time he put the handkerchief away again, he would give the mule a particularly savage dig with his one available spur.

The track descended, climbed again, descended through pine woods, descended, descended. An hour passed, two hours, three; the sun was high in the sky, it was oppressively hot. Three hours, three and a half; and now there were clearings in the woods, steep fields, the stubble of Indian corn, a group of huts, and an old woman carrying water, brown children silently playing in the dust. They were on the outskirts of another village.

'What about stopping here for some food?' Anthony called, and spurred his animal to a trot. 'We might get some fresh eggs,' he continued as he drew up with the other mule.

The face Mark turned towards him was as white as paper, and, as he parted his clenched teeth to speak, the lower jaw trembled uncontrollably. 'I think we'd better push on,' he began in an almost inaudible voice. 'We've still got a long way ...' Then the lids fluttered over his eyes, his head dropped, his body seemed to collapse upon itself; he fell forward on to the neck of his mule, slid to one side, and would have pitched to the ground if Anthony had not caught him by the arm and held him up.

CHAPTER FORTY-EIGHT

July 23rd 1914

ANTHONY had dozed off again after being called, and was late for breakfast. As he entered the little living-room, Brian looked up with startled eyes and, as though guiltily, folded away the letter he had been reading into his pocket, but not before Anthony had recognized from across the room the unmistakable characteristics of Joan's rather heavy and elaborately looped writing. Putting a specially casual note of cheeriness into his good morning, he sat down and proceeded to busy himself elaborately, as though it were a complicated scientific process requiring the whole of his attention, with the pouring out of his coffee.

'Should I tell him?' he was wondering. 'Yes, I ought to tell him. It ought to come from me, even though he does know it already. Bloody girl! Why couldn't she keep her promise?' He felt righteously indignant with Joan. Breaking her word! And what the devil has she told Brian? What would happen if his own story was different from hers? And anyhow, what a fool he would look, confessing now, when it was too late. She had robbed him of the opportunity, the very possibility of telling Brian what had happened. The woman had queered his pitch; and as his anger modulated into self-pity, he perceived

347

himself as a man full of good intentions, maliciously prevented, at the eleventh hour, from putting them into practice. She had stopped his mouth just as he was about to speak the words that would have explained and made amends for everything; and by doing so, she had made his situation absolutely intolerable. How the devil did she expect him to behave towards Brian, now that Brian knew? He answered the question, so far, at any rate, as the next few moments were concerned, by retiring behind the *Manchester Guardian*. Hidden, he pretended, while he ate his scrambled eggs, to be taking a passionate interest in all this stuff about Russia and Austria and Germany. But the silence, as it lengthened out, became at lost intolerable.

'This war business looks rather bad,' he said at last, without lowering his barricade.

From the other end of the table Brian made a faint murmur of assent. Seconds passed. Then there was a noise of a chair being pushed back. Anthony sat there, a man so deeply pre-occupied with the Russian mobilization that he wasn't aware of what was going on in his immediate neighbourhood. It was only when Brian had actually opened the door that he started ostentatiously into consciousness.

'Off already?' he questioned, half turning, but not so far that he could see the other's face.

'I d-don't think I shall g-go out this m-morning.'

Anthony nodded approvingly, like a family doctor. 'That's good,' he said, and added that he himself proposed to hire a bicycle in the village and nip down to Ambleside. There were some things he had to buy. 'See you at lunch-time,' he concluded.

Brian said nothing. The door closed behind him.

By a quarter to one Anthony had returned his borrowed bicycle and was walking up the hill to the cottage. This time it was settled, definitely, once and for all. He would tell Brian everything – almost everything, the very moment he came in.

'Brian!' he called from the doorstep.

There was no answer.

'Brian!'

The kitchen door opened, and old Mrs Benson, who did their

cooking and cleaning, stepped out into the narrow hall. Mr Foxe, she explained, had started for a walk about half an hour before; wouldn't be back for lunch, he had said, but had wanted (would you believe it?) to set off without anything to eat; she had made him take some sandwiches and a hard-boiled egg.

It was with a sense of inner discomfort that Anthony sat down to his solitary lunch. Brian had deliberately avoided him; therefore must be angry – or worse, it occurred to him, was hurt – too deeply to be able to bear his presence. The thought made him wince; to hurt people was so horrible, so hurting even to the hurter. And if Brian came back from his walk magnanimously forgiving – and, knowing him, Anthony felt convinced that he would – what then? It was also painful to be forgiven; particularly painful in the case of an offence one had not oneself confessed. 'If only I could have told him,' he kept repeating to himself, 'if only I could have told him'; and almost contrived to persuade himself that he had been prevented.

After lunch he walked up into the wild country behind the cottage, hoping (for it was now so urgently necessary to speak), and at the same time (since the speaking would be such an agonizing process) profoundly fearing, to meet Brian. But he met nobody. Resting on the crest of the hill, he managed for a little while to forget his troubles in sarcasms at the expense of the view. So typically and discreditably English, he reflected, wishing that Mary were there to listen to his comments. Mountains, valleys, lakes, but on the pettiest scale. Miserably small and hole-and-cornery, like English cottage architecture – all ingle-nooks and charming features; nothing fine or grandiose. No hint of thirteenth-century megalomania or baroque gesticulation. A snug, smug little sublimity. It was almost in high spirits that he started his descent.

No, said old Mrs Benson, Mr Foxe hadn't yet come back.

He had his tea alone, then sat on a deck chair on the lawn and read de Gourmont on style. At six, Mrs Benson came out, and after elaborately explaining that she had the table and that the cold mutton was in the larder, wished him good evening and walked away down the road towards her own cottage.

Soon afterwards the midges began to bite and he went indoors.

The little bird in the Swiss clock opened its door, cuckooed seven times and retired again into silence. Anthony continued to read about style. Half an hour later the bird popped out for a single cry. It was supper-time. Anthony rose and walked to the back door. Behind the cottage the hill was bright with an almost supernatural radiance. There was no sign of Brian. He returned to the sitting-room, and for a change read some Santayana. The cuckoo uttered eight shrill hiccups. Above the orange stain of sunset the evening planet was already visible. He lit the lamp and drew the curtains. Then, sitting down again, he tried to go on reading Santayana; but those carefully smoothed pebbles of wisdom rolled over the surface of his mind without making the smallest impression. He shut the book at last. The cuckoo announced that it was half past eight.

An accident, he was wondering, could the fellow have had an accident? But, after all, people don't have accidents – not when they're out for a quiet walk. A new thought suddenly came to him, and at once the very possibility of twisted ankles or broken legs disappeared. That walk – he felt completely certain of it now – had been to the station. Brian was in the train, on his way to London, on his way to Joan. It was obvious when one came to think of it; it simply couldn't be otherwise.

'Christ!' Anthony said aloud in the solitude of the little room. Then, made cynical and indifferent by the very hopelessness of the situation, he shrugged his shoulders and, lighting a candle, went out to the larder to fetch the cold mutton.

This time, he decided, as he ate his meal, he really would escape. Just bolt into hiding till things looked better. He felt no compunction. Brian's journey to London had relieved him, in his own estimation, of any further responsibility in the matter; he felt that he was now free to do whatever suited him best.

In preparation for his flight, he went upstairs after supper and began to pack his bag. The recollection that he had lent Brian *The Wife of Sir Isaac Harman* to read in bed sent him, candle in hand, across the landing. On the chest of drawers in Brian's room three envelopes stood conspicuously propped against the wall. Two, he could see from the doorway, were stamped, the other was unstamped. He crossed the room to look at them more closely. The unstamped envelope was addressed to himself, the others to Mrs Foxe and Joan respectively. He set down the candle, took the envelope addressed to himself, and tore it open. A vague but intense apprehension had filled his mind, a fear of something unknown, something he dared not know. He stood there for a long time holding the open envelope in his hand and listening to the heavy pulse of his own blood. Then, coming at last to a decision, he extricated the folded sheets. There were two of them, one in Brian's writing, the other in Joan's. Across the top of Joan's letter Brian had written: 'Read this for yourself.' He read.

DEAREST BRIAN, – By this time Anthony will have told you what has happened. And, you know, it *did* just happen – from outside, if you see what I mean, like an accident, like being run into by a train. I certainly hadn't thought about it before, and I don't think Anthony had – not really; the discovery that we loved one another just ran into us, ran over us. There wasn't any question of us doing it on purpose. That's why I don't feel guilty. Sorry, yes – more than words can say – for the pain I know I shall give you. Ready to do all I can to make it less. Asking forgiveness for hurting you. But not feeling *guilty*, not feeling I've treated you dishonourably. I should only feel that if I had done it deliberately; but I didn't. I tell you, it just happened to me – to us both. Brian dear, I'm unspeakably sorry to be hurting you. You of all people. If it were a matter of doing it with intention, I couldn't do it. No more than you could hurt me intentionally. But this thing has just happened, in the same way as it just happened that you hurt me because of that fear that you've always had of love. You didn't want to hurt me, but you did; you couldn't help it. The impulse that made you hurt me ran into you, ran over you, like this impulse of love that has run into me and Anthony. I don't think it's anybody's fault, Brian. We had bad luck. Everything ought to have been so good and beautiful. And then things happened to us – to you first, so that you had to hurt me; then to me. Later on, perhaps, we can still be friends. I hope so. That's why I'm not saying good-bye to you, Brian dear. Whatever happens, I am always your loving friend,   JOAN.

In the effort to keep up his self-esteem and allay his profound disquietude, Anthony forced himself to think with distaste of the really sickening style in which this kind of letter was generally written. A branch of pulpit oratory, he concluded, and tried to smile to himself. But it was no good. His face refused to do what he asked of it. He dropped Joan's letter and reluctantly picked up the other sheet in Brian's handwriting.

Dear A., – I enclose the letter I received this morning from Joan. Read it; it will save me explaining. How could he have done it? That's the question I've been asking myself all the morning; and now I put it to you. How could you? Circumstances may have run over her – like a train, as she says. And that, I know, was my fault. But they couldn't have run over you. You've told me enough about yourself and Mary Amberley to make it quite clear that there could be no question in your case of poor Joan's train. Why did you do it? And why did you come here and behave as though nothing had happened? How could you sit there and let me talk about my difficulties with Joan and pretend to be sympathetic, when a couple of evenings before you had been giving her the kisses I wasn't able to give? God knows, I've done all manner of bad and stupid things in the course of my life, told all manner of lies; but I honestly don't think I could have done what you have done. I didn't think anybody could have done it. I suppose I've been living in a sort of fool's paradise all these years, thinking the world was a place where this sort of thing simply couldn't happen. A year ago I might have known how to deal with the discovery that it can happen. Not now. I know that, if I tried, I should just break down into some kind of madness. This last year has strained me more than I knew. I realize now that I'm all broken to pieces inside, and that I've been holding myself together by a continuous effort of will. It's as if a broken statue somehow contrived to hold itself together. And now this has finished it. I can't hold any more. I know if I were to see you now – and it's not because I feel that you've done something you shouldn't have done; it would be the same with anyone, even my mother – yes, if I were to see anyone who had ever meant anything to me, I should just break down and fall to bits. A statue at one moment, and the next a heap of dust and shapeless fragments. I can't face it. Perhaps I ought to; but I simply can't. I was angry with you when I began to write this letter, I hated you; but now I find I don't hate you any longer. God bless you,   B.

Anthony put the two letters and the torn envelope in his pocket, and, picking up the two stamped envelopes and the candle, made his way downstairs to the sitting-room. Half an hour later, he went to the kitchen, and in the range, which was still smouldering, set fire one by one to all the papers that

Brian had left behind him. The two unopened envelopes with their closely folded contents burnt slowly, had to be constantly relighted; but at last it was done. With the poker he broke the charred paper into dust, stirred up the fire to a last flame and drew the round cover back into place. Then he walked out into the garden and down the steps to the road. On the way to the village it suddenly struck him that he would never be able to see Mary again. She would question him, she would worm the truth out of him, and having wormed it out, would proclaim it to the world. Besides, would he even want to see her again now that Brian had ... He could not bring himself to say the words even to himself. 'Christ!' he said aloud. At the entrance to the village he halted for a few moments to think what he should say when he knocked up the policeman. 'My friend's lost ... My friend has been out all day and ... I'm worried about my friend ...' Anything would do; he hurried on, only anxious to get it over.

CHAPTER FORTY-NINE

January 12th and 14th 1934

It was dark in the little *rancho*, and from noon till sunset stiflingly hot; then cold all through the night. A partition divided the hut into two compartments; in the middle of the first compartment was a hearth of rough stones, and when the fire was lighted for cooking, the smoke filtered slowly away through the chinks in the windowless wooden walls. The furniture consisted of a stool, two kerosene tins for water, some earthenware cooking-pots, and a stone mortar for grinding maize. On the further side of the partition were a couple of plank beds on trestles. It was on one of these that they laid Mark.

By the following morning he was delirious with fever, and, from the knee, the infection had crept downwards, until the leg was swollen almost to the ankle.

For Anthony, as he sat there in the hot twilight, listening to the mutterings and sudden outcries of this stranger on the bed, there was, for the moment, only one thing to decide. Should he send the *mozo* to fetch a doctor and the necessary drugs from Miajutla? Or should he go himself?

It was the choice of evils. He thought of poor Mark, abandoned, alone in the hands of these inept and not too well-intentioned savages. But even if he himself where there, what could he do with the resources at his disposal? And suppose the *mozo* were sent and failed to persuade the doctor to come at once, failed to bring the necessary supplies, failed perhaps to return at all. Miajutla, as Mark had said, was in the *pulque* country; there would be oceans of cheap alcohol. Riding hard, he himself could be back again at Mark's bedside in less than thirty hours. A white man with money in his pocket, he would be able to bully and bribe the doctor to bestir himself. Hardly less important, he would know what stores to bring back with him. His mind was made up. He rose, and, going to the door, called to the *mozo* to saddle his mule.

He had ridden for less than two hours when the miracle happened. Coming round a bend in the track he saw advancing towards him, not fifty yards away, a white man, followed by two Indians, one mounted and one on foot, with a couple of laden baggage-mules. As they drew together, the white man courteously raised his hat. The hair beneath it was light brown, grizzled above the ears, and in the deeply bronzed face the blue eyes were startlingly pale.

'*Buenas días, caballero,*' he said.

There was no mistaking the accent. 'Good morning,' Anthony replied.

They reined up their beasts alongside one another and began to talk.

'This is the first word of English I've heard for seven and a half months,' said the stranger. He was an elderly little man, short and spare, but with a fine upright carriage that lent him a certain dignity. The face was curiously proportioned, with a short nose and an upper lip unusually long above a wide, tightly shut mouth. A mouth like an inquisitor's. But the inquisitor had forgotten himself and learned to smile; there were the potentialities of laughter in the deep folds of skin which separated the quiveringly sensitive corners of the mouth from the cheeks. And round the bright inquiring eyes those intricate lines seemed the traces and hieroglyphic symbols of a constantly repeated movement of humorous kindliness. A queer face, Anthony decided, but charming.

'My name is James Miller,' said the stranger. 'What's yours?' And when he had been told, 'Are you travelling alone, Anthony Beavis?' he questioned, addressing the other, Quaker fashion, by both his names.

Anthony told him where he was bound and on what errand. 'I suppose you don't know anything about doctors in Miajutla,' he concluded.

With a sudden deepening of the hieroglyphs about the eyes, a sudden realization of those potentialities of laughter round the mouth, the little man smiled. 'I know about doctors *here*,' he said, and tapped himself on the chest. 'M.D., Edinburgh. And a good supply of *materia medica* on those mules, what's more.' Then, in another tone, 'Come on,' he said briskly. 'Let's get back to that poor friend of yours as quick as we can.'

Anthony wheeled his animal round, and side by side the two men set off up the track.

'Well, Anthony Beavis,' said the doctor, 'you came to the right address.'

Anthony nodded. 'Fortunately,' he said, 'I hadn't been praying, otherwise I'd have had to believe in special providence and miraculous interventions.'

'And that would never do,' the doctor agreed. 'Not that anything ever happens by chance, of course. One takes the card the conjuror forces on one – the card which one has oneself made it inevitable that he should force on one. It's a matter of cause and effect.' Then, without a pause, 'What's your profession?' he asked.

'I suppose you'd say I was a sociologist. Was one, at any rate.'

'Indeed! Is that so?' The doctor seemed surprised and pleased. 'Mine's anthropology,' he went on. 'Been living with the Lacandones in Chiapas these last months. Nice people when you get to know them. And I've collected a lot of material. Are you married, by the way?'

'No.'

'Never been married?'

'No.'

Dr Miller shook his head. 'That's bad, Anthony Beavis,' he said. 'You ought to have been.'

'What makes you say that?'

'I can see it in your face. Here, and here.' He touched his lips, his forehead. 'I was married. For fourteen years. Then my wife died. Blackwater fever it was. We were working in West Africa then. She was qualified too. Knew her job better, in some ways, than I did.' He sighed. 'You'd have made a good husband, you know. Perhaps you will do, even now. How old are you?'

'Forty-three.'

'And look younger. Though I don't like that sallow skin of yours,' he protested with sudden vehemence. 'Do you suffer much from constipation?'

'Well, no,' Anthony answered, smiling, and wondered whether it would be agreeable if everybody were to talk to one in this sort of way. A bit tiring, perhaps, to have to treat all the people you met as human beings, every one of them with a right to know all about you; but more interesting than treating them as objects, as mere lumps of meat dumped down beside you in the bus, jostling you on the pavements. 'Not much,' he qualified.

'You mean, not manifestly,' said the doctor. 'Any eczema?'

'Occasional touches.'

'And the hair tends to be scurfy.' Dr Miller nodded his own confirmation to this statement. 'And you get headaches, don't you?'

Anthony had to admit that he sometimes did.

'And, of course, stiff necks and attacks of lumbago. I know. I know. A few years more and it'll be settled in as sciatica or arthritis.' The doctor was silent for a moment while he looked inquiringly into Anthony's face. 'Yes, that sallow skin,' he repeated, and shook his head. 'And the irony, the scepticism, the what's-the-good-of-it-all attitude! Negative really. Everything you think of is negative.'

Anthony laughed; but laughed to hide a certain disquiet. This being on human terms with everyone you met could be a bit embarrassing.

'Oh, don't imagine I'm criticizing!' cried the doctor, and there was a note of genuine compunction in his voice.

Anthony went on laughing, unconvincingly.

'Don't get it into your head that I'm blaming you in any way.' Stretching out a hand, he patted Anthony affectionately on the shoulder. 'We're all of us what we are; and when it comes to turning ourselves into what we ought to be – well, it isn't easy. No, it isn't easy, Anthony Beavis. How can you expect to think in anything but a negative way, when you've got chronic intestinal poisoning? Had it from birth, I guess. Inherited it. And at the same time stooping, as you do. Slumped down on your mule like that – it's awful. Pressing down on the vertebrae like a ton of bricks. One can almost hear the poor things grinding together. And when the spine's in that state, what happens to the rest of the machine? It's frightful to think of.'

'And yet,' said Anthony, feeling a little piqued by this remorseless enumeration of his physical defects, 'I'm still alive. I'm here to tell the tale.'

'*Somebody's* here to tell the tale,' the doctor answered. 'But is he the one you'd like him to be?'

Anthony did not answer, only smiled uncomfortably.

'And even that somebody won't be telling the tale much longer, if you're not careful. I'm serious,' he insisted. 'Perfectly serious. You've got to change if you want to go on existing. And if it's a matter of changing – why, you need all the help you can get, from God's to the doctor's. I tell you this because I like you,' he explained. 'I think you're worth changing.'

'Thank you,' said Anthony, smiling this time with pleasure.

'Speaking as a doctor, I'd suggest a course of colonic irrigation to start with.'

'And speaking for God,' said Anthony, allowing his pleasure to overflow in good-humoured mockery, 'a course of prayer and fasting.'

'No, not fasting,' the doctor protested very seriously, 'not fasting. Only a proper diet. No butcher's meat; it's poison, so far as you're concerned. And no milk; it'll only blow you up with wind. Take it in the form of cheese and butter; never liquid. And a minimum of eggs. And, of course, only one heavy meal a day. You don't need half the stuff you're eating. As for prayer ...' He sighed and wrinkled his forehead into a pensive frown. 'I've never really liked it, you know. Not what's ordinarily meant by prayer, at any rate. All that asking for special favours and guidances and forgivenesses – I've always found that it tends to make one egotistical, preoccupied with one's own ridiculous self-important little personality. When you pray in the ordinary way, you're merely rubbing yourself into yourself. You return to your own vomit, if you see what I mean. Whereas what we're all looking for is some way of getting beyond our own vomit.'

Some way, Anthony was thinking, of getting beyond the books, beyond the perfumed and resilient flesh of women, beyond fear and sloth, beyond the painful but secretly flattering vision of the world as menagerie and asylum.

'Beyond this piddling, twopenny-halfpenny personality,' said the doctor, 'with all its wretched little virtues and vices, all its silly cravings and silly pretensions. But if you're not careful, prayer just confirms you in the bad habit of being personal. I tell you, I've observed it clinically, and it seems to have the same effect on people as butcher's meat. Prayer makes you more yourself, more separate. Just as a rump-steak does. Look at the correlation between religion and diet. Christians eat meat, drink alcohol, smoke tobacco; and Christianity exalts personality, insists on the value of petitionary prayer, teaches that God feels anger and approves the persecution of heretics. It's the same with the Jews and the Moslems. Kosher and an indignant Jehovah. Mutton and beef – and personal survival among the houris, avenging Allah and holy wars. Now look at the Buddhists. Vegetables and water. And what's their philosophy? They don't exalt personality; they try to transcend it. They don't imagine that God can be angry; when they're unenlightened, they think he's compassionate, and when they're enlightened, they think he doesn't exist, except as an impersonal mind of the universe. Hence they don't offer petitionary prayer; they meditate – or, in other words, try to merge their own minds in the universal mind. Finally, they don't believe in special providences for individuals; they believe in a moral order, where every event has its cause and produces its effect – where the card's forced upon you by the conjuror, but only because your previous actions have forced the conjuror to force it upon you. What worlds away from Jehovah and God the Father and everlasting, individual souls! The fact is, of course, that we think as we eat. I eat like a Buddhist, because I find it keeps me well and happy; and the result is that I think like a Buddhist – and, thinking like a Buddhist, I'm confirmed in my determination to eat like one.'

'And now you're recommending *me* to eat like one.'

'More or less.'

'And do you also want me to think like one?'

'In the long run you won't be able to avoid it. But, of course, it's better to do it consciously.'

'Well, as a matter of fact,' said Anthony, 'I do think like a Buddhist already. Not in all ways perhaps, but certainly in many ways. In spite of roast beef.'

'You *think* you think like a Buddhist,' said the doctor. 'But you don't. Thinking negatively isn't thinking like a Buddhist; it's thinking like a Christian who's eating more butcher's meat than his intestine can deal with.'

Anthony laughed.

'Oh, I know it sounds funny,' said the doctor. 'But that's only because you're a dualist.'

'I'm not.'

'Not in theory perhaps. But in practice – how can you be anything but a dualist? What are you, Anthony Beavis? A clever man – that's obvious. But it's equally obvious that you've got an unconscious body. An efficient thinking apparatus and a hopelessly stupid set of muscles and bones and viscera. Of course you're a dualist. You *live* your dualism. And one of the reasons you live it is because you poison yourself with too much animal protein. Like millions of other people, of course! What's the greatest enemy of Christianity today? Frozen meat. In the past only members of the upper classes were thoroughly sceptical, despairing, negative. Why? Among other reasons, because they were the only people who could afford to eat too much meat. Now there's cheap Canterbury lamb and Argentine chilled beef. Even the poor can afford to poison themselves into complete scepticism and despair. And only the most violent stimuli will rouse them to purposive activity, and, what's worse, the only activity they'll undertake is diabolic. They can only be stimulated by hysterical appeals to persecute Jews, or murder socialists or go to war. You personally happen to be too intelligent to be a fascist or a nationalist; but again, it's a matter of theory, not of life. Believe me, Anthony Beavis, your intestines are ripe for fascism and nationalism. They're making you long to be shaken out of the horrible negativity to which they've condemned you – to be shaken by violence into violence.'

'As a matter a fact,' said Anthony, 'that's one of the reasons why I'm here.' He waved his hand towards the tumbled chaos of the mountains. 'Simply to be shaken out of negativity. We were on our way to a revolution when poor Staithes got hurt.' .

The doctor nodded. 'You see,' he said, 'you see! And do you suppose you'd be here if you had a healthy intestine?'

'Well, I don't really know,' Anthony answered, laughing.

'You know quite well that you wouldn't,' said the doctor almost severely. 'Not on that kind of lunatic's errand, at any rate. For, of course, you might be here as an anthropologist, say, or a teacher, a healer, whatever you like, so long as it meant understanding people and helping them.'

Anthony nodded his head slowly, but did not speak; and for a long way they rode along in silence.

*

There was light out of doors, and it was cleaner under the sky than in the little *rancho*. Dr Miller had chosen as his operating theatre a little clearing in the woods, outside the village.

'Beyond the range of the flies, let's hope,' he said, but without seeming too confident of it.

A hearth had been built by his two *mozos*, and on the fire stood a cauldron of boiling water. They had borrowed a table from the schoolmaster and some stools, with bowls for the disinfectant, and a cotton sheet to cover the bedstead.

Dr Miller had given him a dose of Nembutal, and when the time came Mark was carried out unconscious to the clearing among the pine trees. All the boys in the village escorted the stretcher and stood round in attentive silence while the patient was lifted on to the bed. Trousered, and in their wide hats, with their little blankets folded over their shoulders, they seemed, not children, but the absurd and derisive parodies of grown men.

Anthony, who had been holding the gangrened leg, straightened himself up, and, looking round, saw the ring of brown faces and the glitter of all those black, blank eyes. At the sight he found his growing apprehension abruptly transformed into uncontrollable anger.

'Go away!' he shouted in English, and advanced towards them, waving his arms. 'Away, you little beasts, away!'

The children retreated, but slowly, reluctantly, with the manifest intention of returning the moment he should turn his back.

Anthony made a quick dart and caught one small boy by the arm.

'Little beast!'

He shook the child violently, then, carried away by an irresistible impulse to inflict pain, gave him a cuff over the head that sent the big hat flying between the trees.

Uttering no cry, the child ran away after its companions. Anthony made a last menacing gesture in their direction, then turned and walked back towards the centre of the clearing. He had not taken more than a few steps when a stone, well aimed, caught him full between the shoulders. He swung round furiously, exploding into such obscenities as he had not uttered since he was at school.

Dr Miller, who was washing his hands at the table, looked up. 'What's the matter?' he asked.

'The little devils are throwing stones.'

'Serve you right,' said the doctor unsympathetically. 'Leave them alone, and come and do your duty.'

The unfamiliarly clerical and military word startled him into the uncomfortable realization that he had been behaving like a fool. Worse than a fool. With the realization of his discreditable folly came the impulse to justify it. It was in a tone of pained indignation that he spoke. 'You're not going to let them look on, are you?'

'How am I to prevent them looking on, if they want to?' asked the doctor, drying his hands as he spoke. 'And now, Anthony Beavis,' he went on sternly, 'pull yourself together.

This is going to be difficult enough anyhow, without your being hysterical.'

Silenced and, because he was ashamed of himself, angry with Miller, Anthony washed his hands and put on a clean shirt which had to do duty as overall.

'Now,' said the doctor, and stepped forward. 'We must begin by draining the leg of blood.'

'The' leg, not 'his' leg, Anthony was thinking, as he stood beside the doctor, looking down on the man sleeping on the bed. Something impersonal, belonging to nobody in particular. The leg. But Mark's face, Mark's sleeping face, now so incredibly calm, so smooth, in spite of the emaciation, as though this death-like stupor had drawn a new skin across the flayed and twisted muscles – this could never be merely 'the' face. It was 'his', his for all its unlikeness to that contemptuous, suffering mask through which at ordinary times Mark looked out at the world. All the more genuinely his, perhaps, just because of that unlikeness. He remembered suddenly what Mark had said to him, beside the Mediterranean, only four months before, when he had woken to see those eyes now shut, but then wide open and bright with derision, sardonically examining him through the mosquito net. Perhaps one really is what one seems to be in sleep. Innocence and peace – the mind's essence, and all the rest mere accident.

'Take his foot,' Dr Miller ordered, 'and lift the leg as nearly vertical as you can.'

Anthony did as he was told. Raised in this grotesque way, the horribly swollen and discoloured leg seemed more impersonal, more a mere thing than ever. The stink of mortified flesh was in his nostrils. From behind them, among the trees, a voice said something incomprehensible; there was a snicker of laughter.

'Now leave the foot to the *mozo* and stand by here.' Anthony obeyed, and smelt again the resin of the forest. 'Hold that bottle for me.'

There was an astonished murmur of '*Amarillo*!' as the doctor painted the thigh with flavine. Anthony looked again at his friend's face; it remained undisturbed in its serenity. Essentially still and pure. The leg with its black dead flesh; the saw there in the bowl of permanganate solution, the knives and forceps;

the fascinated children peering out of the forest – all were some-how irrelevant to the essential Mark.

'Now the chloroform,' said Dr Miller. 'And the cotton wool. I'll show you how to use it. Then you'll have to go on by yourself.'

He opened the bottle, and the smell of pine trees in the sun-shine was overlaid by a rasping and nauseating sweetness.

'There, do you see the trick?' asked the doctor. 'Like that. Go on with that. I'll tell you when to stop. I've got to put on the tourniquet.'

There were no birds in the trees, hardly, even, any insects. The wood was deathly still. This sunny clearing was a little island of speech and movement in an ocean of silence. And at the centre of that island lay another silence, intenser, more complete than the silence of the forest.

The tourniquet was in place. Dr Miller ordered the *mozo* to lower the grotesquely hoisted leg. He pulled up a stool to the bedside, sat down, then rose again and, as he washed his hands for the last time, explained to Anthony that he would have to operate sitting down. The bed was too low for him to be able to stand. Taking his seat once more, he dipped into the bowl of permanganate for a scalpel.

At the sight of those broad flaps of skin turned back, like the peel of a huge banana, but from a red and bleeding fruit, Anthony was seized with a horrible sensation of nausea. The saliva came pouring into his mouth and he had to keep swallow-ing and swallowing to get rid of it. Involuntarily, he gave vent to a retching cough.

'Steady now,' said the doctor without looking up. With an artery forceps, he secured the end of an oozing vessel.

'Think of it scientifically.' He made another sweeping cut through the red flesh. 'And if you must be sick,' he went on with sudden asperity, 'for God's sake go and do it quickly!' Then, in another tone – the tone of the professor who demon-strates an interesting point to his students, 'One has to cut back the nerves a long way,' he said. 'There's a tremendous retraction as the tissues heal up. Anyhow,' he added, 'he'll probably have to have a re-amputation at home. It won't be a beautiful stump, I'm afraid.'

Calm and at peace, innocent of all craving, all malice, all

ambition – it was the face of one who has made himself free, one for whom there are no more bars or chains, no more sepulchres under a stone, and on whom the bird-lime no longer sticks. The face of one who has made himself free ... But in fact, Anthony reflected, in fact he had had his freedom forced upon him by this evil-smelling vapour. Was it possible to be one's own liberator? There were snares; but also there was a way of walking out of them. Prisons; but they could be opened. And if the torture-chambers could never be abolished, perhaps the tortures could be made to seem irrelevant. As completely irrelevant as now to Mark this sound of sawing, as this revolting rasp and squeak of the steel teeth biting into the bone, of the steel blade rubbing back and forth in the deepening groove. Mark lay there serene, almost smiling.

CHAPTER FIFTY

Christmas Day 1934

God – a person or not a person? *Quién sabe?* Only revelation can decide such metaphysical questions. And revelation isn't playing the game – is equivalent to pulling three aces of trumps from up your sleeve.

Of more significance is the practical question. Which gives a man more power to realize goodness – belief in a personal or an impersonal God? Answer: it depends. Some minds work one way, some another. Mine, as it happens, finds no need, indeed, finds it impossible to think of the world in terms of personality. Patanjali says you may believe in a personal God, or not, according to taste. The psychological results will be the same in either case.

For those whose nature demands personality as a source of energy, but who find it impossible to believe that the universe is run by a person in any sense of the word that we can possibly understand – what's the right policy? In most cases, they reject any practice which might be called religious. But this is throwing away the baby with the bath water. The desired relationship with a personality can be historical, not ontological. A contact, not with somebody existing at present as manager of the universe, but with somebody known to have existed at some time in the past. The Imitation of Christ (or of any other historical character) is just as effective if the model be regarded as having existed there, then, as it is if the model be conceived as existing here, now. And meditation on goodness, communication with goodness, contemplation of goodness are demonstrably effective means of realizing goodness in life, even when that which is meditated on, communicated with and contemplated, is not a person, but a general mind, or even an ideal supposed to exist only in human minds. The fundamental problem is practical – to work out systems of psychological exercises for all types of men and women. Catholicism has many systems of mental prayer – Ignatian, Franciscan, Liguorian, Carmelite, and so on. Hinduism, Northern, Southern, and Zen Buddhism also have a variety of practices. There is a great work to be done here. Collecting and collating information from all these sources. Consulting books and, more important, people who have actually practised what is in the books, have had experience of teaching novices. In time, it might be possible to establish a complete and definite *Ars Contemplativa*. A series of techniques, adapted to every type of mind. Techniques for meditating on, communicating with and contemplating goodness. Ends in themselves and at the same time means for realizing some of that goodness in practice.

January 1st 1935

Machinery and good organization – modern inventions; and, like all blessings, have to be paid for. In many ways. One item is the general belief, encouraged by mechanical and social efficiency that progress is automatic and can be imposed from outside. We, as individuals, need do nothing about it. Liquidate undesirables, distribute enough money and goods – all will be well. It is a reversion to magic, a pandering to man's natural sloth. Note the striking way in which this tendency runs through the whole of modern life, cropping up at every point. There seems no obvious connexion between the Webbs and the

Soviets on the one hand, and Modern Catholicism on the other. But what profound subterranean resemblances? The recent Catholic revival essentially a revival of sacraments. From a Catholic point of view, this is a 'sacramental age'. Magic power of sacraments regarded as sufficient for salvation. Mental prayer conspicuously absent. Exact analogy to the Webbs – Soviet idea of progress from without, through machinery and efficient organization. For English Catholics, sacraments are the psychological equivalents of tractors in Russia.

CHAPTER FIFTY-ONE

February 7th 1934

Dr MILLER dismounted at the open door, left his beast with the *mozo*, and stepped into the hut.

Propped up on his bed, Mark watched him enter – a small, erect figure, walking briskly, his blue eyes bright with inquiring kindness, the corners of his mouth alive with the potentialities of laughter.

'And how are all the little patients this evening?' Mark twisted up his pale and still emaciated face into a ferociously sardonic smile.

From the stool on which he was sitting beside the bed, Anthony shot a glance at him, and remembered the serenity of that face three weeks before, in the early morning sunshine among the pine trees. Serene and at peace. But now that life had come back to him, now that he was safely convalescent, the peace had departed, leaving him the embittered enemy of the whole world. There had been hatred in his eyes even before he was strong enough to speak. Hatred for everyone who came near him – above all for old Miller.

'I can't bear his perpetual twinkle,' was what he had said to Anthony later on. 'Nobody has a right to go about looking like the advertisement for a constipation cure.'

But the real reason for Mark's dislike was different. He hated old Miller because of his dependence upon him, because of the unflaggingly watchful efficiency of the man's care. Poor Mark !

How acutely he suffered from having to accept a service and, still more, from being compelled by his own physical weakness to ask for it! How bitterly he resented even affection, if it were given by somebody to whom it was impossible for him to feel superior! His dislike for the doctor had been present from the first moment of his return to consciousness, had increased with every day that the old man delayed his departure in order to look after him.

'But why don't you get on with your journey?' he had asked; and when the doctor answered that he was in no hurry and intended to see him safely down to the coast and even, since he himself was leaving, home through the Canal to England, had protested vehemently that his leg was practically healed, that there would be no difficulty in getting back to Puerto San Felipe, that he himself would probably be taking the north-bound boat to Los Angeles.

But the doctor had remained, attending to Mark and in the intervals riding out to the neighbouring villages to treat the sick. To the convalescent this was an additional source of irritation – though why it should have annoyed him Anthony could not rightly understand. Perhaps he resented the fact that the benefactor of the Indians was not himself. Anyhow, there it was; he was never tired of baiting old Miller with those 'little patients' of his.

Then, a fortnight after the operation, had come the news of the ignominious failure of Don Jorge's attempt at insurrection. He had been surprised with an insufficient guard, taken alive, summarily tried and shot with his chief lieutenant. The report added that the two men had cracked jokes together as they walked between the soldiers towards the cemetery, where their graves were already dug.

'And he died,' had been Mark's comment, 'believing that I'd taken fright at the last moment and let him down.'

The thought was like another wound to him.

'If I hadn't had this blasted accident ...' he kept repeating. 'If I'd been there to advise him ... That crazy rashness of his! That was why he'd asked me to come. He mistrusted his own judgement. And here was I lying in this stinking pigsty, while the poor devil marches off to the cemetery. ...' Cracking jokes, as he sniffed the cold morning air. '*Huele al cimintero, Don Jaime*.' He too would have cracked his joke. Instead of which ... It was just bad luck, of course, just a typical piece of providential idiocy; but providence was not there for him to vent his grievance on. Only Anthony and the doctor were there. His behaviour towards them, after the news of Don Jorge's death, had become increasingly bitter and resentful. It was as though he regarded them as personally responsible for what had happened. Both of them, especially the doctor.

'How's the delicious bedside manner?' Mark now went on, in the same derisive tone in which he had asked after the little patients.

'Wasted, I'm afraid,' Dr Miller answered good-humouredly as he took off his hat and sat down. 'Either they haven't got any beds for me to be at the side of – only a blanket on the floor. Or else they don't speak any Spanish, and I don't speak their brand of Indian dialect. And how's yourself?' he asked.

'*Myself*,' said Mark, returning the doctor his expression in a tone of emphatically contemptuous disgust, as though it were some kind of verbal ordure, 'is very well, thanks.'

'But doing a slight Bishop Berkeley,' Anthony interposed. 'Feeling pains in the knee he hasn't got.'

Mark looked at him for a moment with an expression of stony dislike; then turning away and fixing his eyes on the bright evening landscape, visible through the open door of the hut, 'Not pains,' he said coldly, though it was as pains that he had described them to Anthony only half an hour before. 'Just the sensation that the knee's still there.'

'Can't avoid that, I'm afraid.' The doctor shook his head.

'I didn't suppose one could,' Mark said, as though he were replying with dignity to an aspersion on his honour.

Dr Miller broke the uncomfortable silence by remarking that there was a good deal of goitre in the higher valleys.

'It has its charm,' said Mark, stroking an imaginary bulge at his throat. 'How I regret those cretins one used to see in Switzerland when I was a child! They've iodined them out of existence now, I'm afraid. The world's too damned sanitary these days.' He shook his head and smiled anatomically. 'What do they do up there in the high valleys?' he asked.

'Grow maize,' said the doctor. 'And kill one another in the intervals. There's a huge network of vendettas spread across these mountains. Everybody's involved. I've been talking to the responsible men, trying to persuade them to liquidate all the old accounts and start afresh.'

'They'll die of boredom.'

'No, I'm teaching them football instead. Matches between the villages.' He smiled. 'I've had a lot of experience with vendettas,' he added. 'All over the world. They all detest them, really. Are only too thankful for football when they're used to it.'

'Christ!'

'Why "Christ"?'

'Those games! Can't we ever escape from them?'

'But they're the greatest English contribution to civilization,' said the doctor. 'Much more important than parliamentary government, or steam engines, or Newton's Principia. More important even than English poetry. Poetry can never be a substitute for war and murder. Whereas games can be. A complete and genuine substitute.'

'Substitutes!' Mark echoed contemptuously. 'You're all content with substitutes. Anthony finds his in bed or in the British Museum Reading Room. You look for yours on the football field. God help you! Why are you so frightened of the genuine article?'

For a little while no one spoke. Dr Miller looked at Anthony, and, seeing that he did not propose to answer, turned back to the other. 'It isn't a question of being frightened, Mark Staithes,' he said very mildly. 'It's a question of choosing something right instead of something wrong. . . .'

'I'm suspicious of right choices that happen to need less courage than the wrong ones.'

'Is danger your measure of goodness?'

Mark shrugged his shoulders. 'What is goodness? Hard to know, in most cases. But at least one can be sure that it's good to face danger courageously.'

'And for that you're justified in deliberately creating dangerous situations – at other people's expense?' Dr Miller shook his head. 'That won't do, Mark Staithes. If you want to use courage, why not use it in a good cause.'

'Such as teaching blackamoors to play football,' Mark sneered.

'Which isn't so easy, very often, as it sounds.'

'They can't grasp the offside rule, I suppose.'

'They don't want to grasp any rule at all, except the rule of killing the people from the next village. And when you're between two elevens armed to the teeth and breathing slaughter to one another . . .' He paused; his wide mouth twitched into a smile; the almost invisible hieroglyphs round his eyes deepened, as he narrowed the lids, into the manifest symbols of an inner amusement. 'Well, as I say, it isn't quite so easy as it sounds. Have you ever found yourself faced by a lot of angry men who wanted to kill you?'

Mark nodded, and an expression of rather malevolent satisfaction appeared on his face. 'Several times,' he answered. 'When I was running a coffee *finca* a bit further down the coast, in Chiapas.'

'And you faced them without arms?'

'Without arms,' Mark repeated, and, by the way of explanation, 'The politicians,' he added, 'were still talking about revolution in those days. The land for the people – and all the rest. One fine morning the villagers came to seize the estate.'

'Which, on your principles,' said Anthony, 'you ought to have approved of.'

'And did approve, of course. But I could hardly admit it – not in those circumstances.'

'Why not?'

'Well, surely that's pretty obvious, isn't it? There they were, marching against me. Was I to tell them I sympathized with their politics and then hand over the estate? No, really, that would have been a bit too simple!'

'What did you do, then?'

'There were about a hundred of them the first time,' Mark explained. 'Festooned with guns and cartridge-belts like Christmas trees, and all with their machetes. But polite, soft-spoken. They had no particular quarrel with me, and the revolutionary idea was strange; they didn't feel too certain of themselves. Not that they ever make much noise,' he added. 'I've seen them killing in silence. Like fish. It's an aquarium, this country.'

'Seems like an aquarium,' Dr Miller emended. 'But when one has learnt how the fishes think . . .'

'I've always found it more important to learn how they drink,' said Mark. '*Tequila*'s the real enemy. Luckily, mine were sober. Otherwise . . . Well, who knows what would have happened?' After a pause, 'They were standing on the cement drying floor,' he went on, 'and I was sitting at the door of the office, up a few steps, above them. Superior, as though I were holding a durbar of my loyal subjects.' He laughed; the colour had come to his cheeks, and he spoke with a kind of gusto, as though the words had a pleasant taste in his mouth. 'A hundred villain-ous, coffee-coloured peons, staring up at one with those beady tortoises' eyes of theirs – it wasn't reassuring. But I managed to keep my face and voice from giving anything away. It helped a lot, I found, to think of the creatures as some kind of rather squalid insects. Cockroaches, dung beetles. Just a hundred big, staring bugs. It helped, I say. But still my heart did beat a bit. On its own – you know the sensation, don't you? It's as though you had a live bird under your ribs. A bird with its own bird-like consciousness. Suffering from its own private fears. An odd sensation, but exhilarating. I don't think I was ever happier in my life than I was that day. The fact of being one against a hundred. A hundred armed to the teeth. But bugs, only bugs. Whereas the one was a man. It was a wonderful feeling.' He was silent for a little, smiling to himself.

'And what happened then?' Anthony asked.

'Nothing. I just gave them a little speech from the throne. Told them the *finca* wasn't mine to give away. That, meanwhile, I was responsible for the place. And if I caught anybody trespas-sing on the land, or doing any mischief – well. I should know what to do. Firm, dignified, the real durbar touch. After which I got up, told them they could go, and walked up the path towards the house. I suppose I was within sight of them for about a minute. A full minute with my back turned to them. And there were at least a hundred of the creatures; nobody could have ever discovered who fired the shot. That bird under the ribs!' Lifting a hand, he fluttered the fingers in the air.

'And there was a new sensation – ants running up and down the spine. Terrors – but of the body only; autonomous, if you see what I mean. In my mind I knew that they wouldn't shoot, *couldn't* shoot. A hundred miserable bugs – it was morally impossible for them to do it. Bird under the ribs, ants up and down the spine; but inside the skull there was a man; and he was confident, in spite of the body's doubts, he knew that the game had been won. It was a long minute, but a good one. A very good one. And there were other minutes like it afterwards. The only times they ever shot at me were at evening, from out of the bushes. I was within their range, but they were out of mine. Out of the range of my consciousness and will. That was why they had the courage to shoot. When the man's away, the bugs will play. Luckily, no amount of courage has ever taught an Indian to shoot straight. In time, of course, they might have got me by a fluke; but meanwhile revolution went out of fashion. It never cut very much ice on the Pacific coast.' He lit a cigarette. There was a long silence.

'Well,' said Dr Miller at last, 'that's one way of dealing with a hostile crowd. And seeing that you're here to tell us, it's evidently a way that sometimes succeeds. But it's not my way. I'm an anthropologist, you see.'

'What difference does that make?'

'Quite a big one,' Dr Miller replied. 'An anthropologist is a person who studies men. But you prefer to deal with bugs. I'd call you an entomologist, Mark Staithes.' His smile evoked no answering sign of friendliness. Mark's face was stony as he met the doctor's eyes and looked away again.

'Entomologist!' he repeated scornfully. 'That's just stupid. Why do you play with words?'

'Because words express thoughts, Mark Staithes; and thoughts determine actions. If you call a man a bug, it means that you propose to treat him as a bug. Whereas if you call him a man, it means that you propose to treat him as a man. My profession is to study men. Which means that I must always call men by their name; always think of them as men; yes, and always treat them as men. Because if you don't treat men as men, they don't behave as men. But I'm an anthropologist, I repeat. I want human material. Not insect material.'

Mark uttered an explosive little laugh. 'One may *want* human material,' he said. 'But that doesn't mean one's going to get it. What one actually gets ...' He laughed again. 'Well, it's mostly plain, undiluted bug.'

'There,' said Dr Miller, 'you're wrong. If one looks for men, one finds them. Very decent ones, in a majority of cases. For example, go among a suspicious, badly treated, savage people; go unarmed, with your hands open.' He held out his large square hands in a gesture of offering. 'Go with the persistent and obstinate intention of doing them some good – curing their sick, for example. I don't care how bitter their grievance against white men may be; in the end, if you're given time enough to make your intentions clear, they'll accept you as a friend, they'll be human beings treating you as a human being. Of course,' he added, and the symbols of inner laughter revealed themselves once more about his eyes, 'it sometimes happens that they don't leave you the necessary time. They spear you before you're well under way. But it doesn't often happen – it has never happened to me, as you can see – and when it does happen, well, there's always the hope that the next man who comes will be more successful. Anthropologists may get killed; but anthropology goes on; and in the long run it can't fail to succeed. Whereas your entomological approach ...' He shook his head. 'It may succeed at the beginning; you can generally frighten and overawe people into submission. That's to say that, by treating them as bugs, you can generally make them behave like bugs – crawl and scuttle to cover. But the moment they have the opportunity, they'll turn on you. The anthropologist may get killed while establishing his first contacts; but after that, he's safe; he's a man among men. The entomologist may start by being safe; but he's a bug-hunter among bugs – among bugs, what's more, who resent being treated as bugs, who know they aren't bugs. His bad quarter of an hour comes later on. It's the old story; you can do everything with bayonets except sit on them.'

'You don't have to sit on them,' said Mark. 'It's the other people's bottoms that get punctured, not yours. If you wielded the bayonets with a certain amount of intelligence, I don't see why you shouldn't go on ruling indefinitely. The real trouble is,

373

of course, that there isn't the necessary intelligence. Most bug-hunters are indistinguishable from the bugs.'

'Exactly,' Dr Miller agreed. 'And the only remedy is for the bug-hunter to throw his bayonets away and treat the bugs as though they were human beings.'

'But we're talking about intelligence,' said Mark. The tone of contemptuous tolerance implied that he was doing his best not to get angry with the old fool for his incapacity to think. 'Being sentimental has nothing to do with being intelligent.'

'On the contrary,' the doctor insisted, 'it has everything to do with it. You can't be intelligent about human beings unless you're first sentimental about them. Sentimental in the good sense, of course. In the sense of caring for them. It's the first indispensable condition of understanding them. If you don't care for them, you can't possibly understand them; all your acuteness will just be another form of stupidity.'

'And if you care for them,' said Mark, 'you'll be carried away by your maudlin emotions and become incapable of seeing them for what they are. Look at the grotesque, humiliating things that happen when people care too much. The young men who fall in love and imagine that hideous, imbecile girls are paragons of beauty and intellect. The devoted women who persist in thinking that their squalid little hubbies are all that's most charming, noble, wise, profound.'

'They're probably quite right,' said Dr Miller. 'It's indifference and hatred that are blind, not love.'

'Not lo-ove!' Mark repeated derisively. 'Perhaps we might now sing a hymn.'

'With pleasure,' Dr Miller smiled. 'A Christian hymn, or a Buddhist hymn, or a Confucian – whichever you like. I'm an anthropologist; and after all, what's anthropology? Merely applied scientific religion.'

Anthony broke a long silence. 'Why do you only apply it to blackamoors?' he asked. 'What about beginning at home, like charity?'

'You're right,' said the doctor, 'it ought to have begun at home. If, in fact, it began abroad, that's merely a historical accident. It began there because we were imperialists and so came into contact with people whose habits were different from ours and therefore seemed stranger than ours. An accident, I repeat. But in some ways a rather fortunate accident. For thanks to it we've learnt a lot of facts and a valuable technique, which we probably shouldn't have learnt at home. For two reasons. Because it's hard to think dispassionately about oneself, and still harder to think correctly about something that's very complicated. Home's both those things – an elaborate civilization that happens to be our own. Savage societies are simply civilized societies on a small scale and with the lid off. We can learn to understand them fairly easily. And when we've learnt to understand savages, we've learnt, as we discover, to understand the civilized. And that's not all. Savages are usually hostile and suspicious. The anthropologist has got to learn to overcome that hostility and suspicion. And when he's learnt that, he's learnt the whole secret of politics.'

'Which is ...?'

'That if you treat other people well, they'll treat you well.'

'You're a bit optimistic, aren't you?'

'No. In the long run they'll always treat you well.'

'In the long run,' said Mark impatiently, 'we shall all be dead. What about the short run?'

'You've got to take a risk.'

'But Europeans aren't like your Sunday-school savages. It'll be an enormous risk.'

'Possibly. But always smaller than the risk you run by treating people badly and goading them into a war. Besides, they're not worse than savages. They've just been badly handled – need a bit of anthropology, that's all.'

'And who's going to give them the anthropology?'

'Well, among others,' Dr Miller answered, 'I am. And I hope you are, Mark Staithes.'

Mark made a flayed grimace and shook his head. 'Let them slit one another's throats,' he said. 'They'll do it anyhow, whatever you tell them. So leave them to make their idiotic wars in peace. Besides,' he pointed to the basket-work cage that kept the bed-clothes out of contact with his wound, 'what can I do now? Look on, that's all. We'd much better all look on. It won't be for long anyhow. Just a few years; and then ...' He paused, looked down and frowned. 'What are those verses of Rochester's? Yes.' He raised his head again and recited:

> 'Then old age and experience, hand in hand,
> Lead him to death, and make him understand,
> After a search so painful and so long,
> That all his life he had been in the wrong.
> Huddled in dirt the reasoning engine lies,
> Who was so proud, so witty and so wise.'

'Huddled in dirt,' he repeated. 'That's really admirable. Huddled in dirt. And one doesn't have to wait till one's dead to be that. We'll find a snug little patch of dirt and huddle together, shall we?' He turned to Anthony. 'Huddle together among the cow-pats and watch the doctor trying his best anthropological bedside manner on General Goering. There'll be some hearty laughs.'

'In spite of which,' said Anthony, 'I think I shall go and make myself ridiculous with Miller.'

CHAPTER FIFTY-TWO

July 24th.1914

THERE were four of them in the search-party: Anthony, the policeman, an old shepherd, with the grey whiskers and the majestic profile of a Victorian statesman, and a fair, red-faced boy of seventeen, the baker's son. The boy was made to carry the canvas part of the stretcher, while the shepherd and the policeman used the long poles as staves.

They set out from behind the cottage, walking in a line – like beaters, Anthony found himself reflecting – up the slope of the hill. It was a brilliant day, cloudless and windless. The distant hills showed as though through veils, dim with much sunlight and almost without colour. Under their feet the grass and heather were dusty with long drought. Anthony took off his jacket, and then, on second thoughts, his hat. A touch of sun-stroke might simplify things; there would be no need to give explanations or answer questions. Even as it was, he felt rather sick and there was a griping in his bowels. But that was hardly enough. How many difficulties would be removed if he could be really ill! Every now and then, as they climbed slowly on, he put his hand to his head, and each time the hair felt hot to the touch, like the fur of a cat that has been sitting in front of the fire. It was a pity, he thought, that his hair was so thick.

Three hours later they had found what they were looking for. Brian's body was lying, face downwards, in a kind of rocky bay, at the foot of a cliff above the tarn. Bracken was growing between the rocks, and in the hot air its sweetish, oppressive scent was almost suffocatingly strong. The place was loud with flies. When the policeman turned the body over, the mangled face was almost unrecognizable. Anthony looked for a moment, then turned away. His whole body had begun to tremble uncontrollably; he had to lean against a rock to prevent himself from falling.

'Come, lad.' The old shepherd took him by the arm, and, leading him away, made him sit down on the grass, out of sight of the body. Anthony waited. A buzzard turned slowly in the sky, tracing out the passage of time on an invisible clock-face. Then at last they came out from behind the buttress of rock into his view. The shepherd and the boy walked in front, each holding one pole of the stretcher, while the policeman, behind, had to support the weight on both the poles. Brian's torn jacket had been taken off and spread over his face. One stiffened arm stuck out irrepressibly and, at every step the bearers took, swung and trembled in the air. There were bloodstains on the shirt. Anthony got up, and in spite of their protestations insisted on taking half the policeman's burden. Very slowly, they made their way down towards the valley. It was after three o'clock when at last they reached the cottage.

Later, the policeman went through the pockets of coat and trousers. A tobacco pouch, a pipe, Mrs Benson's packet of sandwiches, six or seven shillings in money, and a note-book half full of jottings about the economic history of the Roman Empire. Not the smallest hint that what had happened had been anything but an accident.

Mrs Foxe arrived the following evening. Rigid at first with self-control, she listened in silence, stonily, to Anthony's story;

then, all at once, broke down, fell to pieces as it were, in a passion of tears. Anthony stood by her for a moment, uncertainly; then crept out of the room.

Next morning, when he saw her again, Mrs Foxe had recovered her calm – but a different kind of calm. The calm of a living, sentient being, not the mechanical and frozen stillness of a statue. There were dark lines under her eyes, and the face was that of an old and suffering woman; but there was a sweetness and serenity in the suffering, an expression of dignity, almost of majesty. Looking at her, Anthony felt himself abashed, as though he were in the presence of something that he was not worthy, that he had no right, to approach. Abashed and guilty, more guilty even than he had felt the night before, when her grief had passed beyond her control.

He would have liked to escape once more; but she kept him with her all the morning, sometimes sitting in silence, sometimes speaking in that slow, beautifully modulated voice of hers. To Anthony silence and speech were equally a torture. It was an agony to sit there, saying nothing, listening to the clock ticking, and wondering, worrying about the future – how to get away from Joan, what to tell her about that accursed letter of hers; and every now and then stealing a glance at Mrs Foxe and asking himself what was going on in her mind and whether she had any knowledge, any suspicion even, of what had really happened. Yes, her silences were painful; but equally painful was her speech.

'I realize,' she began, slowly and pensively, 'I realize now that I loved him in the wrong way – too possessively.'

What was he to say? That it was true? Of course it was true. She had been like a vampire, fastened on poor Brian's spirit. Sucking his life's blood. (St Monica, he remembered, by Ary Scheffer.) Yes, a vampire. If anyone was responsible for Brian's death, it was she. But his self-justificatory indignation against her evaporated as she spoke again.

'Perhaps that was one of the reasons why it happened, in order that I might learn that love mustn't be like that.' Then, after a pause, 'I suppose,' she went on, 'Brian had learnt enough. He hadn't very much to learn, really. He knew so much to start with. Like Mozart – only his genius wasn't for music;

it was for love. Perhaps that was why he could go so soon. Whereas I . . .' She shook her head. 'I've had to have this lesson. After all these long years of learning, still so wilfully stupid and ignorant!' She sighed and was silent once more.

A vampire – but she knew it; she admitted her share of responsibility. There remained his share – still unconfessed. 'I ought to tell her,' he said to himself, and thought of all that had resulted from his failure to tell the truth to Brian. But while he was hesitating, Mrs Foxe began again.

'One ought to love everyone like an only son,' she went on. 'And one's own only son as one amongst them. A son one can't help loving more than the rest, because one has more opportunities for loving him. But the love would be different only in quantity, not in kind. One ought to love him as one loves all the other only sons – for God's sake, not for one's own.'

The richly vibrant voice spoke on, and, with every word it uttered, Anthony felt more guilty – more guilty, and at the same time more completely and hopelessly committed to his guilt. The longer he delayed and the more she said in this strain of resignation, the harder it was going to be to undeceive her with the truth.

'Listen, Anthony,' she resumed, after another long pause. 'You know how fond of you I've always been. Ever since that time just after your mother's death – do you remember? – when you first came to stay with us. You were such a defenceless little boy. And that's how I've always seen you, ever since. Defenceless under your armour. For, of course, you've had an armour. You still have. To protect yourself against me, among other dangers.' She smiled at him. Anthony dropped his eyes, blushed and mumbled some incoherent phrase. 'Never mind why you've wanted to protect yourself,' she went on. 'I don't want to know, unless you want to tell me. And perhaps you'll feel you want to protect yourself still more now. Because I'm going to say that I'd like you to take Brian's place. The place,' she qualified, 'that Brian ought to have had if I'd loved him in the right way. Among all the other only sons, the one whom there's more opportunity of loving than the rest. That's what I'd like you to be, Anthony. But, of course, I won't force myself on you. It's for you to decide.'

He sat in silence, his face averted from her, his head bent. 'Blurt it out,' a voice was crying within him. 'Anyhow, at any price!' But if it had been difficult before, now it was impossible. Saying she wanted him to take Brian's place! It was she who had made it impossible. He was shaken by the gust of futile anger. If only she'd leave him in peace, let him go away and be alone! Suddenly his throat contracted, the tears came into his eyes, the muscles of his chest tightened in spasm after violent spasm; he was sobbing. Mrs Foxe crossed the room, and bending over him, laid a hand on his shoulder.

'Poor Anthony,' she whispered.

He was pinned irrevocably to his lie.

That evening he wrote to Joan. This horrible accident. So unnecessary. So stupid in its tragedy. It had happened, as a matter of fact, before he had had an opportunity for telling Brian about those events in London. And, by the way, had she written to Brian? An envelope addressed in her handwriting had been delivered at midday, when the poor fellow had already started out. He was keeping it for her and would return it personally, when he saw her next. Meanwhile, Mrs Foxe was bearing it wonderfully; and they must all be brave; and he was always hers affectionately.

CHAPTER FIFTY-THREE

February 23rd 1934

HELEN came into the sitting-room, holding a frying-pan in which the bacon was still spluttering from the fire.

'Breakfast!' she called.

'*Komme gleich*' came back from the bedroom, and a moment later Ekki showed himself at the open door in shirt-sleeves, razor in hand, his fair ruddy face covered with soap-suds.

'Almost finished,' he said in English, and disappeared again.

Helen smiled to herself as she sat down. Loving him as she did, she found an extraordinary pleasure in this close and incessant physical intimacy with him – the intimacy that their poverty had perforce imposed on them. Why do people want large houses, separate rooms, all the private hiding-places that the rich find indispensable? She couldn't imagine, now. Humming to herself, out of tune, Helen poured out the tea, helped herself to bacon, then began to sort the morning's letters. *Helen Amberley*. No Mrs. Communist frankness and informality. She opened the envelope. The letter was from Newcastle. Would it be possible for her or Giesebrecht to speak to a group of young comrades on conditions in Germany some time in March? Well, one would have to see. *Mr E. Giesebrecht*. From Switzerland; and surely that thin spiky writing was Holtzmann's. Ekki would be pleased.

'Something from Holtzmann,' she said as he came in. 'I wonder what news he'll have this time?'

Ekki took the letter, and, with that methodical deliberation that characterized all his actions, opened it; then, laid it down beside his plate and cut off a piece of bacon. He poked the bacon into his mouth, picked up the letter again, and, slowly chewing, began to read. An expression of intent and focused gravity came into his face; he could never do anything except thoroughly and whole-heartedly. When he had finished, he turned back to the first page and started reading all over again.

Helen's impatience got the better of her at last. 'Anything interesting?' she asked. Holtzmann was the best informed of the exiled journalists; he always had something to communicate. 'Tell me what he says.'

Ekki did not answer at once, but read on in silence for a few seconds, then folded up the letter and put it away in his pocket. 'Mach is in Basel,' he answered at last, looking up at her.

'Mach?' she repeated. 'Do you mean Ludwig Mach?'

In the course of these last months, the name of this most resourceful and courageous of all the German comrades engaged in the dissemination of Communist propaganda and censored news had become, for Helen, at once familiar and fabulous, like the name of a personage in literature or mythology. That Ludwig Mach should be at Basel seemed almost as improbable as that Odysseus should be there, or Odin, or the Scarlet Pimpernel. 'Ludwig Mach from Stuttgart?' she insisted incredulously.

Ekki nodded. 'I shall have to go and see him. Tomorrow.'

Spoken in that slow, emphatic, foreign way of his, the words had a strange quality of absolute irrevocableness. Even his most casual statements always sounded, when uttered in English, as though he had made them on oath.

'I shall have to go,' he repeated.

Carefully, conscientiously pronounced, each syllable had the same value. Two heavy spondees and the first half of a third. Whereas an Englishman, however irrevocably he had made up his mind, would have spoken the phrase as a kind of gobbled anapaest – I-shall-have-to-go. In another man, this way of speaking – so ponderous, so Jehovah-like, as she herself had teasingly called it – would have seemed to Helen intolerably grotesque. But, in Ekki, it was an added attraction. It seemed somehow right and fitting that this man, whom (quite apart from loving) she admired and respected beyond anyone she had ever known, should be thus touchingly absurd.

'If I couldn't laugh at him sometimes,' she explained to herself, 'it might all go putrid. A pool of stagnant adoration. Like religion. Like one of Landseer's dogs. The laughter keeps it aired and moving.'

Listening, looking into his face (at once so absurdly ingenuous in its fresh and candid gravity and so heroically determined), Helen felt, as she had so often felt before, that she would like to burst out laughing and then go down on her knees and kiss his hands.

'I shall have to go too,' she said aloud, parodying his way of speaking. He thought at first that she was joking; then, when he realized that she was in earnest, grew serious and began to raise objections. The fatigue – for they would be travelling third-class. The expense. But Helen was suddenly like her mother – a spoilt woman whose caprices had to be satisfied.

'It'll be such fun,' she cried excitedly. 'Such an adventure!' And when he persisted in being negatively reasonable, she grew angry. 'But I will come with you,' she repeated obstinately. 'I *will*.'

Holtzmann met them at the station, and, instead of being the tall, stiff, distinguished personage of Helen's anticipatory fancy, turned out to be short and squat, with a roll of fat at the back of his neck, and, between little pig's eyes, a soft shapeless nose like a potato. His hand, when she shook it, was so coldly sweaty that she felt her own defiled; surreptitiously, when he wasn't looking, she wiped it on her skirt. But worse than even his appearance and his sweaty hands was the man's behaviour. Her presence, she could see, had taken him aback.

'I had not expected . . .' he stammered, when Ekki presented her; and his face, for a moment, seemed to disintegrate in agitation. Then, recovering himself, he became effusively polite and cordial. It was *gnädige Frau, lieber Ekki, unbeschreiblich froh* all the way down the platform. As though he were meeting them on the stage, Helen thought. And acting badly, what was more, like someone in a third-rate touring company. And how detestable that nervousness was! A man had no business to giggle like that and gesticulate and make grimaces. Mopping and mowing, she said under her breath. Walking beside him, she felt herself surrounded by a bristling aura of dislike. This horrible creature had suddenly spoilt all the fun of the journey. She found herself almost wishing that she hadn't come.

'What a loathsome man!' she managed to whisper to Ekki, while Holtzmann was engaged in extravagantly overacting the part of one who tells the porter to be careful with the typewriter.

'You find him so?' Ekki asked with genuine surprise. 'I had not thought . . .' He left the sentence unfinished and shook his head. A little frown of perplexity wrinkled his smooth forehead. But a moment later, interrupting Holtzmann's renewed pro-testations of affection and delight, he was asking what Mach thought of the present situation in Germany; and when Holtz-mann replied, he listened, absorbed.

Half angry with him for his insensitive obtuseness, half admiring him for his power to ignore everything that, to him, was irrelevant, Helen walked in silence at his side.

'Men are extraordinary,' she was thinking. 'All the same, I ought to be like that.'

Instead of which she allowed herself to be distracted by faces, by gigglings and gestures; she wasted her feelings on pigs' eyes and rolls of fat. And all the time millions of men and women and children were going cold and hungry, were being exploited, were being overworked, were being treated as though they were less than human, mere beasts of burden, mere cogs and levers;

millions were being forced to live in chronic fear and misery and despair, were being dragooned and beaten, were being maddened with lies and cowed with threats and blows, were being herded this way and that like senseless animals on the road to market, to an ultimate slaughter-house. And here was she, detesting Holtzmann, because he had sweaty hands – instead of respecting him, as she should have done, for what he had dared, what he had suffered for the sake of those unhappy millions. His hands might be sweaty; but he lived precariously in exile, had been persecuted for his principles, was a champion of justice and truth. She felt ashamed of herself, but at the same time couldn't help thinking that life, if you were like Ekki, must be strangely narrow and limited, unimaginably without colour. A life in black and white, she reflected, hard and clear and definite, like a Dürer engraving. Whereas hers – hers was a vague bright Turner, a Monet, a savage Gauguin. But 'you look like a Gauguin', Anthony had said, that morning on the blazing roof, and here in the chilly twilight of Basel station she suddenly winced, as though with physical pain.

'Oh, how awful,' she said to herself, 'how awful !'

'And the labour camps,' Ekki was asking, intently, 'what does Mach say about the feeling in the labour camps?'

Outside the station they halted.

'Shall we begin by taking our things to a hotel?' Ekki suggested.

But Holtzmann would not hear of it. 'No, no, you must come at once,' he insisted with a breathless emphasis. 'To my house at once. Mach is waiting there. Mach wouldn't understand it if there was any delay.' But when Ekki agreed, he still stood irresolute and nervous at the pavement's edge, like a swimmer afraid to plunge.

'What's the matter with the man?' Helen wondered impatiently; then aloud, 'Well, why don't we take a taxi?' she asked, forgetting for the moment that the time of taxis had long since come to an end. One took trams now, one took buses. But Gauguin had precipitated her into the past; it seemed natural to think of taxis.

Holtzmann did not answer her; but suddenly, with the quick, agitated movements of one who has been forced by circumstances to take a disagreeable decision, caught Ekki by the arm, and, drawing him aside, began to speak to him in a hurried whisper. Helen saw a look of surprise and annoyance come over Ekki's face as he listened. His lips moved, he was evidently making an objection. The other replied in smiling deprecation and began to stroke his sleeve, as though in the hope of caressing him into acquiescence.

In the end Ekki nodded, and, turning back to Helen, 'Holtzmann wants you to join us only at lunch,' he said in his abrupt heavy way. 'He says that Mach wouldn't like it if there is anyone beside me.'

'Does he think I'll give him away to the Nazis?' Helen asked indignantly.

'It isn't you,' Ekki explained. 'He doesn't know you. If he did, it would be different. But he is afraid. Afraid of everyone he does not know. And he is quite right to be afraid,' he added, in that tone of dogmatic finality which meant that the argument was closed.

Making a great effort to swallow her annoyance and chagrin, Helen nodded her head. 'All right then, I'll meet you at lunchtime. Though what the point was of my coming here at all,' she couldn't help adding, 'I really can't imagine.'

'Dear Miss Amberley, *chère consœur, gnädige Frau*, comrade . . .' Holtzmann overflowed with bourgeois and Communist courtesies in all the languages at his disposal. '*Es tut mir so leid. So very sorry.*' But here was the address of his house. At half past twelve. And if he might advise her on the best way of spending a morning in Basel . . .

She slipped the card into her bag, and without waiting to listen to his suggestions, turned her back on the two men and walked quickly away.

'Helen !' Ekki called after her. But she paid no attention. He did not call again.

It was cold; but the sky was a clear pale blue, the sun was shining. And suddenly, emerging from behind high houses, she found herself beside the Rhine. Leaning over the parapet, she watched the green water hurrying past, silent, but swift and purposive, like a living thing, like life itself, like the power behind the world, eternally, irresistibly flowing; watched it, until at last it was as though she herself were flowing along with the great river, were one with it, a partaker of its power. 'And shall Trelawney die?' she found herself singing. 'And shall Trelawney die? There's twenty thousand Cornish men shall know the rea-ea-eason why.' And suddenly it seemed certain that they would win, that the revolution was only just round the corner – there, after that first bend in the river. Irresistibly the flood drove on towards it. And meanwhile what a fool she had been to be cross with Ekki, what an absolute beast! Remorse gave place, after a little, to the ecstatically tender anticipation of their reconcilement. 'Darling,' she would say to him, 'darling, you must forgive me. I was really too stupid and odious.' And he would put one arm round her, and with the other hand would push back the hair from her forehead and then bend down and kiss her. . . .

When she walked on, the Rhine was still rushing within her, and, unburdened of her offence towards Ekki, she felt immaterially light, felt almost as though she were floating – floating in a thin intoxicating air of happiness. The starving millions receded once more into remote abstraction. How good everything was, how beautiful, how exactly as it ought to be! Even the fat old women were perfect, even the nineteenth-century Gothic houses. And that cup of hot chocolate in the café – how indescribably delicious! And the old waiter, so friendly and paternal. Friendly and paternal, what was more, in an astonishing Swiss-German that made one want to roar with laughter, as though everything he said – from his commentaries on the weather to his complaints about the times – were one huge, continuous joke. Such gutterals, such neighings! Like the language of the Houyhn-hnms, she thought, and led him on, with an unwearying delight in the performance, to hoick and whinny yet again.

From the café she went on at last to the picture gallery; and the picture gallery turned out to be as exquisitely comic in its own way as the waiter's German. Those Boecklins! All the extraordinary pictures one had only seen on postcards or hanging, in coloured reproduction, on the walls of pensions in Dresden. Mermaids and tritons caught as though by a camera; centaurs in the stiff ungainly positions of race-horses in a pressman's photograph. Painted with a good faith and a laborious lack of talent that were positively touching. And here – unspeakable joy! – was the *Toteninsel*. The funereal cypresses, the white tomb-like temples, the long-robed figures, the solitary boat on its way across the wine-dark sea ... The joke was perfect. Helen laughed aloud. In spite of everything, she was still her mother's daughter.

In the room of the primitives she paused for a moment, on her way out, before a picture of the martyrdom of St Erasmus. An executioner in fifteenth-century costume, with a pale shell-pink cod-piece, was methodically turning the handle of a winch – like Mr Mantalini at the mangle – winding the saint's intestines, yard after yard, out of a gash in the emaciated belly, while the victim lay back, as if on a sofa, making himself thoroughly comfortable and looking up into the sky with an expression of unruffled equanimity. The joke here was less subtle than in *Toteninsel*, more frankly a knockabout; but excellent, none the less, in its own simple way. She was still smiling as she walked out into the street.

Holtzmann, it turned out, lived only a few hundred yards from the gallery, in a pretty little early nineteenth-century house (much too good for a man with sweaty hands!) set back from the road behind a little square of gravel. A large car was standing at the door. Holtzmann's? she wondered. He must be rich, the old pig! It had taken her so little time to come from the gallery that it was hardly a quarter past twelve as she mounted the steps. 'Never mind,' she said to herself. 'They'll have to put up with me. I refuse to wait one second longer.' The thought that, in a moment, she would see Ekki again made her heart beat quickly. 'What a fool I am! What an absolute fool! But how marvellous to be able to be a fool!' She rang the bell.

It was Holtzmann himself who opened – dressed in an overcoat, she was surprised to see, as though he were just going out. The expression with which he had greeted her at the station reappeared on his face as he saw her.

'You are so soon,' he said, trying to smile; but his nervousness and embarrassment amounted almost to terror. 'We had not awaited you until half-one.'

Helen laughed. 'I hadn't awaited myself,' she explained. 'But I got here quicker than I thought.'

She made a movement to step across the threshold; but Holtz-mann held out his arm. 'We are not yet ready,' he said. His face was flushed and sweating with embarrassment. 'If you will return in a quarter hour,' he almost implored. 'Only a quarter hour.'

'*Nur ein viertel Stündchen.*' Helen laughed, thinking of those embroidered cushions on the sofas where the Geheimrats slept off the effects of noonday eating. 'But why shouldn't I wait indoors?' She pushed past him into a dark little hall that smelt of cooking and stale air. 'Where's Ekki?' she asked, suddenly overcome by the desire to see him, to see him at once, without another second's delay, so that she could tell him what a beast she had been, but how loving all the same, how adoring in spite of the beastliness, and how happy, how eager to share her happiness with him! At the other end of the vestibule a door stood ajar. Calling his name, Helen ran towards it.

'Stop!' Holtzmann shouted behind her.

But she was already across the threshold.

The room in which she found herself was a bedroom. On the narrow iron bed Ekki was lying with all his clothes on, his head on one side, his mouth open. His breath came slowly in long snores; he was asleep – but asleep as she had never seen him sleeping.

'Ekki!' she had time to cry, while a door slammed, another voice joined itself to Holtzmann's, and the vestibule was loud with violent movement. 'My darling . . .'

Then suddenly a hand closed on her shoulder from behind. She turned, saw the face of a strange man within a few inches of her own, heard somewhere from the background Holtz-mann's '*Schnell, Willi, schnell!*' and the stranger almost whispering, between clenched teeth, '*Schmutziges Frauen-zimmer*'; then, as she opened her mouth to scream, received a terrible blow on the chin that brought the teeth violently together again, and felt herself dropping into blackness.

When she came to herself, she was in bed in a hospital ward. Some peasants had found her lying unconscious in a little wood five or six miles from the town. An ambulance had brought her back to Basel. It was only on the following morning that the effects of the barbitone wore off and she remembered what had happened. But by that time Ekki had been over the frontier, in Germany, for nearly twenty hours.

A NTHONY had spent the morning at the offices of the organization, dictating letters. For the most part, it was a matter of dealing with the intellectual difficulties of would-be pacifists. 'What would you do if you saw a foreign soldier attacking your sister?' Well, whatever else one did, one certainly wouldn't send one's son to murder his second cousin. Wearisome work! But it had to be done. He dictated twenty-seven letters; then it was time to go to lunch with Helen.

'There's practically nothing to eat,' she said, when he came in. 'I simply couldn't be bothered to cook anything. The unspeakable boredom of making meals!' Her voice took on a note of almost malevolent resentment.

They addressed themselves to tinned salmon and lettuce. Anthony tried to talk; but his words seemed to bounce off the impenetrable surface of her sullen and melancholy silence. In the end, he too sat speechless.

'It's just a year ago today,' she brought out at last.

'What is?'

'Just a year since those devils at Basel . . .' She shook her head and was silent again.

Anthony said nothing. Anything he could say would be an irrelevance, he felt, almost an insult.

'I often wish they'd killed me too,' she went on slowly. 'Instead of leaving me here, rotting away, like a piece of dirt on a rubbish heap. Like a dead kitten,' she added, as an afterthought. 'So much carrion.' The words were spoken with a vehement disgust.

'Why do you say that?' he asked.

'Because it's true. I *am* carrion.'

'There's no need for you to be.'

'I can't help it. I'm carrion by nature.'

'No, you're not,' he insisted. 'You've said it yourself. When Ekki was there . . .'

'No, I wasn't carrion then.'

'What you've been once, you can be again.'

'Not without him.'

He nodded. 'Yes, if you want to be, you can. It's a matter of choosing. Choosing and then setting to work in the right way.'

Helen shook her head. 'They ought to have killed me. If you only know how I disgust myself!' She screwed up her face into a grimace. 'I'm no good. Worse than no good. Just a lump of dirt.' After a pause, 'I'm not even interested in Ekki's work,' she went on. 'I don't like his friends. Communists. But they're just beastly little people, like anyone else. Stupid, vulgar, envious, pushing. One might as well have the fun of wearing a chinchilla coat and lunching at Claridge's. I shall probably end by selling myself to a rich man. That is, if I can find one.' She laughed again. Then, in a tone of more bitter self-contempt, 'Only a year today,' she resumed, 'and already I'm sick of it all. Utterly sick of it and pining to get out of it. I'm disgusting.'

'But are you entirely to blame?'

'Of course I am.'

Anthony shook his head. 'Perhaps it's also the fault of the work.'

'What do you mean?'

'Organized hatred – it's not exactly attractive. Not what most people feel they really want to live for.'

'Ekki lived for it. Lots of people live for it.'

'But what sort of people?' he asked. 'They're of three kinds. Idealists with an exceptional gift for self-deception. Either they don't know that it's organized hatred, or else they genuinely believe that the end justifies the means, genuinely imagine that the means don't condition the end. Ekki was one of those. They form the majority. And then there are two minorities. A minority of people who know that the thing's organized hatred and rejoice in the fact. And a minority that's ambitious, that merely uses the movement as a convenient machine for realizing its ambition. You, Helen – you're neither ambitious nor self-deceiving. And, in spite of what happened this day last year, don't really want to liquidate people – not even Nazis. And that's why the chinchillas and the orchids seem so attractive. Not because you actively long for them. Only because this particular alternative is so unsatisfactory.'

There was a silence. Helen got up, changed the plates and set a bowl of fruit on the table. 'What *is* the satisfactory alternative?' she asked, as she helped herself to an apple.

'It begins,' he answered, 'with trying to cultivate the difficult art of loving people.'

'But most people are detestable.'

'They're detestable, because we detest them. If we liked them, they'd be likeable.'

'Do you think that's true?'

'I'm sure it's true.'

'And what do you do after that?'

'There's no "after",' he replied. 'Because, of course, it's a lifetime's job. Any process of change is a lifetime's job. Every time you get to the top of a peak, you see another peak in front of you – a peak that you couldn't see from lower down. Take the mind – body mechanism, for example. You begin to learn how to use it better; you make an advance; from the position you've advanced to, you discover how you can use it better still And so on, indefinitely. The ideal ends recede as you approach them; they're seen to be other and more remarkable than they seemed before the advance was begun. It's the same when one tries to change one's relations with other people. Every step forward reveals the necessity of making new steps forward – unanticipated steps, towards a destination one hadn't seen when one set out. Yes, it lasts a lifetime,' he repeated. 'There can't be any "after". There can only be an attempt, as one goes along, to project what one has discovered on the personal level on to the level of politics and economics. One of the first discoveries,' he added, 'one of the very first one makes, is that organized hatred and violence aren't the best means for securing justice and peace. All men are capable of love for all other men. But we've artificially restricted our love. By means of conventions of hatred and violence. Restricted it within families and clans, within classes and nations. Your friends want to remove those restrictions by using more hatred and violence – that's to say, by using exactly the same means as were the original causes of the restrictions.' He smiled. 'Can you be surprised if you find the work a bit unsatisfying?'

Helen looked at him for a little in silence, then shook her head. 'I prefer my chinchillas.'

'No, you don't.'

'Yes, I do. I'd rather be a lump of dirt. It's easier.' She got up. 'What about some coffee?' In the little kitchen, as they were waiting for the water to boil, she suddenly started to tell him about that young man in advertising. She had met him a couple of weeks before. Such an amusing and intelligent creature! And he had fallen violently in love with her. Her face brightened with a kind of reckless, laughing malice. 'Blue eyes,' she said, cataloguing the young man's merits, as though she were an auctioneer, 'curly hair, tremendous shoulders, narrow hips, first-rate amateur boxer – which is more than you ever were, my poor Anthony,' she added parenthetically and in a tone of contemptuous commiseration. 'In fact, thoroughly bed-worthy. Or at least he looks it. Because one never really knows till one's tried, does one?' She laughed. 'I've a good mind to try tonight,' she went on. 'To commemorate this anniversary. Don't you think it would be a good idea, Anthony?' And when he didn't answer, 'Don't you think so?' she insisted. 'Don't you think so?' She looked into his face, trying to detect in it the signs of anger, or jealousy, or disgust.

Anthony smiled back at her. 'It isn't so easy, being a lump of dirt,' he said. 'In fact, I should say it was very hard work indeed.'

The brightness faded out of her face. 'Hard work,' she repeated. 'Perhaps that's one of the reasons for going on trying.' After a pause, while she poured the water into the percolator, 'Did you say you were having a meeting tonight?'

'In Battersea.'

'Perhaps I shall come and listen to you. Unless,' she added, making an effort to laugh, 'unless, of course, I've decided to celebrate the anniversary in the other way.'

When they had drunk their coffee, Anthony walked back to his rooms, to put in a few hours' work at the new pamphlet he had promised to write for Purchas. Two letters had come by the midday delivery. One was from Miller, describing the excellent meetings he had been having in Edinburgh and Glasgow. The other, without an address, was typewritten.

SIR, [it began] we have been keeping an eye on you for some time past, and have decided that you cannot be allowed to go on in your present disloyal and treacherous way. We give you fair warning. If you make any more of your dirty pacifist speeches, we shall deal with you as you deserve. Appealing to the police will not do any good. We shall get you sooner or later, and it will not be pleasant for you. It is announced that you are speaking tonight in Battersea. *We shall be there.* So we advise you, if you value your yellow skin, to keep away. You do not deserve this warning, but we want to behave sportingly even towards a skunk like you. – Yours faithfully,

A GROUP OF PATRIOTIC ENGLISHMEN.

A joke, Anthony wondered? No, probably serious. He smiled. 'How virtuous they must be feeling!' he said to himself. 'And how heroic! Striking their blow for England.'

But the blow, he went on to reflect, as he sat down in front of the fire, the blow would fall upon himself – if he spoke, that was to say, if they weren't prevented from attacking him. And, of course, there could be no question of not speaking. No question of calling on the police for protection. Nothing to do but practise what he had been preaching.

But would he have the strength of mind to see it through? Suppose they set on him, suppose they started to knock him about? Would he know how to stand it?

He tried to work on the pamphlet; but the personal questions insistently recurred, thrusting aside those remoter and impersonal problems of colonies and prestige, markets, investment, migration. He visualized the horrible expression of anger on the men's distorted faces, heard in his fancy their violent insulting words, saw hands lifted, falling. Would he be able to prevent himself from flinching? And the pain of blows – sharp, excruciating, on the face, and sickening on the body – how much would he be able to bear, for how long? If only Miller were here to give advice and encouragement! But Miller was in Glasgow.

Doubt of himself grew upon him. To stand there, letting himself be struck, without hitting back, without giving ground – he would never be able to do that.

393

'I shan't have the guts,' he kept repeating, and was obsessed by the fear of being afraid. Remembering the way he had behaved at Tapatlan, he blushed with shame. And, this time, the disgrace would be in public. They would all know – Helen with the rest.

And this time, he went on to think, this time there wouldn't be the excuse of surprise. They had given him warning – 'even to a skunk like you'. And besides, he had been training himself for months past to cope with just such a contingency as this. The scene had been rehearsed. He knew by heart every cue and gesture. But when the time actually came, when the pain was no longer imaginary but real, would he remember his part? What guarantee was there that he wouldn't hopelessly break down? In front of Helen – when Helen was standing hesitant on the threshold of her own life, perhaps also of his. Besides, if he broke down, he would be discrediting more than himself. To break down would be to deny his convictions, to invalidate his philosophy, to betray his friends. 'But why are you such a fool?' a small voice began to question; 'why do you go and saddle yourself with convictions and philosophies? And why put yourself in the position of being able to betray anyone? Why not go back to doing what nature meant you to do – to looking on from your private box and making comments? What does it all matter, after all? And even if it matters, what can you do? Why not quietly resign yourself to the inevitable, and in the interval get on with the job you can do best?'

The voice spoke out of a cloud of fatigue. For a minute he was nothing but a dead, dry husk enclosing black weariness and negation. 'Ring them up,' the voice went on. 'Tell them you've got flu. Stay in bed a few days. Then have yourself ordered to the south of France by the doctor . . .'

Suddenly he laughed aloud. From sinister, from insidiously persuasive, that small voice had become absurd. Carried to such a pitch, expressed so ingenuously, baseness was almost comic.

'Unity,' he said in an articulate whisper.

He was committed to them, as a hand is committed to the arm. Committed to his friends, committed even to those who had declared themselves his enemies. There was nothing he could do but would affect them all, enemies and friends – for good, if what he did were good, for evil if it were wrong. Unity, he repeated. Unity.

Unity of mankind, unity of all life, all being even.

Physical unity, first of all. Unity even in diversity, even in separation. Separate patterns, but everywhere alike. Everywhere the same constellations of the ultimate units of energy. The same on the surface of the sun as in the living flesh warmed by the sun's radiance; in the scented cluster of buddleia flowers as in the blue sea and the clouds on the horizon; in the drunken Mexican's pistol as in the dark dried blood on that mangled face among the rocks, the fresh blood spattered scarlet over Helen's naked body, the drops oozing from the raw contusion on Mark's knee.

Identical patterns, and identical patternings of patterns. He held the thought of them in his mind, and, along with it, the thought of life incessantly moving among the patterns, selecting and rejecting for its own purposes. Life building up simpler into more complex patterns – identically complex through vast ranges of animate being.

The sperm enters the egg, the cell divides and divides, to become at last this man, that rat or horse. A cow's pituitary will make frogs breed out of season. Urine of a pregnant woman bring the mouse on heat. Sheep's thyroid transforms the axolotl from a gilled larva into an air-breathing salamander, the cretinous dwarf into a well-grown and intelligent human being. Between one form of animal life and another, patterns are interchangeable. Interchangeable also between animal and plant, plant and the inanimate world. Patterns in seed and leaf and root, patterns built up from simpler patterns existent in the air and soil – these can be assimilated and transformed by insect, reptile, mammal, fish.

The unity of life. Unity demonstrated even in the destruction of one life by another. Life and all being are one. Otherwise no living thing could ever derive sustenance from another or from the unliving substances around it. One even in destruction, one in spite of separation. Each organism is unique. Unique and yet united with all other organisms in the sameness of its ultimate parts; unique above a substratum of physical identity.

And minds – minds also are unique, but unique above a substratum of mental identity. Identity and interchangeableness of love, trust, courage. Fearless affection restores the lunatic to sanity, transforms the hostile savage into a friend, tames the wild animal. The mental pattern of love can be transferred from one mind to another and still retain its virtue, just as the physical pattern of a hormone can be transferred, with all its effectiveness, from one body to another.

And not only love, but hate as well; not only trust, but suspicion; not only kindness, generosity, courage, but also malevolence and greed and fear.

Divisive emotions; but the fact that they can be interchanged, can be transferred from mind to mind and retain all their original passion, is a demonstration of the fundamental unity of minds.

Reality of unity, but equal reality of division – greater reality, indeed, of division. No need to meditate the fact of division. One is constantly aware of it. Constantly aware of being unique and separate; only sometimes, and then most often only intellectually, only as the result of a process of discursive thought, aware of being one with other minds, other lives and all being. Occasionally an intuition of unity, an intuition coming at random, or sought for, step by step, in meditation.

One, one, one, he repeated; but one in division; united and yet separate.

Evil is the accentuation of division; good, whatever makes for unity with other lives and other beings. Pride, hatred, anger – the essentially evil sentiments; and essentially evil because they are all intensifications of the given reality of separateness, because they insist upon division and uniqueness, because they reject and deny other lives and beings. Lust and greed are also insistences upon uniqueness, but insistences which do not entail any negative awareness of the others from whom the unique being is divided. Lust only says, 'I must have pleasure', not 'You must have pain'. Greed in its pure state is merely a demand for my satisfaction, not for your exclusion from satisfaction. They are wrong in emphasizing the separate self; but less wrong than pride or hatred or anger, because their self-emphasis is not accompanied by denial of others.

But why division at all? Why, unavoidably, even in the completest love, and, at the other end of the scale of being, even in that which is or seems to be below right and wrong, why must the evil of separation persist? Separation even of saint from saint, and separation even of mere physical pattern from mere physical pattern. One man cannot eat for another. The best must think, must enjoy and suffer, must touch, see, smell, hear, taste in isolation. The good man is merely a less completely closed universe than the bad; but still closed, even as the atom is closed.

And, of course, if there is to be existence – existence as we know it – being must be organized in closed universes. Minds like ours can only perceive undifferentiated unity as nothing. Unescapable paradox that we should desire that n should be equal to one, but that, in fact, we should always find that one is equal to nought.

Separation, diversity – conditions of our existence. Conditions upon which we possess life and consciousness, know right and wrong and have the power to choose between them, recognize truth, have experience of beauty. But separation is evil. Evil, then, is the condition of life, the condition of being aware, of knowing what is good and beautiful.

That which is demanded, that which men come finally to demand of themselves, is the realization of union between beings who would be nothing if they were not separate; is the actualization of goodness by creatures who, if they were not evil, would not exist. Impossibility – but none the less demanded.

'Born under one law, to another bound.'

He himself, Anthony went on to think, he himself had chosen to regard the whole process as either pointless or a practical joke. Yes, *chosen*. For it had been an act of the will. If it were all nonsense or a joke, then he was at liberty to read his books and exercise his talents for sarcastic comment; there was no reason why he shouldn't sleep with any presentable woman who was ready to sleep with him. If it weren't nonsense, if there were some significance, then he could no longer live irresponsibly. There were duties towards himself and others and the nature of things. Duties with whose fulfilment the sleeping and the indiscriminate reading and the habit of detached irony would interfere. He had chosen to think it nonsense, and nonsense for more than twenty years the thing had seemed to be – nonsense, in spite of occasional uncomfortable intimations that 'there might be a point, and that the point was precisely in what he had chosen to regard as the pointlessness, the practical joke. And now at last it was clear, now by some kind of immediate experience he knew that the point was in the paradox, in the fact that unity was the beginning and unity the end, and that in the meantime the condition of life and all existence was separation, which was equivalent to evil. Yes, the point, he insisted, is that one demands of oneself the achievement of the impossible. The point is that, even with the best will in the world, the separate, evil universe of a person or a physical pattern can never unite itself completely with other lives and beings, or the totality of life and being. Even for the highest goodness the struggle is without end; for never in the nature of present things can the shut become the wholly open; goodness can never free itself completely from evil. It is a test, an education – searching, difficult, drawn out through a lifetime, perhaps through long series of lifetimes. Lifetimes passed in the attempt to open up further and a little further the closed universe that perpetually tends to spring shut the moment that effort is relaxed. Passed in overcoming the separating passions of hate and malice and pride. Passed in making still the self-emphasizing cravings. Passed in constant efforts to realize unity with other lives and other modes of being. To experience it in the act of love and compassion. To experience it on another plane through meditation, in the insight of direct intuition. Unity beyond the turmoil of separations and divisions. Goodness beyond the possibility of evil. But always the fact of separation persists, always evil remains the very condition of life and being. There must be no relaxation of the opening pressure. But even for the best of us, the consummation is still immeasurably remote.

Meanwhile there are love and compassion. Constantly obstructed. But oh, let them be made indefatigable, implacable to surmount all obstacles, the inner sloth, the distaste, the intellectual scorn; and, from without, the other's aversions and suspicions. Affection, compassion – and also, meanwhile, this contemplative approach, this effort to realize the unity of lives and being with the intellect, and at last, perhaps, intuitively in an act of complete understanding. From one argument to another, step by step, towards a consummation where there is no more discourse, only experience, only unmediated knowledge, as of a colour, a perfume, a musical sound. Step by step towards the experience of being no longer wholly separate, but united at the depths with other lives, with the rest of being. United in peace. In peace, he repeated, in peace, in peace. In the depth of every mind, peace. The same peace for all, continuous between mind and mind. At the surface, the separate waves, the whirlpools, the spray; but below them the continuous and undifferentiated expanse of sea, become calmer as it deepens, till at last there is an absolute stillness. Dark peace in the depths. A dark peace that is the same for all who can descend to it. Peace that by a strange paradox is the substance and source of the storm at the surface. Born of peace, the waves yet destroy peace; destroy it, but are necessary; for without the storm on the surface there would be no existence, no knowledge of goodness, no effort to allay the leaping frenzy of evil, no rediscovery of the underlying calm, no realization that the substance of the frenzy is the same as the substance of peace.

Frenzy of evil and separation. In peace there is unity. Unity with other lives. Unity with all being. For beneath all being, beneath the countless identical but separate patterns, beneath the attractions and repulsions, lies peace. The same peace as underlies the frenzy of the mind. Dark peace, immeasurably deep. Peace from pride and hatred and anger, peace from cravings and aversions, peace from all the separating frenzies. Peace through liberation, for peace is achieved freedom. Freedom and at the same time truth. The truth of unity actually experienced. Peace in the depths, under the storm, far down below the leaping of the waves, the frantically flying spray. Peace in this profound subaqueous night, peace in this silence, this still emptiness where there is no more time, where there are no more images, no more words. Nothing but the experience of peace; peace as a dark void beyond all personal life, and yet itself a form of life more intense, for all its diffuseness, for all the absence of aim or desire, richer and of finer quality than ordinary life. Peace beyond peace, focused at first, brought together, then opening out in a kind of boundless space. Peace at the tip, as it were, of a narrowing cone of concentration and elimination, a cone with its base in the distractions of the heaving surface of life and its point in the underlying darkness. And in the darkness the tip of one cone meets the tip of another; and, from a single, focal point, peace expands and expands towards a base immeasurably distant and so wide that its circle is the ground and source of all life, all being. Cone reversed from the broken and shifting light of the surface; cone reversed and descending to a point of concentrated darkness; thence, in another cone, expanding and expanding through the darkness towards, yes! some other light, steady, untroubled, as utterly calm as the darkness out of which it emerges. Cone reversed into cone upright. Passage from wide stormy light to the still focus of darkness; and thence, beyond the focus, through widening darkness into another light. From storm to calm and on through yet profounder and intenser peace to the final consummation, the ultimate light that is the source and substance of all things; source of the darkness, the void, the submarine night of living calm; source finally of the waves and the frenzy of the spray – forgotten now. For now there is only the darkness expanding and deepening, deepening into light; there is only this final peace, this consciousness of being no more separate, this illumination . . .

The clock struck seven. Slowly and cautiously he allowed himself to lapse out of the light, back through the darkness into the broken gleams and shadows of everyday existence. He rose at last and went to the kitchen to prepare himself some food. There was not much time; the meeting was at eight, and it would take him a good half-hour to reach the hall. He put a couple of eggs to boil, and sat down meanwhile to bread and cheese. Dispassionately, and with a serene lucidity, he thought of what was in store for him. Whatever it might be, he knew now that all would be well.